HEART OF A HEARTLESS WORLD

Niall McGrath

MINERVA PRESS
MONTREUX LONDON WASHINGTON

HEART OF A HEARTLESS WORLD
Copyright © Niall McGrath 1995

All Rights Reserved

No part of this book may be reproduced in any form,
by photocopying or by any electronic or mechanical means,
including information storage or retrieval systems,
without permission in writing from both the copyright owner
and the publisher of this book.

ISBN 1 85863 661 2

First Published 1995 by
MINERVA PRESS
10 Cromwell Place
London SW7 2JN

Printed in Great Britain by
B.W.D. Ltd., Northholt, Middlesex.

HEART OF A HEARTLESS WORLD

CHAPTER ONE

In Shades of Darkness Hide

It was getting dark when Thomas was passing the church. He was walking the lame ewe and wether lamb home, up to Islandreagh, from the grass by the Six Mile River at Shaneoguestown. New Year's Day had a frosty nip in the air. Thomas was whistling out plumes of cold breath. His tune was shrill in the evening gloom. His nonchalance flared inexplicably into joy when he heard a girl's voice softly singing his favourite hymn.

> "God who made the earth,
> The air, the sky, the sea,
> Who gave the light its birth,
> Careth for me."

Peering through the twilight, Thomas saw that it was Pamela Hart. She smiled broadly, entertained by her own singing. He was surprised that a girl like her could sing so well, so strongly. He was impressed that she was familiar with the hymn. His happy heart was swelling, as if to charitably embrace this pretty, grubby works girl, standing before him in her drab frock and dreary coat. His eyes surveyed the figure, from the scuffed boots up to the red, speckled tip of her nose. Pamela was slim but shapely beneath her layers of winter clothes.

> "God who made the sun,
> The moon, the stars, is He,
> Who, when life's clouds come on,
> Careth for me."

She sang with greater confidence and vigour now. Her voice penetrated his mind with a keener force than the grip of the cold air on his bare ears. As he watched her red lips, his eyes flitted occasionally, acknowledging the presence of the pale moon in the evening sky.

> "God who made all things,
> On earth, in air, in sea,
> Who changing seasons brings,
> Careth for me."

She was singing, but her mind was on other things. She was trying to calm her mind and pulse, after the unsettling discovery she had made. Having found herself alone in the building, she had had a nosy around in the Reverend MacIntyre's desk. In a drawer she had found her name in the old Sunday School Register. One of the other black, hardbound notebooks turned out to be really old. Its goldleaf title on the front cover was

PRESBYTERY RECORDS
1831–54

It was a list of marriages.

There was also a thin, inconspicuous book with *'Disciplines'* scrawled in italic script on the first inside page. She thumbed through this, her hands trembling as the word 'fornication' leapt from the page at entry after entry.

> *'Mr and Mrs Nathaniel Chambers appeared before us this day, for ante-nuptial fornication.'*

She had heard that word bandied about by the pastor at the wee Gospel Hall at Burnside, where her father took them to hear the evangelist. Her father reckoned hell-fire and brimstone were better for the weans than this, their mother's church.

Suddenly, one name in particular caught her eye.

> *'July 24th 1859. Mrs Mathilda Manson appeared before us this day for fornication with Sidney Corry. Admitted.'*

Pamela sucked in a breath as she read. What did that word mean again? She sat back in the Reverend MacIntyre's chair, staring at the large, framed certificate on the wall which celebrated the 1840 investigation of the Assembly of the Presbyterian Church in Ireland.

A shiver of indignation ran through her. This was her great-grandmother. The one Aunt Tilda and Great-Aunt Mathilda were named after. The one who had survived the Famine as a wee girl. The old woman who had died the same day as Queen Victoria. She had been married when this happened. Even so, Pamela said to herself, it was none of *their* business.

Transfixed, bubbling up with emotion inside, Thomas let the ewe nuzzle at the white-sprinkled verge as he stood by the church gates to listen to Pamela's lilting melody.

> "God who sent His Son
> To die on Calvary,

> He, if I lean on Him,
> Will care for me."

Thomas was singing the words in his head, but did not dare to say them aloud, for fear of interrupting the gentle sound of her voice with his harsh chords. Pamela moved towards him, approaching from the solid double doors at the front of the church. He noticed for the first time that she had a wilting flower in her hands. The ewe and lamb raised their heads, disturbed by something above them. In one of the bare trees that surrounded the building a branch was rustling. The black shape of a bird cawed once as it flapped noisily into the air. A flurry of frosty drops, like a shower of rice, spilled down to the ground. But it was only a momentary distraction and Pamela continued without faltering.

> "When in heaven's bright land
> I all His loved ones see,
> I'll sing with that blessed band,
> 'God cared for me'."

An immeasurable happiness welled up in Thomas; it was so great it felt like his heart was overbrimming. The lyrics seemed to be directed at him and him alone, as if this was some rite, with Pamela as priestess, he the faithful worshipper. As his eyes absorbed the gentle outline of her features and the cascades of her wavy auburn hair, he was transfixed by her pleasant, earthy aura. The final lines, when they came, seemed to pierce his mind because of the tenderness with which they were uttered.

> "God who made the earth,
> The air, the sky, the sea,
> Who gave the light its birth -
> Careth for me."

Silence. Like emptiness. Like waking from a dream. Like the abrupt fading of beauty, or joy, or perfection.

"What are you *doing* here?"

"What are *you* doing here?"

He watched her intently. She giggled. He thought that she was amused by the way he had raised his peaked cap to scratch his greasy, short-cropped hair. His chocolate-coloured eyes penetrated her eyes. His face was tinged red with the cold; his lean body was trembling slightly.

"What's so funny, Pamela?" he laughed with her.

"You look like the Good Shepherd."

He glanced at the pair of sheep near him.

"The ewe's lame. I'm takin' her home, so's me mother can keep an eye on her. And the lamb doesn't seem to be thriving."

"Have yous land near here?"

"Uncle Isaac's taken the grass by the river, next the weir. And," he stuttered, "what are *you* up to?"

"Mummy provided the flowers for the service this morning. I came to get them, to put in our kitchen. But they're gone."

"They were very nice. I didn't see you this morning."

"No. Mummy and us was goin' to go this evenin', but Daddy insisted we go to the Gospel Mission, like he does when he takes a mind to it. So, none of us was here to gather them up after the service."

He stammered, "One of the ladies must've tidied them up."

"Aye."

There was an awkward pause. The lamb and ewe were gradually moving along the road towards the railway bridge, where the road dipped around a corner.

"Well, Pamela, I'll see you about."

"Aye. Happy New Year, Thomas."

"Aye. Happy New Year, Pamela."

Tittering, she began walking in the opposite direction. He looked over his shoulder and saw her back just before she disappeared beyond the hedge at the Post Office. He sighed loudly as he went through the bridge.

Thomas marched, stick in hand, up the rise to the junction. The temperature was decreasing rapidly, as darkness descended. He tucked his scarf more tightly around his neck, beneath the thick, tweed jacket. He clomped along on the glistening tarmac, crossing the main road. That Sunday evening was gloomy, yet he somehow felt that all was right with the world.

As he went up the Rathmore Road home, Thomas glanced aimlessly across the gloomy fields. The hedges at the far side had been laid, so a still ocean of darkness spread out before his eyes. Going round the bend, he kept his eyes on the plain of shadows. Now he felt cold. It was a stark contrast to the warmth and joy he had experienced not long ago.

There was a figure in front of him. It was a big man's shape. The silhouette was moving ahead of him, going in the same direction. As Thomas followed, he caught up with him.
"Hello."
The shape stopped. Thomas got near to him. In the poor light he thought he recognised the man, but was unsure.
"Do I know you?" he asked.
"Young Thomas!" the stranger acknowledged him.
In the sharp air he could smell the body of the tramp.
"Aye."
"D'ye not remember me at all?"
"Oh, aye!" Thomas stuttered again. "I recognise you now, Paul. Fer a minute there I thought you were oul' Father Time, the Oul' Year himself, packin' off to ... to wherever the Oul' Years go ... I thought that bag over yer shoulder was your scythe! Back with us, then, are ye?"
"I've found my way to the County Antrim again, aye. Like I usually do, this time of year. Is there work at your place?"
Thomas hesitated before speaking bashfully. "Well, you'll have to ask me uncle when we get home." A piece of news sprang to mind. "It's the New Year's party th' night. There won't be much of a gatherin' seein' as this is the Lord's Day. Just Stanford Begley, Esquire, and family, as far as I know. But you'll have to stop in, for sure."
"I had in mind visiting yous. And is everyone at the Orchards well?" he asked as walked the sheep towards the faint glow ahead, which pinpointed the farm half-hidden in the sheltering trees.
Thomas mumbled. "Uncle Isaac's grand. I'm grand. Mammy's much better."
"It was a bit of a scare for you, eh, young'un, last spring?"
"Aye. Well ... I don't know much about it."
"Lots of women have problems. In Jean's case it wasn't so bad a thing. Your mother's a lot better, I trust?"
"She takes weeping fits, now and again. Rambles on about how it's all *my* fault or Uncle Isaac's fault, and how she thinks she's so wicked, to do what she did, whatever she did. I dunno what it's all about." He slurred into silence. "Mibbe ..."
A sin caused it. And no sin goes unpunished.

"Ack, she's a hardy wan. She'll survive. Sure, weren't these things sent to try us."

"I don't understand why she should get like that. Has she anything more than the rest of us to be depressed about?"

"What age are y', 'bout fifteen? You're stretchin' up now, son. Had a birthday recently, did ye not?"

"Aye, last week ..."

Paul rambled on, "You don't live in an ivory tower, do you? You've seen other women run about now and again, actin' hysterical. Your mother wasn't singled out."

"I thought there was some special reason? Some sin she's bein' punished for?"

"Who's been filling your head with that rubbish? Don't listen to it! It's humbug! Absolute balderdash! No science about it at all. I'll tell ye straight, we haven't enough medical science yet to understand things, like cases of bad nerves. Maybe, when you're my age, the doctors will have some sort of a cure. For now, folk just have to grin and bear it. It's her time of life, like manys a woman. If a fox catches a chicken, it isn't because of some sin that chicken's committed, it's just the luck of the draw. Sure, you can explain it by sayin' that particular chicken was the nearest till the fox's jaws, or it was an oul' done hen, but there's nothing *supernatural* about it."

"People are different. We're not animals. We're made in the image of God."

"We may be a more sophisticated species, but we're flesh and blood like any other."

Thomas was troubled by this statement. It was with relief that he was able to avoid the issue, because they were clattering into the yard and so the sheep had to be seen to. Work can be a great therapy, Thomas thought to himself, it takes your mind off niggling things.

There was a light shining through the white of the curtains from the cottage and a chink of yellowness at the byre door, from whence came the noise of a shovel scraping on concrete. The hubbub of conversation welcomed them as they passed the front door. Here, there were people that they knew, people who were friends, who would welcome them in to the warmth of the house and give them sweet, hot tea and fresh, buttered bread or scones or fluffy homebaked buns.

Thomas felt glad again. "Home!" he sighed.

Moving virtually silently, Thomas and Paul guided the ewe and lamb to an empty stable and closed them in. Thomas gathered up a lith of dusty hay. At the pump trough at the back of the house Paul cracked the ice with the rim of an iron bucket, to fetch some water. While he was setting the bucket onto the damp manure in the corner of the aromatic stable and the thin lad was tossing the rustling hay into the wooden manger on the wall, a third figure joined them in the black night. By the triangle of light from the open byre door, which shone across the yard that starless evening, they were aware of the other one's presence as he phumphed a shovelful of tangy turnip shreds in the corner.

"Oh, hello, James. What are you doing here?"

"I'm here to help yous," said the other young man. He resembled his cousin. "When we arrived, your uncle was just finishing the milking, so I'm helping him redd up[1] the byre."

"You'll get your Sunday clothes all mucky."

"I've got your boots on."

"See," stuttered Thomas, pointing, "Paul's come back to us."

"Aye. Welcome back, Paul. How are you?"

"Fine. And are all the Usshers of Umgall well?"

"Grand, thanks. I'm stayin' at th' Holestone, helpin' at Uncle Stan's, at the minute, seein' as he's still not got all the spuds lifted. As usual."

"At this time of the year?" Paul half laughed.

"Well, it's been mild. Till now."

"Is the byre all redd up?"

"Aye, Thomas. Uncle Isaac's away in. The place is clean as a whistle. Is this girl in bad form?"

Slapping the sheep's rump so that she jumped timidly, Thomas replied, "Not as bad as we thought. But the lamb's a poor do-er."

Thomas left the shovel inside the byre and brought the hurricane lamp with him. He was impressed by the precision with which James Ussher had cleaned out the byre. He made a mental note to improve his own standards. He joined the others. Their boots clipped on the frosty ground as they went across to the house.

As soon as the latch clicked, the world was recreated anew. The surge of warmth as they entered was a stark contrast to the chilly air beyond the thin wooden boards of the door. Friendly voices greeted

---

[1] "to redd up" = (coll.) to clean or tidy up.

them, familiar faces smiled in welcome, chairs scraped on the tiles as the folk, in their Sunday best, turned in recognition. Paul was accepted heartily, asked where he had been, was he going to stay awhile?

Thomas sneaked through the kitchen to the wooden bench that sat at the back of the jamb wall. Thomas's mother began fussing over James, getting him to wash his hands in the basin in the corner and entreating him to warm himself by the fire. Thomas, meanwhile, had slithered into a space at the chimney corner. He stared into the leaping flames. The heat reached his cheeks, his chest, his hands. He felt as if he were swooning, diving into the warmth and brightness of home. He scarcely heard them discussing Paul's travels. Paul was telling them he had been to Sligo and Mayo and almost as far west as Tir na n'Og itself. Jean asked Paul if he wanted a drink – there were ribald comments, laughter – *tea*, perhaps?

Drink? In their house? A glance confirmed the novelty: Uncle Isaac and Uncle Stan were clutching whiskey glasses in their laps, as each stared at the fire. Hell-fire raged in Thomas's imagination, fierce as the heat stinging his hands. He saw their insides burning, roaring like the blaze beneath the potato boiler! And their cackling voices: these weren't his uncles, these weren't the men he knew. Thomas's chin shrank against his chest, his head dipping, as if it was too big for the body, hanging heavily like the head of a foetus. Consuming liquor indeed! And on the Sabbath Day! Of course, Paul was known for indulging. What else could you expect of a tinker? But for Uncle Isaac ...! And Uncle Stan ... To drink ... It was a revelation. Mind you, Uncle Stan had had a glass at that party of theirs, last Hallowe'en. Had Uncle Isaac? Thomas couldn't remember ...

Paul took a cup from Jean, and Thomas saw him extend an arm up to the ceiling. The unkempt man tipped the hurricane lamp, hanging above them from a nail in a beam, to pour some paraffin into his cup. The chemical smell wafted down in Thomas's direction. He curled his nose.

"What's the matter, Thomas, don't you like the smell of it?"

Looking up and slowly turning his head, Thomas's eyes sought the face of Aunt Sarah. The purple birthmark on her forehead seemed to throb vaporously.

He briefly became the centre of attention. "Pink poison!" His face flushed.

"Good boy. You've got the right attitude. Drink is the Devil's buttermilk. You've taught your son well, Jean. And don't you think these two lads are more like two peas in a pod every time you see them? James is the spitting image of you, Thomas." Aunt Sarah had command of everyone's attention when she spoke.

Reddening, Thomas mumbled to the bright-eyed strawberry blonde beside him, "You look like somebody too, Mary, but I can't think who just now."

"Only, James is a bit fairer," Aunt Sarah concluded her assessment.

"And his eyes are blue," their mutual cousin Mary bubbled, "but Thomas's are ... much darker."

"You *would* notice something like that," Hugh breathed, unimpressed.

She thumped her brother and he threatened to hit her back.

"Houl' yer whist!" Stan cried. "You brazen hussy," he winked at his daughter.

"Weans should be seen and not heard," Isaac addressed the mantelpiece.

"Their generation's getting beyond that stage, unfortunately," Aunt Sarah commented.

His mother was standing by the fold-down table, near the back window, one hand resting on the rim of the gleaming, white porcelain jawbox sink. Like her sister Sarah, her greying hair was wrenched into a tight bun at the back of the crown. The large mole on her cheek was dull and ugly, spoiling what was left of her looks. For she did look smart in her long, blue, Sunday dress. But while her lips tried to smile, a blur in Jean's eyes betrayed the invisible barrier which so often nowadays seemed to separate her from the external world.

"That stuff's certainly not good for you," Jean retraced their steps in the conversation, as if jolting them back through a brief timewarp.

"Ack," said Uncle Stan, nursing his whiskey, "there's no harm in a celebratory dram once in a while."

"I'm surprised at *you*, Isaac," his mother commented, "yielding to temptation like that. And you a Gray."

Good for you! Thomas was smiling to himself. Go on, Mummy, you tell him! Salvation! This was the way Goodness defeats Evil! Onward Christian soldiers! March tall, proud, chins up, chests out! A Mountie always gets his man! The Sheriff will clean up Dodge City!

Come back, Uncle Isaac, Thomas prayed, into the bosom of our family: leave your sins behind you. He thought, could Uncle Isaac sin? We're all sinners, under Original Sin. Uncle Isaac cursed, now and again: yes, he was only human, after all. Of course he was. Must be. We all are.

Isaac was testing the rim of his tilted glass with pursed lips. "You're better wi'out it."

Nice Uncle Isaac – wouldn't it be a shame if he wasn't flesh and blood? Cold as stone, ice-cold, brittle as glass, inhuman and hard: no heart, no blood coursing through his veins, warming his body, no relation to people at all. Welcome back to the family circle. Uncle Isaac solemnly nodded at her as he said, "Aye, there's Sam Arbuckle as an example to us all."

"What did he do?" asked Thomas.

Isaac leant forward and wagged a finger at his nephew. "The eejit drank all the money he had and didn't stop at that; he had to carry on and drink himself out of the place. Sat on his backside in Barr's and started with the cows, then he drank away the pigs, then the sheep, then the horses, then the very chickens, till there was nothin' left. He didn't have a farthing to his name, there was nothin' left whin the bank soul' his farm. Threw himself and his wife and the six youngsters out on the roadside." He spat into the fire. The spittle hissed. "An eejit, eh, Jean? I warned you about him when you were young."

Thomas's mother began pouring cups of tea. She remained diplomatically silent.

"One of your *beaus*, I remember, Jean?" Aunt Sarah smiled tightly. "One of the young men who courted your mother in her younger days." She directed the latter comment at Thomas.

"It was only a schoolgirl crush," Jean defended herself. "I never had as many boyfriends as *you*, Sarah."

"I've only had one man in my life and that's my Stanford."

"Yous is both exaggerating." Isaac cleared his throat noisily.

Stan laughed to himself. Paul grinned. James Ussher bowed his head and folded his arms.

Ashen-faced, nervously rocking a foot in her shoe, Jean said what she felt had to be made clear to all. "I am sort-of-like a bride of Christ."

"How could any one be so silly as to drink away *everything*?" Hugh asked in an incredulous tone.

Stan said, "There's nicht se queer as folks. Here, here's a wee story for yous. Billy Falk toul' me he was in Belfast, one day durin' the time of the Twenties Troubles it was, an' he had to go a message across town so he was headin' through West Belfast, when suddenly the cart wheel came off. He was just danderin' about, lookin' for somebody to give him a hand when, lo and behold, he got beaten up and robbed by some rips.

"So there he was, lying at the side of the road, covered in blood, when along comes Sir James Craig on his way to the office, at Stormont. Oul' Jimmy takes a deuk over, curls up his nose an' quickens his pace. A wee while later, along comes the Cardinal, goin' to drop in unexpected on some of his surt. He sees this bloody body, looks closer, and is just about to administer the last rites when he spies Billy's Red Hand of Ulster tattoo, so he crosses the road, blesses himself an' scampers on.

"Finally, an ordinary lookin' buddy comes along and stops and tidies Billy up, wets his hankie with spittle, to wipe off the blood, and all that mularky. He hears Billy's been robbed so he gives him a shillin' fer the bus fare home. Billy's about to go on his way and he says 'Thank you so much for helping me'. The bloke says, 'Ack sure, I wasn't in that much of a hurry, the train home to Dublin's not for ages yet!' And that, children, concludes the parable of the Good Free Stater."

Paul toasted, "The Gospel according to Stanford Begley, Esquire!"

"Just a wee parable."

"A corrupted one." Jean glared at the back of his head.

Thomas considered the others in the room as a cup and saucer were passed over to him from the ink-splodged table. Uncle Stan was sitting in one armchair, Uncle Isaac was slouched in his, James was on a dining chair next to Paul, by the table, while his other cousins, pretty Mary and her lanky, gingerhaired little brother Hugh, were next to him on the bench. Those freckles of Mary's reminded him of somebody else; even the curve of her face tickled his memory.

Thomas took his tea, then set his plate, and that towering slice of cake, beside him on the wooden bench. He noticed that Mary was watching him and he swapped smiles with her. Her long red hair seemed to glow as if the light, rather than being produced by the lamp which was ever so gently swinging above their heads, was emanating from her being.

As the grown-ups chatted, Thomas exclaimed to Mary, "Now I know who you look like. A wee bit. Pamela Hart. I saw her this evening."

"Oh, I'm not like her at all. Where did you see her?"

"At the church. It was them that did the flowers this week."

"Really? Do *that lot* go to Dunadry Presbyterian?"

"Sometimes. I don't see them there much."

"So?"

"Eh?"

"So what about her?"

Thomas shrugged his shoulders. "Jus' seen her, that's all."

"Ta very much," Mary gave his thigh a good-humoured squeeze, "for comparing me to someone like *that*."

"Must be the freckles," Hugh grinned. "You're both spotty."

There was a lull in the conversation as everyone began eating buns or sandwiches and sipping their tea. Thomas peered at the fireplace again. His eyes stared without blinking at the black kettle which was suspended above the hob, on a chain from the crane. He was soon in a trance so deep it could have been a timeless state of non-existence.

"What did y' get for Christmas?" Mary asked, nudging him gently.

Looking in her direction again, he answered, "A cowboy buk. A Zane Grey buk. *Spirit of the Border*. Great!" He grinned.

"Oul' rubbish!" said Isaac, sniffling, from across the kitchen. "Here," he pulled a small, bound book from the side of his armchair. "Read us some *decent* stuff."

The book was passed over to Thomas. The friends quietened and all turned to listen as Thomas falteringly recited a poem by Rabbie Burns. His slurring brogue did not do justice to 'A Prayer In The Prospect of Death'. When he got to Uncle Isaac's favourite verse he slid forward and perched on the seat edge.

> "Where human weakness has come short
>   Or frailty stept aside,
> Do Thou, All Good, for such Thou art,
>   In shades of darkness hide."

When he had murmured the last words, the patient faces swivelled back towards each other and the conversations broke out again. Unnoticed, he held out the book for someone to return to his uncle.

"Mummy," Mary said loudly.

Aunt Sarah looked. She saw the arm and took the book. Thomas watched as Isaac received the object from his elder sister and tucked it under the cushion at his back, in the comfy big armchair.

"I got this dress," Mary grinned.

"Yes," Thomas nodded, "I noticed it was new. It's lovely. What about you, Hugh?"

Hugh leant forward to answer him. "New longjohns! And an orange. And a banana. I've never had a banana before."

"I've never had a banana. What's it taste like?"

"Pretty plain. But nice."

"He wouldn't give me any," Mary moaned, "and I didn't get one, because I got chocolate instead. But our new hand, James Ritchie, gave me a taste of his, anyway." She tossed her hair haughtily.

"What's your New Year's resolution?" Hugh asked.

Thomas was holding his triangular hunk of cake before him, about to bite into it. He could hear Uncle Stan telling Uncle Isaac about a ram he had, saw out of the corner of his eye the arms raised to measure out the size of its bag, which Stan was boasting about.

In a flash, a black and white form snapped. The cake disappeared. His hand hurt.

"Christ!"

Thomas leapt to his feet as the border collie padded away between the chairs to the other side of the kitchen. He was shocked at his own outburst.

Isaac reached for his stick, propped up at the table, but could not get his fingers to it. The dog squeezed itself onto the floor at the side of the dresser, so that in one of the rows above a plate tinkled. As it lay by Jean's bedroom door, the dog gobbled the cake.

Thomas sat down, not even looking at his hand. All eyes were upon him.

He struggled to say, "Sorry."

"Thomas!" his mother exploded. "Wash your mouth out with soap! Taking the name of the Lord in vain!"

He lowered his head dejectedly. He burrowed back into his mind like a snail curling into its shell. How could he have done this to Jesus? He hardly dared to think the Lord's name, now, for fear of transgression. Why couldn't he have used just an ordinary bad word? He wailed inwardly, I'll have nailed You to the Cross!

Paul salvaged the conversation and soon Thomas's outburst was relegated to the past. But in his mind, the word, and the way he had used it, blocked out all other consciousness. He saw only a blackness and it was as if the room had ceased to exist for him. A single thought reverberated through his head:

> THOU SHALT NOT TAKE THE NAME
> OF THE LORD THY GOD IN VAIN.

He had sinned. He had broken a Commandment. He had never sworn before. He could not recall even having thought a blasphemy before. He had a couple of times weakened to the extent of thinking a bad word, like 'damn', but never before had he even had a blasphemy in his mind. He felt empty, forsaken. Why? Why had he said that? Now, he was a sinner. He didn't want to be evil! He'd always been a good person; he wanted to remain a true Christian. So, this is what it felt like to be wretched, to be a common sinner. A shock of fear: was he damned to Hell now? He sang silently:

> Amazing grace, how sweet the sound,
> That saved a wretch like me,
> I once was lost, but now I'm found,
> Was blind, but now I see.

And then he felt happy and warm all over: yes, Jesus had died for him. The Saviour had taken this sin upon Himself, even before Thomas had committed it. He smiled, felt ecstatic! He knew more keenly than ever before what it meant to be saved, to be Elect. He was aware of the light again and glanced up at the framed quotation on the wall:

> You have not chosen Me, It is I who have Chosen you.
> John 15.16

Thank you, Lord, his heart sang.

Hugh was absent-mindedly picking at his nose; Aunt Sarah was frowning at Hugh; Mary was taking in a breath, annoyed by Hugh's dirtiness. Thomas's mother was sitting down now, in her rocking chair, beside her sister. The three men were engrossed in a political discussion, Paul at odds with the two farmers. James Ussher, sitting at the fold-down table stacked with sandwiches, cake and buns, was fiddling with a hinged leg beneath the cloth. Help, the dog, was stretched out on the floor by the dresser, her head in her paws. On the dresser, amongst the display of blue delft tableware, sat the Napoleon clock, patiently ticking the seconds. There was peace again.

"What's Mr Ninety-five doing?" Mary asked.

Thomas shook his head. "Me?"

"No," Mary explained, "James."

Ceasing his fiddling, James said, "Forgive me. I was somewhere else. In another world."

With a maternal cock of the head, Aunt Sarah said, "Are you tired, love?"

"Don't think so, Aunt Sarah."

"What about George Ussher, then?" Stan Begley was saying. "Is he a Leftie like Comrade McCann here, or a Fascist?"

James replied, "My father is first and foremost a man of God. Whatever difficulties there are in this world, they are meaningless in comparison to the cosmic battle between Good and Evil. Everyone's policy should be repentance."

Paul upset Thomas, who was listening intently, by laughing. "Religion is the 'heart of a heartless world'." He took a sip of paraffin. "When the workers of the world unite, to overthrow the Capitalist conspiracy, then we will be an invincible force for true morality. Not your false morality of hierarchical and authoritarian regimes, but a world community, with collective farms, where everyone is truly equal and we can reap the fruits of our labour 'from each according to his ability, to each according to his needs'."

Isaac's head bobbed. "There's many a one's ability is to loaf about and then try an' scrounge aff those of us as do a day's work. Why should I work t' keep somebody else in clover when it's hard enough goin' t' keep me own head above water?"

Jean spoke faintly, from the table behind the main circle of seats and speakers, "This socialism is nothing but an excuse for upsetting the apple cart."

Her last words were drowned out as her brother-in-law began to speak, "There's too miny these days think themselves above their station in life."

"There's nothing wrong with trying to improve living conditions for folk, all the same," Uncle Stan pointed out.

"Yes, dear," his wife placated, "so long as it's done in the right way."

"In the Lord's name," her sister's voice asserted.

"Oh, aye, I've nothin' against folk havin' a bit of money about them, if they earn it," Isaac qualified his viewpoint.

Then, old heads turned, slightly taken aback that James Ussher had the temerity to join in on the adult's discussion uninvited.

"Communism is an ungodly creed." His voice had not weakened; he had spoken clearly and loud enough. James sat back on the rickety wooden chair with a self-satisfied glint in his eye. He folded his arms and crossed his legs tightly.

Paul's purple face grinned as he burbled, "Looks like I'm outnumbered here, anyway. None of yous has the guts to admit you don't *really* believe this superstitious stuff about God an' hobgoblins."

Jean moved from behind her brother's chair, so that she stood between Isaac and the tramp.

"It's a mistake to meet the Deil halfway." Her thick lips sealed together resolutely. Her strong tone advised, "Let Satan come to you, if he will. But we should always stand against him, firm in the faith! Like Jesus Christ did: He is our example – He stood His ground, He did not falter," her voice quavered as the emotion rose to a sermon-like crescendo, "though they sacrificed Him on the Cross, still He kept Himself clean of evil, pure in the spirit, innocent of the flesh." She let that last word slither out, on the tide of her tongue and paused, as if waiting for its energy to ebb back from the walls. "He kept Himself true to His Father. Let us not fall short of the Lord's plan for us, that we might be fit to take on the mission He sets each of us in this life."

"Ack, Jean," Paul teased, "sure, didn't he say, on the Cross, 'Father, why hast thou forsaken me?' Didn't he doubt his own mission?"

Aunt Sarah stood up, "Wellll, Stan, time we were go-wing. It's getting late, isn't it?"

The usual entreaties to stay were made, but Stan and Sarah led the three young people to the door. James and Hugh got the Begley's pony and trap ready for their journey home. They said their cordial goodnights and the trap jolted off down the Rathmore Road.

The yard was still. The beasts in the outhouses were quiet. Paul was carrying a lamp and dragging his sack with him across the sparkling concrete, to the steps which arched over the stable door and up to the loft.

"Go and help him sort out his bed," Uncle Isaac told Thomas.

The boy followed the ageing man with a lamp. They went up the high block steps and into the space beneath the slate roof. The loft had only a few lumps of hay and straw in it, with a couple of large boxes by the wall, which were half-full of grain.

Paul set the hurricane lamp on top of an up-turned, wooden crate. He tipped out his sack. A few hardback books thudded out and a couple of creased shirts. He fished around and laid out two blankets on a pile of loose straw. Thomas was peering at the books.

"You want to read wan of these?" he drawled, tired.

"What are they?"

Paul handed a book to Thomas. It was *The Communist Manifesto*.

Thomas stood motionless as he looked at the flyleaf. "Aren't you afraid your Church will excommunicate you or something for reading this?"

"How can they exclude me from a creed to which I do not subscribe? Don't you like the idea of socialism either?" Paul began, filling a pipe from a leather tobacco pouch. "Your mother seems to disapprove of the poor and the rich being made equal. I, however, am in favour of a classless society."

"Everybody's equal in the eyes of God."

"But not under the tyranny of the Capitalist system."

"What's that, then?"

"It's the way we live."

"What way?"

"A minority of idle owners of capital reap fortunes by exploiting the majority of people, who have only their labour to depend upon."

"I don't know anybody who's rich. Farmers own land, but they aren't rich. They aren't lazy, they work for a living."

"Only because the tyrant landlords of the past were persuaded to relinquish their estates. By collective force. The mistake of the proletariat, the peasants and tenants, was that they chose to become little capitalists, instead of forming collectives and establishing a communist heaven on earth. Did it do them any good to kow-tow to the Capitalist system? Look at the Depression we're in. The farmers of Ireland will be paupers so long as they refuse to unite in a brotherhood of the soil. And as for the workers in the factories, they barely earn a living wage, while the owners live in the lap of luxury. Like the mill down the road. Where do all the workers live?"

"In the Rabbit Hutches."

"And where does the mill owner live?"

"Mr Greer? In the big house."

"Exactly. They work hard, and yet they can barely afford to make ends meet, and they live cooped up in tenement blocks. And Mr Greer doesn't work and he has a fortune and lives in a mansion."

"But he owns the mill."

"And I think the workers should own it."

"Oh." Thomas was puzzled. He tucked the book under his arm. "I'll have a look at this, but I don't know if I like the idea of ... Last year, you used to talk about ... Atheism."

"Religion is 'the opium of the people', according to Marx, the man who wrote that book. And I agree."

"What's opium?"

"It's a drug."

"So, religion is a drug which cures our spiritual ills?"

"No. It's a drug people take to help them make it through an unfulfilling existence. It's like ... paraffin." He guffawed.

Thomas bashfully forced a smile. "Well, 'night."

"Aye, gudnight son."

A fortnight later, Thomas was going down to the Meadows at the mill race, down Kaye's back lane. As he was passing through Kaye's yard with the mare he met Mr Kaye. Mr Kaye usually had a distinguished bearing, even if he was wearing his overalls. At the moment, however, he was looking worried.

"The roany cow's down," he moaned, rocking on his heels. "I've sent young Edmund for the horse doctor. They should be here in a minute."

Thomas left the mare tied to a drainpipe and went with him to the shed where the sick cow was splayed out, her belly projecting upwards like a balloon. They heard an engine's roar. It was Eddie on his Norton motorbike, with Davy Sharpe, the horse doctor, in the sidecar. Having struggled from the contraption, and with an air of extreme gravity, Davy inspected the beast. Mr Kaye and his son stood alongside Thomas silently, awaiting the diagnosis. After leaning on one knee to listen to the cow's heart or lungs and tapping various parts of her body with two hands, Davy stood back from the patient and rubbed his bristly chin.

"As I thought. Look's like a knot in th' puddin'." Davy took a green bottle from his pocket and drenched the animal.

"Surely there's a more scientific explanation than that?" Eddie spoke up.

Mr Kaye impatiently told him, "Davy's the expert."

"I've seen it before," Thomas agreed.

Eddie shook his head and left the shed. Thomas followed him to the yard.

"I'm ploughin' th' day. In the Meadows, down th' back loanen.[2]"

"How's things at the Orchards?"

"Everybody's fine. You seen Paul McCann back?"

"Is he? At least he's more sense than our people."

"Eh?"

"You don't honestly believe that a knot could appear in a beast's intestines, do you?"

"A twist could easily happen ..."

"Rubbish!"

"You're wrong, Eddie. Your da and my uncle and Davy Sharpe and everybody else couldn't be wrong."

"No? G' away with you. Go to your ploughing. If you're so smart, I'm not fit for you to associate with."

Thomas walked his mare to the field he had begun ploughing the previous day. He thought about poor Eddie: his friend had always been an odd wee fella. It was being sent to that posh school in Belfast that had been the ruin of him. His head was full of science and weird ideas now. All those fancy notions were no use to a farmer. Eddie should stick to his mechanics and milking and leave the curing of animals to those who had been given that particular gift by God.

Thomas had harnessed Star to the plough and was just rubbing the purple backs of his hands, to warm them before grasping the metal handles of the plough and the long reins.

"Cold hands, a warm heart," he told himself.

A whoop startled him. His eyes darted around the field and hedges, as if he were a rabbit that had heard a shot. The sound was a shout from Paul. He was climbing over wire at the hedge. Paul was billhooking with Isaac in the adjoining field this morning, laying the hedges. Perhaps he's been sent over by Uncle Isaac to scold me for being so slow at getting here?

---

[2] loanen = (coll.) lane.

"Those furrows look a bit uneven," Paul was saying as he approached. "D' you think you've got the plough set right?"

"Dunno," Thomas stuttered. "Right enough, yesterday, every now and then, the soil thinned, so that there was only a sort of half-furrow. But sure, there's nothing you can do about that. It's the field."

"If you adjust the setting as you come to a shallow place, then you can cut deeper and keep the furrows even."

"What, fiddle about with it all the time?"

"Didn't your uncle show you how to plough properly?"

Thomas stared vacantly. "*Him*, show me how to do anything? What need is there? Sure, doesn't everybody just pick these things up as they go along?"

"There's method in my madness," Paul told him.

"Is this why you're called the Prophet Paul?"

McCann laughed. "You think I'm a teacher of agricultural techniques and this is my hedge school?" He cast an arm around about him, to draw attention to their environment. "No. That's just a nickname the people round here have for me. Because of my radical political views. And have you read any of that book I lent you?"

"Aye. A right bit. But it's heavy going. Deep. I don't quite understand it all."

"I'll elaborate on it for you, sometime. Try this anyway."

The casual labourer watched as the lad ploughed a few furrows. He soon got the hang of adjusting the setting. Thomas felt elated. He had learnt how to plough better. He had mastered an unknown art. He felt he could walk behind Star forever, ploughing field after field, for each neat furrow was, in a way, a celebration of life, each sod turned a means of praise.

At lunchtime the two men left the next field, where they had been patching gaps in the hedge. His uncle told Thomas that the men were finished there and that they would be working at the home place in the afternoon. Thomas took a break. He hung Star's bag of oats round her neck. He did not let her out of her harness, which was the routine she was used to. Instead, he threw the blanket over her back. Sitting on a boulder by the ditch, he munched his soda farls and drank his milk. There was a robin redbreast flitting somewhere in the treetops as the sun fought its way into a clear part of sky, to reach its zenith and make the cold day bright.

There was a billow of cloud above him. He looked at it intensely. The wisps seemed to form a face. At first, he thought it was a man's face. But there was no beard. There was a soft jawline and thin cheeks, with small eye sockets and a delicate plumage of hair. He recognised the nose of this vision in the heavens as Pamela Hart's. Elated by the thought that she was special – in some way chosen from amongst the teeming crowd – Thomas stood up, as if out of respect for this sign in the sky. The area was now almost completely silent, except for the trickle of the burn, and so it felt that all the world was empty.

He thought for a moment that he was the only body on the face of the earth, that he was the only soul in creation. There were no Kayes up the lane; there were no Grays at the Orchards; there were no neighbours at Dunadry; there was no congregation at Shaneoguestown; there was no Ireland. There was no church to go to; not even once, like now, certainly not twice on Sundays and Bible Class forbye[3], like the way Mother had insisted most of last year. At least now Uncle Isaac let him stay home on Sunday evenings to redd up the yard ... What was he doing! He was getting carried away by this ... freedom. But it was a pleasant sort of glow he felt inside, all the same. He couldn't help succumbing to it. All that existed at this time were himself, his image of Pamela and the song of the unseen robin. A novel warmth filled Thomas's being, with this notion of his splendid isolation.

When he went back to get Star ready for the afternoon's ploughing, his good day was abruptly altered. He had taken Star's bag of corn from her while she was still fighting to get her tongue around the last of the oats. He took the blanket off over her rump and was stooping near her front leg to lift up the sack, when the mare lashed back.

Thomas swore.

It was not a forceful blow, but it was enough to wind him, for he had been bent over and caught the kick in the chest. He staggered around, holding his arms across his body. When the pain subsided a bit, he straightened up cautiously.

One sin leads to another.
Once a sinner, always a sinner.

---

[3] forbye = (coll.) as well as.

He had done it again: he had used bad language for the second time in his life. Was this the Devil getting hold of him? Maybe he wasn't one of the Elect after all? Maybe he was on the slippery slope down into Hell. How could he escape his shameful self? The throbbing pain in his chest and the worry of guilt in his head were accompanied by a darkening of the sky: black clouds were now approaching over Donegore Hill.

He wanted to carry on ploughing, but the injury would not stop searing. He got the plough going and hobbled along for a furrow, but gave up at the end rig.

He shook his head. "What d' you do that for? 'Cos I didn't let you finish your grub?" he whispered to the attentive mare.

He unharnessed Star, stretching gingerly to undo buckles. Thomas plodded up the rough lane, wincing at every stone he stumbled by. He passed the tumbling down cottages. Should he stop here? No: Eddie had warned him to stay clear of the oul' witch, there. There were nasty people in the world as well as nice ones. So he avoided the cottages as usual.

At last he got the mare along the right of way through Kaye's yard and up the road to the Orchards. He left her in her stable without feeding her or brushing her down. He felt it was an emergency; he just could not muster the energy to brush her down. She wasn't too bad, he told himself. She could do without. It was very dark now and the cold rain would soon be falling. Slouching like a bent old man, he went across the grey yard to the house.

His mother was baking oatcakes on the griddle over the fire. He was about to complain about his aching chest when he noticed the bruise around her eye, by the ear. She looked up at him with a blank expression on her face.

"Did the rain chase you?" she asked, tonelessly.

"What happened *you*?" He drew in a breath, immediately aware that he had breached a taboo.

Jean's red eyes filled with water. "Your uncle and I had words earlier, that's all."

"Have you," he asked timorously, "been havin' one of your," he whispered the rest, "weepin' fits again?"

Her back was to him as she crouched at the fire. He saw her hand go to her face, to wipe her eyes. A word wanted to resound in his brain – Bastard! – but he blacked it out with all his might.

"He shouldn't hit you, it's not your fault you feel bad sometimes." She sniffed heavily. "I slapped him first."

Thomas closed his mouth and turned. Before leaving the kitchen, to shuffle up the jamb passage towards the parlour – beyond which lay his bedroom – he remembered to call, "I'm not feelin' well. I'm goin' to lie down. Will you ask Paul to feed Star for me?" He heard only another sniff as a reply.

In his room he unbuttoned his shirt at the wardrobe mirror. There was a horseshoe-shaped red patch on his left breast. Is this the punishment for my blasphemy, for using bad language? he wondered, as he lowered his back onto the bed. The pain throbbed. He let the pain flow through his chest, accepting it. It began to subside, to feel less uncomfortable. And at that moment his bruise did not appear to be as substantial as the ugly, blackening ring that marred his mother's cheek.

CHAPTER TWO

Graven Images

He was shaking with the cold but carried on, engrossed in his shaving. The sprinkling of snow on the ground made the early morning less dark than it should have been. He could feel the dampness already soaking through the welts of his boots. His thighs felt stiff after yesterday's tramping behind the plough. It was as if the blood in them had frozen. But the discomfort was nothing new and did not annoy Thomas as he shivered at the trough, watching his blue hand draw the blade through the foam by the light of a lamp.

Although his flannel vest was buttoned up at the neck, he flinched each time he reached up to pull the razor against his face. The cold water dripped and soaked the white fabric of the vest, forming clinging patches. A fresh cloud of breath escaped with each slice on the skin. He nicked his chin and uttered a sound. A dark blob appeared. Soon, his blood was dripping onto the vest and onto the rim of the trough. Some drops stained the snow at his feet. He had removed enough soap, so battled with the corner of a towel to stop the bleeding.

"Ye'll wear your face away," Isaac wryly commented, coming up behind him. His galluses were hanging about his trousers and he was bare-chested. His trunk was pale and smooth, in contrast to the lined, leathery face and discoloured arms. He pumped more ice-cold water, splashing the young lad.

"It's freezin'!"

"Cleanliness is next to Godliness, Thomas," his uncle reminded him. "There's nothing like a good, stiff wash in the mornin'. Are you bleedin' yourself?"

"Bleeding horses isn't necessary, y'know. Eddie Kaye showed me this vet-er-in-ary book he has, an' the experts recommend not to do it because it doesn't do any good. Sure, most folks don't anymore, anyway," he said, then hurriedly dipped his toothbrush into the tin of powder.

"We're neet most folks." Isaac splashed his face. "What day is this, that a wean's tryin' t' tell an' oul' daig like me the oul' tricks aren't the best wans? There's nowt like a bitta oul' fashionedness."

Holding his grubby handkerchief to his chin, Thomas went swiftly around the side of the house. In his room he pulled on his shirt and sweater with alacrity. The spot was welling again, so he sat on his bed and held the handkerchief to it. As he did so, his eyes focussed on the framed tract on the wall:

'As Ye Sow, So Shall Ye Reap'.

The wardrobe door was open. He had time to survey the Holy Ghost. It was going to be what Maisie Kaye called 'surreal'. She had shown him some modern pictures in a book that she had got from the library. She was going to be an artist and sit by the banks of the Seine in Paris and paint surreal pictures, and then come home and paint bits of Antrim and Rathmore surreally and become a famous local artist. So he was going to carve bits of surreal sculptures like this, in his spare time, and sell them to holiday makers in the summertime, when the rich English and Americans came over for the Giant's Causeway and the real Guinness.

The Holy Ghost was his first attempt. He had just used the end of a beam that had been lying around. Thomas had shaped it with his precious, horn-handled, razor-sharp Bowie knife – the one they got him last Christmas, when all he had needed was an ordinary foldaway. It was far too good to take to the fields. What if he lost it out of his pocket? He used it sparingly at first, scared to tarnish the blade. But now the spots of rust were beginning to appear in those awkward places near the hinge where he couldn't reach with the glasspaper or oilcloth to clean it. He had used his special knife for this important, arty task of shaping the wood into a cloudy figure with an effeminate face. The head was rather swollen, to compensate for the lack of detail further down. It really did look like a ghost to him. But it was no ordinary ghost: this was a *Spiritual Being*. He stared, in a trance, at the jutting nose and the enigmatic smile of the lips. He closed his eyes and prayed, I have formed You, now You make of me what You will.

"Thomas!" His mother was calling him to breakfast.

The cut on his chin had just about congealed, so he stuffed the handkerchief in his pocket as he went through the cold parlour and round the jamb wall to the heart of the kitchen. Jean was in her usual brown skirt, white blouse and ill-fitting, heavy cardigan. Her figure filled the garments, despite her frail shape. Paul was at the table. Thomas took his own place by the window. Out the back, in the pre-dawn gloom, he could see his uncle, bent away from them, still washing vigorously. He rapped the pane of glass. The elderly man straightened up, wiping himself with his towel. Isaac swivelled to give a thumbs up. A fry was placed in front of Thomas. He dragged his lazy eyes down to the eggs and bacon and potato bread, picked up his fork and stabbed a yolk.

"You've cut yourself," his mother said as she sat down.

"I often cut myself."

Paul advised, "Less haste more speed."

"What are you at th' day?"

"I've the rest of that meadow to plough."

"Still?" his mother asked. "I hope you're not getting slothful."

"The last bit of the last field, for this year."

Isaac came in. He put the rest of his clothes on in his room and then joined them at the table.

"A quare mornin'."

"Aye." Paul nodded. "But fresh."

"Is there anything to do on Saturday?"

Isaac's fork paused in mid-air. "What?"

"Is there much to do on Saturday?"

"What are you on about, son?"

"Eddie was sayin' they need another man for the Scouts football team. I was wond'rin' if I could go and play for them, in Randalstown."

Isaac continued eating.

The morning milking occurred with the same predictability as the sun rising. As well as having his own number of cows to milk, Thomas was ordered out as usual to fetch the cabbages and hay, while the others sat peacefully on their stools. The squilch-squilch as the jets filled the buckets occurred in a discordant chorus. The steaming beasts scrunched their cabbage leaves. It was warm with an ear next to a cow's flank, so Thomas liked the job. Running about for more fodder also kept him from feeling the chill. He always felt there was something special about the byre: it was a *sacred* place. The flickering lamplight, the smooth plaster of the walls and stalls and the sounds of this living industry gave the milking parlour the atmosphere of a cathedral, like the big one in Belfast he'd seen the outside of and often imagined what the inside would be like. Thomas felt relaxed, safe here, at home.

The young fellow was left to sweep out after the milking was over. His mother had gone back to the house to clean up and make cheese or bake and to get the dinner on. His uncle was away on the cart to the Co-op in Belfast to sell a load of spuds. Thomas preferred company when working, but he did not mind redding up the byre by himself after the milking. It was as if sweeping the muck off the stalls, along the group[4] and out through the hole to the midden beyond was a creative process; or a recreative one, making anew the cleanliness of this hallowed place.

As he brushed the goo, he thought out loud, "It could do with a bit of tidying up around the chin. Mind you, I better take care not to cut Him, like I cut myself: draw holy blood, that would never do. But it's a grand carving. I like it. It's *surreal*. Cloudy." It became an internal monologue: and what about your mother's health? Well, it's been fine, just fine, recently. Not a spooky incident with her for a long time. Thank God. Yes, thank You, Lord: You are kind. 'God who made the earth', You care for me. That's why I want to worship You, through this ... image. He stopped for a moment, stood up, resting his chin on his hands on the point of the brush shaft. But what if it's a *graven* image? He thought for a time, staring blankly. The lamp hissed as it burned. Then he resumed his sweeping, singing,

> "It's a long way to Tipperary
> It's a long way to go,
> Oh, it's a long way to Tipperary,
> To the sweetest girl I know -
> God bless her.
> Good-bye Piccadilly,
> Farewell Leicester Square,
> It's a long, long way to Tipperary,
> And my heart lies there."

He mused, "So near and yet so far. So near to ..." *Summerhill* ... "where the sweetest girl I know is. But there's no chance to go there. Not today."

And he briskly set about completing his chore.

---

[4] group = (coll.) manure drain.

Thomas was ploughing in the far meadow, down by the mill. He had stopped at lunchtime. Seized by panic, by a compulsion to get out of that lonely field surrounded by the beastly birds in the bare treetops, he jogged up the back lane, intending to go to Kaye's. At the derelict cottages halfway along the loanen, however, he encountered the old woman at the door of the centre house. Dressed in long black skirts, she had a farmer's cap on and was holding a clay pipe to her mouth. He had never really seen her close up before. He usually only noticed the smoke from her chimney pot. She's a *witch*!

"Hello," she called to him.

"Hello, Mrs Higgins."

"Thomas Gray. And where are you off to, in such a hurry?"

"Nowhere."

"'Mon in." She led the way.

Thomas stepped through the low doorway and into her living room. It smelt musty. It was also dreary, for there was a dense planting of trees around the row of cottages. Mrs Higgins flopped into an armchair by the fire. Thomas sat at the small table in the centre of the tiny room.

"I've got my lunch. Do you want some?" He offered her a slice of jam-covered wheaten bread and the bottle of milk.

She shook her head. "Are you not finished that ploughing yet?"

"I'll get it finished today. We're putting flax in there. It's handy near the dam, see."

"Aye. A wheen of years ago, it was all flax down these fields. I remember when oul' Mr Kaye – this one's father – and your grandfather dug thon lint-hole. My husband gave them a hand."

"When was that, then?"

"Fifty years ago this summer." She exhaled rich tobacco smoke.

"Half a century." Thomas whistled.

"A mere twinkling of an eye," the tiny old woman murmured. As a puff of smoke came down the chimney she said, "Sure, I remember the Hunger."

"The Famine? You're coddin' me."

"Why should I lie? I was only wee, of course. But I remember me father going round these fields lifting the wee small spuds and putting them in his pockets. I thought it was just a game. He kept them as seed, for the next year's crop. It wasn't much, but we lived on it. Survived. Well, some of us. But at least it wasn't so bad here as it was in other parts of the country. But if I had my time over again, I'd go to America, the land of the free. Where a buddy[5] can make a go of it."

"And you'll remember the Great War, then?"

"Of course. And the African one. And the Crimean one. My grandson was killed in Flanders."

"My Uncle Robert died at the Somme. We've got his medals in the cabinet in the parlour. He was Mummy's favourite brother."

"I remember Bobby. He was always at odds with your Uncle Isaac. And Sarah. Sarah and Isaac and Jean and Robert, that was the way they were. Bobby used to look out for your mother. There was Josie, too, a wee imp. Married George Ussher, di'n't she? And the other one ...?"

"Uncle Tom."

"Yes. He was a nice fella, too. Smart. Quiet. Too quiet for his own good. He was always on his own. A born loner. Went bird-watchin', of all things. A smashin' fella! There was just somethin' about him, somethin' that made him stand out from the crowd. He was lost in this place. Belonged in another world altogether. Aye, Tom always seemed happy. Don't know why he cleared off to Scotland. More wildfowl there, mibbe. He died young, too, didn't he?"

Thomas agreed. "He fell off a cliff."

"It's not often I've felt grief so strongly for somebody as wasn't one of me own. For some reason that was one tragedy that pained me. It was like Parnell dyin'."

"Are you a Home Ruler?"

She said in a quiet, steady manner, "Why should I care about the English? They didn't care about me or mine when my mother and sisters were starving to death. My husband was a Parnell man. Michael was a Cath'lic, see. I was his common law wife, because th' wuman's supposed t' take her man's religion, an' I didn't want to an', well, he was worried about it at first, but we reckoned it was all the same God and we were married in the eyes of God, if not of Man."

"You lived in sin?"

Her eyelids rose wearily. "No. We lived in love. I loved him an' he loved me." She smiled, reminiscing. "Aye, an' Michael was passionate about his politics, too. But in those days things were

---

[5]buddy = (coll.) body,person.

different. The Troubles that came later on, in the Twenties, happened in a different world. And it's all changed again, since then. And after this next war's over, it will be all altered again."

"You think there's going to be a war?"

She lifted the kettle from the hob and hung it over the fire. As the stout, bent old woman shuffled back across the room with two cups, the pipe clenched between gums and what few teeth she had left.

"How do you make ends meet?"

"Mrs Kaye lets me hae some spuds an' veg an' rhubarb an' such like. Your mither gives me a bit of meat an' apples now an' again."

"Does she? I didn't know that."

"I've got good neighbours as is good to a useless oul' wumun like me. Save your milk," she nodded. "We'll have some tea. It'll warm our insides."

"Aye. More snow last night." Thomas glanced out the window.

"I lost my Michael in a big fall. He was feeding cattle for a man at Lylehill and a blizzard blew up. He fell in a sheugh[6] and couldn't rise. They found him a week later, after it began to thaw. So, I've been a widow wuman since ninety-three. Forty-two long years ago. And it seems like yesterday. He was only fifty-three when I lost him."

"He was born in 1840, then; the year of the first Assembly." Thomas whistled again.

"What was that, then?"

"When the Presbyterian Church organised in Ireland. There's a big framed chart about it on the wall of the Reverend MacIntyre's study."

"I was Church of Ireland meself."

"What's the difference?"

"Dunno. Our lot stand up and sit down a lot more. That's one reason why I wouldn't go these days, even if I felt like it. I'm too stiff for that caper. Religion is the curse of this country. I think we'd be better off all being pagans again. Civilised ones, mind. Noble savages. Rather than the ignoble Christians we are. I suppose that was what Jesus was on about really: not worryin' about temple rituals and such like, or silly rules and laws and who's been a bad rip an' broke which taboo – but just trying to be good. Be *good*! That was all He meant. Easier said than done!" She smiled sardonically.

The kettle was boiling. She poured their tea. Thomas shared his milk with her.

---

[6]sheugh = (coll.) ditch.

"I hear the Reverend MacIntyre might not outlive even oul' me."
Puzzled, Thomas inquired, "What d'you mean?"
"He's got the Big C."
"The what?"
"Cancer."
"Is that a disease?"
"Aye. It's like the blight: it rots your insides."
Thomas was shaken. His face paled. The thought of someone's organs turning into stinking mulch horrified him. He felt his spine shiver. God will protect him, he thought.
"And I hear there's consumption about Shaneoguestown again. A lot of folk at the Clady Works have it. You wanna keep away from there." She shook her head. "It spreads. And Mrs Logan was telling me the other day, in the Post Office, that these lot in Japan are mostly Fascists, too, now."
"Sure, it's the Italians you have to watch."
"It's the Germans."
"But Herr Hitler's signed a peace treaty."
Mrs Higgins snorted. "Look at his army. And his aeroplanes. You don't spend all that money on those things and not use them. Promises, promises: politicians are good at makin' those. I don't trust them."
"Surely, politicians wouldn't lie about serious things like ... *world peace*. They're our leaders ..."
"That doesn't necessarily make them *nice* people. There'll always be wars, or rumours of wars. Because we're all out of our tiny minds."
Thomas drank his tea quickly. He felt uneasy with this morbid old woman. He explained that he had to get back or Star would be getting impatient. He did not want to think about these things. As he ran down the lane towards the field he decided to think about something nice. When he reached the clearing of the gateway, the sky burst into view.
There was a bright blue expanse, with a blurred sun and a patch of cloud across one half of the sky. The folds of grey above him reminded him of his carving, his image of the Ghost. He prayed to the Ghost to give him an idea, to save him from these dreadful thoughts. He saw the jutting nose of the carving and it transformed into the compact little face of someone he knew: the apple cheeks of Pamela

Hart had appeared in his mind's eye. Thomas felt warm and smiled with joy as he sprang over the hard furrows. As he reached her, Star looked round with a friendly twinkle in her eye. He hugged the mare's neck when he reached her.

"That's my pet," he fawned. "You didn't mean to hurt Thomas, did you? We all kick out, sometimes, like you did thon time. It doesn't mean anything." He embraced her, like a child petting a young animal. "Gooooood Star."

One afternoon later in the week, Thomas went with Paul to the far meadow. Uncle Isaac had gone ahead of them. He wanted the plough transported back to the Orchards and was going to supervise the operation.

As they jiggled down Kaye's back lane on the cart, Paul struck up the conversation.

"Has your uncle bought these meadows yet, at all?"

"No."

"Oul' Mr Kaye won't sell, then?"

"No."

"I bet your Uncle's vexed about that."

"You shouldn't bet: it's immoral."

"I think I'm the best judge of what's right or wrong for me, don't you?"

Thomas blinked, embarrassed. "A sin is a sin," he stuttered.

"Ah, but what is a sin? Have you thought much about the Marx and Engels book you've been reading?"

"Am I gettin' the gist of it, that these continentals want to do away with countries and have one big world? And to eventually do away with governments altogether?"

"Aye."

"But what about criminals? There will always be ruffians. So there'll have to be a government to control them."

"People steal because they don't have something somebody else's got. If material goods were to lose their value, then there'd be no theft. And if everybody got what they needed to live on, then folk wouldn't need to steal."

Thomas glanced at the thawing snow which was gradually sliding down Mrs Higgins's roof.

"But there'll always be evil people."

"And there'll always be community action: people in caring societies will sort out the anti-social ones."

"Marx and Engels go on about doing away with private property and *marriage*."

"Aye."

"But everybody gets married."

"I'm not."

"Well, everybody *should* get married."

"Says who?"

"The Bible. And you can't have women running after any and every man: that's ... disgusting."

"That's not the alternative that I foresee. Anyway, men run after women."

Thomas was blushing. "Maybe some do. But most Christian gentlemen respect their womenfolk."

"You've a naïve view!" Paul chuckled.

"Didn't you ever think of getting married?"

"Oh, once. Sort of. But she wouldn't have me. For a number of reasons. Like, I was, in her opinion, a Cath'lic, and she wasn't. But anyway, even having children hasn't always occurred in monogamous – that is, one man and one woman – relationships. Making women subservient to their husbands is merely a polite form of slavery."

"But I like the idea of marriage. I'd like to have a happy family. It's the way things should be: the wife the home maker and the husband the bread winner. It's only natural ..."

"There's nothing natural about it! It's just an enforced habit in our society. I think women would be happier free from the dictatorship of men. In factories, like the Works here," he gestured with a flailing arm, "the women work, while some of the men are unemployed. That's the fault of the Capitalist system, for a start. And these women in the factories, they get paid less than men, yet they're expected to work as hard and to rear a family as well. That's not just, is it? But these working women and housebound men, do you think these women should dominate the men?"

"'Course not."

"Well, you can hardly argue, then, that the men should dominate the women."

"But you have to be married to have a family."

Paul asked, without looking at Thomas, "Do you know *your* father, then?"

Thomas's face was blank. He stuttered, "I never thought about it before. I think he's dead. I've always imagined that. I think maybe once when I was wee, I did say something about it and I think she said that my Father is in Heaven. I don't bother, it might upset her."

Paul breathed deeply. "Aye. It might."

"At least Uncle Isaac is there to make it seem like a real home. It's his farm, after all. Where'd Mummy and I be, if it wasn't for his Christian charity?"

The cart slapped over the pungent loam, to where the plough was sitting. Isaac was leaning against it, chewing tobacco. He spat it out, sounding as if he was vomiting. The tall, grey-haired farmer stood with Paul as Thomas strained his muscles, to lift the front of the plough into the air. The boy called the young mare and she backed the cart so that he could cog the front of the big plough against it. Thomas went round to the back of the plough and, as Isaac explained to Paul that the mare was called Mrs Simpson because it had been born when the last king abdicated, the boy tried to hoist the rest of the implement into the air.

"Give me a hand," he squeaked.

"Don't be such a baby," Isaac barked.

As Paul helped Thomas to hold the plough aloft for the horse to move the cart back beneath it, Thomas wheezed, "My ribs are still sore after that kick."

"Not do you a button of harm. Liftin's good exercise. Tightens the muscles. You'll just go saft, like a woman, if you don't keep at it. I've a box at the railway station. Will ye go an' fetch it fer me?"

"A box of what?" Thomas asked.

"A box of air."

"What do you want an empty box for?"

"You'll see. Patience is a virtue."

Hesitantly, Thomas said, "But there's T.B. at Clady. I don't want to go near there." He knew that death was something he might catch.

"You're only going as far as Dunadry. And sure, when we go to church, isn't it beyond the tracks."

"Mmm. But it's a holy place. God protects it."

Paul winked at Isaac as he told the lad, "And sure, God'll protect you, too."

So, Thomas and Paul gave Isaac a lift home on the cart and set the plough off in the yard. Paul started cleaning the piece of equipment as Thomas set off down the Rathmore Road for the mysterious box.

He passed Dunadry village and went across the bridge over the gushing Six Mile River, then turned off the main road and drove down the slushy bye-road towards the country railway station. He suddenly decided he would call at Clady, for he had not seen his old school friend Willie Burns for a long time. He might be doing wrong: he might be wasting time, deceiving his uncle or going into danger needlessly, there being T.B. at the terraces.

But as he passed through the dark hollow of the railway bridge and the cart rattled on towards the Works, he recalled Paul's suggestion that God would protect him. Emerging from the shade of the railway bridge Thomas felt the warmth of the day on his neck and was heartened. He turned the clattering vehicle when he approached the line of large old beech trees at the entrance to the noisy works.

Passing the dye-pool at the laneway entrance, Thomas saw that the shallow, rectangular pit had frozen over so that it was now an expanse of red ice. There would be no cloth soaked in here for some time. Some young children were skating on it, in their shoes or boots. A few girls from the Works were standing at the edge of it, in the snow, watching the youngsters and egging them on gleefully. Thomas watched Mrs Simpson at the side of the arc of the semi-circular driveway. As he got down from the front of the cart he glanced briefly in the direction of the noisy linen dying works. The water-driven turbines were rattling monotonously. The big stone-built factory sounded like a sedentary beast, grumbling as it lay resting along the course of the race. Behind the building, the terraces of workers' red-brick houses were just visible. Thomas, however, was interested in the sports at the dye-pool and ran to the red rink beneath the great, shading trees.

His jacket tails flapping behind him, Thomas launched himself forward and slid across the ice. He yelled with exhilaration. At the far side a tuft of frosty grass stopped him abruptly. He tipped forward and grabbed one of the girls' arms to balance himself. The girls were laughing as he caught his breath. With time to collect himself, he realised that it was Pamela he had skated into.

"C'mon!" he yelled, grabbing her gloved hand and dragging her onto the ice. He pushed off and went zipping across the red rink.

Pamela teetered behind him, on the verge of crying out. Thomas bent his knees and skated sideways, round and around, while Pamela held onto his sides and followed like a wagon behind a train. The other girls and kids watched, laughing and cheering and carrying on.

Thomas swung round one last time, causing Pamela to turn and her feet to fly up from beneath her. But he was there to grab her arms from behind and hold her up. He eased her back up onto her feet and they returned to the safety of the grass as the wee ones swarmed onto the ice.

"Hello!" he panted to the other two girls, beaming bright-cheeked. Hetty and Mabel repeated the greeting.

Pamela asked him, "What are you doin' here? I thought you'd be hard at work."

"I've got to pick up a box at the station. I came by to see if Willie's about. I haven't seen him for ages."

Her face grim-coloured, Pamela told him, "Willie was ill. Didn't you know?"

"I knew some of the Burnses weren't at church, but I didn't know why. Nobody spoke of it."

"He's gone," blurted Hetty.

Thomas looked at each of the girls in turn, as if they had conspired to injure him. His eyes traced the outline of Pamela's healthy red-brown hair, her round shoulders in the blue coat, down the line of buttons, spindly stockings, to the mucky snow. He no longer heard the tripping toddlers' shrieks and laughs. His temples were pulsing mechanically. He had no response.

"He's gone already," Mabel said softly.

Thomas raised his face. His eyes were beginning to smart.

Pamela touched his arm. "Didn't you know? Willie and his mother both passed on yesterday. The others are getting a bit better. Mrs Wilson has been lookin' after them."

"I didn't know," he wheezed.

"You'd better stay away from the house for a while. Till they get over it," Hetty advised.

He turned and walked to the cart. He climbed up heavily. Facing the front, he adjusted his peaked cap and flicked the reins. Out of the corner of his eye he could see the girls gossiping and he wanted to turn and say something, or at least to look at Pamela, to have a good look at her so that he could recall her face later. But he could not concentrate.

"That's rude of him," scowled Hetty.

"He's upset," Pamela defended him, following the cart as it rattled up the road, with the dumbstruck Thomas Gray staring straight ahead of him.

"Oh yes?" Mabel winked at her. "Have you a soft spot for Thomas Gray, then, Pamela?"

"No!" she playfully slapped Mabel. "Just 'cos you're too scared-y-guts to skate!" she teased, trying to push Mabel onto the ice.

As she resisted, Mabel was joined by Hetty in pulling Pamela by the arms to the edge of the red ring and catapulting her forward. The wee boys called for them to do it. Pamela whizzed around the dark ice defiantly.

"I'm not scared!" she boasted. "Look, it's good fun."

But the other two big girls began to walk away, leaving Pamela on her own in the midst of the icy playground, singing a silly song and making the weans' faces split with laughter.

Thomas drove along the roads without the hedges or Post Office or church or bridge registering. He was aware of the main road before he realised he had gone too far. He had to swing the cart round to go back to the railway station for the box.

At the station, the noise and teeming activity showed him that life must go on, and this was a solace to him. The Baxters were there, loading coal from a wagon onto their cart. A train pulled in, puffing from its chimney and bellowing steam from the piston shafts at the big wheels and blasting its piercing whistle. The platform was hectic with men sorting out parcels, the station master fussing over a wealthy-looking old lady and a gang of labourers were working on the far track.

Thomas waited for the station master to send the train on and then enquired about his uncle's box. He was swiftly escorted to the side yard, where the long packing case was lying. He was left to negotiate it alone. It was slightly longer than the cart. Having slid it onto the cart, he stepped back and saw how much like a coffin it looked. His cart now seemed like Hennessey's horse-drawn hearse! Was this a sick joke his uncle was playing? Oh, but no: his uncle would not do that. Perhaps this was a reminder that he was only flesh and blood.

Willie Burns had been the same age as Thomas; they had gone to the elementary school together. This was a sign, an omen of death.

As Mrs Simpson swiftly hauled him home, with the long packing case bouncing at the back edge of the cart, Thomas's eyes drifted up to the leafless branches of the planting which was between the roadside hedge and the bank of the river. His thoughts drifted. At first, he tried to remember her face. The long, light brown hair cascading from beneath that floppy, woollen hat. The lightly freckled cheeks dimpled as parted lips flashed white teeth – she had a comely gap – and drew the round chin up; her eyes were a gentle grey-brown, tea colour. The nose was shorter in his imagination that he knew it to be, but he could not force his vision of it to coincide with reality.

But the beautiful feeling transformed into a chilliness, as the picture screen in the sky misted over, then cleared to reveal the Holy Ghost. What had he done wrong? The features were too harsh. How could he improve the body of his masterpiece – this *objet d'art*? He was pondering the imperfection of his creation when he suddenly awoke from his daydreaming to find himself driving along the last stretch of the Rathmore Road, between Kaye's and home.

Thomas woahed the mare in the yard. As the metallic racket of the hooves ceased, shouting replaced one form of discord with another. From inside the house came cries of spite. There was a row. The rough brogue of his uncle drowned out the woman's piteous anger. Isaac came out of the house, closing the front door briskly. With a resolute step, Isaac marched round the side of the house, beckoning with a wave for him to follow.

Thomas had the box tipped up half on the ground, half resting against the trailer, when Paul McCann appeared from down the road. The dog panted at their heels as they carried the long box round to the back of the house. In the vegetable garden, over at the far hedge away from the water pump, Isaac urged them to stand his eagerly expected delivery up on end. They propped it up against a big tree and held it firm as the farmer hammered it tight to the trunk.

"What's the point in that?" Thomas stuttered.

"Wait an' see," Isaac rubbed his nose, then scampered off to get some bits and pieces.

Upon his return, Isaac nailed runner strips of wood inside, then set a ready-made top on them. As he inserted the bucket, the light dawned for Thomas. He grinned approvingly with Paul, as they watched Isaac complete the preparations by attaching to the hinged lid, which was now a door, a make-shift catch, consisting of nails and a short piece of rope.

"Now," Isaac smiled proudly, "to try it out."

He closed himself inside his new lavatory. Paul and Thomas waited patiently, as the sounds from the bucket resonated tinnily.

"There," his voice echoed from within, "that's better than crouchin' at the back of the byre in this coul' weather. Thomas! Go into th' house and bring me some newspaper."

Thomas hared off obediently. The kitchen was gloomy, for the afternoon sun was casting no light in through the garden window. His mother was at the hearth, watching something baking. She was kneeling with a long poker in her hand, turning it slowly, turning it thoughtfully. She started. Her eyes were wide. The lids dropped as she recognised her son.

"What d'you want now?" she snapped. "You're as bad as that uncle of yours, always comin' in t' the kitchen, pestering me. You should be out during the day, doin' some work. Can't you let me get on with *my* work in peace?" She hovered over a boiling pot on the crane. "I'm busy! I'm so busy! I've the dinner t' cook, an' bakin' to do ..." She jabbed a finger in the direction of the table. On it, some flour-sprinkled dough sat in a half-kneaded lump on a board.

He explained what was needed. Without replying, Jean went to the dresser and got some newsprint from a drawer and, slowly and deliberately, cut it into strips with the bread knife. One side of her face was in the shadows. His eyes were fixed on her. Her expression seemed to communicate passive dignity, or lack of complaint.

"I got behind 'cos Mrs Crowe called by. We were talking of oul' times. When her Davy was alive. And our Bobby and Tommy. Before you were born." Her tone was calmer now, dreamier. "The summers were nicer then, the winters more snowy ..." She handed the paper to him and he ran from the house, unable to bring himself to thank her, feeling intimidated by her mood.

"Y' there yit?" Isaac was calling.

"Jist a minute," Thomas replied. "Is Mammy in one of her moods?" There was no reply from inside the box. The labourer beside him looked down at him blankly. "Look at this," he wagged a strip of newspaper to catch Paul's attention. As the hired hand struck a match to light his pipe, Thomas read out, "... In fission, uranium atoms, bombarded wi' neutrons, split into two halves. It was a German physicist, Otto Hahn ... did it. Some women working for him fled Germany and toul' everybody ... A new radioactive process ... it says. ... Could be used to build weapons of unprecedented power ... It's called 'nuclear fission'. What's that mean, then?"

Paul drew on his pipe stoically. "It means a new world order. Whoever gets it first wins the war. Unless, of course, the people rise up in socialist unity and revolt against the tyranny of Capitalism and Fascism in one mighty show of strength and moral purpose."

"But we're not at war."

"Not yet. And if either the Hun or the English gets the houl' of an atom bomb, there won't need to be much of a war. One explosion of that sort could ... I think I'm right when I say I read somewhere ... one would be enough to wipe out a whole city in one go. If it was big enough."

"That's impossible. I wonder, can you read what you believe in the papers?"

"Mibbe you mean that the other way round?"

Thomas thought about it, then replied, "Same difference."

Isaac bellowed, "There'll be an almighty explosion in here if ye don't gie me that paper!"

Paul wryly commented, "By the sound of it there's already been a few explosions in there."

Thomas handed the newspaper strips in through the creaking door. "By the smell of it, there's something dead in there."

Paul was piling turnips into the cradle of the green pulper. The acidic aroma of the yellow slices oozing out at the bottom, as Thomas forced the big handle round and round, seemed to cause a vapour, as if there was incense in the atmosphere.

"Paul, y'know that buk of yours ..."

As he lifted the swedes from the stack in the shed to plop them into the pulper, he chatted, "Aye. Have ye been considering joining the International?"

"When they talk about a Commune, they mean everybody has a room, like, and their own job, and everybody gets an equal say in running things and an equal share of the profits ...?"

"Aye. In Russia there's collective farms. A Soviet, or committee, is elected by the members, and they manage the farm – like a big estate."

"Well, sure, what happens if they don't make a profit? What if they make a loss?"

Paul hesitated. "But you're not talking about it in a Capitalist sense. You grow enough to feed your community. Then, whatever you're best at growing on your soil, you grow extra. You can trade it, with other collectives or industries, for what you need. You get coal; the miners get the food they need. It requires central control, to make sure resources are properly distributed. That's why you need to seize the means of production, distribution and exchange. Rather than sell it to the highest bidder, everybody who needs a commodity gets their fair share. Like the Famine, for instance. The Irish grew grain an' stuff, but the Landlords sold it abroad to pay for their luxurious lifestyles. They had crates of champagne and tons of meat and got fat and bought works of art or squandered it bettin' on horses, having balls and whatnot, and meanwhile the Irish people who did all the work to produce the stuff starved to death for want of a bellyful."

"I understand."

"Economic planning's a tricky business, far above your head ner mine. But at least we have the gumption to know what's in our own best interests."

It was warm as they worked in the shed. The rain was howling outside. The hurricane lamp was fizzing. The pulper ground with a precise swish as Thomas's arms revolved the blade.

"It's these notions of communes that don't square with me. I can't see as they'd work. Sure, why don't they try an experimental one?"

"They did, m'boy, in Paris! In about 1871, for a wee while, they had a Commune there. But the Capitalists outmanoeuvred them and put them out of business."

"Well, did it work?" Thomas asked with increasing confidence in his tone.

"Sure. Instead of toiling for coin, the worker officials gladly undertook the organisation of the economy and the chain of production and distribution, considering it to be a pleasure – rather than a duty or a mere 'job' – to serve their fellow workers."

After a lull in the conversation he asked, "So, a good Communist takes a dim view of art, then?"

"Not necessarily. Art is a necessity, not a luxury. It depends on priorities. Obviously, if you need to bring in the harvest, you should do that before you get out your paintbox or yer chisel."

"Yes!" cheered, Thomas pulped with renewed vigour. He was assured that his Holy Ghost was, at least materially, compatible with Communism.

"And this class business ..." Paul went on, "... that rings true. Do you know, the vast majority of the country's wealth is in the pockets of a handful of people?"

"I don't like the way yer man Marx goes on about the medieval classes, and especially about the '*idiocy* of rural life'. Who's he think he is?"

Laughing, Paul answered, "But the lords and ladies in their castles and mansions and big houses in the Malone Road[7] are the masters these days, and in a way we are their serfs. If we were wise at all, we'd rise up in socialist revolution and swap places with them. Then, we could sit and read poetry or embroider all day, while they pulped the turnips."

Thomas did not respond favourably to the older man's jocularity. "Huh. Recitin' Rabbie Burns fer Uncle Isaac on special occasions is bad enough. I wouldn't want to do that *every* day."

The door opened and Isaac swept in with a blast of cold air. The snow had gone now, but the land was sodden in the wake of the thaw. Paul straightened up from the pile of turnips. He lifted his cap to wipe his sweating forehead with the back of his hand. Thomas wound the handle of the pulper round until his load had all been cut.

"Thomas, young James is here lukin' a hand to fence down at thont field of Duggan's they've taken. There's a big slap[8] in th' hedge and they're bringin' their sows down here soon."

Thomas went off to help his cousin as his uncle took his place at the pulping. So the Usshers had rented the rath field at the bottom of the road. It sounded as if he was going to get the job of keeping an eye on the pig arcs for his friends. Going out from the outhouse to the road, Thomas discovered James was there already, with the wheelbarrow.

"You must be mad, comin' all the way from Umgall with that contraption. It must be twenty miles!"

---

[7]Malone Road = Belfast's Mayfair.
[8]Slap = (coll.) gap.

"Wha'? I didn't walk, y'know. Billy Falk gave me a lift to the top end of your road in his lorry."

"Oh."

They walked down the wet road towards the Duggan's land. It was a breezy day, so Thomas lowered his head into the wind as James clack-clacked beside him with the irritating barrow, full of equipment. The rath field had a high hedge that sheltered them from most of the wind.

As they made their way up the high ground to the hole in the hedge, Thomas told his cousin, "This was the 'dun' of Dunadry, y'know."

"What's that, then?" James asked, concentrating on the homemade post he was sledging into the dyke.

As he held the post for James to strike it, Thomas explained.

"This hump is where the fort in which the chieftain lived was. And the one up th' road's where the King of Dadriada had his court. The rath of Rathmore. He was the ruler of this part of Ulster in the days of the tribes."

"Oh, aye," James remarked, "in *pagan* times?"

"Loadsa folk lived here, in a defended camp. They farmed around the area, an' when an enemy tribe came to steal their cattle or steal their crops, they'd hurry inside the wall with their animals to defend themselves."

"Uncivilised times."

"Aye. I expect it was a bit like the Wild West. They fought over territory, like cowboys and injuns. The boundary between the land of these lot and the one's at the top of the road, at Rathmore, was at Kaye's march hedge."

James continued his sarcasm, "Or wherever the fighting happened to stop."

Thomas took up the billhook and chopped down a scraggly bit of thorn that was growing a good bit out from the line of the hedge.

"What have you done?" James exclaimed.

"I'm just tidying up the place. That bit was growin' out of a root."

"No it wasn't, That's a Fairy Thorn. You've done it now. The Little People will be after your hide. We're *cursed*."

Naw we're not ..." he retorted, without conviction in his words.

"Some great evil will befall us both, now," James warned. "Maybe not for even as long as a twelvemonth, but you don't do something bad like that and get away with it."

Thomas was agitated. "I didn't know I was doing something wrong."

"Doesn't matter," James sucked in a breath. "No sin goes unpunished."

A tense silence descended.

As they began putting a strand of wire across the hole, Thomas thought aloud, "They were sort of the original communists."

James Ussher raised an eyebrow. He continued hammering.

"They were all for one and one for all. All equal. Except, I suppose, for the leader. But there has to be a boss in every society, doesn't there? Like, I'm sure Comrade Stalin has a nicer house than Boris Bloggski. Still, the ancients must've had a better way of life than us: they shared and shared alike."

"Aye. They shared in their heathenness. That was afore the coming of Saint Patrick, don't forget. They still had snakes and demons in them days."

"An' Little People?" Thomas half-heartedly laughed.

Stuffing thorn branches into the gap, around the posts, Thomas's mind pictured bearded warriors charging over the brow of the hill, swords brandished, plaid kilts swishing, their bagpipes wailing. He could hear their battlecries, could feel the thudding of their feet on the earth as they charged towards him, faces contorted, fangs glinting ...

"Uh!"

James jumped too. "What?"

"Nothin'. Just a bad thought."

"A revelation?"

"A revolution."

They were squelching back to the gate when Patsy Duggan's donkey came trotting over. It was a mangy, grey-brown old thing with lame feet. It was a pet. They ruffled its mane and patted its neck.

"Now's your chance," James suggested. "You're always goin' on about how you want to be a cowboy, riding the range. Well, let's see how you would look."

Accepting the dare, Thomas sucked in a breath, took a grip of the mane and launched a leg over the short donkey's back. It took off. He was going to ride like a cowboy!

It whinnied as it galloped, terrified by this violation. Thomas bounced awkwardly on its back, leaning forward and holding onto the mane for dear life. A blur of green kaleidoscoped before his eyes. He could see the new wire ahead; it got nearer and nearer. The wind chilled his forehead. How would he get off? Which way should he go: left or right? He instinctively leant forward and let his legs lift over the mad beast's back.

There was a tremendous thump. He found himself rolling over backwards and felt a fierce bump shake his head. He could not breathe.

James was laughing uncontrollably. He tried to raise his fallen friend, but had no strength. Thomas lay, numbed, lost in the darkness of his throbbing head.

Eventually, the black void ceased to spin and he could see green grass. The grass smelt fresh and its moisture beneath him was refreshing. He became aware of the wind blowing the back of his neck. He was lying face down. He sat up. He could see a horrid face; he knew it was James's, but it was distorted, as if he were a malevolent, unearthly being.

"Ooooh," he moaned. "I feel sick."

Eventually, James managed to suppress his amusement. "Sorry I laughed! You could-a killed yourself. But you should-a seen yourself! You took off like a bat! The sight of you, bouncin' up and down and swingin' about from side to side on that thing! An' then, the way y' skidded along the field and went arse over elbows! Oh! My side's are burstin'. Y'alright?"

"I feel like it's next week."

"Pride comes before a fall," said James, helping him up.

The blue sky, patches of which were just visible behind all those grey cloudbanks, was God's vantage point. He was up there, watching everything that was going on.

Aye, he'd been proud to act the big man, teasing that poor, dumb donkey, so he'd paid the price. Or was it something else? Was it the pride he had, in his secret? His hidden desire – the urge to be something he was not. The vague dream of being the great artist, the sculptor: the ambition to break out of the mould in which he had been cast, to reshape his life – by himself – was that the sin? Maybe it *was* a graven image!

Every cloud has a silver lining, so this one's must be his finding out that good can come out of bad. At least now he knew where he had gone wrong and could put things right: he vowed to himself to destroy the unholy thing, to score it with his penknife. *I'll kill the demon!*

CHAPTER THREE

Tempest

The High Street was teeming with people and animals. It was market day in Antrim town. The rows of high, three-storied shop buildings stared across the broad street at each other, as if the pairs of windows far above the crowd's heads were eyes. To Thomas, the street was all a mass of hats and caps and suits and waistcoat chains and sharp-pressed trousers and sploshed shoes or dirty farm boots. His own corduroy breeches and even his jacket had already been splashed with filth by a careless cyclist. There was a Model T parked down at the garage, near the awesome block which was the Courthouse, but the street was so bunged he could not get a good look at it.

A man in a trilby and dapper suit was milling nearby, sizing up Thomas's three stirks, but did not seem the kind of man to buy beasts. The sergeant passed and he was a likely customer for, although he was one of the well-off townees, he kept a number of cows in a byre at the back of his large bungalow. But he patrolled on. Thomas replied to Davy Turkington's greeting as the neighbour passed up the street with his Clydesdale-drawn cart. One of the town's butchers was driving a beast up the alleyway to his byre in the yard behind his shop. The bustle and fuss of dealing all around was like an incessant buzzing between Thomas's ears. Excitable cattle raised their tails to dirty the pavement. Uncle Isaac usually did the dealing, but he had gone to Belfast on an errand. So Thomas was waiting, as per his uncle's instructions, for a good price.

Jimmy Rodgers from the Ballybentragh approached. Nervously stroking his hare lip, he wished Thomas, "Gud day."

Thomas's eyes flared as he stuttered, "Mornin', Jimmy."

Jimmy pulled a dusty handkerchief out of the pocket of his brown shopcoat. A trail of hay specks floated to the ground. His black trousers had little frays in them, so that patches of white flesh were visible. He tightened the cord around his waist, which kept his buttonless coat from flying free. Jimmy smelt, looked and lived like a tinker.

"Fine stirks. Yearls[9]."

---

[9] yearls = yearlings.

"Aye."

Jimmy made an offer. Thomas asked for more. Jimmy repeated his offer. Thomas repeated his price. Jimmy coughed up a laugh from his lungs. He tapped his stick on the ground. He bargained again. Thomas stuck to his price.

"I know the price of them, and so do you," Jimmy implored the boy.

A crowd was gathering to observe the battle of wits. Thomas was aware of the throng, but ignored them. He was not embarrassed to reaffirm his asking price.

"I've toul' you how much I want. That's what I'll take an' not a penny less."

He had supporters in the audience. They cheered him on by cracking gags. A few took Jimmy's side.

"Ye'll gie me a bit more yet." Thomas was adamant.

"I'll gie ye *nay* more," Jimmy smirked.

"Go on, y' oul' skinflint," a voice from the crowd butted in. "Give him what he's askin' for."

Eventually, Jimmy said, "Take them down thont big field of mine. Here, here's your precious silver." He removed some banknotes and coins from a tatty wallet and stuffed them into Thomas's fist.

"Watch out for the moths!" one of the spectators quipped and a ripple of laughter dispersed the audience.

He had to walk the young cattle back the way he had brought them, for Jimmy was determined to take it out of Thomas by making him deliver them to his farm. But Jimmy only lived a short distance from the end of the Rathmore Road, so it was not much out of his way.

On the road home Thomas felt happy. He had sealed a fine deal. He had also escaped that awful crowd in the town. It was early spring: the hedges were beginning to green and some of the trees were budding. He watched as rabbits sported in Culican's field. Some newborn lambs were lying with their mothers. An Austin truck roared past him; it was Billy Falk's coal lorry, so he waved and saw a hand flap. It's a pity we haven't a lorry or a tractor or a car. He felt a pang of envy, but checked himself.

"Who's that wee lad walkin' them stirks, Billy?"

"The wee fella Gray, from Rathmore. Luk at him: a dreamer. Like meself at that age! I had my head full of big ideas when I'd be drivin' beasts from place t' place. I started as a drover, y'know. At the market in Belfast. Thought I'd be rich an' famous some day. The dreams of children! All I've got's enough t' git by on, despite all me cattle dealin' an' drovin' and lorryin' an' coal merchantin'. Thon Isaac Gray, he's dun alright fer himself. Though he's been up and down on his luck a bit, too. At one time there was three brothers of them."

"Three? I know the oul' couple to see. Didn't know there was more of them at a time."

"Aye. Three boys and their oul' father. They took land all round the country. But the oul' man died, one of the brothers went off to Scotland with some wench, and then the other brother went till fight in the War, an' fell at the Somme."

"They had a run of bad luck."

"You said it, Hugh. And that wasn't the end of it. Sure, there were three sisters of them, too. Two of them married alright, but one, the ugliest one, stayed at the homeplace."

"I thought she was his wife."

"No, she's a sister. Anyway, she ended up havin' that wee fella we just passed on the road. Aye, you could say she's the wife without a husband."

"An' who was responsible?"

Billy told his labourer, "Now you're talkin'. Y'know the way it is, all hush-hush. At first, they though it was mibbe one of their casual han's. You know what them baes[10] are like, not a scruple between them to scratch your left nostril with. But about a year later, one of the wemen that gathered spuds fer Grays fell pregnant, too, and the rumours started flyin', not only was *hers* Isaac Gray's, but the *sister's* cub was, too."

"Holy God!"

"Of course, it was only iver talk. There were so many versions of things goin' round. The woman, Marbeth Manson, married a council labourer, Ben Hart – a bit of a drunkard. So, whether the eejit married her for the wrong reason, or for the *wrong* reason, if you catch my drift, nob'dy seems t' know fer sure."

"Except her."

"An' mibbe not even her!"

---

[10]bae = (coll.) boy.

The lad glanced out at the patchwork of fields at Kilmakee, where the lush green land led down to the Six Mile River. "So, is oul' Isaac Gray a bit of a boyo?"

"He's like all them Blackmouth Presbyterians, as tight as an angel's ..." Ack-huole! He spat out of the rolled-down cab window. "D'you know why they're called Blackmouths?" As the lad shook his head, Billy informed him. "In 1798 the Presbyterians, although they're Protestants, were called Dissenters, because they weren't Church of Ireland like us. Only Anglicans could be part of the Establishment in them days, see, an' the Presbyterians were basically outlawed, same as the Cath'lics. They'd weren't allowed to vote or sit in Parliament or anything like that.

"So, they fought with the Taigs in a rebellion in 1798, against British troops, to try and get the same kind of independence the Americans an' French were gettin', about the same time. Of course, because only the north rose, the southerners didn't, it was easily nipped in the bud.

"The rebels fled to the hills and lived off sloeberries, which gave them a black stain around their mouths. So, they're called Blackmouths. They've an independent streak in them, they don't like anybody tellin' them what t' do. An' at the same time they don't mind tellin' everybody else what to do! Or what *not* to do, I should say, seein' as they're keen on the idea of folk being good-livin'!"

Hugh's head was beginning to sag wearily. "They're a dour lot." He grimaced as Billy blew another heckle out of the window.

Having chased the calves into Jimmy Rodgers' big field, Thomas hurried up the road. It was about time for the milking. As soon as he got to the house he spilled the cash out from his pocket onto the table. His mother counted it but said nothing.

He went out to the field and hollered. Some of the cows were already near the gate, ready to wander in for the evening milking. The stragglers began to plod their way towards the byre. Jean was at the door, in her boots, stool in hand, all set for her quota, when they heard the clatter of the trap. So she went in when Isaac arrived back from Belfast, to tell him the price Thomas had got for the calves.

Thomas was in a mesmeric trance, induced by the way his hand's were rhythmically manipulating the shorthorn's teats, when his stupor was violently disturbed as his uncle opened the door of the byre, slamming it against the wall. Thomas's hands halted.

Isaac was fuming. The old man scraped his boots along the floor as he hurried towards the boy.

"I'll skelp ye!" He began to unfasten his belt.

"Sure, I got a guid price!"

The collar was almost ripped from his shirt as Thomas was lifted up and bent over his uncle's knee. Isaac had a foot on the edge of the stool to steady himself as he pushed his nephew's pliant body over. He thrashed the lad's backside with the buckle. The white cow stepped from hind leg to hind leg.

Tears began to flow as Jean shouted angrily, "Stop it! That's the cow wi' head staggers. You'll set her off."

Thomas's arms flailed like the souples on a hay teader. He got the fingernails of one hand to his uncle's chest and scratched at him. He got his other claw on the cold, bony knee and prised himself up. Isaac's strength was matched. He drew back from the rising boy.

"Don't you come back wi' out a luck penny again!" he bellowed.

"Isaac! He's almost grown," Jean protested. "You can beat a child, but not a stretchin' lad."

"I'll be puttin' him o'er me knee till he's man enough to stap me." He stood back, squaring his shoulders. "You're gonna sell them other stirks nixt, an' if you don't get double th' luck penny, there'll be double th' ruckions." Isaac walked slowly out of the byre, belt hanging limply from his grasp.

The rocking cow's motion slowed as Jean calmed her by petting her.

"You get the tay, Mummy, I'll finish the cows by meself," he said calmly.

"And you can keep your place and honour your elders and betters, young man. You're not fully grown yit, you're only half-roads there. Your uncle's upset about havin' to go and pay the Land Annuity. You know it always riles him, to still have to pay it. As if we've not paid enough, all these years."

"Don't make excuses for him, Mummy. He's just ... bad-tempered."

Jean left the byre.

Alone again, Thomas scratched the cow's head, taking over the job of calming her. Rita's ears twitched. She slobbered as she nuzzled barley.

"Hush, Rita, don't start your punch drunk staggerin' th' day. What's he gettin' stormy for, eh, Rita? No call for it, eh? I tell ye what, though, if he wants a fight, I'll take him on!" His face flared. "It'll be a gunfight at the OK cowshed! Yissir, a shoot out in Dodgey-Dairy City." He sat down again and recommenced the milking with his head against the cow's side, listening to each splash into the bucket as if it was the sound of a distant train on the tracks. "Dern Comanches! We'll show 'em, eh, Rita? For all their savage ways, we'll teach them dirty injuns a lesson. Me an' Ma Smith an' Wesson. We'll teach 'em a lesson."

The following week, Thomas was sent to the Fair in Antrim again, with instructions to sell the sick calf to an unsuspecting customer. He took the beast, its legs securely bound up with rope, in the back of the cart.

Old Star was obligingly trotting along the main road when Thomas noticed a familiar figure walking along the pavement. It was Jimmy Rodgers, swinging his blackthorn stick and singing to himself. A pang of guilt crept through Thomas: here he was, riding high, while the poor oul' buddy had to walk. He stopped the cart beside the country gentleman and let him climb on.

"This is very good of ye, Thomas. Say, are you going to be sellin' the calf?"

"If I get a guid price."

"What's the matter with ut?"

He frowned and said crossly, "I'm takin' it in the cart because I have to go anyway, to get six bags of flour an' a hunnerd weight of sugar fer me ma."

Taken aback by the wee fella's surliness, Jimmy tried to get round him with lighthearted banter. "Don't be tellin' folk that. They'll say you're a Mummy's Boy. Would this critter be a dear price?"

"Aye!" Thomas joked, his face muscles relaxing.

They argued over figures. He saw his chance and started the bidding well in excess of what his uncle wanted. Jimmy brought him down, Thomas took Jimmy up: they compromised. Bursting with pride, Thomas felt elated: it was more than the double Luck Penny his uncle had been slabbering about all week.

"You've learnt your lesson, anyway, I see – to start at a higher price than you intend to settle for!" Jimmy laughed.

Thomas pocketed the money and left Jimmy off in town. He had to leave the animal off in Jimmy's yard on the way home but that was a pleasure, after the coup of selling the ill beast for more than his uncle had wanted.

Upon his return home, Thomas found Isaac in the stable, graiping out matted straw. He displayed the money to his uncle. He tried to sound as casual as possible. "I got your double Luck Penny."

Isaac paused only to stuff the money into his pocket and carried on forking the stinking bedding. "Can you take the harrow up to Begley's? I promised your Uncle Stan I'd let him hi' the lend of it."

Dispirited, Thomas wrestled with the heavy, iron implement to get both sections onto the back of the cart. He let Star do the work of navigating to the Holestone: she knew the route. His backside got stiff. The day was dull. All his happiness had evaporated.

At Begleys, at the townland of Holestone, on the hills that marked the beginning of the Glens of Antrim, James Ussher was there to greet him.

"Afternoon, Thomas! Great day, isn't it?"

"'S'alright. Y' here again? D'ye niver work at your own place?"

"Gotta do a bit of neighbourin' fer your kith an' kin, Thomas," he laughed along with his cousin. "It's only civil."

James had a seed sowing fiddle in his arms. He was checking the wooden box and bowstring mechanism for wear and tear. "I'm about ready to sow the barley. You brought the harrow just at the right time."

"Am I glad to see you!" Uncle Stan was shaking Thomas's trouser leg, grinning up at his nephew, who was sitting at the front of the cart. "But come on in and get a bite of dinner, before we start anything."

"But ..."

"No buts," James smiled.

They led Thomas into the big farmhouse kitchen. Aunt Sarah was at the range in her white apron, ready to dish out the steaming stew. From the table, Mary welcomed him. He sat beside James Ritchie, the hand at Begley's. The friendly atmosphere infected Thomas and he was soon chatting to James about his new cowboy book. He devoured the delicious mince and carrots and potato slices with reverence.

"Is that Paul McCann still at your place?" Uncle Stan asked.

"Aye. He lent me a book, too. By Marx. But I don't know if I agree with it or not."

"Bolshevism!" James Ritchie commented. "That buddy's a known Commie. I would watch him if I was you. He could be a spy, tryin' to undermine our British way of life for the Soviet cause. Don't laugh," he warned Mary, "there's loads of Commies in England already."

"It's not the politics I was thinkin' about," Thomas muttered.

"It's an Atheist creed," James voiced for him.

"Yes," his Aunt Sarah nodded approvingly. "That man is trouble. He's an agent of the Deil. Don't let him lead you astray. A rolling stone gathers no moss."

"He says that religion is like a drug, or drink, that it's a way of numbing yourself to the horror of reality."

"There's nothing horrible about reality!" scoffed James Ritchie. "Just the way he lives *his* life!"

"God protects you from the horrors of reality." James Ussher did not look up when he spoke.

Thomas stumbled over his attempt to express his feelings. "I'm not sure about this socialism stuff. It sounds a bit like what Jesus said. All the stuff about everyone getting a fair chance in life, 'to each according to his needs', and that. But the stuff about religion being only a ... solace, the idea that our faith could be merely the 'heart of a heartless world', I ... think that's ..."

"Balderdash." It was Stanford Begley, Esquire, who summed it up. "Isn't that right, James?" He eyed both his nephew and his employee.

"That oul' tramp Paul gives me the willies," said Mary. "How can he live like that? Wandering from place to place, sleeping in lofts and sheds or at the back of a hedge. No family of his own, no home of his own, no job, or life at all."

"Like a Wandering Jew." James Ussher paused to sip his buttermilk before speaking again. "Some people are predestined to such a life."

"Were ye not at Antrim th' day?" Uncle Stan enquired.

"Yes." Thomas was glad to get his feet on firmer ground. "I sold that poor doin' wee calf we had."

"Surely, if it dies, you'll have tricked someone?" Mary innocently suggested.

Aunt Sarah was setting a plate of buttered scones and pieces of oatcake on the table. As she poured cups of tea for them, she pointed out, "It's up to the customer to pay his money and take his chance. The calf may live, or it may die. It is not in Thomas's power to affect the outcome. If God deems it to die on one person, or live for another, so be it."

"Aye," Stan slurped his tea. "Business is business."

James Ussher said, "I'm sure that Thomas didn't rip the purchaser off."

Thomas's lowered jaw was suspended half-open. "Well ... It was oul' Jimmy Rodgers bought it. He asked me was the calf sick. I didn't say it wasn't." His voice tailed off.

"There you go," James Ritchie interjected.

"Anyway, he ripped me off for a Luck Penny last week."

Stan giggled. "Good man yourself. Don't let anybody get one over on you. It's a tough oul' world out there. It's not the socialist paradise no-hoper dreamers like the Prophet Paul pretend. There's a fine line between 'live and let live' and getting walked over."

"But if you didn't tell him the calf was ill, that would have been a different matter," Mary mused. "That would have been dishonest."

And immoral. This notion was just crossing Thomas's mind. In not telling Jimmy that the calf was actually sick, he believed he had in effect told a lie. The enormity of this wrong-doing was beginning to sink in. As the others chatted gaily, Thomas brooded about his latest shortcoming. It was another sin. It was even *another type* of sin he had committed. The fear of discovery, the shame of guilt, the pain of moral depravity filled his belly with a cold weight, totally destroying the afterglow that he should have felt with the nice taste of tea and crumbly oatcake still in his mouth. This was a serious matter.

If the calf died, Jimmy would shame him in front of the whole community. He'd never be able to trade at Antrim market again as long as he lived! Sure, he had told fibs, little white lies, when he was wee. But he couldn't remember ever having deliberately misled someone about something. What was happening to him? Why was he falling short of the glory of God? Why did he keep doing these evil things?

"What d'you think, Thomas?" James Ritchie was asking him.

Snapping out of his haze, he grunted, "About what?"

"About me emigrating to America."

"You could get a big ranch in New Mexico and drive herds of cattle across the plains and ride on horseback all day long."

"I want to go!" Mary swooned. "I could be a cowgirl, and cook beans and learn to shoot Red Indians and wear a fancy hat and boots with spurs."

"Have a bit of sense." Stan was unimpressed. "If you want to ride a horse, there's our Dapple out in th' yerd, there."

"You could ride shotgun for me, on a covered wagon."

"How unlady-like," Aunt Sarah rejected Ritchie's proposal.

"You should be acting your age," James Ussher told his namesake. "Not keeping the wee girl going."

"I'm sixteen," Mary protested. "I'm grown up."

"Not till you're twenty-one," James Ritchie said, sticking his tongue out at her.

"You'll not be grown up till I say so." Aunt Sarah laid down the law.

Mary smiled coyly at him.

Saturday night was bath night for Thomas. As usual, McCann had gone over to the loft to read before resting his head. As Thomas was lifting the iron bathtub down from the half-loft, above the grownups' bedrooms, which was open to the kitchen, he noticed his uncle taking his coat from the peg.

"What are you up to now?" Jean asked from her rocking chair, where she was darning socks.

"I'm just goin' fer a futther[11] about."

Thomas expertly hopped off the dresser, barely shaking a plate. He set the tub down in front of the hearth and began filling it with hot water from the kettle and all the pots and pans that were arranged around the hobs.

"He's getting too big to wash in the kitchen," Isaac told his sister. "He should take it int' the parlour like ourselves." With that, he went out.

Thomas stripped off his clothes. They felt clogged with dirt and sweat. It would be great, as always, to get a crisp shirt on – and his Sunday suit, after the morning's milking. It was light outside, so rays

---

[11] futther = (coll.) fiddle.

full of dancing sunbeams were cast into the centre of the kitchen, through the yard-facing window, from the west. The spring was definitely here. The room did not feel cold when he was naked, which made the water all the more inviting. There was just enough water for him to splash about in, soaping himself, sitting with his knees poking up.

As he scratched a lather into his crown, he heard a log in the fire drop deeper into the embers. His eyes were closed, but he knew that sound meant that something had altered position in the grate. The next noise, however, came with a force like the shock wave of an explosion.

Crash! Like thunder, glass shattered. Jean looked up to witness a shower of sparkles, like flashes of lightning, tinkling onto the tiles. Thomas heard her scream a cry of fury, like the wild wind. He scooped water over his head creating a deluge to get rid of the soap, rubbed his eyeballs, and looked round the kitchen.

His mother was standing in front of the frantically rocking chair. There was a snorting beast in the room: the white cow. It was staring angrily at him. It took an unsteady step to one side. He saw the window frame and glass scattered on the floor. A draught gave him goosebumps. He stood up slowly, as the cow breathed with erratic gasps and staggered against his mother. It catapulted her against the chair and her body toppled over onto the tiles. The chair, which had been slowing down, tossed itself silly again.

Thomas struggled with his trousers, then sweater. Looking up from fastening his flies, he saw the mad cow over in the far corner, standing on its hind legs, trying to climb the wall. Mad Rita was scraping at the plaster near the ridge with her front hooves. Her mouth and nose were bubbling with saliva.

The door banged open. His uncle rushed in and stared at Thomas, wide-eyed. Before the boy could speak, his uncle had gone to his bedroom. Thomas could see through the ajar door that Uncle Isaac was loading his shotgun.

The cow was down again, on all fours. It suddenly rushed towards him. Thomas dived towards the rocking chair. He got up to see the tail whisking in the air as the shorthorn squeezed her way around the jamb passage and out the front door. Uncle Isaac ran after the beast.

Thomas was near his mother. She was on her back on the floor. He crouched by her. She had a bump on her head. There was a lot of blood gushing over the white sleeve of her blouse. The thick heat of the red plasma nauseated him. He stood up, his head vibrating as his mind volleyed with the dilemma: should he stay with her, or get help?

He quickly tied on his boots and ran outside and to the gate. Down the road, he could see his uncle jogging with the gun, the dog yapping at his heels. Thomas sprinted in the other direction, towards Dr Moore's, brushing his streaming hair down onto his head as he galloped. He was panting when the doctor, dressed in plus-fours, answered his frantic knocking.

"Come quickly! It's a matter of life and death! Rita the white shorthorn's gone mad! She's ... got the head staggers and ..." he wheezed.

"Are you sure it's not the horse doctor you want?"

"No, no. Me ma ... mother ... she's bleeding. And she's out coul'. The cow knocked her over."

Thomas hurried with him to the back of the house and they got into his car. As he drove at top speed to the Orchards, he asked for more details. Thomas struggled to keep his mind on his narrative as he oggled the plush mahogany dashboard and dials.

At Gray's, they found that Jean was semi-conscious. Smelling salts brought her round. Dr Moore cleaned her wound and bandaged it. It was just a graze. He made sure Thomas swept up the broken glass and splintered frame. He found the Gospel quotation in the midst of the debris, its glass cracked. Thomas set it on the dresser with affectionate care.

> You have not chosen Me, It is I who have Chosen you.
>
> John 15.16

The doctor had done his job and was revving up the engine when Isaac arrived back. Thomas was giving his mother a cup of sugary tea when he noticed, through the space where the window lines should have been, Isaac leaning with his head in the car window. As the motor vehicle drove off, Isaac stood watching, grim-faced, the open breach resting over his forearm.

Entering the kitchen, Uncle Isaac demanded, "Where were you?"

"I could ask you the same thing."

"None of your lip," he tossed his cap into his chair. "I had to chase thon beast meself. Eddie Kaye seen it comin' and stood out in the road and it near went through him. He dived into the hedge! I plugged it at the end of their lane." He stroked the barrels. Then, noticing Jean's bandages, he demanded, "Why'd ye get the dacteur?"

"I thought her arm was broke."

"I'm not too bad. Just a bit dazed."

Isaac's face drained of colour; as he yelled, however, it flared red. "Dacteur! Dacteur! We cin't afford Dacteur's bills! Sure, she didn't need that. A bit of lick an' spittle an' she'd be right as rain."

"Well ... I didn't know that at the time."

"Don't be too hard on him, Isaac ..."

"He didn't stop to think," his uncle scolded. "Instead of harin' aff, he should-a looked at you. If there was somethin' serious wrang, you might-a bled to death afore he got back wi' yont bae."

Thomas quickly shuffled into his uncle's bedroom. Raising up the mattress with an aggressive tug, he threw it into the corner of the small room. From out of a brown paper bag that was on top of the springs he brought a handful of banknotes. He rushed into the kitchen, waving them at his uncle's face.

"There's plenty of money here! It's only paper! Gie it to th' doctor! Gie it all to him!" Thomas was bellowing with more rage than he had ever displayed before. He launched the notes into the air. They began to flutter around the flustered farmer.

"Thomas! You're crazy." Isaac snatched at a couple of the floating banknotes.

"That's my mother! If I'm crazy to care about her when she's lyin' knocked out by a wild beast, then yes! I'm crazy. She might-a been killed! I'd give all this money an' ten times more if I thought it' ud help her!"

Thomas grabbed the rest of his clothes and towel and stormed off to his room. Isaac had, during this barrage, stood shocked into silence, looking at his sister, not at the boy.

"What's all the commotion?" Paul entered the kitchen from outside. Seeing the money on the floor, the broken window and the bandaged Jean, he quizzed wryly, "Has there been a burglary?"

Towards the end of March they began planting the turnips and dropping the potatoes. Some of the local women came to the Grays' fields to earn themselves a bit of extra money. Marbeth Hart had always been a hard worker. She had often laboured for Isaac in the past. That Friday evening, free from their jobs at the Works, she arrived with Pamela to earn some pin money. Thomas was busy following the dung cart with Eddie Kaye, scaling the manure in the drills with a fork.

The women, in their full skirts and heavy blouses, and the girls, in a cavalcade of colourful, light dresses, were bent over, hunchbacked, as they groped in their guggerin' bags for seed to drop. Terence, Eddie's young brother, was refilling the hessian pouches. Paul McCann was leading one of the mares, Isaac the other, the two men working as a team to bring the dung from the midden on carts. Isaac had Mrs Simpson because she was the slower of the horses, encumbered as she was by the three-week-old foal trotting by her side. The pause, as Isaac reloaded the cart at the smoking dunghill, let the foal suck.

The field was a hive of active bodies. Some of the women were gossiping. Paul was aloft the cart, graiping down the rank, strawy manure to the lads. As they spread the dung in the drills around them, Eddie and Thomas chatted.

"Is the motorbike goin' okay?"

"Grand. I was at Crumlin last week, for a spin. With Emily," he grinned to emphasise the concluding remark.

Thomas glanced across the brown field to focus on Emily Fleming's backside. "Hae ye any more soccer games, Eddie?"

"We're not in a league this season. That was just a tournament I toul' ye about, at Randalstown. James Ussher was there. Captain of First Umgall. A right player. But our team was more experienced. We've challenged the Clady Works team to a match. But there's a line up agreed already, I'm afraid. I'm glad this is the last of the spuds! An' only our wee corner field to go, wi' th' turnips." He stretched up to relieve an ache in his back. "I see Emily's right an' friendly with Pamela Hart." Eddie gave his neighbour a knowing glint.

"Mmm." Thomas sneaked a peek out of the corner of his eye up at the cart. Paul was walking to the front of the cart to gather up the reins and steer Star back to the gate, for this load was finished. "They're of an age. A year below me at school. Are you takin' Emily for a spin th'marra?"

"Aye. Are you fer goin' a rake?"

Thomas also straightened up as they waited for Isaac to trundle over from the yard. "Dunno if I'd be allowed. Ma wouldn't like it.

Mind you, Uncle Isaac surta owes me one. But sure, I wouldn't wanna be a wallflower," he stuttered.

"Look," Eddie confessed, "Emily's right an' pally with Pamela. Y'know, Pamela sort of fancies you or at any rate she doesn't have any objections to you and ... Emily's gonna try an' coax her t' come too." He wiggled his eyebrows, meaningfully.

Thomas's heart was in his mouth. He choked over his words, glancing sheepishly at Pamela and back at Eddie. "But ..."

Eddie winked.

Thomas grinned, lowering his face to the stones and soil. "I'll come if I can. If she will. But it depends on *their* say-so." He lowered his voice, for his uncle was approaching with the next load of dung.

They soon got a break from the work, when Jean appeared with a basket and a big metal jar full of tea. The basket contained old, chipped or handleless cups and hunks of buttered bread. Some of the working women had also brought a piece.[12] They all gathered round the grassy ditch near the gate. Thomas noticed that Eddie and Emily had got their rations and had wandered along the hedge some way from the crowd of adults. Thomas stood supping his sugary tea, watching with fervid anticipation as Emily beckoned Pamela towards her. Words were exchanged. Pamela glanced at Thomas. Eddie beckoned him.

"We're goin' for a spin on the motorbike tomorrow. Would you like to come, too? Eddie's going to ask Thomas to come along, too." Emily raised her eyebrows. "Go on! I dare you! You said when I asked that you had nothing against him. 'He's alright' you said."

Eddie reassured her. "It's just a day out. Nothing romantic. Just a gang of us goin' for a rake."

"Aye, you pair and," she lowered her voice, "us pair."

"You're not steppin' out with Dickie anymore, are you?"

"No. But I don't want people thinkin' there's something going on between me and him that there's not."

"Not yet," Emily grinned mischievously.

"Oh, don't put her off," Eddie pleaded. "Come on Pamela, say 'Yes'. Just this once. No one's forcing you. You'll enjoy it. Think of it: a zip along the roads on the bike, the wind in your hair, you'll get to see places up the coast road you've probably never seen before, the beaches, the little towns ..."

---

[12] piece = (coll.) snack lunch.

"Oh, alright. Give over. I'll do it. But," she warned him, "you're not to blab about this. I don't want people thinking things I don't want them to about me."

"Sure," said Eddie; "Thomas is a decent bloke, isn't he?"

"He's a bit gauche," Emily told him.

"Where'd you learn fancy words like tha'?" he teased her, stroking her chin.

Pamela bit her lip, before shaking her head and saying, "We used to get on alright at school. And at the Youth Club at the Church an' all." Then, in response to Emily's teasing stares, she added, "Mind you, he's not Clark Gable, is he?"

"At least he's here, with us. Well, almost!" Eddie laughed.

Thomas bowed his head and went to them. Pamela was not smiling: he thought that he was about to be extremely embarrassed, shamed. His stomach fluttered.

"Do you fancy going for a ride on Sunday?"

"Aye. Don't mind," Thomas answered Eddie.

"The girls are coming."

"Sure, there won't be room for us all in your sidecar!" Thomas bravely looked at Pamela. And his heart leapt, for his sentiment was one of pleasure that she was going to go with him.

"It doesn't matter. You can come on your pushbike."

"But my mother's old thing's not been used since ... I was wee, and it's all rusted up now."

Eddie waved his hand, saying, "That doesn't matter. I've bought Willie Burns' old bike off his brother. You can borrow it. The gears are playing up, but I should have her fixed by the weekend."

"I ..." he stuttered, "I won't be able to keep up with a motorbike."

"I'll stick by you! Piece of cake," Eddie told him.

Pamela smiled. Thomas's lips were drawn across his face until it felt his cheeks would rip. He was grinning with joy. The sweet tea and fresh warm wheaten bread filled him with elation. He noticed the cheeps of the birds building nests in the hedgerows, and his head seemed to reverberate with melodies of ecstasy.

"What's this barney you had with your uncle?" Pamela asked him.

"How d'you know about that?" he half-whispered.

"Your uncle was down a while ago to see if Mummy was coming up to drop, and he said yous had a mad cow and that you blew your top, too. I didn't think he'd be shaken up that easily."

"Was he shaken up?"

"Well, I think a bit."

"What have you been up to?" Eddie enquired.

"Nothin'. Just, that oul' cow that you nearly got knocked over by …"

"Aye."

"… It jumped through our kitchen window …"

"I heard about that," Emily said.

"And it knocked me ma over. And she was badly hurt. But all he could think about was …"

Emily's mouth puckered. Pamela's chin was bobbing expectantly. Eddie cocked his head.

In a quiet tone, he continued, "He wasn't there when it happened. So, he didn't think it was so bad. But it was."

"He said you were raging like the cow."

Initially speechless, Thomas stammered, "Well, I was thinkin' about me ma. She was unconscious. And bleeding badly. It looked worse than it turned out to be. Anyway, I was in the bath, in me birthday suit, when our Rita jumped through the winda."

The others laughed loudly. Bemused, but happy for once to be the centre of attention, Thomas laughed with them. The men and women were heading back to their positions in the field. Their gaggling had to end. Everyone would have to work swiftly if they were to beat the dark clouds and get the last of the potatoes dropped before the rain came on. Scaling alongside Eddie, Thomas paused momentarily to stand erect and survey the field of women and girls, his confidence immeasurably boosted. This was *his* field, *his* farm, *his* world; his life was more bearable at moments like this.

One of the heifers was having trouble calving. She was standing straining, her bones already dropped and a trail of bloody matter was being discharged. He walked her back to the yard, put her in an outhouse and got his uncle and Paul.

Isaac began splicing a length of rope. He told Thomas, "Have a feel in there and see why she's stuck."

Paul had managed to get a halter on the heifer. Thomas began to roll up his sleeve. He had not done this before, but did not want to let on. He gritted his teeth as his fingers entered the cow. He pushed his arm on in. Phew! There was a sensation of moisture and heat around his arm. Paul was holding her steady.

"Feel anythin'?"

"I've got a nose. Eye. Ear. Another ear. No, it's the side of another one. Twins. They're stuck!"

"Bunged up!" Paul laughed.

"Give us a feel." Isaac bared his arm.

As Thomas withdrew his arm a sloosh of bloody fluid poured onto the grass. Phew! Rotten eggs. Worse!

"Must be dead," sniffed Uncle Isaac. He felt around for some time. Withdrawing his arm, he said to Thomas, "Run over to the yard and fetch the horn saw." As Paul knitted his brows, Isaac told them, "It's deformed." It was only when Thomas returned with the wire saw that Isaac told them the problem. As he inserted his arm with the instrument, he muttered, "It's got two heads. I'm gonna have to cut one off."

"Impossible."

"You feel." He was adamant.

"Shouldn't we get the vet?" Thomas ventured.

"Vit!" Uncle Isaac snapped. "He'd charge us the price of a cow and a half t' do the same job we cin do oursel's."

"Well, it is a cow and a half," Thomas pointed out.

"A-but there's nithin' gonna come outta this lady alive."

"Deed already," Paul nodded. "It's a risk you're takin' with the cow, but better risk it yourself than risk losin' the cow and payin' a vet t' kill her forbye."

"Aye, it's only an oul' cow," Thomas agreed stoically. "But sure, wouldn't Davy Sharpe be any use?"

His uncle's face widened in amazement. "Davy Sharpe! Th' horse doctor? Sure, he couldn't ... He couldn't ..."

McCann assisted him. "He couldn't cure a chicken of the pox." But his risqué humour extracted no congratulation from the Grays, for it was beyond the pale.

Isaac got the wire over one of the heads and laboured awkwardly through the passage to cut through the flesh. Eventually, he tugged and the wire came out. He rested on the grass for a few minutes.

"I'm beat," he wheezed. "You pull it out son. Bring out the head first. The calf should come easy, then."

Thomas slid his arm in again. He groped around until he made contact with a cold, wobbling nose. He gripped the nostrils and heaved. The light object came easily out of the cow. He swung it round and threw it rolling onto the grass. There it lay, severed at the neck like a butcher's offcut. Thomas took a deep breath and cautiously searched for the legs of the dead calf. He got them and guided them to the end. Once they could see the white hooves, they were able to tie the ropes round the legs. With Isaac and Thomas pulling on a leg each, the calf came tumbling out. The heifer lay down in the shed as it was injected. They stared at the twisted thing, fascinated by the bloody gash at the side where the extra head had been torn from.

His mind was reeling. "Why did that turn out like that?"

A sin caused it. And no sin goes unpunished.

"Just another freak of nature, son," his Uncle Isaac told him. "Ours is to do and die, not to reason why."

Thomas was in Duggan's field in his good clothes. He stepped cautiously through the mud to the troughs and scattered the bag of dusty meal. The grunting, squealing, bustling piglets and lumbering, fat sows were already snouting through the mix of bruised barley and Indian corn. The latecomers that had that been lazing in their corrugated iron huts battled for a place at the feeding troughs. Squelching back from the scene of action, Thomas cast a cold eye upon each pig, to judge its health. None were ill. He walked carefully back to the five-barred gate, where the bicycle was propped against the huge, round, white Ulster pillar.

The rip of a motorbike preceded Eddie and his Norton. He stopped the machine with a splutter and raised his goggles.

"How's it going?"

"All done."

"I'm sorry again about the bike. Couldn't fix th' machine properly because it was late when I was workin' on her and I couldn't get any parts. But as I say, if you ride ahead, we'll catch you up. Y'know, I didn't think your mother would even let you out."

"I didn't say the girls were going. You mustn't tell her that! Sure you won't, Eddie?"

"Me?" he grinned, kick-starting the motorbike.

He was off with a rev and a rip. Thomas disconsolately climbed the gate. He had so wanted to spend all day with Pamela. He thought they would be together on the journey. The thought of learning to ride a motorbike had been beginning to grow on him. After all, he had had a go in Kaye's cattle truck, around the yard, once. Driving was easier than he had thought it would be.

Resigned to his bicycle, he set off down the road and began pedalling along the main road towards Larne. He had sped past Templepatrick village before Eddie caught up with him.

They stopped at the end of Paradise Walk for a short while. The girls were excited to be on an outing. Thomas joked at the state of Pamela's hair, all tossed every which way about her shoulders from the blast across the top of the sidecar. Emily had to shake her hands and legs; being in the pillion seat made her grip onto Eddie for dear life. Pamela said she should cycle and Thomas could go on the back. He didn't mind that she wasn't keen on the idea; he found the ride to the coast road was interesting at his leisurely pace. This Saturday was taking on a special atmosphere all of its own. The trees and hedges and fields and smoking chimneys all seemed to pay homage to God's handiwork. This day was turning out to be splendid. Why then did he sense a lurking malevolence, like the distant humidity in the heavens, if the day was going so well?

They did not stop along the road again. Eddie kept speeding ahead, then doubling back to follow the ferociously pedalling Thomas, as if he were a sheepdog rounding him up. He ushered the cyclist past the port of Larne and onto the small coastal village of Glenarm. Thomas felt sure they were never going to stop. His legs felt tight and his chest was heaving for want of puff. The gears kept slipping, making him double the effort. He halted at the end of the main street, waving at Eddie to go no further. The motorbike turned and roared back to where Thomas was sitting on a low wall, hands on hips, sucking in air.

"Given up?" Eddie asked with a shrill pitch.

As he leant over to tug off the bicycle clips he gasped, "This is far enough. D'you expect me to re idto Timbuktu?"

"I'm frozen," Emily struggled out of the sidecar, rubbing her arms. "And I'm desperate for a pee."

As Emily wandered off across a field at the edge of town, Eddie got a basket out of the sidecar. They had brought a flask of tea and some jam sandwiches.

"This is like tea in the field!"

As Thomas struggled to his feet he dropped a clip. When he twisted over to pick it up, a jag made him jump up straight, swotting at his behind. Pamela was whooping and laughing; Eddie was smirking.

Rejoining them, Emily asked, "What's up, Thomas?"

"She pinched my bottom."

"That'll show you boys what it's like for us girls." Pamela's eyes glittered with self-confidence.

Emily raised her friend's arm as a referee does a boxing champion's. "Three cheers for the Summerhill suffragettes!"

Eddie joked, "Ooh, me next, pinch me now!"

They ate ravenously, unaware in their eagerness of the village's utter silence.

"It's getting very dark," Pamela's voice trembled.

Eddie inspected the sky. "Yes. It's going to bucket."

"It can't. It just can't. It'll take me ages to ride home! I'll be drenched."

Emily smiled pitilessly. "That's life."

"I'd better start takin' the girls back if it's gonna absolutely bucket."

"But we've only just got here," Thomas objected.

Slurping her tea, Pamela choked. Thomas thumped her between the shoulder blades. She winced.

"Not so hard! You *hurt* me. You don't know how easily you can hurt people, do you?" Her tone was blunt.

"You're like your uncle," said Eddie, "too rough."

"Wha' d'you mean?" He tried to comprehend the criticism.

Eddie's analysis was incisive. "You're too caught up in a world of your own to be concerned about other people or what they're really like. It strikes me that you are the only real person in your world. Don't you ever stop to consider other people's feelings?"

"You can talk!" he spluttered. "I do so care about other people," he glanced meaningfully at Pamela, but she was drinking some tea to clear her throat. "*You're* not Mr Perfect."

"Let's not argue," Emily intervened.

"I don't pretend to be perfect. But you always seem to be scared to let people get close to you. It comes over as arrogance. You seem to look down your nose at folk."

"That's great comin' from you, Mr Toffee-nose. *You're* the snob, not me!" he barked irately.

"Thomas, let's not quarrel. We've all got our faults." Pamela spoke kindly but firmly.

He was too taken aback to ask forgiveness. The first spots of rain were touching his head.

"Can we go? It's going to be a wash-out." Emily was stoical.

"Aye," Pamela agreed with her, "I'm scunnered[13] wi' this, too."

"We've only just got here," Thomas moaned. He watched with dismay as the basket was packed away and the youths mounted the motorbike.

"I'll leave the girls back to Summerhill," Eddie told him. "Call in when you get back, if you want."

The engine snarled and raged and then its noise diminished as it sped away from him. Thomas took his time. The rain came down with a plump. The water streamed across his face, tickling his nose and blinding him. He blinked incessantly as he passed through Larne, but the streets were deserted anyway. The world was dark, cold, wet and lonely. The road was long and wearisome. It felt like he would never get home. It felt like there was no such place as home anymore: there was just this dreary, showery road and an interminable stretch of more road unravelling every time he reached a new horizon.

He had reached Templepatrick again, and the wet trees of Paradise Walk. It seemed such a long time since they had stopped here, on the way; it was a world away. And he had thought it was going to be a romantic outing! Turned out it was paradise lost for him. Aye, she touched him, down there, where he was so saddlesore now, and it was nice ... But it was profane: the body is a temple.

There wasn't a soul out here, about the village, just him in the streaming rain. On his own. Was he predestined to be one of the bachelors of this world, like his Uncle Isaac? I don't want to be alone! I want to be with her!

It was a very dark twilight. He tried to escape horrible reality by thinking about something else. But his head kept telling him that this was a punishment: he had told his mother that it was a scoot up the

---

[13] scunnered = (coll.) fed up.

road with Eddie. There was no harm in that, so she had reluctantly let him miss the milking and other wee Saturday afternoon jobs for once, seeing as Uncle Isaac would be back from the sale in Ballymena in plenty of time to give her a hand with the cows. But he had lied and, worse, he had gone gallivanting with two floozies. He had done a terrible wrong. He believed the Holy Spirit had carried him back through this Valley of the Shadow of Death. And to think he had been messing about on poor dead Willie's pushbike!

Get me home safely, Jesus, his heart cried. I won't deceive You, or stray again. Please, Lord, make the sun shine again!

CHAPTER FOUR

The Fields of Islandreagh

Flesh tore as he plucked feathers, index finger curled in, thumb base pressing against it until the knuckle ached. Fluid seeped onto his hand, staining the white down yellow and making the fluffy mass difficult to grip. Isaac worked over the breast, near the limp neck, which was bulging burgundy beneath the skin. He paused, shifting his posture on the three-legged milking stool. Some chickens were padding around the byre, their heads twitching curiously as they inspected the stalls, an empty bucket, a dusty sack, a scattering of yellow meal on the floor. A scrawny one stood on the rim of the group, eyes alert, head cocked, watching him pluck.

"This is a good wan," he said, smacking the bird in his lap on the breast. "Not like thont bag-a-bones." He spat at the scrawny hen.

Jean looked out of the corner of her eye at her brother. He was slacking. "G'wan in an' git yersel' a cup o' tay, Isaac. You've been on the blatter all day."

"M' alricht."

"Did y' get any joy at Kirk's?"

"Aye. I got the right surt-a bolt t' do the job."

"Did ye get the ruck-shifter fixed up, then?"

His veiny face winced irritably as he replied, "Mmm. Did. Bit futthery, but managed it."

"Were you puttin' up spuds this mornin'?"

"I've got to go to the town the-marra wi' a load of spuds for the Co-op. An extra load, he wants. That'll be us near cleared out."

"Is he givin' a bit more fer them?"

"Aye, a wee bit."

"Maybe Thomas'll gie ye a hand to set them up."

"I kin do it mesel'. He's only a wee lad."

"Thomas is almost grown up, now. He's sprung up this past couple of years. He'll soon be the man about the place - you're pushin' it, now."

He glared at her. "Rubbish."

"Anyway, Thomas is just puttin' it on that he's sick. Like he did whin he was at school. He can't be a week sick. It's a disgrace the way he carries on. He's a thorn in the side. I've daubed a mustard poultice on his chest again, any road, just to be on the safe side."

"No wonder he's poorly: them things scorch like Hell-fire."

"Isaac! God forgive you. I sometimes wonder if you are one of His Elect at all. You veer mighty close to strayin' from the straight and narrow path, at times. At least you come bouncing back, just in the nick of time. But you want to be careful: you could be teetering on the kerb just when the Lord decides to call you Home."

"Have I teetered any more nur you, Jean?" he asked with viciously narrowed eyes.

"My Election is sure. I serve the Lord every minute of the day. Why, I've just been prayin', sat here on this stool, pluckin' this chicken."

"Oh? What's on your mind, love?"

She glanced down at the chicken and fidgetted with white feathers. "I was prayin' that I'm lookin' forward to going to the Home of the Blessed, because there no one gets sick at all. I want to see the place where all the trees and flowers are full of freshness and colour in the perpetual summer of Heaven; where the sunshine warms you, but doesn't burn you; where there is vegetables and spuds and all kinds of fantastic fruits galore; where people never upset each other or hurt each other or treat each other like ... beasts."

"You've been mopin' again, Jean."

"Who would want the alternative? Lyin' in your coul', wet grave, with the Undying Worm chewin' at your eyes and wriggling in your ears and curling round your toes an' all."

Her face shrivelled in towards the centre, lines spiralling in to the nose as if to the heart of a vortex. Jean's grey visage took on its most intensely ugly appearance as she contemplated Hell.

"So he toul' ye," he grumped. "McCann. That he's poorly."

"D' you think he's badly ill?" she asked, like a timid little girl.

Isaac shifted on the stool. "Says it's cancer. No cure fer that. But he's always been a whinger. Always exaggerates. Remember he said he's won on a horse in the Gold Cup? For all he won: it was Evens."

"Gambling!" Jean sniffed.

Isaac wiped his greasy hand on his jacket. He pumped his stiff legs. The chicken was almost bare. He tore the last patches of feather from the now cold fowl. When he got up to hang it from the ceiling, he looked down at his sister.

"Aye. Maybe I'll stap for a wee while. I'm punctured. If you don't mind managin' without me?"

"No, no, you go on. I'm happy as Larry, I like pluckin' the chickens. I'll soon finish the rest of this lot off."

Jesus was a man: Thomas had come to the conclusion that Christ had been, as the Prophet Paul argued, a political revolutionary. More than that, He had been a *real* man. He had kicked those scoundrels out of the temple, hadn't He? But Paul went further, said Jesus had lived but had been *only* a man. Thomas could not accept this analysis: the miracles and the Virgin birth and the resurrection all convinced him that Jesus was the Messiah. But He was a go-get-'em Christ, not the Mummy's Boy He's often made out to be. Was there any reason, he tentatively considered, why he couldn't believe in both socialism and Christianity?

"I wish I had an easy life like you," Isaac taunted.

Thomas snuggled down into the armchair in front of the fire with a guilty wriggle. "I'm feelin' a lot better th' day. 'S not my fault I got a coul'."

The luxury of being in the house all day, sipping tea and nibbling oatcakes, was wearing off. He was missing the routine of the milking and the daily bustle of chores. He had not been down the road to feed James Ussher's pigs since Sunday. Perhaps the world had altered somehow since he had been out last? He decided that, like a prodigal son, he would return to his proper role tomorrow. Helping his uncle for a few hours this afternoon would be breaking back into the way of things.

"That'll teach you to g' way messin' about when you should be at home lookin' after what's important. If you're so much better, y' kin come wi' me in a minute wi' the mare. Go an' tell yer mither we're goin' down t' Greer's."

Thomas found her in the cowshed, hanging a bare hen by the heels, from a piece of rope that was suspended over the beam, adding another to the collection. She caught one of the squawking chickens by its cold, bony, yellow legs, twirled it up through the air and caught it around the throat. Its eyes popped and its beak complained as she tucked its beating wings beneath one arm and put pressure on its neck with two hands. The noise ceased as the form in her grasp tensed. The head bulged, the neck snapped and the head fell loose and limp as the wings reacted by flapping madly. She held it out by the feet and it fanned the feathers already on the floor.

Jean took her seat and began plucking the large feathers from the self-willed wings. She held it aside as it shat. Then she replaced it on her lap and her nimble fingers began to make an industrious, rhythmic fustling, as her sniffles echoed in the cold shed.

"Can I have a new pillow?"

"There's another bag of feathers in the loft," she told him. "I've in mind makin' a couple for your bed and mine."

"Isn't Paul usin' that bag in the loft?"

"He's goin' soon."

"Why?"

"Says he's got itchy feet."

"Sandy Thompson had that. He got some powder in the town."

Jean paused, drained momentarily of the power to reply by his naïvety. "His feet are itchy because they're used to being on the move, because he's a travelling man."

Thomas realised his stupidity. He fobbed off his embarrassment by commenting, "I wish I could travel the country like him, seein' new places all the time."

"A rolling stone gathers no moss."

"It's only a dream, not a real idea."

"There's no point in dreamin', son. No point in buildin' castles in the air."

"But it must be interestin' ..."

The rich smell of the chicken dung made her spit as the down tickled her lips. Her brow had become clammy, the work bringing the sweat out of her.

"We're aff to Greer's wi' the mare." His uncle had appeared.

"Oh, right. That'll be a good job to get that done."

Star was in season. Thomas went with his brusque, edgy uncle, leading the frisky mare to Greer's enclosed yard. The courtyard was over the footbridge, at the very end of Kaye's back lane. Thomas hurried at Isaac's insistence. He held Star as Isaac went to the farm manager's office to seek out his friend, Mr Conn.

Mr Conn got Sidney Harper to bring Stonewall the stallion from his box. Thomas stood facing the carriage house and the clock tower as the huge horse sniffed around at the rear of the nervous mare. Isaac chatted about the prices at Ballyclare market with Mr Conn and

Sidney. Impervious to the activity behind him, Thomas dug his toes in and leaned back to hold Star steady. His gaze rose up to the billowing chimney pots of the big house, hidden behind the estate yard, as the big grey Suffolk Punch served with acquired dexterity.

The stallion serves the mare. The mare has to be served to have a foal; animals, brutes. Was that a robin redbreast perched on the chimneypot? Birds and beasts. God put us humans on the earth to mind them. We are superior to them: we are spiritual beings. But we've got bodies too. Was Paul McCann right when he said we are just another species?

Do people behave like ... an-i-mals? Surely not; us, doing *that*? Sandy had told him - and the gang of big boys in the garden behind the playground thon time at school - about touching his stalk and pulling it so hard that the stuff came out. Why? Why do evil things; it was so unnecessary. And Sandy could have done himself damage! Then, Thomas smiled to himself, sheepishly, reflecting on the way he winced when he even brushed his, in the course of dressing or washing. It was an electric pain, like the way a kick in the balls hurts, only ... more delicate, less blatant.

Sometimes he woke up with it stiff and his belly wet and sticky, and wiped it dry with his shirt-tail. Hands smelt of it. First time it happened he thought it was blood, but it wasn't red so he didn't say to anybody about it. Some kind of pus, he had panicked! Wasn't it a sin if such animalistic things - the curse of our baser natures - happened? Surely it couldn't be, if it came out of its own accord! Sure, it sometimes happened even without those lovely visions. No, they weren't omens, they were just ordinary dreams, they were profane: they were earthly dreams, his dreams, not holy messages.

Because people are spiritual beings they have babies in a holy way. We don't have to act like animals, doing brutish things - how was it Sandy put it? - the brutes mate, but people love. He said a girl can't have a baby from *just* kissing. Not ordinary kissing, Thomas presumed, like kissing Mummy or Uncle Isaac. But *real* kissing, the way you kiss a wife. Or a girl! And you have to be careful, Sandy said, because kissing can sometimes *lead* to babies. How? Did the stuff travel up inside you and pass through your mouth, in your spittle? Did the Holy Ghost simultaneously descend upon her and bless her, so that she'd bear a child? Because, of course, we're not like animals; like, his willie wasn't like the big, broomshaft of a thing the horse had. Same, only different; because Man is made partly physical, in earthly form, but mainly spiritual, in God's image. Animals don't have real families, like people; animals don't marry; animals don't kiss; animals don't *love*.

He wondered would he like to be married? To have someone to cuddle, someone to *kiss*. Marriage, he decided, was when the courting kissing stops and the *real* kissing begins. Laawwangeh slobbery kisses. And awh, how he want to kiss *her*, kiss her lips! Daring not even to think her name, he yearned to hold her *right now*, and squeeze her, squeeze her tight!

Oh! Mummy, forgive me for thinking about love. It's not a bad thing, is it Mummy? Animals don't love, he realised, they just do these things because it's in their nature to be dirty beasts. They lie in muck and aren't civilised, like humans. Animals are a lower order: they mate, even brother and sister cat. Through-other lot! But it was a good thing in pigs to have – what did Eddie say it was called? – hybrid vigour. Half-caste porkers! They had more growth about them, were stronger if not inbred. That must be why we're superior to animals; we're not inbred.

We are not animals. We work, which they don't. Well, Star ploughed, but it was him that *really* ploughed because he had the know-how. Star just walked along. Just like dumb animals do, doing their wild things. Like these ones, snorting and huffling behind him, in heat. Like bullocks or heifers mounting each other, playing. Their way of hugging? Brutes: shitting everywhere and fighting and carrying on!

A splatter on the cobbles signified the end. Star relaxed as the stallion was withdrawn to his stable. Before long, his uncle slapped palms with Sidney and the walk home commenced.

His mother had finished plucking when they got back to the Orchards. Thomas gave Paul a hand to get things ready for the evening milking. They began stuffing the feathers into a large sack, as Jean went to the house to sort out the kitchen before the milking.

Coughing severely, Paul asked Thomas, "Are ye back with us in the land of the livin'?"

"I still feel a bit weak."

"I've been a bit poorly meself, recently. I know a Doctor in Belfast. I'm gonna see him soon."

"Are you for travelling on soon, now the planting's all done?"

"Probably. Don't wanna overstay me welcome."
"It must be great seein' all those different towns."
"One town's much like another."
"I wish I had time to explore places."
"You're better off workin' at your own place, here."
"*You* roam the country."
"I started that to get a livin'. What other chance had the seventh bairn of a man with only sixteen acres got? Two of my brothers are in America; one's at the home place. I've a sister in New Zealand and three in England. I was over in Leicester a couple of times to see them. That's where I should-a gone years ago, an' made a go of it." His eyes were struggling against mistiness.
"I thought you were all for Ireland ... an' all that."
"A country's the people, not the rocks and soil. The whole world should join together in Communist comradeship."
"God made the world as it is an' I don't see why we should change it."
"Men made the world like it is. Like men split Ireland. Like men split men between the idle rich and the impoverished masses. There's no God or Son or Holy Ghost about it."
Whispering, Thomas asked, "How can you speak so? Don't you fear God?"
Paul drew his shoulders back and rallied, "I have never seen a ghost, and I don't believe in no Holy Ghost, neither. There's no proof that there's any God. It's just a ploy, a superstition, used by those in authority to keep the workforce, which they have denied an education, from challenging the status quo. Do you believe in the Buddha? Or Ahura-mazda? Or Islam? Why do you cower before the Cross? I'll tell you why - because you've been infected by fear from the cradle. I'm not anti-religion out of spite. I merely think it's a false and irrelevant frame of reality. It's brought more harm than good. Like the Inquisition. Like the trouble here in Ireland. It's all a hoax. Sure, if it wasn't for the Insurrection in 1798, your Presbyterian marriages would still be regarded as fornications and the Presbyterian children as bastards. Is that fair? Is that sensible? Common sense tells you those are some men's rules, not all men's. Certainly not God's. So, why are any children illegitimate at all? Morals are rules we chose, not some Divine Judgement sent down from on high. Away with their old fashioned gobbledegook! Let's design a set of laws that's fair to all.

We're all equal, not because some Bible says so, but only if we agree that everyone is and work to that end. A Marxist interpretation of history sticks to the facts and seeks to alleviate suffering in a practical way. Prayers are only so much hocus-pocus."

Thomas carried the sack of feathers up the steps to the loft where Paul slept. He saw in the gloomy corner the books by the lamp on the wooden crate.

If they were the words of the Devil, why doesn't a thunderbolt come down and strike them, burn them up? If Communism was evil, where did all the souls of the Russians go when they died? They were all atheists, thousands of them. Hell couldn't be that crowded. He began to wonder, was he just a feather, amongst so many feathers in the sack which is our world?

Mrs Crowe had a sore leg, so his uncle and mother gave her a lift home from church in the trap. Thomas said he'd walk home. But he slunk off for a while with lanky Dickie Blenkinsop, over Wylie's stile and along the pad by the river bank. They stopped under the trees where the Six Mile Water was wide and shallow and rock-strewn.

The sun was at its zenith on one of the first really warm days of the year. The heat shimmered, beating like the wings of a haze of insects that would, before long, be rising from the still surface. Dickie lay down, put his hymn book and Bible into alternate jacket pockets and began pulling out stalks of dry grass to suck between his teeth. Thomas took off his jacket and, sitting down, held it over his back with a hooked finger.

"So, you lost the apprenticeship?" Thomas lazily commented.

"Good news travels fast."

"Don't you feel ... ashamed?"

"You mean, a failure? Just because I didn't clean th' mortar aff me trowel once too often? Naw! I hated it! Don't care if I niver see another brick again as long as I live."

"But shouldn't you have tried your best? If a job's worth doin', it's worth doin' well."

"Let somebody else do it! I don't wanna."

"What'll you do now?"

"I'm workin' till Culican's a bit, fer now. I've applied fer a few other things." He rubbed his nose as he spoke. Basking his face in the heat of the sun, Thomas asked, "What do you think of th' day's sermon, then?"

"It sounded alright. Bit high-falutin' for here. Goin' on about Albert Schweitzer – was it? – and *David Strauss*, as if music's anythin' t' do wi' religion," Dickie answered.

"We sing hymns, don't we?" Thomas yawned.

"He seems t' be just as much a rant-and-raver as ever."

"Don't speak like that, Dickie. Be more respectful of the cloth."

Thomas folded his jacket and lay it beside him, extracting the Bowie knife that was slotted into the recess of a tear in the inside pocket lining.

"Where'd you get that?" Dickie admired it, snatching it from him. "It's a wheeker!"[14]

"Present," Thomas told him. Taking it back, he tore up a few blades of grass and began to slice each down the middle. As he did so, he asked tentatively, "Have you seen any of the girls recently, Dickie?"

"What girls?" Dickie asked, admiring the sharpness.

"The ones we knew in school, who else is there? I haven't seen some of them for ages."

"I seen Judy Burns a few weeks ago, at the Youth Club. I had a grand wee chat with her. She was a lucky one, survivin' the consumption. She's leavin' school this year. Makes you feel oul'. Years since we left, already! She's got a job already, helpin' in the Post Office. Goin' full time, soon. Born lucky!"

"Have you seen anybody else?"

"Can't think. You haven't been to the Youth Club fer ages, have you?"

"I don't go at all. I stopped going last year. There's always a certain age, a proper age, to change your ways in things, in life. When you're a child, you think like a child. When you're an adult, you've got to start behavin' like one."

"Lot's of yins go that's into their twenties."

"Well, they're wrong," he affirmed.

"Anyway, you don't go 'cos you're scared t' face th' scandal!" Dickie smirked.

"I don't know what you're on about!"

"I heard you were doin' a line wi' Pamela Hart."

---

[14]wheeker = (coll.) great one.

"Eh! Rubbish."

"It's alright, Thomas," said Dickie, "why should I mind? I haven't been seein' her for donkey's ages. It was niver anythin' special." He threw a clod of grass at Thomas, but missed. "But, right enough, I thought you'd be a ladies' man, too: like uncle, like nephew."

"What d'you mean, about me uncle?"

"Come on, Thomas, I know all about him. Don't tell me nob'dy never toul' *you*? That he ... well, don't quote me, it may not be Gospel truth, but for a start they reckon Pamela's not Ben Hart's daughter really at all, but that your uncle was seein' oul' Marbeth when she got caught."

"Wash your mouth out with soap!" He sat back, shocked.

In his mind he envisaged Uncle Isaac with a bunch of red roses, leaning at the jamb of the Hart's place at the tenements. Marbeth Hart took them, smelt them, thanked him, smiling, and their faces swooned together, about to kiss ...

"How could that happen? They weren't married ..."

"Don't have to be married to get a girl in trouble, you know that! So, you *weren't* told this afore now, about 'im? No odds, anyway. I mean, even if - as I've been told - *you* have been tryin' it on with Pamela, there's no harm in bein' *kissin' cousins*, as it were!" he chortled lecherously. "Sure, isn't that all them surt-a wemen are there for."

"But," Thomas huffed, "even if what you say about him's true, why'd Marbeth marry Ben Hart, then? Surely she'd-a loved the real father of the wean, of ... Pamela?"

"That's the surt of *them*. Some folk like to do ... dirty things, regardless of common decency or morality. It's in their nature. They're not as civilised as you or me. Like them lot at the Rabbit Hutches: a through-other crowd if ever there was one." He shrugged his shoulders and, chucking another bit of white grass stalk at Thomas, concluded, "She might-a been involved with Ben, too, or maybe he just wanted a wife t' luk after the house for him. A woman wud jump at a chance like that. After all, once they're in trouble, who's gonna want them? And I bet oul' Ben Hart couldn't-a pulled a bit of talent with a Fordson tracteur."

"I think that's rotten," Thomas pouted, "that people should heed th' promptin's of th' Devil."

"Unfortunately, it's far from bein' a perfect world." Dickie nodded his head sadly. "C'mon." He got to his feet, "You've listened to enough bull fer one day. An' I want to get home fer me dinner."

They got up, stretching their stiff limbs, and headed for the stile. Nearing the road, Thomas lowered his voice. "Well, it still doesn't make sense t' me. If it was Uncle Isaac's fault, why'd he not marry her?"

"Don't keep on about it, Thomas, it's not important."

"Mibbe not to you. Surely, he'd-a married her if what you said wuz true?"

"A hoor[15] like her?"

"Don't call her names like that."

"'S true, isn't it? I heard she went around wi' lots of men. Kissing them!"

"You know," he said with a perplexed expression on his face, "my mother's still 'Miss' Gray." He waited for him to nod "So what I niver understood was, when they gave the bastards an' such like at school a ribbin' – even Pamela got called names a bit, I see now *why*; then, I thought that was just because the Harts were Stinkers – but, what I mean is, how come nobody ever said anything nasty to me?"

"That's because they're all Stinkers, whereas you're from a respectable family," he assured him. "Sure," Dickie emphasised his point by raising the corner of his top lip, "can you see anybody sayin' anythin' nasty about *your* ma?"

Thomas was with the Kayes, putting up a fence along the march dyke between the bottom meadow and one of the fields they would be grazing this year. There had never been a hedge or a fence here: the stone dyke had been the only boundary. Eddie and Terence had covered it with soil and had planted a zig-zag of hedge quicks along the ditch. They were fencing it on both sides to keep the cattle from destroying the young haw.

Terence was holding the posts as Thomas sledged. Mr Kaye and Eddie were doing the same on the other side of the dyke. As he swung the sledgehammer and each blow rang, Thomas let the rage in him seethe out with the force of the steel head.

---

[15] hoor = (coll.) whore.

He was glad the job was being done: it would protect the Gray's crop. But old Kaye was only doing it because he got given the quicks and posts for next to nothing by a pal who worked at the forest. And he was getting Thomas's labour. Of course, he realised it was jealousy, since the Grays could not afford to splash out on planting new hedgerows. Mr Kaye and his hoity-toity notions about 'good husbandry'! He had more money than sense.

"Good fences make good neighbours!" Mr Kaye laughed, proud of his joke.

His sons laughed dutifully. Thomas forced a grin. Weren't the Grays good enough for the Kayes, that they had to keep them back with a fence?

Terence started going on about the Italians invading Abyssinia. He was enthusiastic and certain that Mussolini was the new Roman Emperor.

"Why couldn't we British be like that again, and get an even bigger Empire? The trains run on time in Italy. And there's no unemployment in Italy."

"That's because they're all forced into the Army."

"What's wrong with that?"

"Not everybody wants to be a soldier," Eddie informed him.

"Not every Italian has a quarrel with the Abyssinians," Thomas argued. "People should live in peace and brotherhood, not invade each other's homes. Like your da says, 'Good fences make good neighbours'. And some people are Pacifists and don't want to be cannon fodder for a dictator."

"Wimps," Terence said in his shrill, pubescent pitch.

It was getting late. They had done well to get the posts in. Thomas felt more comfortable walking back to the yard with Eddie than he had in his presence for several days. The Glenarm incident was forgiven and forgotten: the blame had lasted only as long as Thomas's flu.

Mr Kaye went to the house, leaving the boys to put away the tools. Terence was dipping his muddy sledge in a barrel under a drainpipe, boasting to Thomas, as he scrubbed the soil off, about the marching drill he had learnt at the Scouts.

"This is like the way the Hitler Youth do it," he chortled.

Terence left his sledgehammer and began goose-stepping about the yard. He did it earnestly, not sarcastically. He chirped about what he would do to the niggers in Abyssinia if he was there.

His big brother stepped forward and booted Terence in the groin. As his knees crossed and his hands clasped, Eddie lifted Terence by the collar. Seams ripped. He held Terence up and punched him in the mouth. Thomas heard teeth rattle. Blood began to seep from Terence's lips. He blubbered and his eyes closed, squeezing out salty tears. Eddie let his brother fall to the stony ground like a sack of potatoes.

"What did you do that for?" Thomas put a hand on the moaning boy's shoulder.

"If he wants to play with the big boys, then he better learn the rules of their game. They're not civilised. That's what the Hitler Youth do. And worse. They don't need reasons. Except pure bloody-mindedness. *Get it*?"

Terence sobbed, "Aye."

"It's not like Cowboys and Indians," Eddie said to Thomas. "It's real. People get hurt. Scouts is one thing; armies are a different kettle of fish. Wars are for heroes and fools, not for the likes of you and me. Are you able to give us a hand to put on the wire, tomorrow, Thomas?"

"Aye. I'll be here."

"I'm glad to see your flu's gone."

"It was me own fault. I should-a had a coat with me. I knew it was a bad weekend."

Eddie was alright. Why couldn't he have a brother? Here he was again, wishing he had something he hadn't. Couldn't just be satisfied with what he had. First, it was 'I've no da', then it was 'I've no brother', then it was 'I wanna see new places', then it was 'why can't we have a lorry like Billy's?'. Next, it'll be something else. He was never satisfied! He determined to try and shake it out of his skull, to live properly – live like everybody else – not be drifting into a world of his own all the time, but live in the real world. The world where hard men beat up the innocent? Maybe a dream, like Paul McCann's dream of a better world, *is* allowed?

Why was his head buzzing? He didn't understand enough about these things. Why couldn't he just drop it? Why couldn't he just accept one side or the other? Why did he let these questions race round in his head without end? He wished he could just *forget it all*.

His mother had done the pigs for him, seeing as she was going a message. Returning home, she told him one of the sows was farrowing. It had six or seven so far. As she spoke, Thomas imagined she was Mother Ireland, because her green skirt was the fields at the Orchards, the bottle green cardigan was the fields of Islandreagh, while the little round blue hat was the sky, and that musty, lemony flower splodged on the side at the front was the sun.

She was hanging up her dark grey tweed coat on the peg by the front door. "It's gettin' cloudy," she said, "like rain. But no matter - 'every cloud has a silver lining'."

Thomas ran down the Rathmore Road, anxious to see the new arrivals. He was surrounded on all sides by the green fields of Islandreagh he had just been thinking about. Here they were in reality: the land of Uncle Isaac and the Kayes, Lowries and Duggans. He revelled in a sense of supreme happiness and contentment as he clopped down the road in his big boots, with the tongue-trailing border collie skipping at his side.

When he got there, the sow was standing before her hut, chomping at one of the piglets. Thomas hit the angry brute about the head, so that she ran about, baring her bloody, spittly fangs, and dropped the piglet. He snatched it before she could claw his hand with her heavy, scratching hoof. He stepped over the partition and out of the pen as the squealer raged at him.

The little pink body was wet and warm. Its head was squashed, splattered and marked. A beady eye flashed in the daylight. The crushed head housed no consciousness. It was only a runt, anyway. Thomas flung it, meaning to throw it away from the pen, but the thing landed in the pig-arc. So he hopped into the pen again as the sow sulked in the far corner. Crouching to reach in, he noticed lying in the straw, one on either side of the runt, two bigger piglets. They were at the edges of the flattened straw of the sow's bed; she had obviously lain on them. He scooped up all three of the misshapen bodies and chucked them out, near the hedge, where the dog was soon nosing at them, as if they were scraps.

Jean and Isaac appeared as he was leaving the pigs. Paul was with them, looking smarter than usual with a tie and collar attached to his shirt. His mother had brushed her hair and now also had her good red shawl over her shoulders. Uncle Isaac was sporting the clean, brown shopcoat, the one he wore over his usual attire to special mart sales.

They were all dressed up, as if it was a big occasion. And Paul was carrying his bag.

"Paul's off to the station," Jean called as her son approached the gate. "He's headin' fer Belfast."

"Travellin' in style? Well, 'bye, then, I suppose, all the best. Got your buks?"

"Aye. Cheerio, Thomas. I've gotta head on. The train's due soon. I'll maybe be back wi' yous same time next year again."

They shook hands.

Behind him, Jean quavered, "God willing."

Isaac went with the travelling man down the road. Thomas and Jean watched them from the gate.

"He mightn't be back at all," Jean said. "He's very ill. It's a specialist he's gone to see. Sure, he hasn't been fit all the time he's been here."

"I didn't notice him too sick."

"Doesn't like to fuss. Unlike some."

"How long's he been comin' here to work?" Thomas asked, as they began walking up the road, homewards.

"Oh, a long time," Jean told him.

"He was here a few times when I was wee, then not at all for a few years, then he's been back this past couple. Why's he not stick to a regular pattern?"

"Why indeed?"

"Was he comin' here before I was born?"

"Aye."

"Is he going to die?"

The dog was at her feet, nuzzling for a stroke. She petted it.

"What about the pigs?"

"The sow ate one. A ne'er-do-well. The rest are great. James will be pleased."

He asked hesitantly, "Don't you mind him comin' here, if he's a ... you know ... atheist an' all?" Thomas looked down at the laughing dog.

"He means no harm. I tried to get him to repent years ago. Even to go back to his own lot. But he was not for turning. Not at my bidding. I'm not the gifted evangelist he needs to help him. Your Aunt Sarah might-a done it, if she'd put her mind to it. I've seen her lift up a spracklin' drunk at a perty and sober him up ..." she clicked her fingers, "... like that. She's got a way with people, like I never had."

"Was it Uncle Stanford she converted?"

"No!" Jean laughed. For a short time, she seemed like a girl. Thomas felt an uncanny similarity about her, as if he was in the presence of someone else, someone much younger. "All Stan ever had was a glass of ginger wine."

"He was drinkin' in our house at the New Year. Uncle Isaac and him had that whiskey."

"*One glass*. Sure, he doesn't touch it from one Christmas till the next. Unless it's needed fer medicinal purposes!"

A gruff voice behind them shouted, "What's all this gossipin'?"

It was Uncle Isaac. "Cacklin' like wemen!"

"Is it a crime for a woman to talk to her son?" Jean stuck out her lower lip huffily.

"Yous missed a scene down the road," Isaac rubbed his hands. "We met the Reverend MacIntyre and Paul lit into him because he called him 'McCann'. He said it was a patronising thing, seein' as the Minister called me 'Isaac'. Paul said he didn't care, he was proud to be part of the Proletariat! Said he was an outsider, so he was treated as an outlaw! And he was started bletherin' on about a class war when I slipped away an' left them at it."

"I hope so, too." Jean was annoyed. "You'll have to apologise to the Reverend MacIntyre on Sunday, for causing such a scene."

"I didn't start anythin'. Anyway, the Reverend MacIntyre can fight his own battles. He's got a tongue in his heed with a lick like a big roany cow."

"You'll have to apologise, all the same," Jean went on.

"Aye, alright," he placated her.

Thomas was intrigued by the budding all around him. The grass was growing now and its greenness seemed to pulsate with vitality. Help was at his heels, his mother and uncle by his side and his heart was almost satisfied. Only one thing remained unfulfilled, in his mind, to spoil the tranquillity of Islandreagh. Pamela.

"Are y' going to scrape that byre dur, Thomas? I've got the paint, y'know."

"Aye. Sometime."

"You could paint the door yourself," Jean nagged.

"Lad his t' larn."

"Or are you getting too oul' fer it?" she smiled, teasingly.

"*Me*? I'm in the prime of my life!"

"You're past the big five-oh," she reminded him.

"What age are you, Mummy?"

"Never ask a lady a question like that."

"She's the baby of the family," Isaac told him. "A mere striplin' of ..."

"Doe-on't!"

"Is Aunt Sarah your age, Uncle Isaac?"

"Near hand it."

"If I was born on Christmas Day, why didn't you name me after Jesus?"

"Don't be ridiculous!" Jean exploded. "Don't talk such rubbish. You don't give a sacred name like that, *His* name, to ordinary people."

"You were named after your grandfather," his uncle told him.

"I wish I was older."

"Your youth's the best days of your life," his mother disagreed. "What do you want to grow old for? Things get harder as you get older."

"I thought things would get easier. I thought there'd be more ... success in life."

"The only thing that becomes more abundant is problems," Isaac warned. "What have I managed to achieve since I was your age? Kept my head above water, just about – that's all."

A bicycle swooshed around the corner. Behind them, the racing rider tinkled his bell.

"Ben Hart!" Isaac barked. "Eejit! What's he at, at this time of day, here?" He addressed Jean.

"I was toul' he's workin' fer the Railway these days. But by the smell of him he's been in Barr's."

"He was outta work again, last I heard," said Thomas.

"Don't you be so nosey, gossipin' about other people's affairs," Jean scolded him. "It's not nice."

Thomas was in his room reading St John's Gospel. His eyes were scanning the words, but his mind was not taking in the message. He was looking forward to the Usshers' visit: they would be here soon.

Test-a-ment: the syllables sounded dour in his head, like James Ussher's mountain drone.

> 'For God so loved the world that He gave His
> only begotten Son ...'

Jesus is the only Saviour! Away with doubts! Even the Reverend MacIntyre has doubts occasionally, he had said so in this morning's sermon. It's the Devil trying to catch you. McCann was only a louse. Who pays heed to an oul' tinker when he can't compare to the intelligence of the Minister? And James Ussher is the epitome of Christianity: why couldn't Thomas be like him? he pined. Why was he weak while James was steadfast in the faith? Thomas felt a tremor of fear, for to forsake His way meant damnation. The wages of sin is death, whatever McCann might think.

A clatter on the concrete outside saved him from his study. It was the Usshers' trap. Uncle George, Auntie Josie, John, James and Elizabeth were all here for a Sunday afternoon visit. Thomas hurried into the kitchen.

The sunlight was beaming through the repaired kitchen window. He felt light-spirited. Auntie Josie was nattering to Mother. There was a welcome from everybody and for everybody. Christian people in fellowship! This was what it was all about. This was desirable. He sat in his place, on the hard bench by the fire, glad to see the familiar faces around the grey kitchen. His eyes drifted down to the grate.

Worms in your ears and maggots crawling through your eye sockets! The sod being spaded on top, blocking out the sunlight! Instead of sunbeams, shafts of flame: fire! Fire! The alternative was Hell-fire.

"That's a grand litter of pigs, this week," James was saying.

"Aye," George agreed. "It's good of you to look after them for us. Thanks."

"No problem," Uncle Isaac nodded graciously.

"So, the travelling man's gone?" Josie was saying to Jean. "He doesn't stay in one place for long."

"Have you had any ewes lambed lately, yourself?" George asked.

"Aye. 'Mon. We'll take a look." Isaac got up and pulled on his cap.

James and Thomas followed the men out. Isaac led George over to the paddock, beyond the Far Orchard, where the apple trees were just beginning to blossom. Their sweet scent filled the mellow country air that warm afternoon. Rather than join the men, Thomas and James went out the gate and wandered along the road.

"I saw wee Maisie Kaye on the way. I've spoken to her at somebody's party, once. She's very nice. Well-mannered."

"Maisie goes to a good school. Wish I'd the chance to learn more."

"You can never learn too much," James nodded.

"I always think I'm missing something. I can't always get things straight in my mind."

"How do you mean?"

"This mornin', the sermon was about doubt. Sometimes I don't know enough to be sure of what I believe."

"The truth has been revealed."

"I'm told it has, and I feel it has, but I just can't see it myself, yet. When yer man McCann left, he had an argument about religion with the Reverend MacIntyre. You know the way he's a Communist and doesn't believe in God. But you've got to admire him, he can stand up for himself against the best of them. I wish I could understand all those books he reads."

James was walking with his hands clasped behind his back. "Huh. I have no wish to read the Devil's propaganda. All that sinful living those Reds preach! The only book you need's the Holy Book. I'm sure the Minister roundly foxed the old tinker, for all his books an' big words."

"I wasn't there. I don't know."

"A little bird tells me there's a wee girl's the apple of your eye," James teased.

Thomas knitted his eyebrows. "Who?"

"The wee girl Kaye, of course. I saw Edmund at a soccer match and he said you've been calling in to chat with her."

"Oh, that was ages ago. I was just shelterin' from the coul' an' rain when I was workin' down Kaye's Meadows, earlier in the year, that's all. Maisie's keen on art. It was interesting. For a while. In small doses. But she was into this new stuff from France, Surrealism. It's about making the real stand out by putting it in an unusual background. Like, paintin' a picture of a cow in a purple field, or somethin'."

"Or an Orange field?"

Thomas laughed with him. "That wouldn't be so unusual. But this art lark, it's alright for the likes of her, but us ordinary people haven't time for all that."

"Oh, I dunno. Art is an expression of sophistication ..."

"That's what I mean."

"No, I mean of society's progress towards the ideal. Art's a sign of civilisation."

"There you go. The Kayes are civilised enough. They're proper people. But us Grays are a rougher clan. She's much too good for the likes of me."

"Nonsense!" James laughed. "Don't put yourself down. You're as good a fella as any."

"I'm useless!" He bowed his head and buried his hands in his pockets. "I always get things wrong. I'm useless. I only learnt to plough properly this season."

"But you have learnt! And the years will improve your skill. Experience is what life's all about."

Thomas's eyes were beginning to smart. "Experience of what? I've never experienced life. I'm in my sixteenth year already and what have I achieved? Nuffin'. Can't even adjust a plough properly, at my age!" He was angry with himself. "Eddie Kaye's only a year and a bit oul'er than me and he can fix motorbikes and drive the lorry and all sorts. I can't. I've never even ..."

"What?"

"It's too embarrassing ..."

"You can trust me."

Thomas stared mournfully into his cousin's pupils. He could see his own sad face reflected on the glassy sheen of James's grey eyes. He spoke in a low tone. "I've never had a girlfriend. Not a real one. I ... I feel incomplete ... You won't know what I mean, because you're ... so decent a buddy. But I ... I long for love. For a friend. Like, I feel ready to marry – after all the getting to know each other and engagement and particulars. I don't want to end up a crusty oul' bachelor like me Uncle Isaac. I want a happy family life like ... like a real family, because of not havin' a real da meself, you see. But you wouldn't understand that kind of weakness. You are so much more self-controlled than I am."

James looked up. "You over-estimate my strength of will power, I think. No one is perfect. Most people find it necessary to marry rather than to burn."

"You remind me of the Minister. You are so ... righteous?"

James almost laughed. "No I'm not. What advice can I give you? So you feel you need ... a friend. Well, God will provide. Won't He? Trust in Him." He wagged a finger, pointing vertically. "He feeds the birds, doesn't He? The lilies in the field ..." James gestured towards a patch of daisies over the hedge, "... are clothed."

"Let's turn back," Thomas urged. "I don't want to go near the rath field today. It gives me the willies."

"Oh? Because you fell off Duggan's donkey?"

"No," said Thomas, turning to walk back the way he had come. "Something else. Bad thoughts."

"We stopped to look at the pigs on the way up. Thank you so much for keeping an eye on them for me."

"You won't tell anyone I said all this, will you?"

"It's perfectly normal to have feelings. And it's common decency to respect privacy. We're for starting the renovation of the house, soon. Are you gonna give us a hand?"

"Aye, surely. Whenivar I can."

There was a couple up ahead. A boy and a girl. Thomas thought from a distance that it was Eddie and Emily, out for a stroll. As they got closer, he realised whose gay laugh it was, whose smiling mouth, whose glinting brown hair it was, streaming over her shoulders like an array of spring petals. His heart thumped as the couple came near them. James was talking about the pigs, but Thomas was merely mouthing replies. She saw him! Suddenly, they had drawn level and she was looking directly at him!

"Hello, Pamela." He spoke sternly.

She forced a smile. "Good afternoon, Thomas. Hello, James. Are you well?"

Harry Murtagh halted beside her. "'Lo."

"Yes, thanks," Thomas answered, faking enthusiasm. He battled to think of something to say. "How's things with you? Saw your da the other day," he blurted out. "On his bike. He was in a hurry."

Pamela attempted to keep the conversation alive. "Another boring Sunday afternoon."

"On the contrary," James disagreed, "It's good to have a day of rest."

"Well, Saturday afternoon's enough for me to rest up."

"You won't be saying that," James continued, "when you've a family of your own to rear and floors to wash and socks to darn and meals to cook."

"My ma still has cookin' an' tidyin' up after the weans t' do, an' t' luk after the weans themselves."

She glanced at Thomas, who lingered. He stared at Harry, who was shuffling the gravel with the welt of his shoe.

"Are you not singing for us, today?" Thomas grinned broadly.

She blushed. "I can't, not now you've embarrassed me."

"Some other time. When it's not bucketing!"

Her perplexed look showed that she did not know how to take his oblique reference to their Saturday at Glenarm. Thomas moved and they all began to move on. Shoes scraped on the tarmac. Saying their good-byes, Pamela and Harry walked on. James was droning in his ear while Thomas strained to hear what they were talking about as Pamela drifted away. Can't make it out! "Give over!" he snapped.

James blinked. "Sorry! What's wrong, now?"

"Sorry. I didn't mean to be short with you. I was thinking about something else."

"It's alright."

But James was quiet for the rest of their journey. He must think I'm crazy! And I am: for someone ...

They rejoined Uncle George and Uncle Isaac, who were still in the yard. The men were leaning on the cart, yarning. James and Thomas stood patiently, listening as the men discussed the pros and cons of tractors. Thomas's gaze wandered. There was a bad smell coming from the pile of wet straw at the front of the cart, in front of him. He leaned forward and poked it with his fingertips. He uncovered pale cat dung.

"You're in the shit!"

Who said that? Thomas looked round. Their conversation was carrying on as if nothing had happened. He must've imagined it. His mind playing tricks on him? An evil thought. Bad language, how could he? But it came from nowhere, he hadn't willed it. Maybe his suspicion was true – maybe we are predetermined to do certain things, good or evil, regardless of how hard we try to be good.

He wiped his fingers in what clean straw there was. James was listening intently to what his father and uncle were saying. Thomas stood idly, folding and unfolding his arms. The smell of the catshit was wafting up to his nose with each inward draw of air. Someone's stomach gurgled; but still they did not go inside. The men's voices were just a drone to him now.

In his imagination he could see Pamela walking down the road, through the railway bridge. She was passing the church now and the recollection of her singing filled his heart with sorrow, because Harry was beside her.

CHAPTER FIVE

The Love of God

He spotted a small figure with a shotgun across the field. He marched towards the hunter. As he approached, he saw that it was wee Terence Kaye. As they met, the tang of gun oil wafted.
"Hunting rabbits."
"Bit early in the mornin' for that."
"It's the early bird catches the worm."
"What are you at?"
"Moved the cows down to the bottom meadow. Our place is gettin' short of water already."
The two lads ambled up the back lane. The bird's nests were now barely distinguishable in all the foliage. There was a heavy wisp of peat smoke coming from Mrs Higgins's chimney.
"She's up early. You'd think an old woman with nothing to do would have a lie in."
"Old people eat less and sleep less."
"It feels like Sunday this morning."
"Why?"
"There's not a great deal needin' done th' day. Me uncle's gone to Belfast to see the man at the Co-op. He said fer me t' enjoy it afore the busy time hits us! I could go up to Ussher's and give them a hand with their buildin', I suppose. It feels like Sunday because I feel ... free. I haven't had the chance to relax much recently. Too much on me mind."
Terence tittered. "Like what?"
"This and that. But today, I feel as if a great weight has lifted from my shoulders. It's warm, sunny," he raised his voice, "the air's so fresh!"
"With this stink of her peat?" Terence meant the witch's fumes. "You're barmy."
The boys were near Kaye's yard. Terence went into an outhouse; Eddie's workshop. The dismantled Norton was there, bits and pieces strewn about the black floor. The whiff of grease seemed to cling to the walls.
Terence pulled a cartridge from his pocket and split it with a knife on the bench. Thomas watched intently. Terence spilled out the

gunpowder into a pile and discarded the wadding. He repeated the process with more cartridges, until he had a sizeable mound. Holding a jam-jar at the lip of the bench, he brushed the grey powder into the pot. Lifting a five-gallon can, he took his load out round to the stockyard at the back of the byre. Thomas followed.

Terence tipped out the gunpowder onto the stony ground. He tugged a handful of hay from a stack and laid a trail from the powder. The petrol was sprinkled liberally over the dry hay. He plucked a coggly, rusty tin bucket from a patch of weeds and placed this over the pile of powder.

"D'you think this'll work?"

"We'll soon find out," he sniggered.

Terence pointed out a large boulder by the byre wall. Thomas went over and crouched behind the rock. Terence brought a packet of matches out of his pocket. As he struck one, Thomas tightened himself into a ball. Terence's feet pounded along the stockyard. He pushed against Thomas, behind the big stone. There was a pregnant silence. Thomas was blowing a safe. He had a red 'kerchief tied across his nose and mouth. Running Water had lit the fuse, they were gonna ride off with the loot. The earth shook, the explosion rang in their ears: tremor and report.

The posse's shooting swirled round him in a vortex of carnage. Horses rearing. Bullets whizzing past. Some of his gang had fallen. He was running, leapt onto his horse's back. Galloping off – Running Water and Big Chief Paleface, WANTED DEAD OR ALIVE, $10,000 – leaving behind the screamless bleeding bodies of the other bandits.

A thud in his chest: I'm hit!

Blood between his fingers. 'Kerchief falling off as he floated to the ground. Taste of moist dirt. From the ragged red wound his heart pumping blood into a puddle ...

A clatter ricocheted at the boulder. Uncovering his head and straightening up, Thomas inspected the remains of the bucket. It was torn and twisted, lying at the front of their defensive stone.

Terence was wide-eyed. "That was some bang!"

"What's happened? Are you alright, Terence?"

Mrs Kaye was puffing. She was flapping like her flowery frock. Seeing they were uninjured, her shaky voice demanded, "What's the reason for this?"

"We were just messin' about." Terence submitted to her wrath.

"Your father'll give you a good hiding when he hears about this, my boy! And as for you, Thomas Gray, you should be ashamed of yourself!"

"But I didn't know what was going to happen."

"Don't try to bluff with me. You're grown up now, you should be more responsible than this. You're a bad article, Thomas Gray, leading my boy astray. Your mother's going to hear about this right away."

And she marched him resolutely up the road to the Orchards, to tell Jean Gray what he had done.

―――――

It was Communion. At Dunadry, as at other Presbyterian congregations, the Eucharist was celebrated twice a year. Thomas had attended the last one as an observer, sitting up in the gallery with the others in the Communion Class. He had been to Communion classes in the weeks leading up to this event. He mouthed the things the perspiring Reverend MacIntyre expected, but in his heart Thomas did not feel the Spirit. He believed he should feel an intense emotion, a state of bliss and satisfaction, he should know the Spirit's presence. But as yet he did not.

The building was plain. The windows were arched, with many small, diamond-shaped panes of frosty glass. The pastel-painted walls were bare. At the front, to one side, the pulpit dominated the raised area. The blue velvet cloth that hung from the lectern stand on the pulpit was decorated with a colourful burning bush motif and the legend:

ARDENS SED VIRENS
(Burning but alive)

On the wall front, behind the pulpit, to one side of the door that led up through the church complex, to the Minister's study and to the hall beyond, was a plaque. It recorded the names of the men from the congregation who had fallen in the War, '1914-1919'. *Robert Nathaniel Gray* was one of those proud inscriptions.

The new electric lights, suspended from the high rafters on thin chains, made the room so bright and unlike home or outhouse. The choir were seated behind a rail to the right. Between them and the pulpit was the font. In the centre of the front, raised area, decorated with a bowl of flowers, was the Communion Table. The carved back of the Chair faced them, with its shiny tacked leather back. That's how to turn wood. I wish I could carve like that. The Communion Table itself was also a heavy, Gothic piece of furniture. Along the front was the elaborate inscription:

'THIS DO IN REMEMBRANCE OF ME.'

This morning, the Reverend MacIntyre looked pale and weary. In the children's address he recited the miracle of the feeding of the five thousand. This angered Thomas. Sycophantic! Palestinian peasants stuffing their faces! This had nothing to do with religion, with spiritual experience!

"All things bright and beautiful,
All creatures great and small,
All things wise and wonderful -
The Lord God made them all.

Each little flower that opens,
Each tiny bird that sings -
He made their glowing colours,
He made their tiny wings."

He didn't like this dreary pace. These hymns needed more oomph! He watched disdainfully as his mother warbled from the book and his uncle repeated the lyrics from memory, his mouth forming the words in a slow, deliberate manner.

"The purple-headed mountain,
The river running by,
The sunset and the morning
That brightens up the sky,

The cold wind in the winter,
The pleasant summer sun,
The ripe fruits in the garden -
He made them every one."

The wee-est children went out to the Sunday School; it was time for the real people, the real Christians to get on with the business of summoning up the Spirit.

The Minister began by reading from Luke, chapter twenty-two. The Elders came to each pew in turn, to offer the silver plate to the brethren. The tiny slithers of bread were passed along the rows of the faithful. He saw Mrs Smylie, the widow woman, take the bread.

As the plate came nearer his pew, Thomas became agitated. *'This do in remembrance of me'*: that was for the disciples alone, surely? For us to ritualise a single symbolic gesture was heathen! His mind had a snowstorm within: yes, no, yes, no – he could not decide. Mrs Smylie, who had doubted for years, had finally submitted to the love of Christ. Or to the wiles of the Devil?

He knew he wouldn't take part in a Roman Catholic Mass, for he was informed that they believed in silly, superstitious things, like transubstantiation and the Pope's infallibility. Why then should he accept the rules of these men? Wasn't this just as silly and superstitious? The men in dark suits had reached their pew. Decide! Decide!

His mind was dizzy. The silver plate, hot under the electric lights, was hovering before him. Thomas breathed heavily. His eyes flickered wildly. The Reverend MacIntyre was wiping his brow. Thomas's cheek twitched.

Thomas's legs pushed him up. He leaned over and slithered out of the pew, past the Elder. He staggered to the door, his brow dripping and his breathing laboured. He did not look back until he was pushing against the door at the end of the aisle. His mother's head was bowed, she was slipping the bread into her mouth. Uncle Isaac's head was turned, his fierce eyes were glaring at Thomas. The boy put his shoulder to the door and burst out.

The door banged behind him. The vestibule's coolness refreshed him. It was dim there, in contrast to the bright church. He passed through the grey porch and drew open the great front doors.

Sunlight blinded him. He breathed deeply. He felt much better now. Across the road the shady trees and lush grass led down to the river's edge. Thomas closed the double doors behind him and sauntered across the road. He leaned his elbows on the stone wall and gazed admiringly at the drifting waters.

A whisk behind him caused him to look round. Geoff Archer, an Elder, was on his bicycle and pedalling through the bridge with a sense of urgency. There was soon peace again.

This was his Temple: nature. God is everywhere, not just in a church, an ugly oul' building like thon. God's a Spirit, not a symbol – like the Cross, or the burning bush. God exists. Here. His God was a personal God, an individual God; his God was unique for him, and everybody else's God was unique to them, but it was, at the same time, all the same God. The flux of life, like the flowing river, is the Spirit. Rituals are no substitute for genuine spiritual experience. Man-made ceremonies of bread and wine are evil: they are a corruption of the sacrifice Jesus made. His mate Jesus! Who died for his sake. He was born the same day as He was, so they'd something in common. There's something special between them. Thomas was a chosen one. He understood Him completely. And he wanted a pure faith, untainted by the hand of Man. Only nature, only the real world, could provide this paradise, this new Eden, this Heaven, he believed in.

He was disturbed by the clatter of heels on the road. He saw that his mother had followed him out.

"You didn't have to leave too."

"The Reverend MacIntyre collapsed. Geoff's away for the doctor. He looks serious. It was very stuffy in there. Those new lights make it very hot. You could've tried to hold on a bit longer, disgracin' us by walking out like that!"

"I felt like I was going to throw up." Thomas sat up on the wall. He struggled to explain how he had felt. "I couldn't stick it any longer. I'm sorry if it embarrassed you."

"Can't be helped. Shall we go?"

"Let's go along here, it's cooler under the trees."

> Where human weakness has come short
> Or frailty stept aside,
> Do Thou, All-Good, for such Thou art,
> In shades of darkness hide.

They took the path by the river. The day was beautiful and the Sunday peace relaxed Thomas's mind. He was absorbed in the sensual experience of the sun's warmth, the perfume of the primroses and the gentle gush of the shallow waters.

His mother began to sing in her familiar, scratchy, unskilled way:

> "The Lord's my shepherd, I'll not want.
> He makes me down to lie
> In pastures green; he leadeth me
> The quiet waters by.

> My soul he doth restore again;
> And me to walk doth make
> Within the paths of righteousness,
> E'en for his own name's sake.
>
> Yea, though I walk in death's dark vale,
> Yet will I fear none ill:
> For thou art with me; and thy rod
> And staff me comfort still."

Her voice was as crude as ever but it did not matter. To Thomas, at that moment, it seemed an angelic melody. Thomas's heart welled up with joy. He just had not felt right about it, that was all. If he felt better about it, he could do it in six months time. But at least for now he was being honest. He had his doubts about Communion. End of story.

This he had no doubts about: the happiness he was experiencing at present was the peak of pleasure. And the countryside they passed through as she sang the psalm was so gorgeous, so special. It was home. He loved this land and he loved these people, despite all their imperfections. That, surely, was enough.

He daydreamed of dipping naked into the cool, calm stream. He imagined the slippery hardness of the stones beneath his soles, the lapping of the current at his shins. The breeze teased his testicles. His lithe white body glided forwards and downwards into the water. He plunged his head beneath the surface like a waterbird diving for its prey.

Resurfacing, he wiped the water from his face as drops rolled down over taut pectorals and joined the ripples running round his midriff. He opened his eyes to behold beauty incarnate: Pamela was before him, slipping her dark dress from her shoulders and letting it drift to her ankles. The white lace of her petticoat trembled as she stepped away from the frock and leaned down to untie her boots. Her round flesh glistened golden beneath the high sun. She rolled down the stockings and peeled them from her toes and cast them aside.

She sat on the grass bank, chin on her knees and arms around in front of her smooth legs, watching her water god splashing in the stream. Her teeth flashed as he beckoned her. So she rose and the white underwear flew in the air and her beautiful body arched and dived into the deep dark part of the river. Bobbing up again, she brushed her auburn hair from her face, upon which the droplets of water gleamed like a new scattering of freckles. With a smile, she began to swim towards him ...

Thomas paused to kneel by the water's edge and scoop up a drink in his hand. His mother joined him. She sprinkled a handful of water over his head.

"Ah!" he tensed, as icy fingers probed down his collar. "Don't! It's coul'!" His mother's concave face curled in amusement. "I couldn't go through with it," he confessed. "It didn't feel right. You won't tell Uncle Isaac, will you?" His eyes pleaded. "He'd lose the bap.[16]"

Jean smiled and carried on singing the psalm. As they went up the Rathmore Road, Thomas joined in. Dr Moore's car raced past them. Geoff was with him. That was a glorious sight! What a machine! Who needs the power of God when you can have that kind of horsepower!

"My table thou has furnished
In presence of my foes;
My head thou dost with oil anoint,
And my cup overflows.

Goodness and mercy all my life
Shall surely follow me:
And in God's house for evermore
My dwelling-place shall be."

Jean and Thomas were home for some time and the roast lamb was ready. Thomas was at his place at the table, eagerly watching as his mother spooned out the cauliflower and white sauce. Reaching for his glass of milk, he looked up as his Uncle Isaac came in, and knocked the glass over.

Flicking her son on the arm with a cloth and then wiping up the spilt milk, Jean asked her brother, "What kept you?"

Solemnly placing his Bible on the dresser, Isaac told them, "The Reverend MacIntyre's deed. It was a stroke got him, in the finish up, fer all his fight agin the cancer. Dacteur Moore came and luked at him, but there was nithin' he could do."

It was May Fair Day in Ballyclare. Mary Begley was with Jean. She was showing off her blue dress, with the white border around the

---

[16]bap = (coll.) head ie. to get angry.

shoulders and down across the bodice. The sleeves also had white lace. She had on thick, blue stockings, which obviously had been expensive. Jean and Mary were being frivolous, keeping each other going about finding a fella. Mrs Simpson was in fine fettle, trotting along briskly. Uncle Isaac drove impassionately as ever.

The morning was pleasant and he was looking forward to the bustle of the market town. Thomas was anxious about his hands spoiling everything: they were black, streaked with bituminous paint. He had been lopping it onto the hayshed roof a few days ago. They hummed of petrol, yet despite all his scrubbing he had been unable to get the tar off.

They had hardly got off the trap when a small girl tugged Thomas's sleeve. "Job?"

Isaac glared at the urchin. "Nay jab," he replied.

There were coconut shies, ballad singers, bagpipers and pillsellers all competing for attention. The clamour was greatest around a bare-chested sword swallower. He criticised the crowd and in the same breath badgered them for money. Faces jolted everywhere: women in fancy hats, men in bowlers, small boys in shorts, girls with their hair in plaits or pigtails. Jean and Mary went off together to search the stalls. Thomas followed his uncle, who went to the sheep pens and spoke to a farmer selling a flock. An elegant, well-dressed lady in an exquisite lilac frock passed Thomas. Her high cheekbones and hair pinned up beneath her hat gave her a regal air; her grace captivated him. Her aquiline nose was cutely sprinkled with minute, light moles. His eyes glistened as they followed her. They diverted as she receded into the distance and a short, stocky man with a dark moustache approached. He was carrying a bundle under his arm. The man tipped his cap to Uncle Isaac.

"Frederick Nelson, at your service, sir." He seemed to have a local accent, but it was dominated by an American burr.

"Oh, aye. Where're ye frame?"

"Born an' bred in Banbridge. I was in America until a month ago. Decided it was time to return to the Emerald Isle."

"Oh, aye." Isaac scratched his throat. "So, yer lukin' hired?"

"I am indeed."

"What kin ye turn yer hand te?"

"Ploughing, sowing, reaping, livestock and bloodstock, plumbin', carpentry, electrical work, mechanical work, I'm a real Jack-of-all-trades."

Uncle Isaac looked about him. There seemed to be no other men waiting for a job, only some weedy wee lads and lassies. He cleared his throat and began dealing for a term. The man was satisfied by an offer. They shook hands. Isaac sent Thomas to find the women.

Wandering amongst the crowd, at last he caught sight of Mary.

"Where's me mammy?"

"Chattin' to Mrs Duggan. Are we going already?"

"Uncle Isaac's lookin' at the sheep. He's hired a man. Fred Nelson. He looks like Herr Hitler."

"Getaway!"

Eventually, they were heading back to Islandreagh in the trap. They gave Patsy and Mrs Duggan a lift, so the cart sat low on its springs. The new man made little small talk, merely replying in a vague, general way when asked questions by Jean and Isaac.

Jean put the kettle on when they got back to the Orchards. Fred got out a stereoscope, consisting of a rack and handle, a slide and a pair of screened lens-prisms. He took out a box and inserted a picture in the stereoscope. He explained that they were like the movies, only stills, but realistic because it was a viewer which made the picture three-dimensional, so the scenes looked like they were real, and he thought it was better even than the big screen.

Uncle Isaac looked in the viewer at a picture. As Fred told him which American place it was, he grunted. The first view was passed to Thomas and as he stared into the viewer a grey, fantastic world of gruesome and incredible shapes was before him. What was this? All grey. No sense to it. What was it called? Fred had said it was the Petrified Forest: a fossilised wood. Suddenly, the stones were trees! He could see it now. And it was ... unreal. He was there: in the Petrified Forest, in America, the Land of Dreams and Huge Things and Fantasy and Where Anything Is Possible. And then he was back in the smoky kitchen. Four dull walls, the familiar furniture, craggy Uncle Isaac and rugged Mummy and Fred's shiny, marble-like face.

The next scene was the Grand Canyon. The deep ravines were a startling contrast to the previous place. And an aeroplane – like the Spirit of St Louis – was flying between the clifftops, far above the abysses that seemed to descend to Hell itself. Uncle Isaac passed another picture: the Empire State Building in the centre of the New York city skyline with all its skyscrapers. How could people live in such a grey world? All grey buildings, grey streets, even a grey sky! And the long Golden Gate bridge, set against a bright sky and dark water. And a group of Red Indians in their feather head-dresses, gathered around a totem pole - the chief had a peace pipe! Thomas gulped down his tea, the adrenaline flowing as he swooned into these new worlds, these new realities. He was in Washington DC, gawping at the White House, when the gruff voice disturbed his state of altered consciousness.

"It's time t' gie an' bring in the cows, Thomas."

"Awww!"

His mother consoled him, "You can look at the rest of them later. It's time the milkin' was done."

"I'll go with you," Fred volunteered.

The Yankee accent lifted Thomas's mood again. He had a new enthusiasm. Thomas changed into his work clothes and then went with the new man off down Kaye's back lane to the Meadows to bring in the cows.

"So, Uncle Isaac didn't buy any sheep," he said as they walked.

"No. He dealed for a pen, but wouldn't give what the guy was asking. But there wasn't much left, it was all scrawny stuff when you got there. You arrived too late in the day. But just in the nick of time for me. I thought I was going to miss out on getting a job."

"Destiny prevails, eh?"

Fred's chin jolted upwards. "I don't have much faith in such notions. There's no such thing as predestination, in my book. Lady Luck is chance, not supernatural premeditations."

"Lady Luck wears a lilac dress."

"What do you mean?" Fred inquired.

"Nothing," he mused. "Aren't you religious?"

"I don't know about religion. I think it's impossible to prove such things one way or the other. I like to think we can get by with the right philosophy, regardless of the truth or falsity of particular explanations of why we're here."

"Where were you in America?"

"Utah. I was a miner, and a drover, for a time."

"A real life cowboy? In Utah? Like, the Green River valley, like in *Robber's Roost*?"

"Well, Zane Grey is hardly like the real thing. Life on the range is not as glamorous as it is in books. Anyway, I worked in a copper mine most of the time. I went out there after the Great War. I was in the Navy during the war. Thought America would make me a millionaire. But, the Depression scuppered those plans."

"And now you're back home."

"Home to earn a bit of money and get myself started and settled for good. And I want a place of my own, eventually. I may never get it, but by God I'll try."

"Ah!" Thomas pointed a finger. "You *do* believe in God."

"Who knows about such things. They don't concern folk in their daily lives. You just try to muddle through the best you can."

"I've always thought there was something about religion that was ... suspect. I'm not sure if I believe in it."

"You don't have to be sure either way, at all, do you? You can settle for being agnostic, can't you?"

Thomas hollered for the cows to come to the gate. "No," he told Fred. "I think I want to know for sure. One way or the other: I want to believe with all my heart and all my mind – or *not* at all."

"I've heard it said that the Catholic Church reckons ninety-per-cent of people don't make it to Heaven. That's not much of a catch, is it? We might as well all live a wicked life, if only one in ten is going to get through the Pearly Gates, regardless of how well or badly we live. I'm not interested in moral élitism. It's necessary to be pragmatic in this world, in this life."

"Ah, but they say a similar thing about Presbyterian notions about Predestination. Some say, if you don't know whether you're Elect or not and if, according to Calvin, it doesn't matter whether you live a good life or a bad life because if you're Elect you'll get to Heaven regardless of how good or bad you've been, then why bother bein' good-livin' at all? But the Reverend MacIntyre used to say we still all have free will and are responsible for our deeds and, sure, isn't it better to be nice to each other rather than cause trouble because there's enough heartache in the world as it is already."

"Yes, I'm familiar with Calvinism," Fred said ethereally. "They've both got much the same idea, I suppose. After all, Calvin was a Catholic priest."

"*Was 'e?*"

"Till he joined in on the Reformation he was. After his father died he felt free to leave the Catholic fold. Fathers can be oppressive, sometimes. And uncles?" he humorously quizzed, not expecting a reply.

Thomas hollered again. They began walking and the cows streamed after them. The lane was shaded by the high hedges. Mrs Higgins's smoky chimney made them cough. The cows all followed them loyally.

A flying cat squealed. It landed on its feet in the yard. Jean Gray was at the half-door, scowling. Eddie laughed to himself. She'd lost the bap about something. The door banged shut and the latch slammed its jaw fiercely.

Thomas was at the gable wall, whitewashing the cottage with a yard brush. Eddie sauntered over and stood by as Thomas raised the broom up towards the peak beneath the eaves. His jacket and trousers were spotted white with the watery solution. He watched Thomas stroke the wall again, until the last area of pebbledash was covered and glistened. "Y'haven't mixed that very well."

"Do richtly," Thomas insolently replied. "Haven't much lime."

Shaking his head, Eddie said, "Shoddy. Say, are you still interested in going t' Man, then?"

Thomas mumbled something.

"Aw come on. I've the boat over arranged an' all. You can't let me down now. I've even the B and B fixed up."

"Well, I'll ask when I think they're in a good mood."

"I've bumped into Fred. We've got a new hand, too," Eddie told him. "He's okay, but he's a bit slow. No common sense."

Thomas's eyes swivelled skywards. "Paul McCann once toul' me there's no such thing as common sense. It's only what people know, collectively. So it's a relative thing. Relative to what society as a whole knows. What's common sense to someone who knows something's not always clear to somebody who's not had the same kind of experience." He scratched his light stubble.

"What are you on about? You think too much."

"You must lack common sense if you can't see it, like everybody else can, when a beast's got a knot in it's puddin'."

Eddie ignored his argument. "Have you asked them about the races, then? I was down at Ardglass the other day and the boat's all fixed up. Do you get seasick?" He chortled; he was excited. "Terence was last year. Both trips, across and back! He's giving it a miss this year. It was a cod, to see him ralfin' and hueyin'."

A familiar tune could be heard, first of all faintly, then it increased in pitch. Fred Nelson was approaching them, whistling as he returned from the fields for his dinner. He walked with his back straight, arms swinging smartly by his sides. His trousers were mud-caked, but he had a smart bearing. His clipped moustache and trimmed hair, the new looking cap and the well-cut clothes gave him a distinguished look. His gait was assertive and confident. He was singing.

> "In Dublin's fair city,
>   Where girls are so pretty,
>   I first set my eyes on
>   Sweet Molly Malone.
>
> She wheeled her wheelbarrow
>   Through streets broad and narrow,
>   Crying 'Cockles and mussels,
>   Alive, alive-o!'"

"He seems a right bloke," said Eddie. Seen some things in his time. He was a Down man, Isaac had told him. And he knew he was an Orange man. A good sort. A hard worker, Isaac said. A tight bae. Though somehow he seemed out of place here.

"'Lo."

"Hi, there, Eddie." Fred was grinning. He slapped the young man on the shoulder. "Is the lunch ready, Thomas?"

He stuttered, "Aye, should be. Think so."

"How do you like this part of the world, then, Fred?"

"Come with me," he beckoned, winking.

The two lads followed the thick set little man across the yard, out the gate and down the road a few yards. Fred extended an arm, making a sweeping gesture. Over the hedges, seemingly at the end of the dark line of the road, the countryside was visible. The lush fields rose to gradually mingle in the tussle of dense treetops that were hiding the foot of the hill from sight. The hazy blue pyramid of Divis dominated the horizon, framed by the greenery. Above it were splodged white wisps of cloud, as if they and the pale sky had been painted on canvas. As the temperature changed the mountain in the distance blushed purple.

"That's what I like about this part of the world: the scenery is magical. It is beauty in its purest form. Forty shades of green! Nature, unsullied by the hand of Man. I went for a stroll on Sunday, found myself at the top of Rickamore Brae. You can see the green bubble of Donegore Hill from up there, and even the rock of Tardree nestling on its back, like a baby in the crook of its mother's arm. From up there you can see Lough Neagh shimmering and even across to the rolling Sperrins beyond. Such a vast, wild beauty – it *humbles* me. We are like planetary bacilli, compared to the size and splendour of our environment. It is grander than any one of us could ever be."

"But America must be nicer," Thomas said. "Your pictures of the Petrified Forest and the Grand Canyon ..."

"Ach!" He waved a wrist contemptuously. "The America I know is deserts and dustbowls, rocks and concrete tower blocks. The grass is greener *here*." He marched off, heading for the Orchards, to get his dinner.

Thomas was still gazing at the mountain in the distance. He swapped a glance with Thomas. He placed a hand over his brow, to shield his eyes from the now intense sunlight. Divis had changed colour again. It seemed to be glowing intensely, like a beating heart. He was thinking that Fred was right, we never appreciate the good things around us. Or, usually, not till it's too late. Sweet Jesus, this place is beautiful! It's so sunny, warm, *warm*! He felt happy, free and at peace. Relaaaxed!

"Mmmmmm! Szsnisff. Pfe-mmmmmmmmmmpfh!"

"What are you sighin' about?"

"It's nice."

Eddie raised an eyebrow. "Aye. Ask them, anyway."

"Eh?"

"About the races. Say, what did he mean, we're bacilli?"

"He's got this theory, that people, individuals – this is gettin' to be a lot of philosophisin' fer one day – we're not as important as the race as a whole is. Somethin' the Nazis are in to. He gimme a load of articles about it, pictures of the Führer and stuff." He had his hands in his pockets and was engaged in kicking a stone on the road as he spoke, eyes downcast, intent on what he was doing as his mind rummaged to retrieve Fred's chat. "What's needed is to breed a race of Supermen. Men that are better than ordinary men. 'The good of humanity lies in its specimens', y'see. Modern science has gone forward in such leaps and bounds, we hae te reassess our values. Our morality. Since it's now possible to produce a Master Race – like Herr Hitler says, why, not do it? Why be stuck with weaklings, like spastics an' Jews an' Slavs?"

"And Celts? And Anglo-Saxons?"

Thomas looked up. "This is Fred's idea of the future. May well turn out like that, for all I know. It seems to be like human nature, to want to improve all the time, for each generation to progress. Something about it doesn't seem quite right; but I can't put my finger on it. Goes against my grain, that's all."

"Jesse Owens is a nigger an' he won at the Olympics. No wonder the Nazis were upset: that shows how silly their racism is. It's all a matter of culture, not racial superiority. We're not better or worse than each other, we're just different, that's all. If the Fenians want a Free State, good luck to them. They're Irish. But I'm British and so's the rest of the northern counties. They can't change that. We can't make each other into something we're not. You've got to live and let live."

"I thought you'd be a bit more staunch than that."

Eddie leaned over and whispered, "Only when the going gets tough. If they give us peace, we'll give them peace. Simple. But if they want a fight – we've got to stand up for our rights. There's not much point in living if you're not free to live the way you please. That's why these Germans are gonna cop it. I don't want t' be German, or a slave for Germany. Do you, Thomas?"

"No!"

"Fight the good fight!" He clenched his right hand into a fist so tightly it became coloured by the blood within.

"Well, I'd better hurry up or I'll be late." He extracted himself from Eddie's sermonising.

He spotted Help in the field. He halted to whistle. Her ears reacted. The head turned. The mouth opened in gay recognition. The dog bounded towards him. He noticed that one of Patsy Duggan's wee heifers had broken into their field. It was licking a cow's flank. Their big, black, curly-haired Galloway bull approached it, began sniffing at its tail, then jumped on the tiny beast. The creature toppled under the weight. But, when it rose, the bull mounted again and its back arched as it served the young animal. Careless. Patsy would be vexed when he found out his calf was ruined. But that was his tough luck; it was his hedge.

Thomas saw a four-poster bed in the middle of the field. Marbeth Hart was on it, naked, squatting on all fours, with her rump up in the air. Uncle Isaac was striding across the field towards the bed, leggings and mucky boots slopping as he marched forward, determined eyes aiming from beneath the peaked cap. Reaching his target, he straddled her like a Tom cat would a writhing moggie.

He denied it: the vision vanished as Thomas shut his eyes. He gripped his head, his sore head, in his hands. He was feeling a stabbing pain, as if he had been struck by a pickaxe. Ah! He understood now; this was what was meant by the sins of the flesh, when people behave like animals, rather than loving each other, with all their hearts and all their minds. He was gently amused by the thought that he couldn't see the Reverend MacIntyre and Mrs MacIntyre, oul' Emily and Rab, ever having done the like of this.

There was a simple explanation; nice ladies don't do disgusting things like this for, after all, to have babies all they have to do is kiss their husbands in a wifely sort of way, whereas whores and dirty old men do these bestial things purely out of carnal self-indulgence. It's true, one sin leads to another, all right: you start off by picking your nose, and before you know it you're pulling your stalk, like Sandy, and then – fornicating. He had it straight in his mind now.

Jean opened the creaking door. A fustle: Thomas lying on his bed, facing the window. A fistle: the hurricane lamp glowing on the bedside cabinet.

"Yer uncle's not back from Auntie Sarah's. The church hall has to be opened up for the Youth Club and the boiler put on. Nip down and do it for him, darlin'."

He gawped and shook his head. "I don't wanna ..."

"You should take yourself out, son. It's nice to see you so keen on your Bible readin', but it's Saturday night. Leave it now. You can see your friends and lock up before you go. Save Uncle Isaac going down when he gets home."

Thomas got off his bed. "Alright, I'll go. But ... Mummy ... I don't ... I don't like crowds."

"Nobody likes throngs of people. But sure, there's only your friends down there. You want to see them."

Once she was gone, Thomas tucked the scrapbook under the bed and extracted the Son from its hiding place. He brushed flakes of wood from the effigy. Thomas quickly set his carving in the wardrobe and tidied himself up. Pamela and Harry were sure to be there. Face them, face them! Who were they? Nobodies. But she was ... More fish in the sea, Thomas told himself. Nicer girls than her. And you are young, handsome, rich, a fine, respected member of the community! Cheer up. Looking in the mirror to comb his hair, he caught his own eye; trust in Jesus,

He will carry you through.

"Here, I've found this by the chair." Mrs Crowe passed it to Jean. "'A fork on the floor, a stranger at the door'," she recited, hearing the front door.

Glancing across the kitchen and then back to the kettle over the fire, Jean said, "That's Thomas away out to the Youth Club. Hidin' himself away in his room evenings! Not natural. To not even sit with Isaac an' me an' Fred an' enjoy a bit of crack[17]. Or even go down the road to the Kayes' anymore. Since he got told off about that gunpowder. If he'd have got in with that wee girl Maisie it would've been a good thing. They're right folk, the Kayes. I dunno what to do with him sometimes. You seen him at Communion? I hope he *was* sick; I hope to God you-know-who wasn't puttin' strange ideas in his head. With any luck *he* won't be back, anyway. He'll mibbe be dead, soon."

"Jean! I'm surprised at you."

"Oh, I don't *wish* him any harm. What I mean is, it seems inevitable. He's not getting any younger."

"Well, you can't be blamed for bearing a grudge against him ..."

"I don't bear a grudge against anybody ..."

"... after the way he treated you."

"Aye!" she said sourly. "Men! Leading you into temptation, leading you astray. He was the Devil in disguise. And I was weak: I was at that age when you're scared you're about to be left on the shelf and still try to resist the Lord's plan for you. It amazes me now how could I have seen anything in *him*." She shook her head.

---

[17] a bit of crack = (coll.) conversation, merriment.

"To err is human. It wasn't your fault, Jean. I heard Thomas was seen with, of all people, Marbeth's girl."

Jean's gaze pierced her visitor's eyes. "A wheen of those young ones, Edmund Kaye and so on, knock about on the bikes an' that. That girl of Ben Hart's might've been there, but it wasn't what the usual rubbish-talkers reckon. You know the way youngsters pal about."

"I hope you're right."

"Even if there was something to it, it wouldn't matter too much. After all, she is *Ben's* daughter."

Cautiously, Mrs Crowe asked, "*Is* that the way of it?"

"Definitely. Just look at her. The breedin's obvious."

"Yes, I think you're right, though she looks more like the mother than Ben. But sure, anyway, why'd he-a married Marbeth if she wasn't his? Well, anyway, how have you been yourself?" she asked, taking the offered cup of tea.

Jean's head wagged. "Can't complain."

Thomas walked down to the church along quiet roads. Everyone was at their tea still. It was too early for them to be abroad. The solitary atmosphere refreshed him, helped to cool his burning cheeks.

At the main road a passing car blared. Dr Moore waved. He waved back. The noise subsided and the birds in the trees along the river, behind the village, uttered a rendition of their familiar, happy tune.

Thomas liked the railway bridge. It was like the arch of the gateway at the castle in Templepatrick: the entrance to a magical, mysterious place. He passed through the slice of tunnel and went round the corner to the church. The grey building stared sullenly out of its two front windows. It was a sleeping dragon, he decided: sometimes it would bellow fire and brimstone, snort smoke and spit flame, rise up on its hind legs and swat pesky varmints – cattle rustlers or savage injuns – from the terraces and the like. In the end, it would snap at everyone.

He unlocked the boiler room and started up the central heating. Thomas fuelled the boiler and checked that it was set right. An easy job. He imagined being a worker in a factory, in a big industrial plant where you had easy work all day, like checking machines were working properly. Or would he be bored and wish he was back out in the sunny fields? Or back out in the cold biting wind and slicing rain, wrestling with animals or slopping through mud and shit?

He went round to the side door and opened up the hall. He went into the kitchen, which always warmed up quickest. Thomas jumped up onto the top of a low cupboard and sat waiting. He was resolved to face what would come. So, Pamela wasn't to be his. It didn't matter. It was God's will.

> 'Thy will be done
> on earth as it is in Heaven.'

Footsteps. Someone else.

"Thomas."

"Harry. Isn't Pamela with you th' night?"

"Pamela? No. It's Harriet I'm seein', not her sister. She's coming down later on."

Could it be true? When all seemed lost, He provided a miracle!

"Pamela?"

"Harriet. Dunno about Pamela. She's more or less stopped coming. Getting too big, she says. And her younger than me. What about you? Haven't seen you down for a while."

"Been busy."

"Wanna box?"

"What sort of box?"

"No, boxing." He raised his fists. "I'm showing the lads how to fight. Come on, the gloves are in the hall."

"Fighting, in the church hall?" he queried, following Harry to the hall.

"It's good clean sport, not brawling."

A few others had arrived. They helped lace up the two boys' gloves. Harry danced around a bit. He instructed Thomas to hold his hands up in front of his face all the time. They tried a few tester throws. Then Harry started to box in earnest.

For a time Thomas was able to circle with his opponent and protect himself from punches. He hit Harry's gloves a few times. He struck at Harry's body. Rapid blows struck his arms and chest. Thomas felt he was getting the hang of it. He was aware of the door opening and a girl coming in. Pamela!

Pain! Seering round his face. Blackness; flashes of light; sensation of falling; a jolt like the time he came off Patsy's donkey. Spinning room. Harry's face swaying like a garden swing. At last his sight focussed properly.

"I ... I must've fell."

There was a peal of laughter. The whole hall was laughing. But it was not sinister; Thomas laughed at himself, too. He looked round for the girl, for Pamela. He wanted to share his happiness with her.

Then he saw that the girl had red hair, that she was not his brunette. Her nose had a bump; the face was more like their father's than their mother's. It was Harriet Hart, not Pamela. He had been mistaken. His mood collapsed once more.

"Want another round?" Harry grinned.

"I'd be round the bend to think I could take on an expert like you." Thomas held out his hands for someone to untie the gloves.

So much for wishful thinking. No Pamela. But at least now he knew she wasn't Harry's girlfriend. Now he knew there was still a chance! A ghost of a chance. Good old God; He had fixed it for him to get down here tonight, to discover that the way forward was still open. My destiny awaits me – still!

They played some basketball, bringing the high hoops out from the storeroom. Thomas sat with Sandy Thompson as they caught their breath and drank pop. Sandy was one of the ones in charge of the Youth Club now.

"What's your big brothers all at these days?"

"Billy's in Australia, John's finishin' his apprenticeship, Robbie an' George are still at home wi' us."

"There's a lot of yous, at the one wee place."

"Aye. I'll maybe luk fer a trade meself, soon. You don't know how lucky you are."

"Most of our ground's only taken."

"Harry tells me you're doin' a line with Pamela."

His mouth felt dry, despite the lemonade. "Why'd he say that?"

"Admit it, you're on the prowl."

"Don't be dirty. That's not true."

"I didn't think you'd bother with her, right enough."

"Don't you think she's worth bothering about?"

"One of them Stinkers?" He pointed his bottle in Harriet's direction. Shaking his head, he said, "They're the sort you don't think twice about. Last time I seen Pamela she was at the end of Summerhill loanen, at thon tumbled down cottage where her da keeps the goats." He paused, smiling broadly to himself. He laughed and told Thomas, "And your uncle appeared and started keepin' her goin' about givin' him a kid! She was flummoxed."

"He'll've been gettin' her ma an' all t' gie us a hand wi' something. Them 'uns still works till us."

Sandy got up and blew a whistle. He organised the last game of the night. "This is the way I want you to do it," he announced.

Pearl Fleming played the piano as they all went round in a big circle, singing:

> "The farmer wants a wife,
> The farmer wants a wife,
> Heigh-ho, my dearie-oh,
> The farmer wants a wife."

When the music stopped, each boy grabbed a girl and rushed to the centre to nab a chair and set her on his knee. Thomas got Harriet before Harry Murtagh could reach her. But Harry grabbed Mabel and manhandled her onto the last free chair. Those who had missed out on a seat were out and sat round the walls of the hall, watching the frantic competitors.

After several runs, it seemed a competition had emerged between Harry and Thomas for Harriet. He noticed that Sandy was nodding to Pearl when to stop. And it was always when Thomas was further from Harriet than Harry was. Sandy grinned at him, wickedly, a couple of times.

He was doing this on purpose! Because Harriet was Pamela's sister and so he was mocking Thomas. The farmer was himself. And farmer Gray's 'wife' was Pamela. Was Harriet. Thomas swore to himself: I'll show you, Sandy!

They got down to one chair and one girl: Harriet. And two boys: Harry and Thomas. His heart was racing as the piano played.

It stopped. Thomas's hand sought Harriet's but she drifted away from him and levitated onto Harry's knee, on the chair. The rest of them were cheering loudly and clapping as Thomas faced the dreaded shame of this defeat.

Holding out their prize – a big fruit cake to share between them – Sandy said, "Hard lines, Thomas. Looks like you're one farmer that's not going to get a wife."

They were shearing sheep at Begley's. There was a narrow walled race, just wide enough for a single animal to walk along, at one side of the sheep pens. James Ritchie chased a few sheep along this crush. Young Hugh Begley and his father were clipping with hand shears. Thomas was gathering up the discarded fleeces and stuffing them into large, square canvas sacks. Fred Nelson was catching a sheep to clip it. His arms were smeared with sheep dung.

"You're a more agile bloke than that Paul McCann, anyway," Stan told Fred. "Paul works for Isaac Gray from time to time. He's away down south, now. Supposed to be very ill, isn't that right, Thomas? And he's a Commie, isn't he?"

Fred glanced up. "I'm most certainly not one of them! I swing the other way. I'm a firm supporter of Moseley."

"Really? Why's that, then?"

Thomas listened intently as Fred introduced his political beliefs. "Life is all about the will to power. Everyone is trying to succeed, to assert their authority over somebody else. Life is one big competition. A race for survival and domination. It's the strong versus the weak. The Commies, like Christians, believe in herd morality, in slave morality. The way I see it, we should just compete and let the strong get on with making the best of themselves. How else is mankind to progress? Certainly not by letting the weak and effete hold the strong back with their fear-based regulations. Let the 'Supermen' stride on!" He clacked his shears in the air. "If you or I aren't fit to compete with them, good luck to them. That's life. The law of the jungle. Not nice, I admit: but it's the way of the world. Let the strong be masters of their own destiny, I say. Let's have a master morality, not a slave morality."

"Get a houl'-a that lamb," James nodded at Thomas, lifting a knife from the wall of the pen.

Thomas reached out and grabbed the end of its tail. As it skipped forwards to escape, its tail became taut. James placed the rusty blade between two bones and put a little pressure on. The lamb jerked forward as the long end of the dirty tail fell limp in Thomas's hand. He flung it onto the pen wall, from which it slithered down onto the gravel of the worn yard.

Fred was clipping a black ewe. As he held her, her front feet dangled in the air, submissively. The shears divided the wool from the animal. When he had finished, he let the ewe scamper to the bloody-tailed lamb. They were chased back out to the field by Hugh.

Thomas hesitantly asked, "What's the master morality?"

"Whatever the Superman says it is. After all, it's the boss that calls the shots, isn't it?" He winked at Stan.

Laughing, Stan said, "In that case, get your backs into it! C'mon, Thomas, git yer coat off. Aren't ye roasted in thon jecket?"

He muttered, "Aye. I'll take it off in a minute. You sound like you would be on Adolf's side," Thomas commented. "But sure, the British are near at war with the Germans."

"Yep. But should they be? Aren't we Aryans, like them? What are the Slavs but second-rate beings. Do we ally ourselves with sheep or cattle? The Nazis believe in being cruel to be kind. To rid the world of the weak and let the Master Race thrive: that's what you do on a farm, isn't it? The sickly animals snuff it, the strong are the valuable ones."

Thomas considered this point. "But there's been great Jews. Like Einstein, an' thon buddy Freud."

Fred's sharp eyes watched the snipping blades of his shears.

"Phuh. What they done anybody could-a done. They were just lucky to be the first to get into print and publicise themselves, that's all. For all we know, they might turn out to be all wrong, anyway. What is needed in the modern world is leadership with vision, with the vigour to revitalise society and create a new order, a new world where the only virtue is ability, where the only criterion is strength. We need the kind of motivation the Germans have had. Look at their industry, look at their autobahns. Look at Italy's improvements in drainage and land reclamation and getting the trains to run on time. I don't want to hold anyone back who's a better man than me."

"Can't just not care," Hugh piped up. "You've got to look after the old and the young and the handicapped. They may be weak, but they're *people*."

"The individual is of little relevance in the face of the furtherance of the species."

Stan argued, "The species can only be improved by raising up all of the people. The improvement of life for a few exceptions isn't much use."

Fred straightened his back, releasing another ewe. "Oh, I don't know. It's pretty easy to tell the sheep from the goats." He shared a laugh with Stan Begley.

"There's no answer, is there?" Thomas said loudly, angrily.

Taken aback, Uncle Stan told him, "Well, I've my answer, and Fred's got his. And I'm sure you've got your own. So it's a case of an abundance of answers, rather than too few."

Thomas went across the yard to the back of the byre. He undid his flies and took up position at the wall. With one hand he slipped the notched piece of wood from his inside jacket pocket. The Son was a small carving, just a bearded face with deep eyes. It was scored across with vicious grooves now. He dropped it in the long grass at the byre wall. Like the Holy Ghost, this attempt at art had thrown him into a bout of despair. It was no good: he could not do it, he could not sculpt. Why was he a failure at art? Thomas stared down at the injured face. Why could he not get things right? Why did everything he touched seem to crumble?

As he urinated he recalled the discussion. Fred's beliefs sounded at the same time both nasty and intriguing. He did not like the sound of it, yet it *was* realistic. It was close to the experience of life he knew. Why then, did his heart crave something else? Why did his mind keep railing at the thought that there was no perfection? The crude resemblance of a face stared up mournfully, seemed to snarl like a medieval monster rather than smile like a benevolent Saviour. *Was* life always sordid and mundane, or *was* there a transcendental quality which penetrated into the material sphere, into this earthly life?

But it was when he tried to think about it that everything seemed to fall to pieces. It was like a throbbing in a tooth that would persist, however hard he tried to forget about it. His mood turned against all this striving for Art and even the striving for Truth. He hated the sight of the carving; he hated the thought of religion; he hated feeling he had to know and believe in the proper meaning of life. His head was aching with perplexity. I must get it out of my out of my mind, he told himself. I must squeeze it out of my heart!

CHAPTER SIX

The Love of Man

His mother was wearing her best dress. She even had on her fancy hat. His uncle was tidied up, had shaved, seemed a cleaner complexion. The sail in the trap was fun because they were all dandied up and the neighbours they passed on the road looked up at them enviously.

The short church service was followed by a bit of crack as the beaming groom, James Ritchie, tried to explain to Thomas how to take photographs with his box camera. He had trouble making Aunt Sarah say 'cheese'; she looked so sad, though she didn't cry.

They went to Begley's for sandwiches and tea. A small gathering: even the Usshers didn't bother going on to it. Thomas looked around him at the pictures on the parlour walls: a family photograph, a fading picture of a stallion, the portrait of the King. The table and sideboard were stacked with plates of sandwiches and wee buns and bowls of trifle, with piles of small plates and saucers set out for the guests to help themselves. The milling strangers made this once homely place sinister; it was so noisy with chatter and cluttered with bodies he didn't know.

Mary was wearing a cream dress, with lots of frills and lace and a compact little matching hat which had a now pinned up veil attached. Her crimson cheeks were dimpled by her uncontrollable smiling. She was sitting by her new mother-in-law, while James, in his suit, stood at hand. Thomas smiled too, for his favourite cousin looked so pretty and happy. Her face seemed to radiate joy. She blinked nervously, shy amongst the crowd. He noticed that across the room his mother was talking to Aunt Sarah. She put her arm around her shoulder; Aunt Sarah raised a handkerchief to her eyes. Now the tears, he thought.

"Want some pop?" Hugh held out a bottle.

"Thanks. I see your mother is letting go at last."

Hugh glanced. "No option."

Thomas sipped some lemonade. They listened as Stan had a few words with his daughter.

"Where's me new son-in-law?"

"He's just nipped out to the hedge, Daddy."

"In that case, I've something I want to tell you, Mary. Once upon a time, there was a wee farmer who had a son and a daughter. The son was a right lad, helped out at home an' all. The daughter, she decided she wanted to rake about and see a bit of what life is all about. So, off she set with her oul' bag in her paw, and headed off away, ooh away miles away, as far as Cushendun. And she had lots of charm and grace and beauty, so she doled it out to the chaps, as they sat sipping afternoon tea and nibbling wee buns and enjoying jolly nice things, living it up, y'know. And when they saw she'd no more charms, that they'd had the lot, they all cleared off to some other tea house, and she was left there, all on her own, with only the dregs and without even a crumb. In fact, she ended up having to wash the dishes to pay her way.

"So she said to herself, 'Wouldn't I be as well off back home with me oul' ma and me oul' da, givin' them a hand about the home place as stuck here, slavin' me guts out for somebody else.' So she wheeked up her skirts and she set off down the coast road home again.

"And she was headin' up the loanen when her oul' da saw her comin' and he ran out and give her a big hug and tuk her in and she had a clean up and changed her oul' rags fer a decent dress and he got the mother t' roast that bit of beef they'd been savin' fer Christmas and they had a big feast.

"And the son, he gets in later after doin' the milkin' and says, 'What's goin' on here! What's that hussy doin' back here? Sure, she was off galavantin', with her wild livin' and chasin' after the mickey dazzlers and all that carry on, and here she is back and yous throw a perty! That's not fair, 'cos yous niver throw a party fer *me*, an' I milk cows and lamb ewes and graipe muck and do all that. What's the big idea?'

"And the oul' da, he puts his hand on his son's shoulder," Stan put his hand on Mary's, "and says, 'Son, you're here and this place is as much yours as it is the wife's 'n' mine. But your sister was gone from us, an' now she's back with us, and no matter what she's done, we'll still always love her.' And that, my dear, is the Parable of the Prodigal Daughter, according to yours faithfully, Stanford Begley."

Mary moved her face towards her shoulder and, kissing her father's hand, said softly, "Esquire."

Hugh told Thomas, "They're fixin' up that cottage at the bottom of the loanen. That should do them till he gets some money gathered up.

Will you give us a hand to dip some sheep while you're here? You can put a pair of James's leggin's on ye."

When Thomas went into James's room to put on the working clothes, the groom was changing too. He was changing into his working clothes. Without speaking to each other, the two young men went out to the yard. James carried two brown suitcases. Uncle Stan took the luggage from him and then hauled his daughter and wife up beside him.

"Mind yous luk after the place! See yous Monday!"

He shook the reins and the colt responded to his clicking tongue. The trap sped down the lane, scattering the last of the departing guests. Hugh and James strode off down the fields. Thomas ran to catch them up.

"Where are they away?"

"Newcastle. For a few days at the seaside," Hugh told him.

"But aren't you going?"

James Ritchie replied, "There's far too much to do. Mon bae, let's get these sheep rounded up."

The Begleys had constructed a wooden walkway at the end of the walled crush, so that the sheep had to drop into a wooden box, the size of a trough, at the end of the race. The box was full to the brim of pungent, creamy dip. James dipped a stick in the box and stirred the pale liquid. He wiped his face as the vapour stung his eyes.

Hugh dragged each sheep in turn from the race and as Thomas and James got a hold it dropped into the dip. James held each sheep under, then dunked it again. The chemical mixture poured from the ewes' sides, dribbling as they ran across the yard to huddle in a group by the gate, where they waited to be let back out to the field. A few old blackfaces clenched their tongues between their teeth and tried to bounce into the air, over the box. But James and Thomas forced them all to submit to their parasite-killing bath.

A sudden recollection made Thomas beam with delight. "I am fer goin' to the TT races in the Isle of Man," he boasted.

Hugh's mouth opened in disbelief. "You lucky sod. How'd you wangle it? Wish I could go."

"Why not ask? I did when me ma was in a good mood and I managed to coax her when Uncle Isaac said it was fine to go for a few days, seeing as Eddie'd already arranged it. Just think, I'm going to stay in a hotel," he enthused, "and eat in restaurants and watch the motorcycle races and, and ..."

"Go dancing," James prompted.

Thomas paused to consider the idea. "I hadn't thought of that. Aye," he stuttered, "dance."

"And spend a fortune." James kept his eyes on the sheep. "How'll you afford it?"

"I've been given a wee bit. A belated birthday present."

"I dunno, you spent a week lyin' about pretendin' to be sick, now you're off on a holiday! You know what you are, Thomas Gray, you're inconstant." His face was serious.

Inconstant. Lazy. A sinner. Was he? But Mummy and Uncle Isaac said it was fine. I'd worked hard and deserved a break. 'Do it while you're young,' Uncle Isaac said. 'You're only young once. You'll spend long enough toilin'.'

'You're a good boy and help us,' Mammy said.

Inconstant. Means? Fickle. Flighty. Was he? No more than everybody else. I'm weak. Too weak, I suppose, according to Fred. He felt he should be stronger, tougher. Uncle Isaac was never sick. He didn't complain if he got a cold, he just got on with it. Thomas thought he needed to buck himself up, make himself into a Superman like James Ritchie or Uncle Isaac.

He caught the next sheep with increased vigour: he flexed his arm muscles, tearing the jumping ewe from the air, and plunged her deep into the dip.

"Go easy!" Hugh shouted. "Which are y' tryin' to do: knock her brains out on the side of the bax, or poison her?"

The blue tint of the flax field had long since faded away and they got it pulled without much trouble. A couple of the older women – Mrs Hart, Mrs Fleming – had come for that job, but not the girls. But today, they were here with their mothers for the spreading out.

The folk were gathered in the field, waiting, as Thomas donned his leggings and set out across the pungent lint hole. He held his chin up as he waded through the reeking, dirty water. Help lapped at the strong liquid as Thomas rippled the pool. He went to the edge, where a dam of sods separated the lint hole from the burn, and cautiously groped under the murky surface of the long, narrow pit and began passing out the beets of flax. His head soon began to swim, the stench made him so dizzy. He noticed with satisfaction Pamela's anxious looks as he dipped down to his neck in the stinking water. His arm muscles were soon aching. He took a break and watched them setting the steeped beets upright around the field, to drain.

There was a yelp. Isaac had given Help a clout round the ear with a beet, to stop her drinking the dam water. There was a peal of laughter as the border collie began zigzagging up the field.

"Did y' do her a brain injury?" gasped Thomas.

"She's drunk on the dam water," Pamela pointed out with amusement. The dog collapsed at her feet and she petted Help.

Thomas joked, "Must be as good as paraffin, this stuff."

Isaac barked, "Take that dog away outta the road t' the yard an' lock it in the shed."

Fred said, "You take her, Thomas. You've been in there long enough. I'll relieve you."

Thomas peeled off the leggings, left them sodden on the earth for Fred and went over to Help. The black and white collie was half-snoozing. He carried her to the place where the wee grey Ferguson tractor – which his uncle had bought recently – was parked, at the gateway. She was struggling, not knowing what she was doing. Pamela was nearest, so it was her he asked to sit on the back with the animal to stop Help crawling off as he was driving along.

Pamela sang a lullaby to the dog on the way. Oh, for a dog's life! Thomas thought. Listen to her, spoilin' that thing. Had she a kind word for him? At the Orchards he carried the ill dog to its bed in an outhouse. He lay Help down on her bed of straw. Pamela stroked the now sleeping collie very gently.

"Will she be alright?"

"Oh, aye. Now that I think about it, I think she did the same thing afore now, a wheen-a years ago. But I was still at school, then." Images flashed in his brain of the schoolroom, the rows of desks, the pupils' faces – all blank, except one. "D' you think she'll be sick? I wud be with as much of that mucky water in me as she's had. I can taste it yit."

Should he make a move now? Ask her ... what? To be his girl. No: too blunt. To be ... She began to move towards the door ... see him sometime? She was away already. He followed, closing the door of the outhouse and watching her beautiful back as they crossed the yard.

"Maybe I should tell me muh ... mother what happened." He went into the house.

"What do you want?"

Pamela jumped at the gruff bark. Looking round, she saw Jean Gray appearing from the byre.

"We brought the dog up from the field. It's sick after drinkin' the dirty dam water."

"Where's Thomas?"

"Gone int' the house to look for you."

"You stay away from him, y'hear?" she said angrily.

"Eh?"

"I know your game. Y' think I was born yisterdae? You keep your filthy paws off my lad. He might be starry-eyed for a while, like all youngsters, but he'll soon see through *you*."

Pamela was just about to snap back. She was trying to think of something smart to say, when Thomas came out.

"Ah! Eh, Mummy," he approached her, and stuttered, "Help's ... sick. She was drinkin' the lint hole water."

"Aye. So Miss Hart was tellin' me," she said severely. "She'll live. A load-a fuss over nithin'."

"Uncle Isaac toul' me t' lea' her home."

His mother wagged her head and walked to the front door and went in without replying.

Going to the cart, Pamela asked, "What's up with her?"

"Nothin'."

"I don't think she likes me."

Giving the starter handle of the tractor a few turns, it started into life. He shouted over the rips and roar of the engine and through the exhaust fumes, "Everybody likes you."

Pamela sat leaning against the mudguard and holding the lip of the metal seat. Her warm body bounced at his side - so close to him - as a jet of hot air from somewhere spurted up his trouser leg. "You'll be heading for the Isle of Man soon."

"Tomorrow."

"You're so lucky! Wish I could go on a holiday. I've never been anywhere special."

"You will be. Someday."

"That's a nice thought."

He began driving towards Kaye's yard. Perhaps he should stop on the back loanen and ask her? Ah but, he was going to the Isle of Man tomorrow. Maybe he should wait till he got back?

He was slowing down, taking the bumpy lane easy, and was just about to step hard on the clutch and turn round to face her – he could see himself throwing his arms round her, squeezing her to his breast – when the old witch came out of her cottage. While they were stopped, Pamela told her all about the poor wee dog. And Mrs Higgins droned on about Uncle Isaac's wee grey Fergie, "a quare contraption if ever there was one." Containing his anger, at last they were able to extricate themselves and he drove on.

Aw well, no hurry, it would do when he get back. Maybe it was for the best. It must be the Lord's will that Mrs Higgins appeared when she did. Maybe she wasn't a witch, but an angel – because any agent of the Lord is an angel. Sure, wasn't even Lucifer originally an angel, before he fell from grace? This was a sign, telling him to wait until was the time was right, by Him. Patience is a virtue.

Aye, you gotta get to know the girl first. You can't just mosey up the aisle without havin' done a line or two first. Take it easy, pardner, he consoled himself. He pushed back the throttle lever as the tractor bounced violently through the rutted gateway. Our day will come, he told himself; Thy will be done.

A lovely blast of night air was cooling his face, as the fishing boat sped across the glittering undulations. Despite the penetration of the breeze, Thomas felt no better. He held the wooden rail with tense determination. How he wished it was the banister rail of a house, like Begley's, or the hotel, the one they were going to, or anywhere on firm land.

The boat was rocking from side to side on the water. Steadying himself, he felt his dry throat fill with nausea. There came a hot flush to the back of his ears, his eyes bulged, white foam washed away the bitter tasting vomit as he burst forth over the side.

Another retch, beside him this time, not from him, brought him out of his energyless daze. It was Hugh, coughing up his Scotch broth. Thomas wiped his tender lips with a damp, oily cloth. His pale face surveyed the weather deck, as he made his way to the dim light of the hatch window, using the lashed down motorcycles to propel himself forward with a shoulder-wrenching lurch. He left Hugh to the swirling Irish Sea. Like an old man, Thomas stepped cautiously down the wide ladder.

The flap slammed shut above him. The cabin was gloomy, but the warmth was a welcoming friend. The churning in his guts was subsiding. His spirits were picking up again already. Nonetheless, he sank onto a half-padded sack on the floor and held his stomach with one hand, while with his other hand he wiped his throat, then fanned his clammy face, as if swatting imaginary flies.

From the table, Eddie snorted, "You look awful. Here, have a bit of bread."

Thomas looked up through slitted eyes. The lamp was swinging above Eddie's head, alternately brightening his grinning face and casting it in shadows. He felt he needed to get something inside him. At least it would be something to bring up. All that was left after this evacuation in three instalments was a bile that resembled calf scour.

"Huh." He held out a hand.

Eddie passed some dry wheaten and said, "It can't be that bad. You must feel better after a good boke."

"Wanna die!" Thomas gasped, setting a tiny piece of bread on his tongue.

"Maybe he wants a drink?" said Ernie, who was the other motorcyclist making the voyage with them.

"Here, wet your whistle with this."

Thomas nodded in appreciation as he took the sarsaparilla. After a gulp, he said with a stronger tone, "I'm used to it now. It's Hugh you wanna worry about. He's that tall he'll be airsick as well as seasick."

"We'll be there in half an hour. It'll be getting steadier from here on in. Anyway, it was worse last year. I was in a worse state than you are. I pity you. I'm glad I'm not unwell this time round. Just you wait and see, in a wheen of hours it'll be light and you'll see the island and it'll be beautiful. Nice hills and scenery. Quaint wee town. The marra night we'll go to a dance and chat up lots of pretty wee wenches. This lovesickness, your pining for the mermaids, will be long forgotten."

The hatch slammed and a bump announced Hugh's return. The boat had rolled and he had gone feet first down, without touching the ladder. He picked himself up and snarled as the two elder boys laughed.

"Don't you still feel sick?" Thomas asked as Hugh took a pew beside Eddie.

"I feel okay. It was just a sudden pain tuk me and I had to go and throw up."

"I've felt rotten the whole time," said Thomas dragging himself to his feet.

"You wanna see it when its really rough!" teased Eddie.

As they approached Douglas, the boys went up to watch the berthing. The fishermen tied *The Maiden* alongside. Thomas hurried to get his feet onto the pier. But he had to turn back and help Eddie and Ernie to get their bikes off the boat. Then, Hugh and he carried the cases along the dock in the early morning darkness.

"What we want now is a big feed of bacon and eggs," said Ernie.

"I just wanna sleep," moaned Hugh. "My head feels fuzzy."

"Yup," Thomas agreed. "My belly thinks it's still at sea."

The excitement of being away from home in a new place, in a new country, was deflated somewhat by the darkness. It was nippy and the streets were lonely. As Eddie wheeled his bike up the road he just missed a black cat with no tail. The legends were true! The cat cursed at him and sauntered proudly on its way with its backside struggling defiantly.

They found their guesthouse: *Shalamar*. Eddie and Ernie wheeled their motorbikes round to the back yard. Ernie went boldly up to the front door and rapped it. A light appeared at an upstairs window.

"What are you doin'? You'll upset them, at this wee hour."

"How else are we to get in? Anyway, I know oul' Mrs Heggarty. She's a light sleeper. Catnaps in the day, too. She knows we're arriving at this time."

The door opened. An enormous woman with flabby jowls bared her yellow teeth. "Men! Come in."

She chatted away, telling them where everything was and what everything was. She had a bog-soft Irish accent. She told them her house rules. They were shown to their rooms. Mrs Heggarty lit a lamp in each of the two rooms, which had two single beds in each.

Hugh was fussed over: the tall lad got the three-quarter bed in the bigger room. Eddie was already standing in there, so Thomas was swept out on an invisible tide of air by the bulk of the landlady and cast into the other, pokey wee room, with the stranger.

Ernie yawned long and loud. Thomas yawned. He began to undress. Thomas felt so weary, he didn't think about being embarrassed as he stripped to his longjohns. He swooned into the fresh, ever so soft, luxury spring-mattressed bed. His last faint awareness was of the fizzing lamp on the dresser being blown out by his bare-chested room-mate.

"Mmhah!"
"She's frae Wexferd."
"Uh?"
"She's a right daecent oul' bird, really."
Light rushed into his head. He turned his face towards the wall. Ernie was shaking him again.
"I'm awake," he groaned.
"I'll see you downstairs. Breakfast starts in ten minutes."
Thomas turned over and rose from the bed. He rubbed his eyes and looked around for his clothes. They were on a chair at the foot of the bed. He pulled on his socks and trousers and went over to the dresser to wash. A scoop of cold water over his face and head lifted some of the heaviness. Drying off with a towel, he peered around the room before shaving.

The walls were *very* yellow. The wallpaper was a sickly colour, patterned in diamonds of curling beige vines, with mustardy flowerheads at the crosspoints. The embossed design mesmerised him. High on the wall between the bed-heads was a curious picture. He moved closer. It was a Renaissance-style portrait of Jesus Christ. The crown of thorns was drawing blood around the Messiah's brow. A faint halo capped the holy head. The expression on the face was one of sorrow. A salty tang prickled his nostrils. His hunger was rampant.

The breakfast was like a party: everyone chatting, Mrs Heggarty bringing plates stacked with grub, the tea strong, the toast crisp and warm. The freedom to go out into the world stunned Thomas. He had no cows to milk, no chores ahead of him, just a blank day, sunshine and a few bob in his pocket. The feelings of insecurity were forgotten and he wanted to get out there, get out there into the big, wide world!

"C' mon, you baes. Hurry up." They were still eating toast.
"Houl' yer horses," Eddie told him, "us kings of the road need our fuel, y'know."

They headed for the practice race, which would decide their starting positions in the Lightweight competition. Eddie and Ernie took their bikes to the front of the B and B and kick-started them. Eddie's Norton ripped into life. He revved her up. Ernie roared off on his Triumph, his goggles on his nose pinched in the wind. Thomas watched Eddie mouth something and then he too was off with a raging wail.

"What did he say?"

"Didn't hear. But don't worry, I know the way," Hugh informed his cousin. "He toul' me this morning."

They found a vantage point at a long stretch a little way off from the start line. Thomas and Hugh stood with their hands in their pockets, looking about them wide-eyed, as a few other spectators arrived. It was a warm, bright morning. Thomas inspected each new sight about the town and countryside, overwhelmed by the novelty of his surroundings. The clamour of engines in the vicinity created an atmosphere of expectation that glimmered like the fumes. Hugh held a hand up to shade his eyes as the bikes assembled for the start of the trial run. The buzz of the swarm of machines increased.

They were off! Hugh tugged Thomas's sleeve and their bulging eyes moved with the hurtling shapes that were heading towards them.

A group of young people had stopped near the lads to watch the first racers. Folk like you to be civil, he told himself. They would think Hugh and he were ignorant Irish bucks, not even saying good-day. Was this Eddie coming? No, these were the experts. He would be in the last half of the starters, since it was only his first race. Wow! Screaming bikes passed, in a flick of turbulence and smoke. There was a pause between huddles of racers; the next lot were on the line. Out of the corner of his eye he spied the blonde looking round again ...

"Morning."

She smiled. "Good morning." She had an English accent. Posh. Nice. Ultra-polite. "Are you supporting anyone in particular?" Part-ick-u-lar: she licked the word between tongue and teeth, tossing it delicately towards his ear.

"Ahh. Eddie Kaye. He's fairly new. It's only his first year racin', though he was here afore, t' watch. We're just here for the cod, [18]really. And you?"

---

[18]cod = (coll.) fun.

"My brother Robert is competing. He's just gone by ..."

"Aye. Yous were all wavin' and cheerin'."

"Robert's in twelfth place at the moment."

"He must be good."

"He's been here a few times. I'm Margaret." She held out her hand. "And you?"

He stared at the hand; his features set like stone. He watched as his own scarred hand moved out. He felt a soft warm thing, and shaking it sensed it was as delicate as a newly-hatched chick. Be careful, you fool, his mind screamed, this is no time for a good oul' Presbyterian funeral bone-crusher of a handshake. This hand was part of a living body, it was coursing with life. The skin was so tender. The touch sent an electric tickle through him.

He introduced Hugh and himself. Margaret was with her friends, Sally and Olivia. Her brother's mates were at the startline. Perhaps they would care to find a good spot further along the route? Hugh gave Thomas an enquiring, boggle-eyed, wink.

What was that thing Paul talked about once – *déjà vu* – feeling you've experienced something before. Margaret, in her pretty blue frock, with the fair locks, friendly, distinguished, confident manner, and lilting voice – she seemed so familiar, yet he *knew* he'd never met her before. In this life. Paul had gone on about Hindus and living several lives – said maybe we come back as some breed of animal or other, or as another person. It sounded like rubbish but, he wondered, why had he hit it off so well with her? Maybe they were soulmates.

As they were walking on their way to find another good place to watch from, the girls chatted with Thomas and Hugh. They were so open, Thomas was incredulous. They were getting on like a house on fire. He felt the rage of the passion of life within, a new ecstasy. They were nice girls, nice people to know. And Margaret, in particular, was an absolute angel.

The din of the motorbikes began to increase. They had taken a shortcut and waited to see some action. Two bikes were neck and neck. As the bikes roared by, Margaret's brother edged in front of his rival. They were able to see the Triumph press on as the pair of them receded into the horizon. Up a hill, at the end, Robert was way out in front of the other chap! The girls jumped, cheering, elated. Margaret held Thomas's shoulder as she sprang on her toes, laughing and shouting. A hint of perfume competed with the petrol and mown grass. He looked round nervously. Their eyes sparkled at each other. Blue: she had those luminous kind of eyes that have a throbbing life of their own, that glisten like clear water on a brilliant day. A trickle teased his spine.

"I haven't seen Eddie at all," Hugh said to his cousin.

"What sort of bike does your friend have?" Sally with the red hair was taking an interest in him.

"A Norton."

"Ooh, my favouwite!" Her lisp made Hugh grin and blush. "There's a good place further along. You can see the finishing line from there. When they've completed their route, we can cheer them on as they take the flag."

"Shouldn't we try and spot Eddie?" Hugh suggested.

"He'll be alright. Sure, he's only a novice, anyway. He won't get anywhere. Come on, I want to talk to these girls."

"Mar-gar-het!" Hugh mocked.

They spent the afternoon chatting. The sun was beating down as they sat in a field by the road, which was the track, on warm grass that had been nibbled short by sheep. The hedges were full of nests. It was a far cry from the way he usually spent his time in fields, working – this was a place of leisure and ease. They were from Leicester. Their daddies sounded like well-to-do businessmen. Robert was in the family firm, an engineer. His pals were fellow enthusiasts. The girls were just finishing school this year and had been allowed to come along since they'd studied so hard in their final year. Olivia had done *particularly* well; she was hoping to go on to train as a teacher.

"Here come the leaders!" Hugh yelled, jumping up.

The first handful of competitors battled it out for the places. A huddle of bikes was led by Margaret's brother. He was sixth!

And all of a sudden it was over. The noise was tremendous as the engines converged, for the last riders had appeared and the crowd was flocking towards the circle of competitors.

"We'll have to go and congratulate Robert. I expect you will wait for your friend?"

"Eh ... yes."

"Perhaps we'll bump into you later?" Margaret smiled at him. "We usually go to the Blue Monkey in the evenings."

"'Bye." He watched them disappear into the crowd around the best riders and their bikes.

"You're smit."

"Wha'?"

Hugh elaborated. "You're a smooth operator. What time do we have to meet them at?"

"Dunno."

"Anytime. Where's Eddie? I see Ernie." He pointed.

They went over to yarn to Thomas's room-mate. They waited but Eddie did not show up. He had been behind Ernie. The biker went back along the course, to see if Eddie had broken down. No sign of him. They decided to go to the boarding house and wait there for him. He'd surely show up soon.

"I wanna go an' lie down."

"In the middle of the day?" Thomas was astounded. "Don't you want to explore?"

"We can do that th' marra. I only got a couple of hours sleep, I couldn't settle in the strange bed," the younger boy complained. "I'm beat."

In their room Thomas lay on top of his bed as Ernie washed. Lighting up a cigarette, Ernie droned on about motorbikes and the race and engines and oil and chains and gearboxes and the race and last year's race and the problems he had then with the pistons and how the Triumph was going much better this year and wasn't Eddie's Norton a wheeker and he thought he did quite well this year, considering the gearbox was dodgy but it had stood it well and when he was in the race itself he would give it all he'd got because he was quite well placed, he'd only ever been placed better once in a race, that was at home, and since this was *the* Tourist Trophy itself it was quite an achievement, didn't he think so?

"Surely."

The yellow wallpaper was the colour of scour. The wee calves would be sucking Jennifer and Myrtle and Daisy and the other ladies would be meandering towards the gate because their elders[19] were full to bursting. Help would be lolloping at Uncle Isaac's heels, going down the lane in his jacket with the collar twisted up, fetching the cows for milking. The byre would be vibrant with the warmth of the big-framed beasts. The squilch of milking, the clunk of buckets, scrape of stools, Mummy's inspiring smile as the cows munched with rubbery mouths and rocking backsides.

---

[19]elders = (coll.) udders.

And he would have a better chance of seeing *her*. Her! His soul rose out of his body: he was flying, looking down from the sky at the island and the sea, then grass, land, again. And there was Shaneoguestown – the railway bridge, the church and Post Office, Clady Works, the school – he swept past them all and down the lane at Summerhill to the Rabbit Hutches. And there was Pamela, standing with a hand shading her eyes, her frock blowing in the breeze, a smile on her pretty face, the wavy auburn hair gently moved by the wind, looking up at him as he circled around her head. Swoosh! He dived hands first, shrinking as a spirity wisp of smoke, he entered her heart like a duck slipping bill-first into a pond ...

Sickly yellow and beige swirls, a corner of paper loose up near the cobwebby ceiling, the white faded to grey, the dresser scraped, the bed jingling as you twitched. The mirror reversing the religious painting on the wall above him. It was watching him. It was glowing: the red patch of blood on the forehead, the yellow circle, the brown hair and beard, the sad face mouthing a melancholy message to him. The choking stink of tobacco heavy in the air.

"Let's go and get something to eat. I'm starvin'. There's a good place I know just down the road."

Action again, at last. They were going to a fancy restaurant, perhaps? Good job he had some cash in his pocket. Thomas forced his stiff body up from the shaky bed and followed the man. They got Hugh and headed down the road. The fresh, salty air was reviving. Thomas was a bit downhearted to discover Ernie had brought them to a fish and chip shop, but he was so hungry he didn't think twice about it. Lots of salt and vinegar, all wrapped up in newsprint: a novelty. They dandered down to the shore to sit and admire the Irish Sea as they tucked into the floury chips and the succulent, steaming flesh of the fried cod.

"This is the life," Hugh smacked his lips.

Out there, across the sea, was home. Westwards. The Land of Promise. The Emerald Isle. Ireland. Ulster. James Ussher wouldn't waste his time chasing after bike races and lying about in guesthouses and eating out of fish and chip shops. A big plate of boiled spuds, butter melting into a yellow lubricant on the white fluff, a sprinkle of salt. A slice of cold beef. A big beetroot, weeping purple juice when you cut into it. Mummy's oatcake, crumbling when bitten, flavoured with a thick coating of butter. The yellow of home was a tasty colour;

here, the yellow smelt like the discharge that spewed out with a stillborn calf. At least at this spot the waves were gentle, stroking the coast in a friendly way. And the sea was murmuring with the same melancholic melody as his heart.

"He's probably fallen in with a crowd of Norton enthusiasts. He'll be back for his wash and brush up and night on the town."

"Are we going somewhere?"

"The Blue Monkey," said Hugh, tapping Thomas's boot with his own.

"Oh?" Ernie queried. "Why there in particular?"

"Because of a certain Margaret, in part-ik-u-lar," Hugh teased.

"Just to see, chat ..." Thomas's stammering was at its worst.

They ribbed him.

Should they be going into a pub, a den of iniquity? But these were English girls and the English have this custom, of going to the pub. Not ladies, surely? It's an Inn, Thomas recalled: a hostelry, not a pub. Besides, it was *déjà vu*, it was fate, his destiny. God had ordained them to meet. Was she his wife? Oh, to hope against hope, to hope that there could be some hope of it, and of her, for him. To go or not to go? *They* were going: not just the girls, but Ernie and even Hugh. He must go. If he didn't, he wouldn't see her ever again. Of course, the decision was easy, simple, there was no alternative. The sun was warm and the evening bright, the clouds on the horizon were orange, turning to pink and red, as the twilight soaked into the sky. The water was calm, as was his mood. There was no fury in his head, no incessant turmoil in his heart. Peace perfect peace! he closed his eyes and said a silent prayer, drifting into nothingness ...

"Are you dreaming of your sweetheart?" Hugh hit his cousin.

"Do you know where this puh ... place is then?" he anxiously asked Ernie.

"While ye've a tongue in your head ye kin ask."

"I know where it is," Hugh surprised them.

They left the shore and went in search of the Blue Monkey. They went through Douglas's streets of houses, with shops and children playing in the side streets and old men nodding and women in their aprons, arms folded, and the holidaymakers obvious from the smart clothes they were wearing. They found the pub and were soon enveloped by its malty aroma. Ernie led the way in.

He ordered Hugh a ginger beer and got himself a pint of bitter. Thomas insisted on sarsaparilla, which prompted the barman to call him the Sarsaparilla Kid. Thomas told him he was a friend of Zane Grey. The crack was good.

Ernie said to Thomas, "Cough up, then."

"But I haven't enough money on me. I didn't know things would be so dear." He whispered, "Mibbe he'll take a bit less?"

Laughing at his fluster, Ernie paid for the round. They sat in a snug and shortly the girls arrived with the bike enthusiasts. They made room for Margaret and her friends. She had changed into an elegant green frock. Her teeth were dazzling white between cherry lips. She sat beside Thomas and their words were one language, there was no uneasiness between them. Ernie launched into a tirade of bike talk with Robert and this mates, while the others girls asked Hugh lots of questions about the hills of Antrim and the Giant's Causeway and he told them an elaborate tale about human sacrifices in the dead of night at the Druid's stone that was near their house. Thomas had never seen the Holestone at Holestone up close, only from the road, so he listened as intrigued as the young ladies.

"Is there anyone here knows an Edmund Reginald Kaye?"

The voice repeated the question loudly as the chatter died. They saw that it was a race marshall who was making the inquiry. Ernie said he did. The conversations picked up again as the marshall approached their table.

"Can you come with me please. I'm afraid your friend has had an accident."

"Oh, God!" Margaret breathed.

"Excuse us, folks," Ernie spoke for them. "We'll have to see yous tomorra, after the other practice race, eh?" He shook hands with Robert.

Thomas stared glumly at Margaret.

"I hope your friend is alright."

"Thanks." He got up reluctantly. "See ya."

As they walked from the pub to the marshall's motorcar – a plain old Ford – he explained that their friend had been taken to hospital, that was all he knew. But he had heard that it had been a bad accident.

"I didn't see it myself, but one of my colleagues told me his front wheel caught a pavement kerb, the bike flipped up and did a somersault in the air above his head. Apparently, the bike landed on top of him. I'm afraid it doesn't sound good."

They were driven to the hospital. Thomas felt Hugh's body shaking as they sat in the back of the car He strained a few times to look at the instruments and levers and all, but gave up because it was giving him a crick in the neck. He wasn't upset. Eddie was probably dead, he thought, but he wasn't really worried. You either live or you die. If the motorcycle landed on his head, he'd be a mess. Shouldn't he be sad? Shouldn't he cry? Why *did* he die?

A sin caused it. And no sin goes unpunished.

A lesson to me? Thomas pondered. Because we've been in a pub, a drinking den, chasing after women – the cause of the fall of man. Aye, and they were women that would go in a pub! A nice accent didn't make her heart pure. The Devil had told him to go to that place, Thomas reckoned. The Devil must've whispered in his ear: sins of the flesh – warm Margaret – and intoxicating liquor and lazing around at the seaside and lying on your bed in the middle of the day. When you should be at home, working, doing something useful.

Eddie was hurt. Mmm. Hugh was scared, he could tell; Death frightened Hugh. Is there a fate worse than death? Thomas realised there is: losing your soul to the Devil before you die. Because you have the chance here to right your wrongs. Did Eddie die pure? He had been a bit arrogant, but he had never been malicious. Could he really be dead?

The news was that Eddie had suffered a broken neck. They had brought him to the hospital but he was dead on arrival.

They were taken to the morgue to identify the body. It was an eerie place, like a butcher's coldstore. A sheet was lifted and the contusion of the neck was noticeable. Like a chicken with its gullet pulled. Eddie's face ashen, waxy. Sleeping. Gone. *Never to return.* Thomas felt cold, empty, but no grief, no sense of loss or sorrow or pity. Somebody was dead. Hm.

Having returned to their yellow room in the guest house, Ernie announced, "I can't race after this."

"You should, it doesn't affect you that much." Thomas urged him to take part.

"No. I must not."

The following day Ernie arranged for a fishing boat to take them and the bikes and the coffin back across to Ireland. He sent Thomas to the Post Office with instructions to telephone the Kayes and ever-so diplomatically break the news. Thomas used his Bible-reading voice to inform Mr Kaye of his son's accident and passing on.

They were due to sail that evening, the evening of the first real race. Ernie said they shouldn't go to watch the races out of respect. Mr Kaye appeared; he had come over for a few hours, to sort out the formalities, then go back with them. The boys weren't much bothered about missing the races. Thomas spent a long day, bored mindless, chucking stones into the sea with Hugh, as Ernie and Mr Kaye sorted out the paperwork with the authorities.

Time dragged. This was time Eddie hadn't got, thought Thomas. He just wanted to be home, to get the meeting with the weeping Kaye women over with and to get back to the routine of milking and working and milking, so that the world would feel right again, so that life could get back to normal.

In the early evening, when it was still warm, he saw Margaret buying an ice cream at a shop near where he and Hugh were playing skimmers.[20] He dawdled over, his nerves tingling.

Sally and Olivia went over to talk to Hugh.

"I heard about your friend. It's so horrid."

"He was only a neighbour." Thomas shrugged his shoulders. "We have to go back th' night. With the corp ... coffin. We spent all day at the boardin' house, sittin' in that awful room. Just came out for some chips. How did your brother do today?"

"He came nowhere."

"We'll be going soon."

She held out her hand. "Well ..."

As he touched her hand, she leaned forward and kissed his mouth. Her lips lingered just long enough for him to appreciate their soft, wet warmth. As she ran off to catch up with her friends, Thomas's heart skipped a beat; he hoped he hadn't opened his mouth too wide, for he was afraid it might cause her to have an unwanted baby, a love child, like in the way God breathed life into Adam.

But that fear soon subsided. And he was aware of his lack of any feeling, either for Margaret or because of Eddie. Why did he feel only numbness? It was better to have no feeling: it only hurts if you have feelings. Better to be hard. Like Uncle Isaac: you lose a beast, you

---

[20] skimmers = (coll) ducks and drakes.

lose money, you try for better luck next time. You lose a neighbour, these things happen.

To lose Mother? To die himself? To be in a cave; dark, reeking of sulphur; a human-like shape ugly-faced, evil-leering, red-horned and red-tailed beast! Stoking the fire with Eddie Kaye's body; stuff him in there with a pitchfork! And you're next, Gray! The beast's grinning, cackling! The heat's overpowering. And he felt the pricks of the fork, stabbing him in the chest – get in there, Gray – eternity in Hell-fire!

"I saw yous!" Hugh berated when he returned to the water's edge. "Sally and Olivia nudged me, so I saw! Kissing her, indeed! You little tinker!"

"So wha' if we *did* kiss?"

"Now, Thomas, you know these things can lead you into all sorts of trouble if you're not careful. What did she say, anyway?"

"Nothin'."

"Not seeing her tonight before we go?"

"Grow up: we've to mourn."

Thomas turned sharply. She was gone. He could've at least got her address. He stared at an advertisement for Lifebuoy soap that was on the wall of the shop. What was the point? She'd be in Leicester and he'd be at Islandreagh. Besides, he had Pamela waiting for him.

Back in the boarding house, he sat and read the evening newspaper for a few minutes after tea before going for the boat. Ernie was still packing.

The I.R.A. bomb thirty cities: mailbombs and bombs in the London Underground. Civilians killed. More death! Pact of Steel between Germany and the Soviet Union. Ah, here, here they were, today's results. Lightweight T.T.: *First*, E.A. Mellors, on a Benelli, in three hours, thirty-three minutes and twenty-six seconds. Averaging over seventy-four miles an hour. He mused, what's it like to die at that speed? *Second*, E. Kluge, on a D.K.W.; *Third*, H.G. Tyrell Smith, on a good oul' Excelsior. No mention of the accident here: yesterday's news, already. He didn't even die in the big race, went out in the warm up. 14th today. Yesterday was the 13th of the 6th: Death's number and the Devil's number! It must've been predestined to happen.

And he must've been destined to be here. Why? To see what other girls were like? For all her hoity-toity elegance, Margaret was nowhere near as nice a girl as his Pamela. Going to a pub, indeed!

This was the Christian message: it didn't matter how much money her father had, or how posh she talked, she couldn't compare to Pamela. Pamela might be just a wee Irish 'peasant' girl, but she was a better person that that stuck up cow could ever be.

And the yellow walls seemed to close in on him, throbbing and bubbling like a cesspit. And the Christ on the wall changed into a Devil and cackled away. Thomas looked in the mirror at his own grumpy face. He felt weary, bored, was glad not to be spending another night in this rotten room, with Ernie and his jabbering on about bikes and the bedstead jangling and the walls supturating[21] with that vomity yellow pattern.

As Ernie clipped shut his case, Thomas sighed, "Let's get out of here."

Thomas was doing a bit of neighbouring[22] at Usshers'. They had taken the roof off the cottage and were adding a second storey. When Thomas arrived on Terence Kaye's bicycle, which he had borrowed again, James and John were just throwing down the last of the old rafters that had held the thatch. The house seemed so different now, it was a shame it had been stripped like this. It looked dead.

They had moved the furniture into an empty stable. The family were living in various outhouses for the summer. It brought back memories for Thomas of sleeping in the tickling straw in the stable loft when their home at the Orchards had been renovated, when he was small. He had hated the move, the uncomfortable loft, the strange surroundings, living like a tinker, like McCann.

James was red-faced already. "Thomas! Hie bae! You got here just in time."

John asked, "Have you been on this Ferguson much yous bought?"

The conversation erupted as the work commenced. Local news was swapped. The lads were knocking the plaster off the gables. Thomas clambered up the ladder to the makeshift scaffolding. Chisel in hand, Thomas hammered at the grey mortar on the stone walls. As he lay perched on the top of the house hammering, Thomas looked across the plain below. He saw the hills in the distance and the shimmering shores of Lough Neagh.

---

[21] supturating = becoming viscous, like pus.
[22] neighbouring = (coll.) unpaid assistance with labour.

"Ahh!" he breathed in the fresh air with a sigh, like that of a seafarer returned to land. "Like the first glimpse of Canaan!" He addressed James, who was on the other gable.

Between them the shell of the house's empty rooms lay open like a young bird's beak. "It's all rock or bog round here." James was less idealistic.

"Ah, but to be up here, on top of the world!"

James and John hammered away as Thomas admired the view. James pointed out a particular field. "We had to put barley in the wee bog, to satisfy these new 'Dig for Victory' regulations. There won't be much of a crop if it's a wet year, but what else can we do?"

"Do you think it'll come to war?"

"Best to be prepared, in any case," John said.

"If there is one, I shall volunteer," James told Thomas.

"I didn't think *you'd* leave home."

"Some of us have to go."

John told Thomas, "The British cavalry's in action in Egypt and Palestine, at present. That's where the action's gonna be, in the Holy Land: it'll be Armageddon."

Thomas's head spun. He felt shaky at that height. "Don't say things like that."

James nodded grimly, "Haven't you read Revelations? The Anti-Christ is here, on earth – he's Mussolini. They've got that air force and gas weapons and bigger artillery than you or I could imagine. Fire, poisoned water, blinding explosions: mass destruction, just like the Scriptures have prophesied. But sure, what does it matter? When the old world order is swept away, why then Jesus will return, in a *blaze of glory*. And the new order will be here, the true millennium of peace and harmony and brotherhood. There's nothing to fear, except maybe our own inherent evil."

"That's true," said Thomas, meaning to have one last lingering look across the lush Irish landscape before concentrating on his work again. "I often feel I am my own worst enemy."

The posse came riding across the plain, jumping the hedges as they cantered in formation towards the homestead. Hadn't he suffered enough? Did they have to come for him now? He'd run and evaded them before. He'd been settled for years, had a wee wife and young 'uns at her skirts. A peaceful rancher now. No more bank robberies. Running Water was back with his tribe, in the tepee at Holestone.

They were getting nearer. Should he get the shotgun down from above the mantelpiece? Or go quietly: let them take him to the old oak tree there, and string him up at sunset?

They heard the trap returning. Uncle George was in a temper. The cob had lost a shoe. He was impatient to get started into work on the house himself. He was fixing up a new pump in the scullery. Harry Aiken was coming over to give him a hand. He complained about having to be bothered about going to the blacksmith's. He asked Thomas would he go?

So Thomas hurried over to Louis Brown's with the horse. The forge was as dark and warm as ever, and grimy Lou was cheerful, as always. He had on his thick leather apron, spotted black where sparks had burnt it. His heavy boots shuffled as he worked.

The cob was walked onto the stance made of railway sleepers and Lou set to work. A shoe was measured, heated, the great bellows squeezed so that in the fire, in the hearth beneath the large, tunnelling chimney flume, the incandescent coals seethed. The whitewashed walls were stained with soot around the interior of the forge. The blacksmith hammered at a red-hot shoe on the anvil. It was dipped in the fizz-trough. The angry hiss of the steam made the gloomy forge seem like Hell. The new shoe was nailed onto the cob's hoof and the other shoes tightened. A file was used to rasp away any jagged edges.

"Is that gate mine?" a man asked.

Lou glanced up, his mouth full of nails. He grunted.

"The rivets are every which way. He's done this bit wrang, so that bit's turned out wrang ..." he moaned. "It's a buckled shape of a thing. What's your apprentice up to? All that young feller of yours does is make mistakes. An' one mistake leads to another." The farmer continued, "You don't expect me to hang thon by the roadside, for all the neighbours to laugh at, do ye?"

The young lad at the bellows turned his face away.

Finished with the cob, Lou let the hoof fall to the floor. Taking the spare nails from between his teeth, he replied, "Then hang it between fields. Goodness sake, the lad's gotta learn somehow."

"Not at my expense," the farmer argued.

Uncle George's cob was backed out of the forge and into the daylight. Thomas sized up the tall, scrawny man with the disdainful demeanour. The face was covered with grey bristles. The pale eyes had a cold, hard colour. Thomas waited for the farmer to relent.

"You'll pay up," big Louis Brown flexed a round arm. He rolled the shirt sleeve up tighter.

The farmer snorted. He handed over some money. "This is all you're gettin'. I'm extrectin' discount, due to the poor quality of the workmanship. I haven't any time for the below average."

Lou was rattled. "Put your gate on your cart and get outta my road. I've a young man here to teach a trade to. And when he's your age and mine, I reckon he'll be a better man than you or me, regardless of your attitude."

CHAPTER SEVEN

False Idols

Bent double, he crawled along the drill. The cabbages in the potato field had grown well, he noticed, as they thinned out some of the biggest ones. Some were six feet wide now. Light green and fluffy. Fred Nelson was nearby, working with characteristic thoroughness. As he moved over the dry earth, the labourer whistled the tune of 'Danny Boy'.

"It's remarkable the way stuff just grows, isn't it?"

"It's the minerals in the soil that make it fertile," Fred replied, amused by Thomas's comment. "Science can explain everything."

"Can it? Well, where did the soil come from?"

"It's weathered rocks and decomposed vegetable and animal matter. Nature recycles its rubbish. Waste not want not."

"But how did it all start?"

Fred shrugged his shoulders. He hacked at a particularly large cabbage with his knife. It was eventually detached and thrown aside, to be gathered up later.

"I wonder what it was like in the beginning. When there was no one about. Before Adam and Eve were ..." He held up a taste of moist soil and let it crumble through his fingers, "... moulded from the clay."

"Eve was made from Adam's rib! If you believe that old tale."

"Do you doubt the Bible?"

"I believe in evolution. As for the Bible, it might have some symbolic significance, but I can't see that it's literally accurate. I read a bit about these archaeological excavations they did at Babylon and Nineveh and so on, and it seems the Bible has the gist of things but is a much later version of stories that weren't all originally Hebrew at all."

"Babylonians! Heathens. They worshipped false gods. I trust in the Word of God."

"But you can't dispute that evolution is a convincing explanation of life on this planet."

"My ancestors weren't apes!"

"No. But our species developed along similar lines. You must accept that we show all the characteristics of animals."

Thomas wagged his blade at Fred, heated by the subject. "Look you, oul' Paul McCann tried to tell me this stuff about us being animals. So we're earthly creatures. I accept that. But we're more than they are, that's why we're here doing what people do and they're over there," he gestured to the next field, "chowin' grass. We've got spirits. It's our soul, the breath of life God breathed into us when he created Adam, that makes us in God's image. There must be a God: how else could it all start? God is the alpha and the omega, the beginning and the end." He rested on his hunkers, satisfied with his argument. "What else could the Bible's message be, other than His message to us, His way of letting us know He exists?"

"It's a for-instance. God is a metaphor."

"God is love."

"Love is God, you mean? God is an abstract emotion? In that case, the concept 'Love' is your God. You worship Love?"

"God is more than an abstract concept!" Thomas stuttered. "God is real. God is ... Almighty."

"A Supreme Being?"

Thomas warily agreed.

"And do you think Heaven and Hell exist, then? I mean, as real places, like Umgall or Holestone?"

"They're real places, but not like places here. They're in a different plane of existence, in a spiritual ... space. Outside our time and universe. What else could Heaven be?" he laughed.

"Heaven is only an allegory. Like the legends: you don't believe there really *was* a giant Finn MacCool, do you?"

Thomas stared blankly. "We just can't say there wasn't."

"Have a titter of wit. In the seventeen hundreds, some smart alec worked out from the begets and begots in the Old Testament that the world was created at nine a.m. on Sunday the twenty-third of October, four thousand and four B.C.."

"Well, if that's what the Bible says, it *must* be true."

"Yet there's all these dinosaur skeletons that are millions of years old."

"The scientists could easily be wrong."

Fred laughed. "You're impossible. Look, the earth goes round the sun, right?"

"Yes."

"The earth goes round the sun once and that's a day?"

"Aye."

"Well, if the sun was only created on the fourth day, like it says in Genesis, how could there have been three days before there were days?"

"Ah! Easy one! God is omnipotent. He can make a day whatever length He wants. Just because things are the way they are now, doesn't mean to say He can't change them."

"What about the laws of nature?"

"If God makes them, He can break them."

Fred squealed and fell forward, burying his face in the heart of a large, soft cabbage.

"Thomas! Fred! Come and gie us a hand." It was his mother.

"What now?" Her worried tone disquieted him.

"More trouble?" suggested Fred. "Haven't you had enough lately?"

"What do you mean?" he asked as they walked across the field.

"Eddie Kaye's accident."

"Oh, that."

"I thought you and he were great chums?"

"There's a cow stuck in the sheugh," Jean called when they were nearer to her. "I seen her earlier, through the winda, goin' fer a drink. I forgot the sheughs are dried t' gutters 'n' sloor. I was knockin' about and didn't notice the Roany again, so took a look. And there she was, up to the uxters.[23]"

"That's all," Fred sighed.

"Don't take that tone with me, Fred Nelson," Jean reprimanded him. "I'm not one of your sailor cadets to be ordered about by a wee corporal like you."

"Sorry, I'm just tired and irritable, Miss Gray, after the big bicycle ride I was on on Sunday. But there aren't corporals in the Navy ..."

"I don't care what they have or haven't got. And you wouldn't be tired if you rested on th' Sabbath Day, like everybody else. Apart from which, I want me cow outta this sheugh."

"What'll we do?" Thomas asked.

"Haven't you ever had a cow in a sheugh before?"

"Not a live one."

"What do you do with dead ones?"

---

[23]uxters = (coll.) oxters, armpits.

"Let them lie there. Till Uncle Isaac gits a spare minute t' drag it out."

"So, get a rope. I'll nip over and get the tractor."

Jean led them to the cow's field. Thomas got the good rope from the hayshed and arrived at the sheugh as Fred came putt-puffing across the field on the wee grey Fergie.

"Where's Uncle Isaac?" Thomas asked his mother.

She shook her head gravely. The cow was in mud up to her joints. A layer of water lapped around her head. She slurped. Fred made a noose and put it around the cow's neck. He secured the other end to the drawbar of the tractor.

"You'll strangle her."

"It's a running knot. She'll be okay."

He drove forward, taking up the slack. The rope caught around the back of her skull, tightening at the sides of the jawbones. Her head followed the tractor, her neck stretched, gradually her front legs eased out of the glarry. Her back twisted round. She rolled over onto her side as her feet slithered out of the clay like four snakes from their skins. She gasped as the rope squeezed around her face. The weighty body was dragged up onto the grass. Fred stopped and let the rope slacken. Thomas freed the beast's neck. She lay where she was, weak from her ordeal.

"Poor Roany." Jean patted her flank.

Fred shouted at the cow, slapping her rump. "Gie up!"

Roany stumbled forward, got on her knees, then raised herself up onto her feet. She staggered, then steadied herself. She shook her head, then began to graze.

"Would you look at her. After all that, she just gets up and walks away. The oul' bitch!" Fred had to excuse himself in the lady's presence.

But Jean was happy because Roany had been saved. She strode off across the field to the yard, singing merrily:

> "There is a green hill far away,
>   Without a city wall,
> Where the dear Lord was crucified,
>   Who died to save us all.

> We may not know, we cannot tell
>   What pains He had to bear,
> But we believe it was for us
>   He hung and suffered there.
>
> O dearly, dearly has He loved,
>   And we must love Him, too,
> And trust in His redeeming blood,
>   And try His works to do."

"What did I tell you?" Fred told Thomas. "We soon shifted her. You can't beat technology when you need to solve a crisis. We need far more of these things." He hit the big rear mudguard arch so that it resounded dully. "I can foresee the day when there's no horses in the country ploughing, or anything."

Thomas scoffed, "You're talking fiction."

"She's shivering. She might get pneumonia. We'd better take her in to the shed."

"She'll be alright."

"Better safe than sorry."

As they walked the coughing cow towards the yard, Fred commented, "The Germans are superior to us because they believe in technology. Look at all the aeroplanes they have. And they're breeding themselves into Supermen, while we're becoming a bunch of weaklings."

"Christianity is all about the meek inheriting the earth."

"Meekness is nothing to do with unfitness. The unfit-like idiots shouldn't be allowed to breed. They only contaminate the race with impurities. We select the best cattle, why not the best people? It is always the few Supermen in society, like the Mussolinis and the Hitlers, who lead the way and make the world leap forward, instead of struggling along, burdened by the mass of wretches. Like stupid cows who waste our time by jumping into ditches." He slapped the roany cow's rump.

Thomas was seized by a revelation. "Jesus Christ was no weakling. Jesus was a hard man. He turned the moneylenders out of the temple, didn't he? He stood up to the sharks an' shysters. That took courage."

Fred pursed his lips noncommittally.

"The new Minister's preachin' for the first time on Sunday. The Reverend Dr Marsh. Brave and young-looking, so he is. It's the first time in our congregation's history we've had a Doctor of Divinity."

"Clergymen preach the word made flesh. I prefer to believe the flesh made the word. Man's objective in the end is to enjoy the ecstasy of perfection."

"Man's chief end is to glorify God and enjoy Him forever," Thomas corrected him. "Have you forgotten your Catechism?"

"Man's chief end is his back-side! I would rather put my faith in somebody who has a place in the present day, who has shown the way forward. Don't you think we should believe in men, in Supermen, rather than in ghosts?"

"We all end up as ghosts. But I suppose leaders are necessary for runnin' a country. You've got to do what the boss says, right enough."

"Man! You must believe in the leader. If you don't, the only alternative is anarchy."

They put the cow in a shed. She lay down heavily. Thomas had a bright idea and nipped into the house to get his uncle's bottle of poteen, specially for the purpose of. He drenched the cow with several large swigs.

It was time for a cup of tea, so they chatted with his mother. She was harping on about how glad she was that Roany was safe.

"Aye, she might get a chill. Best she's kept in. What on earth's that dreadful racket?"

Thomas went out to the yard to investigate and came back in, holding his side, laughing so much that he had tears on his cheeks.

"Roany's flat out like a wino, snorin' her head off!"

After the morning milking, Thomas found his uncle backing Star into the shafts of the potato sprayer. The main body of the contraption was a wooden barrel, set lengthways onto large iron wheels. At the back, rubber tubing delivered the contents of the barrel to pairs of double nipples that were situated at regular intervals along copper pipes. Star's brasses were polished and the leather had been rubbed down so that it was shining much more brightly than usual.

"You goin' to a show?"

"This is oul' Star's last workin' day. Thought I'd doll her up a bit. Make her look the part."

"Why's it her last day?"

"I've soul' her. The man's comin' for her tomorrow. She's not held and she's gettin' oul' and sure now we've the tracteur, we don't need 'er."

"Where's she goin', the knackers?"

Isaac nodded.

After the sprayer was safely through the gateway, Thomas extended the booms, the ends of which had been constructed to slot inside the middle section so that the implement could pass through the pillars.

Once in the field, Thomas stood on a little platform at the side of the barrel. Here, there was a hand pump. He forced in up and down, up and down, as Star trundled along the drills. The air soon became stagnant with the vapour of the chemicals, as the booms delivered the liquid to both the tops and the undersides of the potato plants. Isaac sat on a metal seat, steering the mare and mutilating a folk song about the Famine as the monstrous axle creaked steadily forward on its course. The sprayer rolled on, as Thomas pulled the plunger up, pushed it down, up, down, up, down, pumping out the eye-stinging spray that would kill the fungus that would blight the spuds.

When the barrel became low of spray, Thomas signalled for his uncle to stop. At the end of the drill, they heaved up a metal drum and poured the contents into the funnel at the top of the sprayer tank. Once they had refilled it with the dissolved bluestone and soda and the gauze filter had been tipped out clean of sediments, they were back in business.

"What'll ye do about the tractor? You can't hook it onto this thing. And it' ud go too fast, surely?"

"Son, you must be the most useless bein' in the world!" Isaac was vexed. He tapped his temple with an index finger. "There's a sprayer machine you can get that's made specially fer tracteurs."

The hiss of the jets along the booms responded to Thomas's regular movements. Suddenly, he slipped on the wet platform. He tumbled forward, head first, between the shafts.

There was a jerk. His vision shuddered. A dizzy swaying blurred his comprehension. He saw brown legs, brown earth, chains and horse shoes and realised that he was suspended above the drill. The back of his trousers had caught on a cleet of the chains that reached across the chasm to the mare.

The sprayer had halted after the jolt. Thomas was twisting very slowly from side to side, his head a couple of inches from the back hooves of the horse. His uncle told him to pass him up the knife. Thomas stretched his hand to the inside pocket of his jacket and tugged the Bowie knife from the recess in the lining where the long-bladed implement resided. He held it up, straining his shoulder socket. The weight disappeared from his fingers and, above him, his Uncle Isaac leant forward and sawed through the caught bit of material. Thomas heard a rip and he fell onto his hands and knees. He swiftly turned as he got up between the horse and the sprayer and levered himself onto the platform again. His uncle hauled him up by the shirt.

As he got back into position, his uncle passed him back his knife, horn-handle end first.

"Well, git pumpin' lad. There's half the fiel' t' be done yit."

Thomas noticed the black birds' cawing. He felt the sun on the back of his neck and sensed a blister developing on the inside of his thumb. Up and down, up and down, up ...

"Don't pump so hard. You'll use up the stuff too quick. D' ye hear me? I won't warn ye again."

Thomas called Fred's name as he entered the loft. Fred had swept it tidy. There was no loose straw anywhere, now. His clothes were hanging along a rail he had fixed up. He had a hammock and had borrowed a chair from the kitchen. He was sitting beneath the skylight, reading a book. When Thomas entered, the pock-marked face looked up and was caught by the sharp glare from the skylight.

"Are ye goin' wi' us?"

"I think I'll give it a miss."

"You said you were brought up in missions," said Thomas, lying on a sack of straw, scattering some of the contents as he made himself comfortable. "It'll be a bit of crack."

"Why are you going?"

Thomas pondered this strange question. "I *want* to go. To praise God. To thank Jesus Christ," he mentioned the latter reverently, "and to encounter the Holy Spirit. Come with us."

You might get saved.

"The only thing I need saved is money. I'm gonna get my own wee place, someday soon. They say 'a rolling stone gathers no moss' an' I've rolled long enough. I'll do it, I'll get my place. Because I've the will to. The will to power. I have the power over my own destiny. With nobody givin' me orders, to be my own boss, that's my ambition. Religion is fine as an expression of culture, or for moral law, but the way *you take* it ..." He shook his head. "Like these wee Gospel missions that I knew as a cub, they're founded on sand, because they go on about a superstitious kind of faith. They literally put the fear of God into you. I think we need a positive attitude. That's why *Il Duce* and *Der Führer*," he clenched a fist, "have the right idea: strength, hard work. No namby-pamby nonsense, like these English toffs or Yankee swankies. Pure, honest-to-God sweat!"

Thomas took the book from his hands. *Beyond Good And Evil*. Philosophy. Wasn't it a bit beyond him? Look at this stuff: he couldn't read that! At least yer man Marx wrote in plain English. This was weird writin', this.

"You'd be interested to read Nietzsche. He says 'God is dead'. Because the modern knowledge of history and science shows that most of Christianity is superstition and ritual. I don't need to sing hymns and pray to feel good. Now and again I might take a nip of spirit – of the Bushmills variety – but really all religion is is a way of accepting one's circumstances as they are."

"That's blasphemy! Or sacrilegious, or somethin' bad."

"Only if you're right and there is a Supreme Being."

"If God's dead, then He must've been alive!"

"It's a play on words – it means the notion that there was a God is dead, is no longer realistic, because it's illogical. If God isn't dead, then that's only because He was never alive. Because there's no such Being. 'God' is only an expression of the belief that there's an external power that influences our lives. We've more ken now than the people of Biblical times. We don't think like primitives, like these African tribesmen, do we? There's no god in a stone, or god of the wind, or god of the water. Physical science explains how things work. The universe is just a body, it has no soul. Like I say, God is only a metaphor; a label in life for that ineffable influence, that experience we call Destiny."

"How come people have religious experiences, then?"

"They *say* they do. They are mistaken."

"But you've got to believe in something."

"I believe in me. In my future. Things are as they are, and if I want to change them, make life more enjoyable, I've got to do it for myself. I admire a man that shows how it can be done. If you want to make a go of it, too, you can. All it takes is the guts and the drive."

"We can't do anything without God." Thomas struggled to express his point of view. "God lives in my heart, I feel strong when I believe an' weak when my faith falters. If I go out to plough and God doesn't fancy the idea of me ploughin', I just can't. Everything goes wrong."

"Rubbish. Things don't always go according to plan. But if you persevere, you will succeed in the end. You need to work hard, learn the skills of your trade, pay attention to detail like servicing machinery - prevention is better than cure - and not give up just because you stubbed your toe getting out of bed this morning and think it's an evil omen."

He held the book out to Fred, who waved his hand, signalling for Thomas to borrow it. "I don't like these mission preachers much. They slabber too much. Shoutin' and gettin' on. The Reverend MacIntyre used to a bit, but he wasn't too bad. This new man, Dr Marsh, is the opposite. He talks above your head. He talks like the way this bae writes."

"Don't worry about it. Slog on, you'll get the gist, then the deeper understanding will come. I had to struggle at first. Like Herr Hitler, in the early days, being spat on and gaoled for his principles. But he showed them he was right. Nobody said life was going to be easy. A life is the pursuit of knowledge followed by the pursuit of power. You're still at the learnin' stage. And if you want to make your ambition become a reality it's going to involve some suffering." He also passed Thomas a newspaper on the front page of which was a photograph of the German leader.

Thomas grinned as he got up. "Suffering's good for the soul!"

What was his ambition? To know what the truth is. To know God. And Pamela - he wanted her. And he needed God's say-so to have her, to win her heart. If God existed, which he believed, then he wanted Him to give him a sign. So that he could be sure; sure of Him - and sure about her.

James Ussher was going with them. He was waiting in the kitchen, chatting to Uncle Isaac. Jean was tidying up the last of the dishes when Thomas returned to the house. They heard the latch click and the door close and then the parlour door opening and he soon entered the kitchen. He sat down on the jamb bench, in his usual place.

"Is he coming?"

"He's reading."

Uncle Isaac said, "James tells me this bae sometimes does a bit of faith healin'."

"Does he?"

James elaborated. "Cecil Bates went to him a couple of years back for the laying of hands and it cured his bad leg. He was lame for nearly twenty years, but now he can jump about like a jack rabbit."

"Will he be doing miracles tonight?"

"Isaac!" Jean scolded. She was kneeling at the hearth, poking the fire. "Don't be naughty. It's not a freak show we're going to. The Lord's business is serious business."

"Give over will ye, I didn't mean it like that."

"Are you going?"

"I've got to go down the road and see if I can gether up a few hands for the haytime."

As they walked that pleasant summer evening along the country roads, Jean told James, "That's a nice new suit you've got. You look like a proper Christian gentleman in that. We'll have to get Thomas a new one soon. The one he's in's getting past it. Those sleeves are a bit short."

"They're alright. I like this suit. Why should I change it?"

"Oh, son, you can get a better suit than that."

The hedges were thick and full, overflowing out onto the roads. Their dark green contrasted with the lighter green of the foliage on the trees. A gentle breeze accompanied them down and round the twisty bye-ways to Burnside, where the mission tent had been erected in a field beside the Orange Hall. As they reached the field they met dribs and drabs of people. Men in their Sunday-best suits – black, brown, blue or grey – and wobbly women in abundant dresses, or tiny old women still huddled in heavy coats and pinned-on hats, or girls in flowery frocks, their shiny bare calves captivating the starlike eyes of the smart young men.

Thomas and James flanked Jean Gray as the end of a row inside the shady tent. She leaned forward to tap Mrs Hutchinson on the shoulder and swap pleasantries. Looking about him, Thomas spotted Mr and Mrs Hart.

Ben Hart in a suit! And at a Gospel mission. This was good news: he must be changing his ways. Poor Mrs Hart, her clothes looked so drab. The hardship showed. This is what poverty looks like, he thought. The wages of sin. Could they really be as bad as everybody says they are? There was Harriet beside them. He sucked in a breath. Where was Pamela? Not here? Wait ... with Hettie across the other side. The big girls together. She was here! Thank you, God! he prayed. This was his sign, the omen he had hoped for! And it was a good one. Oh Lord, You do abide with me.

The talking fell to a cough-punctuated silence as the grey-haired evangelist crossed the platform and placed his material on the lectern.

"No sin goes unpunished!" he bellowed. He thundered into his sermon, condemning their sins. He shouted and shuffled about, shook his fists, foamed at the mouth, beginning by denouncing drinking, smoking, gambling, fornication and swearing.

As the lay preacher ranted, Emily got out an envelope and a pencil and scribbled a wild head on it. She titled the caricature: 'Mr H.F. Brimstone'.

She sneaked it onto Pamela's lap. They tried to quell their giggles. Pamela took the pencil and wrote: 'Still griefing?'

Emily wrote in reply: 'A bit.'

Pamela wrote: 'Don Armour fancys you.'

Emily mouthed a denial at her friend before writing: 'I had a run in with S.T.'

Pamela scribbled furiously: 'Stay AWAY. He's TROUBLE.'

Emily assured her: 'And too rough. Don't worry, nothing happened. And D's much nicer!'

They giggled in unison. Pamela drummed the end of the pencil on her lap. Both kept their heads up for a while, pretending to listen to the sermon. Pamela glanced over at Thomas Gray. The preacher was waving a Bible in the air and crooning about finding salvation through the Lord Jesus Christ. Thomas's head was bobbing as he took in the powerfully delivered words.

At last, she scrawled: 'I'm right of boys.'

Emily gave her a disbelieving stare. She wrote: 'T.G.?'

Pamela put: 'Just friends. His ma doesn't like me.'

"... and so, when you stand before Almighty God on that Judgement Day, will *you* be able to say, 'Take *me*, Lord, You know I've been a good man; gather me up into Your arms, hold me to Your bosom, Lord'? If you want to be loved by God, and by Jesus Christ, and by the Holy Spirit, first of all *you* must love Him. You must love Him, too."

A sudden pinching of her face accompanied Pamela's furtive writing: 'Boys are ALL beasts.'

But she scored it out as Emily tried to see over her arm what she had written. Pamela scrunched the brown envelope into a ball and let it fall. She rolled it with her foot under the seat in front as they got up to sing the last, rousing choruses.

Happy songs, lively songs, not dour, sad old hymns, but cheerful tunes. Clap your hands! If Jesus loves you and you know it, clap your hands!

The preacher called for those who felt moved by the Spirit to come forward. For those who had denied Jesus all their lives but who now wanted Him in their hearts, or those who had once loved Him but who had since strayed from the path. There was no response for a short time, but the preacher carried on at the top of his voice, calling them to Christ.

George Kirk was the first to shuffle to the lectern. A few more bodies began moving towards the front, with their heads bowed. Then, Thomas noticed Ben Hart go forward and kneel at the platform. The preacher touched his head. Thomas's head was still buzzing as the rest of them began slowly crowding up the aisle to the flap.

"It's a magic atmosphere."

"A bit rowdy," said James.

"No faith healin'," his mother commented.

Outside, the sun was almost down. The evening was now grey and chilly. Thomas looked around for Pamela, hoping to sidle in her direction. She was here and he was here and He was here and all was well. It was meant to be like this.

His mother and Mrs Crowe stopped to talk with Mrs Wallace. They nattered for ages. Thomas and James stood dutifully with her, looking at their toecaps and saying 'hello' to faces they knew. The imaginary smell of oatcake warming on the griddle and the taste of hot tea made Thomas lick his lips. Soon, there were only a few stragglers left at the mission tent.

Were the Harts still there, waiting on Ben's interview with the lay preacher? Or had he missed them? Perhaps God had planned it that way. Tonight, Thomas got the message: she was a good Christian from a Christian family like his. After all this time, weeks, months, of being unsure, of not knowing if she was the right woman, at least now he knew.

On the way home they walked with Mrs Crowe to the widow woman's house. They had just commented on the tranquillity of the fading twilight when a tirade from behind a high, thick hedge disturbed the peace.

James shouted, "What's all this bad language in aid of? Houl' yer tongue! There's ladies present."

A man's voice from behind the bushes replied, "Sorry. Didn't know there was anybody listening. I forgot meself. I'm looking for me pipe."

"George Kirk!" Jean berated the hedge.

"Aye. Jeannie Gray? Aye, it's me. I left early, determined to give up my wicked ways, like the bae said to," the hedge explained. "I chucked the oul' pipe over the hedge and said to huh ... heck wi' it. But I no sooner got home and sat down and twiddled me thumbs than I was up and had me cap pulled on and rushed back to git the dratted thing. I can't bear the thought of going to bed without a draw of baccy first."

In his room, before undressing, Thomas furtively drew the scrapbook from under the bed. He wasn't going to be like George Kirk! He wouldn't let his sin get a hold of him. *He* could kick a bad habit. He opened the scrapbook at the first page and tore a newspaper cutting of the German Chancellor from it. He could resist evil. He tore the cutting to pieces. No false idols for him. He went through each page, destroying the annals of history: Munich, Austria, the visit to Rome and the picture of the Putsch, which Fred had given him. He tore them all up until all that was left on the empty pages were the hard splodges or ragged places where the spots of glue had been.

His uncle was just going into his room, at one side of the dresser, and his mother into hers at the opposite end. They paused as he sped round to the fire and dumped the shreds of newspaper on the embers. He answered their goodnights, staying to poke every last bit of print into the flames, until each shred of paper had shrivelled to a thin black leaf. Now he could sleep.

Uncle Isaac and Thomas were at the gate of the wee meadow, finishing sharpening the blades of their scythes. Thomas stopped and looked up. His uncle rasped with the stone a little longer. When he stopped, Thomas took the rough implement from the elder man and set them on top of the pillar. Uncle Isaac took off his jacket and hung it on the point at the front of the gate. With the wooden handle of the scythe between his legs he spat on his palms and rubbed them together. Thomas held his scythe in position and once his uncle had begun to mow, in one direction around the outside of the field, he followed at a staggered interval.

The sun was high and their white shirts were soon soaked with sweat. The grass was hard. Its tall stems swooned straight, like felled poplars, the heavy seedheads flopping like a branchy top. The women were arriving along Kaye's back lane, going to the nearby hay field, to help Fred turn the crop with pitchforks.

Thomas snatched glimpses of the two women and the two girls: Emily and her mother and Pamela and her mother. Pamela was smiling, chatting to Emily when they came down the lane. Passing the gate, they had waved to him. He had looked round. His uncle had had his back to him, so he had quickly raised his hand, but they were soon passing through the other slap[24] and he wasn't sure whether they had noticed him wave or not.

He worked ferociously, wanting to be finished so that they could get onto the next job, one that meant being nearer the girls. His uncle told him to take the lead, he was getting too close behind. Isaac took a break, going over to the sheugh to scoop up a drink of water.

Their arms were sore by the time they reached the centre of the wee field. The stiffness from several day's mowing was forgotten, however, for this was the last of it for this year. Thomas stopped and stood aside. His uncle turned to strike at the last tuft of grass in the middle of the sweet-smelling, dusty field.

"Leave it!" Thomas cried. "There's a corncrake's nest in there."

He cut down the patch Thomas had left. As the nest shook, the young birds fell out and tumbled away from the upturned nest, which broke on the ground.

"Luk's bad on its own," his uncle muttered. "Waste not want not."

Thomas pulled a spiteful face and gritted his teeth as he bottled up his resentment.

---

[24]slap = (coll.) gateway, gap.

He got no chance to work near Pamela or to talk to her during most of the afternoon. Then his mother brought a basket to the field, at tea time. They all huddled together, near the gate. Pamela chatted cheerily with him, as they shared in the group's yarning. Was she still interested in him? He couldn't tell. At least she wasn't avoiding him.

In the late afternoon, as it began to cool a little, they rucked a field that had been cut a few days ago. The sky began to redden. There was a twittering of birdsong. The dust from the whinned hay[25] irritated the throat, eyes, nose, neck. Hands had blisters, backs twinged. The light, crisp hay was swept up as the tips of their pitchforks flashed in the haze.

Emily's and Pamela's faces were puffy and pink with exertion as they gathered hay, sweeping it up with their forks. Thomas was working with Mrs Simpson, dragging a paddy[26] on long chains. It gathered the hay into its five points. Now that it was cooler, the mare was less restive, since she was sweating less and so clegs[27] did not nestle on her back. Each time Thomas reached the ruck he lifted the handles of the paddy. The wooden points stuck in the ground and the back lifted up and, tumbling over, righted the handles. With the long reins, he directed the horse from behind to where Marbeth Hart was tramping the centre of her gradually rising ruck. Uncle Isaac and Fred were working at one of the rucks, the women at the other. Uncle Isaac liked his rucks built big, so big that the shifter would strain.

When a sizeable expanse of the field had been cleared, Thomas and Pamela found themselves working at one side of the field, while the others were at the other end. Pamela had gone to gather up a line of hay the paddy had missed. Thomas called over, was she going to get a drink of water at the burn? She stuck the fork in the ground and he left Mrs Simpson standing, to join her at the stream.

His heart was pounding. He watched as she knelt down and washed her tanned face. He saw that the others were busy away across the other end of the field. Sitting up, she stared at him.

As he wiped a droplet from her chin with his finger, he said, "You're dripping."

She smiled. "The water's lovely."

---

[25] whinned hay = (coll.) sun and wind dried hay.
[26] paddy = hay rake.
[27] clegs = (coll.) gadflies.

His heart hammered more furiously. Should he say it? It was silly thing to say, but what did that matter?

"You're lovely, too."

She bowed her face, as if hiding a smile as she got up. He gulped a few handfuls of water and hurried after her. She turned and he stopped. She touched his cheek with one hand, to steady his face as she brushed the water from his lips with her raw fingers. He believed their eyes were communicating a shared happiness. Long after they parted again, his inner joy kept him working with replenished fervour.

The darkness was upon them before the last of the hay was raked to the foot of the last ruck. All the others had congregated around it now. Mrs Hart was on its summit, receiving the last forkfuls from the men. Jean, who had stayed after bringing the tea, was walking backwards, away from the ruck, pulling some hay from the base with a grass-rope twister. As she began wrapping the rope around the peak that Marbeth had just lapped, the youngsters moved away from the scene of activity. Emily said that she was going to fetch her cardigan, which was hanging on the hedge, and scampered ahead.

"I'm done in," Pamela sighed.

As Thomas watched her shadowy form glide onto the ground a tremor of pleasure flowed through him. He thought she smelt comforting, like the sweet hay, and he was captivated by the way her face was elevated so that it caught the moonlight.

"Isn't it nice with the stars scattered across the sky."

The gentle, feminine tone thrilled him. He felt joy, perfect contentment in the twinking, starlit gloom. Elation clouded his head like an opiate.

He wished it could be like this forever. How he loved her completely; how happy he was! It would be Paradise to walk back up the dark lane with her, knowing she was by his side; to wash in the bowl of soapy water she has just used; to chat as they drank refreshing tea, and hear her gentle voice; to go upstairs with her, rest their weary limbs between the same, fresh sheets, hold her in his arms, cuddle her tightly; to fall asleep in each others arms, knowing that they were in love with each other; to have her with him *always*. That would be *living*.

Pamela was taking oxygen in through her nose and expelling with gradually decreasing pants. In the dark distance, the silhouettes of the others and the ruck could be seen at the top of the field. The murmur of their merry chatter battled unsuccessfully with her rhythmic breaths in the night air. He imagined her heart fluttering, the way Help's feels when he stroked her at the ribs.

"Time to go home," she whispered.

"What are you whispering for?" he whispered. "C'mere."

He lurched forward to where she was and snatched at her. She struggled as he tickled her sides. They both giggled. She rolled forward as she wrestled with him, so that her hair caressed his face. In the darkness, a fumbling hand brushed the soft side of her hot breast. As he tickled her more she pleaded for him to stop, so he was obedient and drew away.

He sat rigidly, to ask her quietly, "Can I come down and see you some evenin'? Can I see you, Pamela?"

The others were leaving them. His mother was waving her arm and shouting sternly that they were heading for the gate. They got up.

Stepping ahead of him and shrugging her shoulders, Pamela whispered, "Maybe, sometime. We'll see, Thomas."

CHAPTER EIGHT

The Lord's Day

Isaac, Fred and Thomas were neighbouring to Begleys', at the Holestone. They were cutting the corn with sickles. The field was sheltered by a planting, the cooling breeze could not reach them and they felt it stifling. The fetid air seemed to be throbbing the way Thomas's temples were pounding. The shade from the direct sun was little comfort to the sweating Begleys, who were binding the sheaves and hutting.[28]

Stan protested to Isaac. "Sure, why don't I go borra Jackson's reaper? It'ud be much quicker and easier."

"Aw, loss too miny seeds. This is a cleaner jab."

Thomas was within earshot. "I'd use a reaper on the tractor. What else did you git it for, to sit about an' be luked at?"

"Houl' yer whist!" Uncle Isaac snapped. "Mibbe nixt year."

"Ye've got a tracteur, Isaac?"

"A Ferguson. Got rid-a Ster. She didn't houl' her last servin'. The oul' herse was done. But I hivin't surted out all the complications of this new tracteur yit. I don't wanna bust it whin I've ainly gist got it. If you git something wrong, it kin cause worse problems. One mistake leads to another, an' a wee mistake can result in a big mistake."

"The only way to learn's by trial and error," said Thomas.

Stan took Isaac's side. "If you're reckless, you may soon find, Thomas, that your errors will cost you dearly."

They took a break in the late afternoon when Aunt Sarah brought out a basket.[29] Isaac told Thomas he had better head home, it would be time for the milking and his mother would appreciate a hand. Aunt Sarah suggested that Mary could take him in the lorry, it would be quicker than the bicycle.

It was not long before the cattle truck appeared on the road. Thomas ran over and scaled a weak place in the hedge, where there was only a single strand of barbed wire. As he hauled himself up into the sheepy-smelling cab he noticed her bulge.

"How's married life?"

---

[28]hutting = piling sheaves.
[29]basket = (coll.) basketful of snack meals.

"We've the wee house fixed up better already. James is workin' like a nigger, but it's worth it. The roof was poor, but the patchin' James done should do for a while. I suppose you know," she changed her tone, "I'm expecting a baby."

"Congratulations."

"Isn't it noticeable?" She glanced down at her belly.

"Well, now you mention it."

"It has to be, I suppose. I'm looking forward to having a wee nipper, and I think Mummy's happier about it now."

"Didn't Auntie Sarah like the idea of being a granny?"

As they reached Dunadry, Thomas asked her to stop at the shop. He had to do a message for his mother. When he entered, he found that Pamela was there. There was some small change in her, a thicker neck, perhaps, or her build was heavier? She was maturing. She had already been served. They exchanged hellos and he told her to hold on, he had a message for her. She said she would and went on outside. He made his purchase and was hurrying out when Elsie called him back: he had forgotten his change. He took it and had to swap some more small-talk before escaping.

At last he could speak to her. He looked over at the Austin lorry. Mary was staring up the road, as if in a trance. Pamela's dull eyes searched his. Her tanned flesh was like unpolished bronze. She did not smile.

"I'm sorry I haven't been down to see you, but we've been so busy with the harvest."

"I know."

"I *will* come and see you, soon. I ... want to."

She started to shake her head. "I don't think we should ..."

"I know what you're worried about ..."

"You *do*?"

"Aye. And it doesn't matter."

"Of course it does."

"No, it doesn't. I don't care what people think."

"I do! And you should."

"Nonsense. Life is what you make it. You have to be happy in yourself, no matter what anybody else thinks. If you don't respect yourself, nobody else will. My mother told me that once and if she can struggle on, despite all her troubles, so can me an' you an' anybody."

They stood in awkward silence, briefly.

"Your Mummy doesn't like me," Pamela confided.

"What makes you think that?"

"It's obvious. I'm a Hart."

"It doesn't matter who your family is or what they are, everybody's equal. Sure, didn't Jesus say the Gentiles were every bit as good as his own people? An' we're *all* Gentiles."

"Yes!" She began to brighten. "Y'know, Thomas, you've cheered me up a lot. You're a *good* friend."

"Well, I want to be good to you ..." he stuttered. Glancing at Mary's disdainful stares from the lorry, he asked, "I'll come down for a chat, eh? Th' night, eh?"

"No," she replied. "There's a dance at Orr's Barn on Saturday night. I'm allowed to go. I'm trying to get Emily to go. She's down in the dumps at the minute, like she has been on and off since Eddie's accident. Don't let on, but I'm tryin' t' fix her up with Don Armour. I can't really see you before Saturday. And anyway, Mummy wouldn't like it if you ... for *any* boy to call..."

"I understand," he said, stroking her arm. She ceased smiling, so he snatched away his hand. "And of course, you're thinking about somebody else's happiness as usual, before your own. I'll come on Saturday. I'll come to the ... to Summerhill and meet yous. If you like."

"Well ... or along the road, at the end of the Clady?"

Thomas stood watching her as she left him. Pamela was about to back away when he said, "Are you alright? You seem sad."

"Just got something on my mind. Nothing important, really. I'm worrying about nothing." She tried to laugh. "I'm making a mountain out of a molehill."

"I'm getting a lift with Mary Begley - Mary Ritchie - in their lorry. Uncle Stan got it fer shiftin' sheep in. An' he's started transported fer other folk, forbye. I reckon he'll make a mint, it's far handier than walkin' beasts hame. Mary's expecting a baby now."

"Oh? Why tell me that?"

"Just sayin', I thought wemen were interested in them surt-a things. We've been cuttin' corn th' day, at the Holestone."

"I hope it stays dry for yous. Well, suppose I'd better let you get on." She ruefully began to move away from him.

Mrs Jacobs was walking towards the shop. "Aye. I'll see you."

When he clambered back into the lorry, Mary teased him, "Chatting up my *alter ego*, were you?"

He blushed. "Just being sociable." As the engine revved, he asked her, "Your *altar* what?"

"*Alter ego* – my other self. Don't you remember, at the New Year you said I look like *her*."

"Has everyone an *alter ego*?"

"I dunno. But you certainly have."

"Have I? Who?"

"Can't you guess?"

They spent a day piking[30] the hay. Thomas brought the rucks from the fields on the ruckshifter. Fred had tinkered with it last weekend and lo! it was adapted for being pulled by the tractor. They soon got several rucks in to the yard and built on the stone bottom in the stackyard.

When the pike got too high for the men to reach up, Isaac sent Thomas in to fetch Jean, to stand halfway up a ladder and pass the pitchforks, loaded with hay, up to the top. He waited for her as she was lacing up her yard boots.

"Didn't think we'd git it piked this early in the year."

She replied, "Make hay while the sun shines."

"You've been kept busy this week, Mummy, with all the cookin' and this forbye."

"Better at something than at nothing. 'The Devil makes work for idle hands'. Sure, us oul' folks can't graft like you young bucks. You're the worker of this house."

"Mummy ... I was thinking, I might go out th' night."

"Oh *aye*? *Aye*, take yoursel' out a rake. Where're y' goin'?"

"Th' dance at Orr's Barn."

She had finished tying her laces and stood up, stamping her feet on the floor to make them comfortable. "Oh. Good. All your friends will be goin', I'm sure. *Aye*, young 'uns ought to go to dances. Ah! The August Ball at Orr's Barn. I went several years in a row. Great crack! The highlight of the year. Wish I was young again."

"You're not *that* old."

---

[30]piking = piling into a large rain-proof mound.

"Ah, but I feel it, at the moment. But don't be late. And don't be hangin' around with any of those scuts from the tenements. Bad news, all of them. Socialise with your *nice* friends, like Maisie Kaye."

"She'll hardly be goin' there."

She nodded. "Mibbe not."

Fred smiled to himself each time the revamped ruckshifter returned to the Orchards, with a jiggling mound of hay on the back. Proud of his handiwork, he was describing to Uncle Isaac the equipment, but soon strayed to the international situation. Thomas listened to the political discussion as Fred, brandishing his pitchfork with all the inherited resolution of his tribe, vigorously demolished the ruck.

"We're taking the wrong side. We shouldn't be against Germany. Them Irish rebels have bombed Coventry. I was there, once. Nice place. Nice people. Bombin' innocent people! That's not war."

"The Germans are a bit ruthless. Look at the way the Nazis killed their political opponents. Killed them for disagreein' with them. That's not democracy."

"Some things are more important than democracy, such as the defence of the country. They were enemies of the state. Like Communists!" He spat through the dust. "An' anyway, the masses need strong leadership. I don't profess to know what's the best solution in political issues, because I don't have the knowledge the politicians have. Let the experts get on with runnin' the country, I say. The Fascists are working for the people. Britain should be workin' for a stronger economy and for improving the Empire. Not letting people starve in dole queues. A political master should act like a master and rule. These lot we've got, bunch of spineless ... It's an abdication of responsibility. Lord Carson knew how to lead. A show of force, that's the way."

Uncle Isaac had his turn. "They're a load of hooligans. Trouble-makers. Greed, that's all it is. Power for themselves. Stealin' other countries' territory t' make theirs wealthier," he mocked. "I've nothin' against Britain fer she's done alright by us, but she's done us harm, too. Why am I payin' land annuity all these years? Because we're still payin' the absentee landlords for the privilege of workin' our own land! My da toul' me what it was like, when he was a young man and they were tenants and times were hard and you slept with the fear of a knock at the door in the night because the rent was due and you were lucky to scrape a few shillin' together and might-a been evicted onto the side of the road and the house knocked down as you stood by the gutter wi' your wife and chil'ern weepin'."

"That was then. It's the people that are the backbone of the country now. One People, One Country. It's progress."

"I heard the Germans are moving troops to the Polish border," Thomas interrupted them. "D' you think they're calling our bluff?"

Isaac said, "They'll take Poland over like they did Austria."

"But will we go to war?"

Fred sounded melancholy. "We shouldn't and I think the top brass know it. But they've made a silly promise and it's not like them to back down."

"They'll come up wi' some con, some agreement."

"What do you think, Mummy?"

Jean looked up at him from the ladder. "I don't like that bae Hitler. He looks ... wrang. I think our side's right to stand up to him. Where'll they go next? You can't have people invading other countries and taking them over. That's not right. I dunno about Poland, but I wouldn't want to be German and I don't think the Polish folks do either."

They finished piking in time to milk the cows. Isaac sent Thomas over to Kaye's, saying he had promised to send him over to give them a hand with something in return for the help with the hay.

Driving into Kaye's yard, Thomas groaned inwardly. Two horses were harnessed to the gearing mechanism of the barn thresher. The horses were walking in their circular path outside, led by the Kaye's man. Their track was well turned over by the hooves as the horses dragged the pyramid-shaped metal mechanism round and round. From inside the shed, the revolving beaters blattered monotonously.

Thomas went inside and climbed the ladder up to the loft. Terence was bagging the grain, as the seed came out of a chute. Mr Kaye was filling the thresher. Thomas took up the long handled fork and began tossing the pile of straw that was being discarded by the machine. As he forked, the dusty chaff fell down through a hole, into the hayshed below. As he worked, as the thumping-thudding-thundering of the beaters droned, his mind was beating another theme around.

It was like there was a war of wits keeping them apart: what people would think. Her people, his people, all the people round here. Did she see him as friend or foe? Friend, she said. Yet he felt they weren't really allies. He saw her as white, she saw him as black. Maybe this going to the dance was a pact between them? That wasn't enough! But it had to start somewhere: he had to be a friend and see her and talk to her if he was going to get anywhere with her. Let love grow, like a flower – it takes a long time for the seed to sprout and for the plant to grow. And the bloom would be only a short-lived thing? But it would be so beautiful ... It would be worth it, wouldn't it?

But he couldn't dance, what would he do at Orr's Barn, anyway? All those people laughing at him because he had two left feet. What would he say to her, anyway? He was too shy to think of anything amusing. But he didn't need to be smart. God would put the words in his mouth. Or would've, if he had been going. Not now; now he was here, doing this. Fate had intervened. Why couldn't he have her? Why couldn't he have a little bit of happiness? And she was so pretty.

"We're only doin' a wee bit th' night. You needn't-a come over at all, Thomas," Terence told him.

He stood upright. "Really?" he said loudly.

Mr Kaye nodded. "Just tryin' her out to see if the old machinery's still operating properly. We'll have an extra hand on Monday. Gerald's away tonight. Likes his Sunday's at home. Visits his parents in Larne. A right ride from here, eh?"

"Aye," Thomas agreed. Dare he ask? "Are you sure you're not doin' much? Only, I was fer goin' to the dance th' night and will be a bit rushed, changin' an' all."

Mr Kaye intoned over the drone of the machine, "You go on. There's no need really." As Thomas set the fork against the wall of the dusty, murky loft, Mr Kaye beckoned him closer with a finger. He said into Thomas's ear, "And don't do anything I wouldn't do." He scrunched up his face into a leer.

Thomas pulled the throttle lever full down gleefully and the tractor roared up the road to the Orchards. He swung it round into the yard, still belting along. There was a horrid howl. He was shaken up as the wheel bounced over something. He braked. Oh no! Poor wee thing, Help!

"Christ Almighty!" At the byre door, Fred swore.

The little man came running across the yard to the incessantly howling dog. He laid his hand on its shoulder and spoke to the dog. Thomas bent over her, his face strained with the anguish of guilt.

Uncle Isaac heard the commotion and appeared. He touched the dog's leg cautiously. "It's broke. Thomas, run in and get the shotgun."

"No! Why?"

"The bitch is no use fer work now."

"No!" Thomas repeated, as the dog whined feebly.

"Quit yer gulderin'."

"There's no need to put her down. We had a dog at home got hit by a car and it lay in the shed for a few weeks and then it was able to hobble about alright. The bone knit together of its own accord," said Fred.

Isaac relented. "Don't expect me to nursemaid a *daig*." He eyed his nephew ferociously. "Load-a fuss over nithin'. Plin'y more daigs in th' country."

Fred got a sack and they set Help onto it and Fred carried her into a shed. She was lying in a corner out of the way. Thomas brought a syringe and a bottle of morphia and gave her a jab. Her moaning soon subsided and her eyelids slithered together.

"All she needs now," said Fred, '"is plenty of T.L.C."[31]

The Usshers had called in: George, Josie and James. Uncle Isaac was still arguing about the same old political stuff when Thomas went back to the kitchen after washing and dressing. As if Europe was all that was of importance. He was driving Thomas nuts with all this talk of war and politics.

"What will be will be." James gave his analysis of the world scene as Thomas combed some Brylcream into his hair.

"Does James want to go to the dance with Thomas?" Jean volunteered. "Yous don't have to stay long."

Thomas prayed. James declined. He was obliged to stay, having come to visit them. Thomas's chest heaved.

"Remember the harvest parties we used to have," Josie said to her husband.

"Are ye not havin' a perty this year, Isaac?" George asked.

Josie teased, "There's niver any harvest parties at Islandreagh."

"Quit your raggin'," Isaac blustered. "I don't hear of any perty at Umgall the year, either."

"We've only just finished renovating the house," George said.

"All the more reason," Jean teased, "for a party."

---

[31] TLC = tender loving care.

"Perties!" Isaac had had enough of the subject. "Fool nonsense."

He was ready, now. Clean, smart, combed, dressed to the nines. He'd done the trick with that girl in the Isle of Man, hadn't he? He could do it with Pamela, too. Would he get to kiss her? Oh, Thomas, get these dirty thoughts out of your mind. He shot his eyes in his mother's direction. She glanced glumly at him. Her eyes were bleary, baggy. Sorry, Mummy. I didn't mean to be rude. My soul's in a tizzy. She was alright, wasn't she? She wasn't a bad girl, really, was she? *Were* they a through-other crowd, the Harts? Don't say that. It's the individual that's important. She was nice, really, wasn't she, wee Pamela? And if they had to wait till the wedding night for patty-fingers and the huggin' and kissin', what odds? He could wait till it was the proper time. Mummy, my heart's burstin'. You can see that. I can't help it. And this feeling wasn't wrong, was it?

He took one last look in the mirror, said his goodbyes and went out. The night was warm and pleasant. It was dull, but felt right. That's better. He felt better now: the collywobbles had gone already. He put his hands in his pockets and his shoulders relaxed. He stepped lightly, grinning as he went down the Rathmore Road.

The mellow evening was filled with the scent of late summer flowers. The low sun was tinged orange and the light clouds were lined pink. The sky was a pale blue. He had got it wrong in the past, he had messed it up with her. But things were alright now. Hadn't God fixed it for him to get away on his own tonight, when he thought he was going to be stuck at Kaye's till after dark? Hadn't He made James stay at home, to let them have some privacy?

Leaving Summerhill, Emily and Pamela let the others walk on ahead of them. Pamela eyed her friend like a startled ewe. When they spoke, they both did so in low voices and with their eyes darting about them, like sentries keeping a lookout at the frontline.

"It doesn't show, very much," Emily encouraged her.

"It will very soon," Pamela sighed.

"Have you told your ma yet?"

"Didn't have to. The sickness. She wasn't angry. Just ... drained of energy. Here we go again, sort of thing."

"Did you tell her who it was?"

"It's nothing personal, that I don't want to tell you ..."

"I don't mind that," Emily assured her. "But, surely you should tell your mother."

"I explained to her why I don't want anything to do with him. That's what made her angry. I was surprised by Daddy. I thought he'd be round there, trying to force him to marry me. But when I toul' Daddy that I *hate* ... the father, he just accepted it. Said I was to live me own life. And after he went out he niver even blethered about it when he was drunk. Mummy wanted me to marry him or take him to law or something. Maybe she's letting it rest at the minute, thinkin' I'll come round."

"But you won't?"

"Oh, I *liked* him, I suppose, I wouldn't be in the state I am if I didn't. That's my trouble: I like them too much, boys."

"Pamela!"

"Ssh!" She warned Emily to keep her voice down. "Pamela, you're ... you've *no* shame. Eddie an' I liked to ... snog, and sometimes he ... was a bit *too* friendly, but I always made him stop before things got out of hand."

"I didn't know it would lead to this."

Emily pulled a face.

"Honest, I didn't. I was never told. I more or less knew you could do it, some of the girls at work talked about it a bit. But nobody ever said it was what made babies. I thought it was just, you know, a bit of fun. And Mummy reckoned if she didn't tell us, we wouldn't make *her* mistake. But I made it without even knowin' ... I thought maybe I was doin' something I shouldn't, you know the way something nags at the back of your mind. But when I was close to him, he was so warm an' strong an' *there*, I just, "Pamela elevated her face skyward, "lost control. It had happened before I knew what was going on."

"I can understand that. Right enough, there's load's of ones I know don't know about it right." She let her voice drop so low it was scarcely audible. "Eddie told me one of his friends at school, th' big school, had a biology book all about it. And some of them didn't know. And boys are supposed to talk about them things more than us. Eddie said the townees were so naïve. Even he hadn't the gist of it properly, till he seen the book. An' him livin' on a farm!"

Pamela smiled with her. "Aye. It's all around us, an' we don't even cotton onto what's in front of our noses."

"Well, you never think, do you? Mummy told me. I was so shocked. And embarrassed. At the beginnin', to think of her and Daddy, doing *that*! Is it ... is it really nice?"

Pamela wagged her head uncommittedly. "Well, at first I didn't really notice. He knew what was going on an' thought I did, an' I didn't. Then ..."

"You did it *more* than once!"

"Don't breathe a word to anybody!" she pouted.

"I won't. Honest to God, Pamela, I wouldn't do that on ya."

"Well, I was curious t' see what it was really like. And, right enough, when you sort of get to know how to do the thing right ... I think it's ... great."

"And all this time you still didn't know ... what would happen?"

"No. I know it sounds," she blew through pursed lips, exasperatedly, "*silly*, but I thought it was just part of the game, like the kissing. And as for babies, I never even thought about where they came from. Well, you don't when you're young, do you? It's not something that concerns you, you think all that has to do with marriage."

"I'm so sorry for you! I'm glad my mummy told me. She'd kill me if I did ... that, y'know."

"Why? *I* don't regret it."

Emily raised her hand to her mouth.

"No! *So what* if it 'gets you in trouble'? It's nice."

"Oh, it is not a nice thing. It's wicked."

"Unless you're married?"

"Yes."

"I can't figure that out."

"Why *not* marry him, then, if you like him?" Emily sought to re-establish order. "You don't *love* him, is that your feeble reason?"

"Can't I just have friends, not be tied to one man? Why do I have to live like everybody else? What makes you think gettin' married is the be all and end all? He's not fussed ..."

"That's no reason. Do what your ma says, make him! I would!"

"... and neither do I want to, either," she snapped. "I don't care what folk think. Why should I change, do something like that, when I'm content as I am?"

"You're a fool to yourself. Sure, won't things soon change when this wean appears."

"I don't want to live like my ma lives, workin' all hours God sends, with him to look after and a herd of weans gurnin' at her all th' time. One's alright, I could cope with one. But I want - I want to be *free*, too; independent, to have a life of my own, to be my own boss. Not have some man tellin' me what I can or can't do. Not have him comin' in drunk and ... wanting me when he feels like it." She shook her head, speaking determinedly. "I'll get by on my own. If oul' Mrs Wilson can afford to live on her own, so can I. I'll be able to have friends round when I want, or be on me own if I want."

They paused as they reached the entrance to the Works. They saw that the crowd of youngsters had stopped up ahead and were hanging around at the bit of waste ground between O'Hara's cottage and the end of the Clady Road. There, beneath the great trees, Emily touched her friend's shoulder and looked earnestly into her eyes.

"Pamela! What about God? What about doing things the way we should do them? I know we mess about at the wee mission and take the mickey out of the preachermen, but this is serious. If you don't live your life right, you'll go to Hell. What kind of life will your child have, bein' brought up without a da? Gettin' called names at school? Your ma's right, get yourself a man. Whoever you get, it'll be a damn sight better than ... It won't be that easy, rearin' a child on your own. Your ma had the right idea, when she got lumbered ..."

"Don't you believe *those* lies! I thought you were my friend. I know what they say about my ma an' Mr Gray an' it's all a load of baloney! She never tried to hook *him* at all! That was only rumours that got about because Jean Gray *thought* there'd been something goin' on, but there *hadn't*. My daddy *is* my daddy!"

"Oh Pamela, I didn't mean that stupid gossip. What I'm saying is, she made sure *your daddy* did the right thing by her. She's got him to bring in money – when he's got a job, at any rate. But if you don't have a man and have to work, who'll rear the wean? Who'll do the men's things about the house?"

"The men's things about the house? You mean, what your da an' my da do: leave smelly socks lyin' around, dirty dishes at their backsides, get full an' spew up all over the scullery?" She shook her head. "I'll get somebody who'll look after it for the time I'm at work. Doesn't Mummy work an' copes with all us lot alright? Mrs Wilson can watch it when it's wee, or Daddy when he's not workin' ..."

"If he's not busy spewin' up."

Pamela spun round, trying to ignore Emily's pragmatism. "I've thought about it and I'll be thinking about it some more. I haven't had time to decide about anything yet." She faced her friend again. "Will you go on ahead with the rest of them? I've to meet somebody here."

"Is it ... Don?"

Facing her friend, Pamela said gently, "Now I *am* only thinking about myself, while here's you, pinin' away! Don said he'd be there early, to help set up the stage. He'll be waiting for you!" she cajoled. "All you have to do is just go up to him and say 'Hello'. It'll be alright. Don't be nervous. I'll be there in no time. I've just to wait for somebody."

"*Him?*"

Pamela shook her head. "I toul' you I'm not sayin' who he is. But there's no secret about who I promised to walk with. Thomas - and don't look at me like that," she wagged her finger. "I saw Thomas at the shop an' you know what he's like, always nervous about these sort of things, so like a good friend I said I'd stay with him th' night. He's nice to me, so I like to be nice to him. So you an' Don have t' sit with us durin' the dance."

"Oh, I don't intend to be sitting, I hope to be swept off my feet!" Emily pirouetted at the roadside. She danced on, to catch up with the departing crowd, laughing and waving to Pamela as she went.

As he was sauntering through Dunadry, Thomas met Dickie and Lennie Blenkinsop. Like himself, they were spic and span. Dickie was yarning he had got a letter informing him that he was accepted by the RUC[32] and was going soon for training. They met Sam Agnew at the railway bridge. He was as scruffy as ever, despite the effort to dress up. A clod of muck splattered on Sam's jacket pocket. A face cried in glee from the railway line, on top of the bridge, grinning down at them like a gargoyle: Sandy Thompson. When he came down to the road to pick up his bike Sam went for him. Sandy fended him off, almost falling over with the bicycle. Dickie told them to quit. Lennie Blenkinsop told his brother to give over, he wasn't a peeler yet.

At the Clady Road they encountered a gang of their friends, who were just heading for Orr's Barn. Dickie sidled over beside Brenda Nixon and started telling her all about the job he'd got. Thomas saw Emily and made for her.

"Aren't you going to go and walk Pamela?" she asked. The other girls tittered. "She's back thonder."

---

[32]RUC = Royal Ulster Constabulary.

Lennie yelled at him, "Didn't know you were such a ladies' man, Tommy! Got any tips for us?"

"He *is* a tip," said Sandy, "he's an' oul' tuppin' ram like his uncle!"

Ignoring his mates' remarks but sensing his cheeks blush as hard as they were able, Thomas said quietly to Emily, "Aye. I better find her." He turned and went in the opposite direction. He heard a wolf-whistle, more indistinct comments from the lads and then Dickie telling them to mind their manners in front of the girls.

But once the crowd had parted from him, he felt confident again. What did he care what they thought? He was the one who had to be happy with himself, not them. To pot with them! It's my life.

He saw her ahead of him, waiting under the big trees at the entrance to the Works. That shady lane could have a consoling serenity when the factory was quiet. This evening the dye pool was coloured black, like a dark, primordial ocean lapping against the long grass.

But his eyes were feasting on Pamela, in her gorgeous lilac frock. A matching ribbon decorated the light tresses of her hair. She was wrapping the white cardigan in front with her hands dug into the pockets. He saw now that her evanescent eyes were more grey than hazel. Perhaps Pamela's eyes were like the mountains, he thought, and changed colour as the daylight waxed and waned. The bulge of her bosom, the baggy woollen cardigan that hid her waist and hips, the summer colour of her round arms and legs and face, all her visible form pleased his senses. Her mouth was open a little, pursed expectantly. The moist lips seemed to quiver as she looked him up and down, her eyelashes fluttering slightly. White teeth peeped through the crevice of her soft features. As he stepped nearer, her scent greeted him. And then the light faded, as the sun disappeared behind a puff of passing cloud, casting his vision of her into dullness and shadows.

"I was in a rush th' night. Thought I'd miss you."

She moved nearer him. "You're here now."

They began walking towards Orr's mill. Thomas had his hand in his pocket. He felt her touch his elbow. She was linking her arm through his. As she bumped along beside him he got used to her presence. She soon felt like a part of him.

"What have you been up to?"

"The weans are all sick with the flu. Imagine, bad colds in the summertime. They're a nuisance. I've been trying to keep them quiet. Mummy's at the end of her tether."

"You must be a jinx: I got the flu that time we went to Glenarm on the bikes."

"Yes, that's right!" She laughed with him.

They were passing the elegant, thatched cottage where the Works' owners lived. An apple tree in the grounds overhung the road. Pamela stretched across the sharp-clipped hedge and plucked one of the small green fruit from a branch. She held it up to his mouth. He shook his head. Withdrawing the offering, there was a crunch as she bit into its hard flesh. Trying not to wince as she swallowed, Pamela said, "It's bitter," and had to throw the apple away.

They soon reached the scotching mill at Straidballymorris. A lane led them to Orr's big old stone barn, near the stream. It was getting gloomy, making the strains of music and the clamour of the dancers seem eerie in the shady laneway. One of the great wooden doors of the barn was ajar. Lennie was at the door, smoking with Sandy Thompson.

Lennie nodded his welcome. "You found her then."

Thomas grinned with embarrassment. "Did."

"Oh, our Pamela's always there when y' want her, 'n'at right, Princess?" Sandy ran a hand over her hair.

"Don't be so beastly!" she retorted, scowling and snatching her head away. She hurried Thomas inside.

Thomas followed her to where Emily was sitting on a bench along the side of the barn. An array of hurricane lamps were hanging from the wooden beams, a bit like the way the church used to be lit, before they got the electricity installed. The band were on a platform at the far end. There was a drummer, a piano accordion player and old Gordon Fraser with his tin whistle. The instruments wailed into harmony. Couples took to the earthen floor. Thomas looked around him, nodding a greeting to those he knew, not interested in her gossip with Emily. Don Armour strutted over and asked Emily for a dance. As the beaming Emily rose, Thomas caught Pamela's attention and spluttered the same question.

Thomas's feet struggled for coordination. Pamela whispered for him to take simple steps, not the bold plodding he was attempting. She humoured him with a left, right, left. There was an improvement, which they acknowledged by exchanging joyful smiles.

As they sat down, she asked, "How's your mother keeping?"

"Fine," Thomas answered. "The usual. Better than last year. She's fine, same as usual. We got a new tracteur."

"Aren't they very expensive?"

"But it's essential to have one, nowadays. It's worth its weight in gold. We're motorin' on, the year. Got all the hay in with her, all piked already. Just a bit of corn to thresh. Just think, there'll be no more trampin' after the plough now, I can sit in comfort on me wee grey Fergie!"

"I fancy another tramp."

They danced again. Holding her back, feeling her warmth, smelling her feminine odour. Inside he was reeling with a sense of wonder and happiness. They wafted around and around, gracefully following the rhythm that was being scratched out by the men on the stage.

The band took a break and so there was an interval for refreshments. They got tea and sandwiches and buns and rejoined Emily.

"Where's Don gone?" Thomas raised his eyebrows mischievously.

"Out for a cigarette with Sandy."

"I didn't think those pair would be friends," Pamela said.

"No," Thomas agreed. "But they both smoke."

Herbie and Irene sat with them. They told them they were engaged now. The wedding was going to be at Easter. Irene excitedly discussed the plans with Emily and Pamela. Herbie blethered on about their schooldays, the good summer they'd had, the corn crop was grand.

James Mateer arrived with his fiddle and boasted that the temperature was about to soar and the stour rise. They all danced livelily. At last, Pamela begged for a rest. They found a place by Robina and Davy. They worked at Clady too, so Thomas listened politely as they complained with Pamela about the new foreman.

And then it was time for the last waltz. So soon? The time had flown. And it had been great! As he took her in his arms again he looked at the outline of her face: the tender skin, delicate nose, enticing lips, the bobbling Adam's apple. Their bodies swirled as if mere appendages: he felt as if he was a spirit, floating through the air, linked to the one he loved by this peak of excitement.

"I feel great!" she said, resting her head on his shoulder as the music wheezed to an end.

The floor began to vibrate with the shuffle to the exit of the young people and the older couples and the grey-haired bachelors and prim spinsters and widows. Drawing apart from her, Thomas noticed how many of the locals were glimpsing at him and Pamela out of the corners of their eyes as they passed. Luk at them smirking, that pair of oul' wemen, whispering to each other, are they passing comment about us?

They sat down for a while, as the throng departed. Pamela and Emily became engrossed in a conversation about dresses. Don yarned to Thomas about how well the soccer team was going to perform this coming season.

They made their move when the crowd had gone. At the doorway, Pamela slipped her smooth little hand into his and he felt a rush of blood to the ears as a certain pride began to circulate within his being. Don and Emily were hand in hand and all four of them praised the evening's fun as they strolled along on that sultry summer night. Don lived not far down the Clady Road, so asked Emily in for a cup of tea. Emily hesitated, but Pamela told her to go in. They all wished each other goodnight and the door clicked shut.

Suddenly there was silence, for the sound of all the others had long since drifted with them, away towards the village or to Summerhill. And so now they were alone in the moonlit night. They walked on, slowly, through the desolate darkness of the countryside.

"I thought it would be pretty boring, run of the mill, y'know," Pamela confided. "But it's been really great." She squeezed his hand. "It was my first time."

"I've not been afore, either. I hope I didn't show you up by dancin' poorly?"

"Don't keep putting yourself down, Thomas," she lectured in a friendly way. "You did as well as any of the rest of us there. I like dancing with you. And look," she raised a leg, "I've still got all me toes."

Pausing for her to regain her balance, Thomas felt their bodies brush together. She linked her arm through his again.

"I'm glad you're happy ... with me."

"Yes!" she laughed. "And I'm beginning to realise I'm very pleased that you're pleased that I'm pleased with you."

"And I'm pleased ... I'm pleased you're pleased that I'm pleased that you're pleased, too!"

As they reached the path by the thatched cottage, Pamela wheeled him around the corner. "Let's go by the Hidden Drive."

"It might be a short cut for you, but it isn't for me."

"Aren't you walking me home?" she teased.

The pad took them along a bank of the Clady River. A steep drop led down to the rocky stream, where the silvery water was trickling in the half-light. The dry twigs and old acorns under their shoes rustled as they walked. The huge trees that lined the path created a web of branches overhead, so that the drive was always damp, cast as it was in perpetual darkness.

A loud shaking disturbed the treetops. "Whassat!" Pamela hissed, stopping and clutching him.

"Don't be frightened. It's only a bat."

She had her arm across his chest. Her warm fingers were on his shoulder. The warmth of her body was pressing on him. They were close, so close, together. He raised a hand and held her near.

"Aren't you going to court?" she said softly.

Her eyes were flashing. He closed his own eyes and leaned his mouth forward towards hers. He could feel her body burning against his, felt he was going to explode, burst into flames of passion. Her wet lips met his. She was pushing into him. He felt her thighs against his. He was tipping back, so forced against her to keep his balance. Her lips were flowing over his face like water upon water in the stream. Their teeth clashed painfully. She was kissing like a wild thing, gripping him to her.

Was this right? It felt wrong. What was wrong? What was niggling? She rested her head upon his chest. Her heart was banging, vibrating against him. It wasn't the way he had thought it would be. She was too forward. This was too ... brutal. There was no tenderness, no sleepy cosiness. His throat felt dry.

She moved her lips towards his and the frenzy began again. His lungs were straining, he could not breathe! He forced himself apart.

He stammered, "You're too ... quick."

She leaned back and they stared at each other. "How do you mean, Thomas?"

"You're not doing it ... ladylike. You're too bullish."

She loosened herself from his arms. "Don't you give me this 'ladylike' stuff. It all boils down to the same thing, no matter who it is. Why d'you have to spoil it? Leave me be!" She started to run off.

He ran after her for a few paces, then stopped. Having given up, Thomas spent a long time sitting dejectedly on one of the big stumps, letting his mind go blank. Eventually, he roused from his trance. If he let her go, it wouldn't matter, she'd cool off soon. He could apologise tomorrow. Women! He glanced at the moon and noticed it was already waning. It was tomorrow already! It was Sunday. He looked up at Orion. Was that it? It was the Sabbath Day: *His* day, not ours. Thomas understood! He could tell her that everything was alright, it was just that *He* came first!

Pamela stopped along the road at the small, humpy bridge, where the Clady mill race crossed the road to meet the river. She was catching her breath after her running when she saw a light, a bicycle lamp: someone was approaching.

"Hello, Princess." Sandy Thompson hopped off his bicycle and rested it against the bridge wall.

"I thought I toul' you t' get lost?"

He grabbed her from behind, around the waist, squeezing himself to her. "Aren't we still mates? You're no fun th' night." He was squeezing his cheek close to hers, trying to nuzzle.

"Some friend you turned out to be." She struggled free. "See this," she touched her stomach, "this is fun, too. You ought-a try it."

Opening his arms wide, he apologised, "I'm a man, I'm not built that way. But I'm glad you are."

He reached for her again, more gently this time. This time, he managed to contain her less vehement struggles. They stood by the wall of the bridge, looking out at the myriad of sparkles on the surface where the moonlight was reflected on the babbling water.

"My ma wants us to get married."

"You *toul'* her? You swore you wouldn't!"

"She *noticed*. Sandy, *everybody'll* notice soon."

"I toul' ye, you keep your mouth shut an' I'll see right by you an' slip you a few poun' now an' again." Then he spoke in a harsh tone. "You squeal on me, you dare shame me, an' I'll deny it. I'll make people think you're the worst slut in creation. You can't prove a thing against me, but I could blacken you ..." He gripped her jaw tightly, then pressed his mouth to hers again. The kissing intensified.

Pamela drew back. "Don't you waste your threats on me, Sandy. I'm not all *that* fussed about marryin', anyway."

"Prin-cess!" he whispered. "I don't wanna be nasty to y' fer the sake of it. But you gotta keep it under your hat – my ma' ud *die* if she thought I'd ... been a bad boy."

She extracted herself from his arms. Breathing deeply and sniffing, she said, "I don't know what I ever saw in you."

"I don't know what you see in Gray."

"You're *both* a pain in the neck! Only for completely different reasons." She looked away from him, towards the gushing river, and continued, "I feel comfortable with Thomas ..."

"Do you feel comfortable now?" he caught her again and tried to caress her.

She resisted initially, but his lips found hers and soon her arms clung to him instead of fighting him. They kissed long and feverishly. Her mouth moved rhythmically with his. She slid her hand from his waist – which she was able to feel through his thin shirt – down the rougher, thicker fabric of his trousers and, pushing her palm against that bulge, felt his whole body stiffening. But as he began to explore her, when his fingers slipped beneath her cardigan to stroke a breast, she curtailed the petting. "Don't! Not here. Som'dy might see."

"Who's here to see? Come on, Princess ..."

"There's somebody!" Hearing the footsteps getting louder, she unravelled herself from him and trotted away in the direction of home.

"Who the Hell's that!" he breathed to himself.

The shadow reached Sandy. "'Lo there. What d' ya say, Sandy?"

"What're you doin' here this time-a night, Tommy?"

"Is that somebody else thonder?" he peered into the darkness. "I thought I saw somebody."

"There's not a soul about, y' stupid bastard!"

"There's no need to snap at me like that! I dunno what's raggin' you, but there's no need to be callin' *me* names."

"Why not? It's true, isn't it? Who d'you think sired you, some knight in shining armour? Your uncle an' your ma, all alone in that house together, an' she has *you*." He prodded his chest. "Not just a bastard, but an *inbred* bastard."

Thomas lunged forward, grabbing his throat. They wrestled. Thomas hit Sandy as they were bent by the wall. He went down on one knee, stunned. Thomas stood back, calming down.

Sandy croaked. "There's no call for you to kill the messenger. I'm only repeatin' the stories I've heard." He coughed a little, but had soon regained his composure. As he mounted his bicycle, he said, "It's after the witchin' hour. See you in church th' marra. Or, I should say, *this* mornin'."

On his way home Thomas walked rapidly, expending his anger in exercise. He thought he would stop and take a look at James's pigs. One of the sows was due to farrow. He crept over to the pens and stepped over a partition. He approached the arc in which the pig in question usually lay. As he peered through the poor light an ugly creature gnashed and leapt forward.

White fangs, like horns: it looked like the Devil's head!

It was the boar, in a vicious mood. Its snout sought his calves. Thomas beat at its ears and ran to the partition. It almost got him; he stumbled. He felt the wetness at his trouser leg. He managed to clear the wooden barrier before the big tusks found their target.

From outside the pen he shouted manically at the angry pig. "You brute! You brute! You! Could you do that, to your own sister? To ..." he choked on phlegm. "Y' beast!" he screamed.

It gnarled back at him.

He stared up at the stars with a questioning look. "You have intervened?"

When he arrived in the yard, his temper was already dissipating into tiredness. He heard whining. Of course, poor Help was in suffering. He went to the stable and injected her with a little more morphia. He put his hand on her head and drew it down. Her heart was beating gently. She licked his hand, the big brown pools of her eyes displaying devotion, her unadulterated affection.

The weather was turning muggy. Thomas was gathering potatoes from slippery drills, chuffed to be in charge of the schoolchildren who were dotted about the soil like gulls. In the next field, his uncle and Fred were doing a bit of neighbouring, repaying Kaye's favour by helping at the threshing. They wanted to get the last of it done today, for there was rain coming. The canopied steam engine chugged away, pisting as it drove the belts, powering the thresher as it grinded the grain and spilled out straw. Fred was loading up a cart with the sacks of oats, ready to take to Jackson's, to be set in the drier.

With the churning of the machinery nearby, Thomas scavenged in the muddy potato field, hurrying to get the drills dug before the bad weather was upon them. The youngsters were full of sport and there were plenty of jokes being told and the mood was good. Thomas was engrossed in the earth, his eyes sifting through the soil for potatoes, his hands rejecting stones, when a pair of slender shins appeared in front of him. He glanced up as he got off his knees, saw the young ones were watching from a little way off. He faced her with a blank, accepting stare.

"You're a hard man to satisfy, Thomas Gray."

"What do you mean, Pamela?"

"When friends falls out, it's the fella's supposed to do the chivalrous thing. Instead, here I am. To apologise. I'm sorry I was bad. I didn't mean anything by it. It was all rubbish, surely you realise that?"

"If you say so." He had difficulty finding the words.

She seemed to be oblivious to the dilemma which gripped his heart: he had these tender feelings for her, she was so lovely, but he had been told she was his uncle's illegitimate daughter and also the country was full of this talk about him being – he hated to think about it at all – he himself was the product of an incestuous relationship, so they shared the same blood and for him to even *think* about her ...

It's a sin.

She reached out and touched his arm. "Please don't be angry with me. I've had so much on my mind recently, I can't think straight. Do you forgive me?"

His face took control of itself and softened into a smile of relief. "I'm sorry too. I was being too snooty. I think it was just ... I was goin' to come down an' see you. Honest, Pamela. But I thought ..."

She moved closer to him, so that they were almost nose to nose. She whispered, "And as for the ... kissin' ... please don't think I throw myself like that at anybody." Her voice quavered. "I got carried away. I hope we can still be friends, Thomas ..." She was standing so very near to him and reached out and held his hand for a brief moment.

A surge of happiness flowed through Thomas. "The way I see it," he stuttered, "you're more than an ordinary frien', you're my sister in Christ."

One of the schoolchildren came over. "Mister Gray, we're gonna stap fer a minute an' hae our pieces."

"Aye, right, Tommy," he replied impatiently.

"'Lo, Pamela," the wee boy chortled, as he began hobbling back towards his pals.

"Hello, Tommy," she answered pleasantly, as the boy ran off.

"There's something's come between us ..." Thomas strained, trying to utter the unspeakable.

So, he had seen her with Sandy, she thought. "I know what you mean. But let me put your mind at rest about *him*. It means nothing. Not to me, anyway."

Aware of the drone of the engine nearby, Thomas lowered his voice. "You mean ... *him*?"

"It doesn't matter who he is, does it?" Thinking she now knew exactly what he meant, Pamela assured him, "But I hope you won't let that come between us, Thomas. Let's be mates."

She seemed quite nonchalant about it! But then, noticing her dejected look, he thought she needed comforting after all, so said, "I'm sure it was all a big mistake. An' I'm not bothered, I mean, we can't change what happened in the past. But we can forgive. And try to forget."

A shout made Pamela turn her head towards the road. "Harriet's waiting for me. We're just goin' up to Granny's a message." Her deep eyes delved mistily into his. She whispered, "Come an' see me and we'll talk some more, about pleasanter things, eh, Thomas? But let me know when you're coming, so's we kin meet at the goat house at the end of the lane, where it's private."

She strode across the mud and departed without looking round from the gate. Thomas went over to where the helpers were.

A wee boy asked, with his mouth full, "Is she your girlfriend, Mister Gray?"

"No! Just a freen'."

He munched on a slab of soda bread. Staring up at the ominous dark clouds that crowned Donegore Hill, he tried to sort out his inner turmoil.

Come on rain, bucket down, he pleaded. He needed his head shired: he needed to clean his brain of the mucky filth, let the sediments of sin settle at the bottom of his heart, so that his system would be pure again. He felt so sad, so lost, bereft of his dream. But at least now he had her as a special friend, even if he was still grieving for the loss of her as a lover. How could she accept the sordid truth so nonchalantly?

It cheered him up that they got the field cleared and he could glance back with a satisfied nod as they took away the jiggling load of potatoes on the cart. The sack of spuds were soon all in the outhouse. The sky was getting very black as the school children lined up in the yard for Isaac to dole out their money. The clamminess of the atmosphere was becoming unbearable.

The sultriness continued as they milked. Thomas's head was pounding. It seemed that the weather would never break, that this stifling tension would last forever. The sweat sat molten on their brows like the butter on their lukewarm spuds as they ate their supper.

Fred went to the loft, after the evening's chat in the kitchen. Thomas said he was going across to take a look at the dog before turning in. His mother decided she would go to. She cajoled his uncle into going with them to see how much better the collie was getting. Lying on her bed of straw, the invalid had begun to eat again and was slapping her tail around, raising dust, enjoying being spoilt by so many all at one time.

Even Uncle Isaac gave her a paternal pet. Help panted and blinked her appreciation when he fed her a biscuit. "There y' go," he glanced up at Thomas as he spoke to the dog, "you'll be trying to catch your tail again in no time."

Thomas stared into those glassy orbs and saw Pamela. She was running across a ploughed field, smiling, staring at him with beckoning eyes. They met, embraced, kissed a kiss that lasted for eternity. Beautiful Pamela, loving Pamela ... Aggh! Get this evil out of your heed! He felt drained of energy and emotion, was so sorry to leave poor Help on her own. Her wide, dark eyes seemed to weep as he closed the outhouse door.

Crossing the yard to the house again, Jean said to her brother, "I can feel a spit of rain."

"At last," he grunted. "It's about time. I'm swelterin'."

Thomas lay listening to the patter on the roof. He pushed his sheets down his chest. It was too humid to sleep. The shower increased in severity. There was a flash. A rumble of thunder, a long, low, grumbling, as from a dissatisfied bull. More lightning. The thunder getting worse. A flash! Crash in the heavens. A building roar: the storm was soon raging. The power of the winds and the plump of the rain disturbed him terribly. At his window, the branches of the cherry tree were being whipped, sending shadows scurrying about the panes like rats. Thunder boomed again.

It was too hot. He leapt out of bed, flapping his nightshirt at the collar. Thomas tiptoed through the parlour and out to the kitchen. As he reached the jamb, a flash of lightning illuminated the text on the wall:

You have not chosen Me, It is I who have Chosen you.
John 15.16

He felt cooler out of bed. He climbed into his uncle's armchair, curling his bare feet up beneath his body, huddling into the seat and clasping his arms across his chest. He felt parboiled. He was drowsy. He stared at the red glow amongst the black coals and the white ash of logs in the grate. And the storm beat on, as if it would never end.

The eye of the storm was upon them. The stridulousness of the atmosphere felt even more unbearable than before. Between two thunder cracks he first noticed the jangle of bedsprings. Someone else wasn't able to rest? He puffed, wiping sweat from his brow.

The creaking became frequent, increasing into an incessant riot as the horrific noise of the heavens ranted outside and above and all around. In the grate a charred log moved, fell into the heart of the smouldering ashes, as the rain crashed onto the slates. It was as if God had opened the window of the firmament and the celestial waters were all coming tumbling down upon them, as if a second flood was being let loose, reneging on the covenant – because mankind deserved no mercy.

And he was frowning; but the bed ceased its metallic groaning as the steady splatter of rain outside on the concrete yard and upon the roof replaced the fury of the tempest, so his face eased. It was subsiding as quickly as it had developed. The window panes were only tinkling now, not rattling as before; the drainpipes were gushing less wantonly; peace was returning.

A floorboard thudded. A door knob was turned. Someone else couldn't stick the steamy night? His eyes remained transfixed on the glow of the fire. A heavy tread moved along the cold stone floor as the wind swept a wave of rain against the kitchen window. A plate on the dresser behind him tinged as the steps paused. There was a deep breath, heavier than a sigh. Then the pat-pat was repeated. He heard a door close. A bed jangled again.

There was only the rain and the dying wind and the dropping temperature to disturb his mind's vacancy. Or, was there was some other, muffled sound, now? Was that a whining? Just his imagination? Noises in the night, harassing his memory, were forming deep currents, demanding attention as they ebbed under the surface of his consciousness, eroding the foundations of his being, like the way sea and wind weather rocky shores.

As he sat immobile, his eyelids became heavy. He couldn't even sense himself blinking. It had gradually quietened. The rainclouds had moved on, but were still blocking out the moon and stars, so that the kitchen was pitch black, except for the faint glow of the fire. There were no longer any shadows creeping around the walls like evil spirits.

He hauled himself from the armchair. He stopped and stood for a while staring at his uncle's bedroom door.

Why?

He turned and padded back to his room. Drowsiness enveloped him like the cool sheets. The once unbearable cacophony had become a mere murmuring of rain. Islandreagh absorbed the shower as he slept. The soil was moistened; the plants soaked up their watering gleefully, and all the beasts in the fields got their matted coats washed clean, shired by the downpour.

CHAPTER NINE

Idle Hands

"Get a bucket there, Thomas," Uncle Isaac ordered.

It was Sunday. The friends[33] were visiting. James and John Ussher were in the Far Orchard with Auntie Josie and Mary Ritchie gathering apples. Uncle George and James Ritchie had stayed inside with his mother. The afternoon was bright but breezy. Thomas reappeared in a hurry, carrying a white enamel bucket, complete with its vented lid.

"Uck, Thomas!" his uncle cringed.

"It's alright, it's clean."

"Ye can't use the po bucket. There's one in the house by yont daig. It'll do."

He went back and fetched the dog's water bucket. He helped gather the windfalls that James and John were lifting. Fred was plucking some of the few good apples from the branches, so they could have some to eat as well as for Auntie Josie's baking.

Jean came rushing out. "You missed it! I toul' ye yous would! It's happened. Mr Chamberlain's just been on. We're at war."

"Yeehah!" Fred shouted.

James Ussher laughed and pranced around the trees that were weeping with fruit. He stuck out his arms and soared around in circles, imitating an aeroplane.

"I'm gonna divebomb Berlin!" he screamed.

Thomas copied him, shouting, "I'm the Red Baron. I'll stap ye."

They had a dogfight. James akkah-akkah-ed Thomas, who spiralled theatrically and crashed to the ground.

"Daft eejits," Isaac said to Josie and Mary.

"What about you, Fred, are you goin' to sea again, to take on the Hun?"

From the ladder, which was resting against a tree, Fred Nelson responded, "Huh! I've beaten them once already. Let these young lads have a turn."

James said to Thomas, "I'm going to join the RAF and do my bit. What about you, Thomas? Are you game?"

"Haven't thought about it."

---

[33] friends = (coll.) relatives.

"What's there to think about? Civilisation is in peril. Your country needs you. See, even Fred's on our side now. Wimp!" He thumped Thomas on the arm.

"Why are you agin the Germans now, Fred?"

"I've read recently about some of the things the Nazis have done. I've got to thinking. They've let themselves get out of hand. But, anyway, war is the ultimate trial of strength. May the best men win!"

"Thomas," Uncle Isaac called from the orchard, "come an' give me a hand, here."

He was up the ladder with a basket, picking the last few good apples from the tree. Thomas began lifting the last of the windfalls, filling the buckets with the apples that were scattered around their best tree.

"Whit's th' matter with you, recently? You've been very quiet. Are ye in love or somethin'?"

He said bluntly, "I just haven't anything to say to *you*."

"What have *I* done wrong? Right enough, I've noticed you're still pally enough wi' yer ma an' Fred, there. What've *I* done t' make y' single me out?"

"You know fine well."

"I do nit! Whatever it is, it must be in yer imagination." His uncle chatted away, regardless. "Your grandfather had a great interest in the new knowledge that the scientists have discovered fer us," he said, as he shook on the ladder. "I was called after one of them. The daddy of them all, in fact. Do you know the story about the apple? About Sir Isaac Newton sittin' under a tree and an apple fell on him?" He dropped an apple near Thomas, who covered his head with an arm. "Nothing floats up, everything falls to the ground. Gravity." He held out the wicker basket in one hand and an apple in another. "If I drap them together, which will hit the ground first?"

"Oh ... we were toul' this in school, I think. Mmm. The basket. Must be. It's bigger. Because it's heavier, that's it."

Uncle Isaac let go of both items. They landed simultaneously. "They land at the same time. See? It's nothin' t' do with weight. And the interesting thing is, they don't fall, they're *dragged* towards the centre of the earth. Things aren't always as straightforward as they seem." He tapped his temple.

"I know all this," Thomas muttered.

"Do ye?"

They took the apples to the potato house. Isaac put the good ones into a sack by the wall. Thomas made to tip in the windfalls. His uncle stopped him.

"Hie bae! Don't put the bad apples in with the good ones. You should keep them separate. We'll gie them to the calves. Apples is like folk: y' have t' get rid of the bad 'uns, or they'll ruin those that's good."

Before long, he went in, leaving Thomas to redd up the last of the windfalls by himself. Everyone else was inside, excitedly discussing the news. Mary Ritchie and her cousin came back out and helped him finish off.

"Aren't you interested in the war?" James asked him.

"There'll be wars an' rumours of wars," he replied, "but none-a that'll redd up these apples fer me."

They soon finished the job together.

As they lay on the grass beneath the trees that fine afternoon, Mary said playfully, "I know, let's play Mummies and Daddies, like we used to when we were wee, at your place on days like this." She flopped over and tousled James Ussher's hair.

Defending himself, he replied, "Aye. I'm Daddy. An' you're Mummy, for sure." He gestured to her stomach. "That's baby number two. Thomas can be baby number one."

"Yes, after all, he is your *alter ego*. But he's a *big* baby!" she made James laugh hysterically.

"Shut up! Shut up!" Thomas yelled. "Stop this dirty talk. Yous are cousins."

"So!" Mary dismissed his prudishness. "Cousins can kiss." She slobbered on James's cheek, making him screw up his eyes and mop his face. "It's not as if we're brother an' sister or somethin'."

Thomas leapt to his feet, panting angrily for some reason known only to himself.

"C'mon," James kept the peace. "Forget it! Let's go in an' get our tea. Let's not fight over nothin'."

"It's not nuthin'!"

Thomas was seething like they had never seen him before and they were amazed.

Grubbing for turnips was unpleasant when the air was cold and the soil tore at the hands, when the wet stones scraped skin off the fingers and his nose dripped, with the chill down his neck niggling, when it was all damp around his knees and soaking through the welts of his boots uncomfortably. At least the field they were in at the Holestone was sheltered a little from the north wind by the slope and the thick hedges, even if these had already begun to shed their soggy, tarnished leaves.

"The e-lec-tric-it-y is coming up our road," Thomas told his uncle.

"Good fer yous," Uncle Stan replied. "It's a blessing. I couldn't live without it now. They're installing it at Umgall, too, aren't they? Didn't George wire the house when they renovated it, to be ready for the connection?"

"Fred is wiring up our house. Reckons he was a bit of an electrician in the States. Uncle Isaac's all interested in the new-fangledness of it and is tinkerin' away with him. Strikes me as being dangerous. I hope Fred knows what he's doing."

"He's a bit of a blow."[34] Hugh gave his opinion.

"As long as he doesn't blow yous all sky high," Stan grinned.

"Where James th' day?"

A pregnant pause was ended by Uncle Stan's uncomfortable reply, "He went to Liverpool on the boat and joined the Army."

"Did he ... *leave* Mary?"

"Not permanently, nothing dramatic like that," Uncle Stan ventured. "He went to earn the King's shillin', to have summat to send home fer t' rare the wean on."

Hugh added, "Did you know James Ussher has applied to the RAF?"

"Never!" Thomas straightened his back. "He talked about it, right enough. But I thought it was just talk."

Hugh also stood up straight and quizzed, "What's wrong with that? Sure, you know what he's like."

"But ... how'll they cope at Umgall?"

Thomas bent down again to the task in hand.

Uncle Stan answered him, "They've big strapping John there, who'll likely be getting married soon. There's hardly enough room for both of them, anyway."

---

[34] a bit of a blow = (coll.) a person who boasts, exaggerates.

"Are you going to join up, Thomas?" Hugh asked. "You're near hard the right age to join, if you got permission."

"I niver thought about it."

"He's the only lad about the place. Like you, Hugh. A place soon goes to pot without a young man about it."

"I'm not going to war," Hugh smirked. "I'm too young to die."

"You're only a schoolboy," Thomas teased.

"Leavin' nixt year!" he countered. "Can I go to the T.T. races again next year, Daddy? See if those wee English girls are there that Thomas was chatting up."

Thomas blushed. "Rubbish. Was just being sociable."

"A right ladykiller is our Thomas," Hugh went on. "Did y' hear, Daddy, about his courtin'?"

He lifted a large clod and chucked it at Hugh. The lump shattered as it struck the ducking lad's long arm.

He cried, "You shut up! I'm not seein' nobody at all! Shut it!"

"Lads!" Stan was put out. "Calm yourselves. This is Ulster, not Flanders. Git on with it!" He pointed at the earth, his expression fierce with disapproval.

The two youths grubbed through the drills for the turnips.

Thomas's fingers poked into a rotten one. The mulch stuck to his fingers, a stinking, sticky, creamy goo. Like pus.

"In the dirt again!" The mocking voice laughed manically.

Who said that? He wiped the putrid matter on his trouser leg and carried on tearing up the soil, his heart still racing.

"Wait till I tell yous a wee story." Stanford Begley Esquire orated: "One day, Thomas Gray was out in the field sowin' corn wi' his fiddle, in the Thorny Forth fiel' there, and the seed it flew away out and bounced all roads and directions about the place.

"Some of the seeds over by the laneside saw a big dark man in a black cloak with a floppy hat pulled down over his eyes. He toul' them, 'You'll be alright here wi' me.' So they went, 'Weeee! C'mon boys, away over through the hedge here an' out to the lane.' And then along came big Hugh Begley, wi' his big feet, and stamped all over them, and crushed them till their guts spilled out, and they all went, 'Agghh!' and died.

"Some of the rest of the seeds, they fell on the rocky bit at the head of the Thorny Forth. They said to each other, 'We're grand here boys!' and stretched themselves out and sunned themselves. And sure enough, they began to grow. But then it was 'Oh, I'm parched!' and 'Oh, I'm as dry as a dog's nose.' So, they shrivelled away up to nothin' and died of thirst.

"Another wheen of seeds went over yonder nixt the bracken, and began to sprout in amongst the weeds thonder. But the bracken and the thistles and the nettles all ganged up on those seeds, and said, 'Oi yous, we was here first. Git away t' blazes!' And the weeds throttled the seeds, 'Aggh!', and they were all strangled to death.

"But most of the seeds bounced into the drills where they were supposed to be goin', and grew up into big tall, ripe stalks of corn.

"So, the Parable of the Seed is, if you fall in wi' bad comp'ny that leads you astray so's that you're ripped off, or if you are lazy, or if you don't set yoursel' up amongst your ain surt, you'll end up in dire straits. But if you stick to your proper groove in life, then you'll live the way you should do. Sure, the Reaper'll get you in the end. But isn't that the way it's meant t' be?"

As ye sow, so shall ye reap.

A grey mistiness began to shroud the land around them. The hedges began to drip with condensation. Their shuffling and infrequent murmuring resembled the slow gait and chanting of some religious order. The Reverend Dr Marsh had talked about the war on Sunday.

> Onward! Christian soldiers,
>   Marching as to war,
> With the Cross of Jesus
>   Going on before.
> Christ, the Royal Master,
>   Leads against the foe;
> Forward into battle;
>   See! His banners go.

The dutiful thing to do. Defend the liberty of others. Selflessness. Should Thomas go and see England and France and earn some money, have adventures, experience the camaraderie? Be a pilot! Or a tank driver – bobbing over the tops of trenches, the turret gun blasting. Die? Die in a hail of bullets? Or be killed in a dogfight. Or blown to smithereens by a bomb. James had gone, knowing God was with him. If Thomas went, he would be protected, too. And what did it matter if he did not survive – who would mourn for a snivelling wretch like him? It would be escape! Escape from his dreadful past! He'd get away from Islandreagh! See the big wide world. Maybe see the wonders of the USA! Make a new life for himself, have something of his own! Not be stuck in one, small place, on an oul' farm, grubbing for turnips and spuds. What was it Paul called it? Praxis! Action! Define your own life.

> Fight the good fight with all thy might;
> Christ is thy strength, and Christ thy right.
> Lay hold on life, and it shall be
> Thy joy and crown eternally.

He got home late from Begley's. It was dark and the mist had been followed by a heavy shower. It was good to get in to the warmth. Fred was in the kitchen.

"They've gone to the hall. There's some church social on. Your grub's there, should still be warm enough. I just stayed to deliver the message. I'm off up to Barr's for a stout. I'll see you later."

Before Thomas got a chance to expel an answer from his open mouth, Fred was past him and out the door. Gone drinking? Not often he did that. There were spuds and turnip and a bit of mutton on the plate on the hob. He put it over the fire, to warm a bit more.

He sat at the folded down table near the window, waiting for it to heat up. He never much noticed the clock on the dresser, but because he was alone he was aware of its steady ticking. The animals in the yard were quiet tonight. No milking this evening: he had been home too late. Small mercy.

Silence. No life: no Mummy jabbering or Uncle Isaac clearing his throat or Fred telling them about the USA. As quiet as the grave. Is this what it is like to be in your coffin, six feet beneath the clay? Silence.

He checked the spuds – still not ready. He sat at the table again. Silence. Boredom. He didn't want to look at the paper or go near the carving or go to this social – he was too tired to go all the way down there on a cold, wet night like this.

He went over to the dresser and knelt down. Reaching into the back of the cupboard, he found the bottle of whiskey his uncles had been sampling at Christmas. He took it to the table, eyes alert, ears straining for warning sounds – they might return unexpectedly, miraculously. He carefully poured a teacupful, right up to the brim. Then, he scooped up a cupful of water from the basin in the jawbox and carefully poured it into an empty delft jug that usually held flowers. He poured the water along the spout of the jug and dribbled it into the bottle. He screwed the cap on tight and returned the bottle to the dresser cupboard.

Stealing! Thomas you're wicked! Why was he doing this? Was it a sin? But Uncle Isaac drunk it at New Year's. Uncle Stan took whiskey too, and he was a nice man. It was a bit of fun, that was all, a bit of crack. No harm in trying it once. The Devil finds work for idle hands? He knew he was stealing from Uncle Isaac, but reckoned he would never know. This was the spirit, this adventurous mood. Praxis! Action! Haha!

He tipped half of the whiskey into a second teacup, then filled both to the brim with water from the jug. He rubbed his hands gleefully. He tore a piece of bread from the slice on the table and chewed it. He raised the cup in both hands, to his lips. He slurped in a mouthful and gulped it down. He noticed a sting in the throat: he blinked, almost coughed. How did it taste? Mellow, sharp, like wet fire. Fire water!

He used a folded tea towel to carry his plate to the table. He sprinkled on some salt and plonked a big lump of butter in the heart of each spud. To dispel the unpalatable taste of the lukewarm potato, he took another draught of the whiskey. This was the high life! Like Adolf Hitler in his big office, the servants bringing in the tray of goodies - 'Bottle of wine, mein Führer?' 'Nein, ze Irish schvizkey, pliz.' He ate quickly, for he was very hungry and anyway the food was not as pleasant half-cold as it was when his mother cooked it. He drained one of the cups as he ate. He soon felt no sting at all. He could handle this!

He took his bare plate to the basin and slipped it into the cold water. He got out the jar of Jeyes Fluid from beneath the corner work area and dropped some into the cup, which he then sniffed. He gave it a good wipe; they'd never know. He took his other cup of whiskey with him and lowered himself into his uncle's armchair, expelling a wheeze of relaxation as he did so. He spread out his legs, until the fire began to roast his toes through the stocking soles. He gazed lazily into the cup in his hands before him.

"Good medicine," he said aloud to himself.

What was he going to do about Pamela? Better go and see her sometime, he decided. After all, she'd be back to work for them sometime. If *he* could face Marbeth and Pamela day in, day out, so could Thomas face Pamela. If *he* could live like this, with Mummy here and Mrs Hart and Pamela coming to work every now and again, and the whole village *know* about it and not say anything – not take him out and lynch him, burn him at the stake or anything! But on the contrary, they made had him an *Elder*! Ah! Christian forgiveness was a wonderful thing. But Thomas still had difficulty convincing himself that he was not to blame. Then, those pertinent words of the Lord's came to mind: 'Forgive them, for they know not what they do'. And he knew that he, too, had not known what he had been doing. So, even though he was guilty under original sin, was responsible for his actions because he had free will, at the same time his slate could be wiped clean. Like Master Brooke rapping him over the knuckles thon time in school for notching 'Vote Liberal' into the desk with his penknife. Was *that* all he deserved – a wee reminder that he'd done wrong and then it was business as usual?

As he rapidly sipped the rest of the alcohol, he recalled their kissing and her hand touching his and smelt her sweet odour and felt his loins stirring. He couldn't help it if he fancied her. Lazily, he set the cup on the floor by the chair. His willie felt caught beneath his longjohns, so he slipped a hand down his trousers to make himself more comfortable. He lay there, gently stroking his warm parts, enjoying a bliss that was like that peacefulness that comes before a deep sleep.

She pinched him! He turned and held her arms, with firm hands. He grinned. Her smile showed that she shared his feelings. He leant forward and their lips met ... She was so, so nice. His willie was straining now, it had come alive of its own accord. He rubbed his palm against it, squeezing it against his belly, for this was a contenting sensation. Images flitted into his mind, filling his consciousness.

He was reliving all his moments with her, real and imaginary: her singing in the winter cold, her touch as they skated, her figure in the fields, the slight disappointment of their short stay at Glenarm – but she joked about it with him, holding his hand in her warm hand, when they walked to the dance. And, of course, after the dance, they had gone along the Hidden Drive together – forget that argument – and she had squeezed herself to him, her body heat warming him, as his lips pressed against her wet, succulent mouth, with her tongue writhing near the tip of his, as her thighs pressed against his, trapping his willie like it was now trapped between his pulsing palm and hot belly. He knew he shouldn't be thinking these things but his will power wasn't strong enough yet for him to resist – just picture her a wee bit longer

... He was twitching with excitement. His stones felt full, hard. He brushed away vigorously, becoming more pent up with every furious stroke.

Her bulging bosom, her freckly nose, wrinkling when she laughed, those tender hands, touching his side, ticking the hairline near his ear, as her beautiful face caressed his ...

> Oh what can little hands do
> To please the King of Heaven?
> Those little hands some work may try -
> Though I've forgotten the reason why!
> I'm *firm* in the faith, haha!

He was sweating, gasping. Look at her eyes, look at her body. Kissing, kissing, kissing! Look at her, look at her, *look* at her! His mind exploded. His body shuddered. Spasming like an epileptic, he was thrown about in the armchair. His eyes widened with tension and shock. He jittered into a heap. He bent forward, raising his hand from his soreness. He felt and smelt the creaminess and, unbuttoning himself with his other, shaking, hand, he mopped himself with his grubby handkerchief.

"So," he gasped, "is that what Sandy meant?"

He sat forward – feeling his red face burn even more, near the fire – and threw the handkerchief onto the glowing bits of log. He took a swig of the whiskey, then drained the second cupful. As the cotton cackled and fizzled, his brain became flooded: was it Leviticus where God said to the Israelites not to sin by throwing their seed onto the fire? And if she was his sister, then he had had lustful thoughts about someone he should not have and that was ... unfathomably sinful. The flames became a blur as his eyes watered.

Was there no hope of salvation from what he had done? He told himself that it had been accidental, that it was forgivable. But still he felt guilty, because he had done it, just like he had taken his uncle's whiskey, without bothering to stop and consider that what he was doing was wrong, was breaking another Commandment. Another one! How many had he violated now? His shoulders began to heave as the sobbing overpowered him. Thomas wept for the stolen innocence of youth.

Stirred by the fear that they might soon return, he got up wearily, to wash the crockery with the Jeyes Fluid, scrubbing his hands thoroughly as he did so. He stood swaying, feeling the drunkenness beginning to weigh down upon him. He sniffed the cups several times as he slouched across the room, to hang them from their hooks on the dresser. He yawned a long energyless sigh. It was definitely time for bed.

As he shuffled towards the jamb passage the floor seemed to tilt up on him as he was traversing it and he staggered against the wall. His shoulder knocked against something. He leaned against the wall, trying to prevent it from falling, but the thing slithered to the tiles regardless of his efforts to trap it against the wall. He blinked exaggeratedly, to examine the object. It was the dusty and now glassless, framed text:

You have not chosen Me, It is I who have Chosen you.
John 15.16

Thomas was in the yard, waiting for his mother to sort out the apples she wanted him to take down to the shop, when Billy Falk and his man Hugh arrived. Having parked the lorry at the roadside, they met Thomas in the yard.

"Hello there, young fella. We're here to see about scrap metal," said Billy.

Thomas greeted them. "Oh, aye."

"We're here on Government bisnis. Y'see, everybody has to gather up any oul' bit of scrap they can for the war effort. It's all going to be melted down and made into weapons and equipment for the boys at the front."

"My cousin's gone to the Air Force."

"Grand," Hugh humoured him. "Y'know that big cannon at the head of Antrim town? It's been taken. They'll make him a whole aeroplane outta that lot. But even an oul' busted bucket will do. Everything and anything. Got the picture?"

"Yissir," Thomas playfully saluted.

"We'll be comin' round in a few week's time to gather it all up. Get hoakin', eh?" As they headed for the lorry again, Hugh added, "Tell yer da for us we called, will y'?"

"He means yer uncle," Billy said to Thomas.

Thomas forced smile, taking it as a genuine mistake. But then he gasped when he realised that they might have been insulting him, by referring to *the secret* about his uncle.

"Whit are you doin' there, wi' yer jaw hengin' like that, like a yawnin' daig's?" his mother shouted from the half-door.

"Billy Falk an' his man were here. They're collectin' scrap for the war machine."

"What machine?"

He put a finger to his nose. "A secret weapon."

"Don't you use that tone with me! Here, here's these apples. Get on with you an' get them delivered."

Thomas drove down to the village on the tractor, to deliver the apples before milking time. At the bottom of the Rathmore Road he met Jimmy Rodgers for the first times for ages. He acknowledged Jimmy apprehensively.

"Where've you been hidin' all this time?"

"What d' ya mean?"

"I haven't seen you since you soul' me that calf, in the springtime. You niver even gie me a hand wi' the hay this year. What's the reason fer it?"

"I thought me Uncle Isaac seen you, he said you said you didn't need ..."

"I'm only coddin' y'! Did y' hear the latest?" said Jimmy. When Thomas shook his head, Jimmy told him, "About yer man Thompson from Ballysculty? He'd deed."

"Dead! He can't be."

"Died in his bed. Whether he was asleep or not at the time, I dunno!" he winked. "His heart give out. I'm nat surprised, with all the bairns he's got an' all the wemen he's chased."

"Mr Thompson? Did he chase women? Sure he's good-livin'."

"He might-a made out he was. But sure, when he was a young man, he was niver doin' anythin' else but sniffin' round skirt. They reckon he'd had a couple-a wemen since he got married an' all."

"Oh, I couldn't believe that of him."

"Would ye listen to me, corruptin' your young ears." He laughed. "That's bad of me."

"Jimmy," Thomas began warily, raising himself up a bit on the tractor seat, "Y'know that calf you were talkin' about, that we soul' ye, what iver happened to it?"

"Oh, it's a grand calf! Thrivin' well. Best do-er iver I bought. Cheap at half the price. I'll get me turn out of it, by God I will."

"I thought it might-a been a poor do-er."

"Are we talkin' about the same beast? It got a touch of scour t' begin wi', you kin hardly expect anythin' else of a dropped calf. But then it just ate and ate and grew and grew." Jimmy was all smiles.

So it was a relieved and happy Thomas who delivered the apples to Elsie in the shop. She mentioned that she'd heard about Sandy's father's death, it was the talk of the village. He had finished and was just setting some empty boxes beside him by the wheel arch. Turning, he saw a familiar figure at the far end of the village, so quickly drove round by the other road, to ambush her along the path. He left the tractor running, with the brakes on, and made his way along the pad by the river at Dunadry.

Passing the bleaching mill, a memory was re-enacted: a boy and a girl, heading home from school, were swinging on the scaffolding at a wall that was being repaired. The girl could not reach, so the boy lifted her by the waist until her hands grabbed the bar. She was light; it was like tossing a pancake in the air. She swung, smiling, laughing, shrieking. She had no strength and slipped to the ground. She had no muscles, no fat, no shape at all; all she was was bone and tears.

Snapping back into reality, Thomas looked up from the path to see Pamela before him, carrying a big brown paper bag.

"Running errands?" he asked, interrupting her humming.

"For me mammy," she copied his snidey tone. "I wasn't at work th' day, not well." They wandered along the path by the river's edge. "Want a sweet? I've got a craving for them these days." She offered him a boiled sweet, clutching her bag awkwardly in the crook of one arm.

Taking one from her palm, he commented, "Right enough, you'll be as fat as Emily before long."

Setting her shopping down by a boulder, she ran a hand over her belly. "Why be so hostile, Thomas?"

"Sorry."

They were beneath the dark trees. The rattling of the mill machinery, the constant moan of his tractor and the gush of the race were competing with their voices. Pamela sat down on a large stone. Thomas plonked himself beside her. He sat watching a spider in a tree trying to make a web. The outline of the design had already been constructed, but the wet branches meant that the insect kept slipping and hanging in mid-air at the end of its silvery strand. It reeled itself up, only to fall again. Eventually, it abseiled down to the branch beneath and ran towards the trunk, disappearing from sight.

She stared at him expectantly. "So, you've noticed I'm expecting a baby."

"*You are*? No, I didn't ... well, I suppose I did just ... I can't believe it." He spoke hollowly, faintly, shocked by the news. He kept thinking, this was his *sister*. "I can't believe it. But you're ... well ..." Not daring to mention the unspeakable, he muttered, "... it seems so wrong."

She opened her arms, letting her belly protrude from beneath the thick coat. "And it's not alright for me, but it is for your cousin Mary?"

"But ... well, for a start, she's married."

"Only just. And what difference does it make, anyway?"

"It makes *all* the difference. It's not natural to have a child ... like this. How can you be sure? Surely, you can't be havin' a baby, there must be some mistake?"

She sighed long and low. She couldn't be bothered going over with him all that she had so many times in her own mind. "Well, that's just the way it is."

Still in a daze, staring at the sky, here bathed the words, "But, Pamela, we only kissed ... once."

She was drawn into a lighter mood by his misconception, so she placed a hand on his shoulder and tried to reassure him.

"*You're* not to blame!"

"Don't blame *yourself*," he urged her. "I'm sure it wasn't your fault, Pamela. It must've been predestined, or something."

She thought his simple response was touching. Certainly, she knew, she had been an innocent victim of *his* lust. She laid her head on his shoulder, relief bursting from her. "Thank you for caring about me, Thomas. It's good that you're so nice to me. Yes, I think you may be right," her flashing eyes penetrated his, "I don't think it was something I could've prevented."

"An act of God," he said. "But, I think it's incredible how it happens, that women get pregnant, just from ... doin' that."

How had he done it? Had he breathed into her as they kissed, or something? Had his seed sprayed into her through his spittle? Had the Holy Ghost descended upon her, there, as they leant against the tree root, in the middle of the Hidden Drive? Thomas pictured that fateful kiss, when they had been oblivious to the process of incestuous procreation, which he now reckoned they had been unwittingly indulging in. It was all too terrible to contemplate.

"It doesn't make any sense to me. It's like a miracle."

"Aye, it was a bit of a shock to me, too, when I discovered that there's more to it than just a bit of fun." She laughed, recalling her naïvety about what she had been doing with *him*. "But, you never know where these things lead to."

A sense of maturity and responsibility stirred in him and, thinking he was doing the honourable thing, Thomas proposed: "So-o, I expect you want to get married?"

She thought hard about *him*. "No. It wouldn't be right."

"No. No, I suppose it is impossible. But ... don't you care what people will say?"

"That's my problem."

Flabbergasted, he said, "You're taking it very well."

"I've had time to get used to the idea."

"What'll you do?"

"Dunno. But I'll muddle through, somehow."

"Look, I've got to go an' milk the cows. Can I talk to you about this again sometime?"

"Yes, yes, you go on."

"D' you want me to walk you home, or anythin'?"

"No, I'll be fine."

So, he headed home, his heart feeling heavy.

Like father like son.

Had he followed in his dirty oul' uncle-father's footsteps? Was history repeating itself? But his crime had not really been his fault. Had his uncle also been oblivious to *his* sin? Or had the oul' goat done it *knowingly*? This was terrible, terrible! But he would just *have* to live with it, grin and bear it.

As ye sow, so shall ye weep!

Fortunately, his mind was saved from dwelling too long on this terrible revelation because Hugh Begley appeared in the yard, just as Thomas was mucking out after the milking. He had come in the trap. Uncle Stan had bought a new gelding and Hugh was trying him out. He offered Thomas a spin.

Hugh drove at a keen pace. He flicked the reins and the springs of the trap rocked. Thomas gripped the side as the trap sped faster and faster along the Belfast line.

Another trap up ahead was moving steadily, but Hugh caught up with it. It was getting dark and the lamps at either side of the trap were a poor guide. Hugh began to pull out to overtake the other trap. Its driver urged on his steed like a courageous charioteer. There were lights in the distance, but Hugh raced on beside the man in the top hat, wheels rattling, heading on a collision course.

"Careful," Thomas warned, "it might be a car."

Hugh cracked his whip. They drew ahead of the bloke in the top hat. Hugh swerved his gelding over in front of the beaten vehicle. Swoosh! The lorry roared past them.

Thomas breathed deeply. Yet he felt exhilaration, not fear. Live dangerously! Mission accomplished! This was the thrill of the chase. Hugh turned the trap at Paradise Walk.

"How was that, then?"

"This is living! Hugh ... Y'know, they say Adolf Hitler likes fast cars, an' I can see why. This is like the sail I had in Dr Moore's car. Hugh, I'm not sure about it yet, but I'm thinking of clearing off. Joining up. Get a bit more excitement. Broaden my horizons. Get away from this place."

"I'm content to dig for victory," he replied. "Don't say to anybody, but between you and me and the four winds, I think you'd be silly to go off an' be cannon fodder."

"I've messed things up, here. If I stay here, I'll just sink deeper and deeper into the Slough of Despond." He sighed.

"Miseryguts! What on earth are you moping about?"

"It's personal. I just need a new start, y'know? A breath of fresh air."

"Right!" Hugh grinned, flicking his whip once more.

God was by Thomas's bed. He was lying on the bedspread with his feet at the pillows, his head propped up by one hand. It was still rough. He would take his time with this one. This was the Big One: the Father. It had to be perfect. The other two were no use. But practice makes perfect. He would get this one right, for sure. It would be as surreal as anything.

He reached for his Bible. He closed his eyes and opened the book, letting it fall to whichever page Destiny ordained. His nostrils flared as the dry mustiness of the pages – like the smell of a rained-on, sun-dried newspaper you find in the hedge at the roadside – caused his throat to itch. And his finger sought out St John, chapter twenty, verse twenty-seven:

> 'Then saith he to Thomas, Reach hither thy finger, and behold my hands; and reach hither thy hand, and thrust it into my side; and be not faithless, but believing.'

Here was hope! He didn't understand what it could mean to him, yet, but he knew he must have faith, he must believe that God had preordained this turn of events for some *good* reason, even if he was unaware as yet of what it was.

"Thomas! Milkin'!" his mother called.

He got off the bed, setting his Holy Bible on the bedside cabinet. He hurriedly took the carving over to the wardrobe and set it inside, on the shelf, before going to the hall for his boots.

It was time for the grand switching on. They hadn't quite finished wiring up the house yet, but the byre was ready. Thomas was intrigued. He flicked the black switch. The 60 watt bulb burst into light. The byre was basked in brightness, as if it was a summer's afternoon, rather than the early evening gloom. Every nook and cranny was starkly visible. There were no shadows in the corners, no dullness anywhere: all was light. Like the church on a winter's evening, it remained strong and did not fade away or wisp as lamplight does. Because this was man-made light. This was praxis, action, defining your own destiny.

"Put that out! Wastin' 'lectric in here, burnin' money. The lamps'll do. I'm nippin' round fer a word wi' Patsy Duggan. Thont bull of his is in our fiel', mibbe he wants it shifted afore the cows go out again. I'll be back in a moment. Yer mither's away t' call the cows, y' kin go gie her a hand."

Thomas went to the fields to call the ladies in for their milking. In the field next to the one the milkers were in, he saw his mother already across the field, near the far hedge. She was bringing in a lame cow and its calf, clearly unaware that Patsy Duggan's bull was prancing towards her from behind a big whin[35] bush. Thomas shouted

---

[35]whin = gorse.

and she looked round to see the bull snorting and lowering his head, while he menacingly flexed a foreleg.

She hared off, darting along the hedge, with Patsy's red bull bounding behind her. The lame cow was hobbling in the other direction; the startled calf was galloping ahead with its tail in the air.

His heart skipped. As Thomas ran forward, the adrenaline streaked through him. He paused with a gasp of relief as he saw the bull halting. His mother and the lolloping cow slowed their pace once they were halfway across the field. The bull pranced around in the corner, grumbling and shaking his neck. As his mother reached the gate, he asked, "Are you alright? Didn't you know it wuz there? Uncle Isaac's gone round to see Patsy about it. Did it give ye a fright?"

"I'm not afeared of him," she snorted, giving the bull the evil eye. "What's he doin', goin' round there, anyway, crawlin' to them? He should make them come an' chase the thing away outta amongst our yokes, back over till its own side. It's all right for them Duggans, there's a whole brood of them," she said pugnaciously. "They kin afford t' lose one. But there's only you an' me an' your uncle here."

Thomas soothed her, "I suppose, when it comes down to it, family's the most important thing."

Fred had been talking about Buddhism again. The idea of reincarnation seemed weird. If Jesus had been the earthly incarnation of God, why had He never mentioned karma? Probably because it was an occult phenomenon, not part of the creed that Christians were supposed to follow. He reckoned Fred was trying to cloud his thoughts with doubt. There were many gods for the Hindus, he had said, as many Hinduisms as there are Hindus. And there were all the ancient Greek and Roman and Celtic deities. If our God existed, could these gods? Thomas tried to convince himself that there was no alternative to God: the ancients were just wrong, just interpreted it all in a primitive way. They were stupider than us. Maybe now, in nineteen thirty-nine, people were smarter than they were in Jesus's day. Maybe now it was time for a new religion? Yet Jesus had showed the way: selflessness – love others, be good to them, do good for and to them.

And how he would like a better life, himself! A happy wee life somewhere, with a wife and youngsters. With Pamela as his cuddly bride, of course. Maybe he and Pamela could run away to the States?

He could be a rancher and love Pamela, as a knight of the range loves his coquette, living in the splendid desolation of the Wild West. But that would hardly happen, for she couldn't possibly be his now. And yet ... there was Uncle Isaac and his mother ... here, together, in this house ...

"Isn't America the land of freedom and opportunity?"

Fred was abruptly stirred from his milking. "North, south, east, west – home's best."

"But surely dreams can come true in America."

"Reality is always imperfect in comparison to one's fantasies. But dreams aren't real experiences."

"If the world was all Socialist run, surely there'd be no class conflict and no poverty."

And no moral hypocrisy ... like, concerning marriage, Thomas pondered.

"Balderdash. Besides, co-operatives are a much better idea than a state-run affair. There's the incentive for the individual as well as the workin' together. Wealth, like all things, is best in moderation. The kind of wealth the landlords had, that's obscene. And so is the poverty we all know too well. An honest day's pay for an honest day's work. That's the ticket."

A little while later, Thomas spoke again, boldly asking, "Fred, what's the best way to handle wimin?"

Fred chortled as he milked. "From the far end of a bargepole!"

His voice was shaking as he asked, "How do you make a girl stay in love with you?"

Fred sat back on his stool, surprised by the question. "Are you doin' some serious courtin', Thomas?"

"No. Just curious. Fer when I need t' know, y'know."

"Whisper sweet nothings in her ear. Tell her she's the most beautiful woman in the world. Flatter her. But don't be too hot and bothered, either. Make her think you might have more than one iron in the fire. Or, if all else fails, forget about her. None of them are anything but trouble."

Forget about her? Could he? Was there more to life than romance, than this sad craving for love?

When Isaac appeared, Fred told him there was a wake he'd like to go to. The boss was obliging; he hurried away, hoping to get a lift to Banbridge with Jack McGuigan.

As the streams of warm milk squished into his bucket, Thomas was summoning up the courage to speak. His mother had finished her cows and had gone to the house to get the supper ready. There was just the two of them there: it would be man to man.

It was time. How many times had he sat on this stool milking? How many mornings and nights in this byre? Seven, wasn't he, when he started? Here before school; then in the evenings before tea and bed. He didn't so much leave school as just not go back after the Easter break – they were so busy with the spud dropping – a few years back, when he was twelve. No such thing as him getting the chance to go for a scholarship. Not that he was sad to get out from under Master Brooke's cane!

But there had been some good crack. It was nice to be in the open fields, not stuck in a factory or office. Bare brown fields, turning green, then golden; then dry and cut; ploughed again. Calves born, lambs skipping, growing into yearls, then big beasts. An egg; a scaldy chick tweeting; then a fluffy big hen itself.

Did he want to be here when he was *his* age? he asked himself, staring at his uncle's bent back. Grey-haired, stiff, belly getting soft. He couldn't stick it that long! To be in this same byre in forty years time – still here by hurricane lamp, because he was too tight to put the electric lights on! – with the stools scraping on the floor, the strones of milk jarring in his skull! This was so tedious! He had to get out of this. Escape! Soon! To find fresh air. To breathe!

His thoughts were displaced: it seemed as if he had voided his body and was watching someone else. He witnessed himself walk from the unfinished cow to where the other man was working. He poked his uncle's shoulder with an extended index finger. The lined face looked round.

"I'm not staying here. I want to join up."

The old mouth opened, exposing yellowing teeth. "I'm going t' go like James Ritchie did, to Liverpool, and join up over there. Not hang about here, waiting for ages for an acceptance letter like James Ussher did ..."

"What's got into you?"

"You need to ask?" he hammered out each syllable.

"Your mother's the one that would have to sign the papers."

"Aye, but you know rightly if you coax her to, she will," he said firmly.

"I wudn't be so sure about that. But sure, there's no sense in your goin', Thomas ..."

"I want you to tell her to let me go!"

Isaac moved, the stool fell over, clattered. He gripped the sleeves of Thomas's shirt. He was on his knees, in the dung. "What are you sayin'?" His face was screwed up. "What's got into your head?"

Thomas tried to step back, but would have dragged the elderly man with him. "I'm fed up with this place. I want to go places and see things."

"We're lost wi' out you." He suddenly sobbed. His eyes were watery. "I can't look after this place on me own. I need you. Don't do this ... There's nobody else. Don't leave us, son. We need you. It's all yours, anyway. It's all for you."

"Son! Son! *Am* I your son, am I?"

"I've always treated you like a son, haven't I? I've no *real* fam'ly of me own, so this place," he moved his arm, "it'll go to you, you know that. Who else is there to get it? Nob'dy. Would you just desert your ma, would you just leave your home an' fam'ly an' go away an' end up mibbe killed in a French field and be buried where there's nob'dy t' even put a flower on your grave? Don't do what Bobby did. I know I might be rough on you at times, Thomas, but I can't help the way I am. I've not done anything deliberately, you know that, don't you? Am't I fair? You got goin' to the Isle of Man, eh? You've not got it as bad as some round here ..."

"I want a *real* father!" He shook him.

"What's done is done, son. I tell ye, I tried at the time to prevent it from happ'nin'. But I just wasn't able ..." he bowed his head. "I tried to explain to your mother what would happen ..."

So it was true! "Shut up! Shut up! I don't wanna hear this!"

"What's happened can't be undone. But let it be. What's important is what we have here and now. You're young, you've your whole life ahead of you. Don't let these wee worries spoil it. Look what you kin do with this place ..."

"But I don't know nuffin'. I can't even plough properly."

"You can plough a darn sight better than I could at your age. If you wait till you're eighteen, you can go-a your own accord, then, if your heart's still set on it."

"Th' war'll be over be then!"

"At least wait a while an' think about it. I wouldn't stop y' goin', if y' really wanted to; but your ma'd take some convincin'. And I don't want t' lose you, either. Don't go, Thomas." He kept repeating it and repeating it as he clung to the young man. He kept on crying, "Don't go! Don't leave us!"

Thomas began to weep, too. "Alright, alright!" he bellowed.

He tore himself away from his uncle's grasp. Shaking, too frightened and embarrassed to look round and have to face the old man's emotion, he sat at his stool again. He buried his face in the cow's comfy flank and began to milk again.

Having finished his cow, his uncle got to his feet and, as he wiped his face with a grubby handkerchief, his shaking voice reiterated, "Don't leave us, Thomas, please."

CHAPTER TEN

Severed Branch

The dark days had arrived. The evenings were shorter, the mornings colder. The plants all around were beginning to shed the signs of life. The weeds were withering. The countryside was shrivelling as time trudged towards the most miserable season.

The big saw was rrrassping. Fred and Thomas were tugging and thrusting the serrated blade between them, sawing at a twisty old apple tree. A strained creaking warned them that it was time for the tree to totter and faint. It toppled gently, tossing its rusty head of leaves as it lay down. They moved along to another victim.

"No! No!" Jean was coming running towards them. "Mother's orchard! Daddy planted those trees when they were courting, for her. You can't cut down Mother's apple trees!"

"Shut up, shut up, shut up!" he bellowed at her.

Jean stopped in her tracks. Her face had been full of pain; now, it displayed surprise. A wary fear began to crease her eyes.

"Go away int' the house and leave us in peace!" His face was red, bloated with anger.

"You calm yourself," she remonstrated, sobering up herself and leaving them.

"Is she in one of her funny moods?" Fred asked.

"She's a pain in the neck," Thomas snapped, bending back to the saw.

"You shouldn't be so hard on her. And it's not like you to be ratty, Thomas."

"She'd try the patience of a saint!"

Fred laughed heartily. "Why are we chopping down her precious orchard, anyway? Your uncle never said anything to me about it. I hope you've not taken it off your own bat to do this?"

"No. He toul' her we were for fellin' them. They're done. No yield. Too oul'. Sure, apple trees are there t' produce apples. If they don't, they're no use."

"And oul' people?" his eyes pierced Thomas's slyly.

"How'll we ever get these roots out, that's what I want to know. We'll kill ourselves diggin' all these up." He looked around at the white stumps in the grass. "Maybe we could pull them out with the tractor?"

"There's tarry stuff you put on them and it stops them budding and they rot away. They just crumble to dust."

Ashes to ashes, dust to dust.

Thomas muttered, "Killing trees instead of men."

"Much more preferable," Fred commented, as the saw ate its way through another trunk. "Y'know, the pioneers in America had such big trees to clear, they ringed the bark and the trees died and then they were easier to remove. But they had to dig up the roots. Of course, we have chemical compounds now, to do the job more quickly. Poison them. That's progress. We learn tricks, that's what makes us superior to dumb animals. Like rabbits: they don't pass on their knowledge from generation to generation, they still keep getting caught in traps. Or your dog: she drinks lint hole water year after year and keeps on getting a sore head. When will they ever learn?"

"There's plenty-a ones around about does a similar thing! An', anyway, I bet Help won't bite at tracteur wheels again."

"Aye. Intelligence is a matter of degrees. Each to his own level. Like, it takes a buddy like Hitler to run a Reich. Could you run a country? I know I couldn't. Nature imposes limits on all of us. Like, we can do this kind of job and women have their housework."

"Mummy helps gather spuds. And thin turnips. And ... But I know what you mean. I couldn't have a baby, could I? Unless God caused me to have one, through a process whereby His supernatural, spiritual will transcended the physical limitations."

Fred was rendered silent for a moment. "Aye, well," he stood back as another apple tree fell, "I wouldn't know about *that*."

Thomas was sitting on the wide window sill in his room, dressed in his suit, whittling at his piece of wood. In her present state of mind his mother had forgotten about the visit until her brother had reminded her at the last minute and now she was scurrying about in the kitchen, cooking and cleaning and panicking. The point of the Bowie knife jarred a line into the figure. God – no: the Father. He looked up as he heard the motorcar outside. He put his statuette in the wardrobe and went to join the party in the kitchen.

The Reverend Dr Marsh's beard was neatly trimmed. He sat in Uncle Isaac's chair, waiting for them to pay court.

Thomas was more interested in seeing his wife up close for the first time. At church she sat at the front and slipped out halfway through to take the children's Sunday School. She had flowing red hair, was slight of build, young, jolly, reminiscent of a summer bloom. He was captivated by her charming face and friendly smile.

The conversation began with the weather and the news about Warsaw falling to the Germans. Safe subjects. Uncle Isaac brought up some Elders' business with the Reverend Marsh: a window in the hall was broken, has been boarded up but should be fixed before the winter gales came along.

Jean ushered them to the parlour for dinner. The table was spread with the good china and Granny's silver cutlery. The family photographs had been dusted and Uncle Robert's medals in the cabinet had been polished. Fred politely seated Mrs Marsh. A course of soup was served. The Reverend Marsh said grace.

Thomas noticed some old photographs on the top of the cabinet which he had not seen before. His mother must have dug them up out of somewhere. One had the brothers side by side: Uncle Isaac as a lanky young man, in loose shirt and trousers, beside Uncle Robert in his Army uniform – negative medals – and Uncle Tom, before he ran off to Scotland and fell off a cliff.

The other was of the sisters. This black and white picture was of three skinny teenagers with their hair in plaits. Aunt Sarah and Auntie Josie and Mummy when they were schoolgirls, before he was born! The wee one with the round eyes and the pert little nose had a mole on her cheek, so it had to be Mummy. She had had a smoother face then, a fresher complexion. She looked like ...? Reminded him of Pamela! A bit. Not quite as pretty, though? And so his thoughts were filled with her. And with his distress and anger, that his desire had been frustrated, because she could never be his. For them to be friends was little comfort to him.

"I see you have been clearing the paddock," the Reverend Dr Marsh commented.

"It was Mother's apple orchard. But the trees are so old," Jean told the guests, "they were almost completely barren."

"What a pity," Mrs Marsh sympathised. "I do so love the scent of apple blossom in the springtime."

Her teeth were pure white, her tongue a salmon pink, her eyes emerald green, her voice as succulent as strawberries. Thomas studied her face intently. Yes, a likeness of Harriet Hart, only much prettier. A hint of freckles on the bridge of her nose, though it was straighter than Harriet's, more like Pamela's. And her posh accent was so ... cultivated.

"I'm told," Dr Marsh chatted, "that the olive trees on the Mount of Olives have grown from the bases of the same ones that were growing there so fruitfully when the Lord Jesus Himself walked this earth. Margaret and I were fortunate enough to be able to visit the Holy Land a few years ago. Weren't we, my dear? And we also visited the pyramids in Egypt, while we were in that part of the world."

Margaret! The same name, same manner, same angelic voice as his English lover. Coincidence? Or Fate? Should he take her in his arms, sweep her off to Scotland, to the romantic, heathery highlands, there to live a simple crofter's life poor but happy, with his angel Margaret?

This is a nice bird, Fred was saying to himself as Thomas drifted into an unrealistic reverie. How did an old coot like this end up with such a corker? He was a university man, though. And these Holy Joes were all into the psychological conditioning lark. Talk of eternal love and peace and hope and joy – women were suckers for that stuff. Sweet nothings. Fred peered over his soup spoon as he sucked the homemade broth through his teeth. She had a nice handful, firm and pearshaped, just the way he liked them, with the nipples pointing up. And her a clergyman's wife: God forgive me! And young Thomas looked like he had the hots for her, too. Dream on, sunshine! Fred laughed to himself. Aye, you and me both.

"Thomas, now that everyone's finished, will you give me a hand to fetch the main course? Please excuse us.

He collected the soup plates and followed his mother to the kitchen. She served the beef, potatoes and vegetables and he carried them through to the diners in the parlour as Uncle Isaac poured them each a glass of ginger wine.

"I expect this war will have an impact on prices," the clergyman said to the farmer.

"Yes, indeed."

Jean blurted, "There's only one lad here. If there were more of us, we could spare a soul. But our family's made its blood sacrifice already, in the last war." She gestured to the photograph of her brothers. "Robert died for us. He fell at the Somme."

Mrs Marsh smiled, appreciatively. Uncle Isaac looked out the window. The Reverend Dr Marsh produced his handkerchief and blew his nose. Fred poured himself into his glass of wine.

"Uncle Robert died with his boots on," Thomas blurted.

Mrs Marsh smiled, uncomfortably. His uncle swapped a stare with Fred. The Minister took a sip of *his* ginger wine.

The guest bridged the gulf of silence as they ate. "And are you a native of these parts, Mr Nelson?"

"I'm from the County Down. In fact, I'll be returning there when my term here's finished. I've got another job lined up nearer home. Back to God's own county, at last."

"Yes," Uncle Isaac said, "the wanderer returns."

"Will you be on the lookout for a new man, then, Mr Gray?"

"Oh, we can cope over the winter. There's a casual labourer usually comes this way about Christmas time, stays a while. Good ploughman."

"I thought Paul was dead," Thomas whispered to his mother.

"No, dear," she answered. "Not yet, that I've heard."

"I see from my records, Thomas," the Minister went on, "that we don't have you as a Communicant. Would you like to come to classes next week?"

"I've done all the classes," he stuttered. "Just I was sick last time."

"Something you 'ate?" Fred said to his plate.

"Or *drank*," Isaac said, comprehending Fred's inflection but fearing that his sister might not and would think Fred was criticising her cooking.

Be sure your sins will find you out.

The whiskey! There, he'd been found out. Thomas leapt to his feet. "Forgive me! But I didn't know it was wrong!"

His mother calmed him. "Thomas! There's no need to burst out like this. You couldn't help being ill."

He sat down, his face masked with worry. Had Uncle Isaac been tuning in just then? Maybe he was switched off, now. He prayed for forgiveness and for protection from his uncle's wrath. He bared his teeth, chewing some meat like a dog.

"I like this presbytery very much," Dr Marsh volunteered. "I find my colleagues all share my outlook. I'm not fond of these newfangled interpretations. Liberal wish-wash. 'There's nowt like a bit of oul'-fashionedness', as my father used to say. I just can't see that the fundamentals of the faith as revealed in the Bible could be in need of being *improved* or tampered with. I pride myself on my academic ability, yet do not see why other theologians feel they need to revolutionise our doctrine. Our religion is about ..."

"Love!" Thomas blurted out. Mrs Marsh's surprised smile made her look *so* pretty, it embarrassed him.

"... Yes, it is. But, primarily it is about the Salvation of Jesus Christ, as recorded in the Holy Bible."

"And the creation of Adam and Eve, as recorded in the Bible," Fred just couldn't contain himself any longer. He breached the social taboo and got a bit too near the quick, by asking, "Is that *literally* true?"

Jean glared at him. Isaac chewed furiously. Thomas's eyes were still straying in Mrs Marsh's direction as often as he thought possible without looking suspicious.

"Male and female, created He them. And though weak of the flesh as we are, it is also true to say that God cares about we mere mortals. He sent his Son to show us the Holy Way. God was in Christ. And so the Word was made flesh. And that is how we have been saved from our sin, from the weaknesses of our earthly nature."

Thomas experienced a sensation of wonder and joy. Yes, weak as we are, He forgives us. He had been weak, he had nearly succumbed to the worst of sins, but His grace saved him! This rapturous feeling was enough for Thomas, he did not need to listen much to the rest of the conversation. Besides, he had heard his mother's small talk and his uncle's yarns all before, and even Fred's stories about his adventures in America were becoming stale.

His mind was tired; he could not concentrate on anything. He felt an emptiness, like a sleepiness, sweeping him into the future and into the yard, where Mrs Marsh shook hands with Help, who was on her feet again, limping round in excited circles, and almost toppled over when she sat down, to hold up a skew-whiff paw. Why had she run to this strange lady? She was nice; but she was not real, she did not exist, not for him. He wanted a *real* woman, like Pamela. They were soon gone and he was glad to be waving at them from the yard gate as they headed off down the road, for he wanted only his bed and the oblivion of his fantasies.

The Begleys had been slow, as ever, getting their potatoes dug at the Holestone. Stan had taken the bit of land that Isaac Gray owned up there, since it was so handy to them. The wet weather had arrived and Uncle Stan was panicking about getting them lifted. Fred and Thomas were sent to give them a turn.

Mary had come to spend a while with them, too, for Hugh's break from school for the potato picking had ended and Aunt Sarah was a stickler for doing what should be done. Thomas asked her, "How does it feel to be a mother?"

"Tiring! The wee brat had me up all night."

"You shouldn't call your child that!"

"It's only a joke. I don't mean it. Don't you start. Mummy's bad enough."

"Are you happy married?"

"Sure. Who wouldn't be? Though I suppose it depends who you marry. I mean, James is my sweetheart. But I couldn't imagine being married to ... well, someone older, fer instance."

"What d'ya mean by older? Sure James *is* older than you."

"Yes, but I mean *really* old. Like Daddy's age."

"I heard that, girl. Less of your lip. You're as young as you feel. Right enough, this stoopin' quare an' ages you."

"Hey, Fred!" She sat back on her heels. "You've got streaks where you've been scratching your face. It looks like war-paint! You're a Red Indian."

Thomas got up to whoop and do a war dance. Mary clapped her hands. Uncle Stan looked over, but ignored the eejit. He said, "Fred's in love with Mrs Marsh. I saw you, lookin' at her like that, when they were at our house."

"I'm not like you, dreamin' about women and never doing anything about it. 'Faint heart ne'er won a fair lady'."

Thomas dropped to his work again. He drew out of the wet soil a slither of bone. Old, dry, yellowing bone. He showed it to Uncle Stan.

"Oh aye, that could be anything. Animal or human."

"Human?"

"Aye. There was a church and graveyard here, centuries ago." Thomas threw the bit of bone away. "We shouldn't be digging them up."

"There's no remains now. They'll have all rotted away to nothing long ago. But she's still a good field for growin'. Fertile. But sure, as I say, that bone could be of anything."

Fred interjected, "It might be a bit of dinosaur bone. Imagine the days before the Ice Age when the hills of Antrim were volcanoes and big dinosaurs roamed freely!"

Thomas dispassionately replied, "Sure, dinosaurs are no use to nobody. What were they here for?"

"Same applies to us. What are we here for? No purpose at all, as far as I can see. It's up to each of us to chose a life for ourselves."

Thomas went over to the edge of the dry ditch and relieved himself. He was shaking his willie when he slipped on wet grass and tumbled forward into the hedge. His arm caught a bramble, but he went into the bottom of the sheugh. He felt jags. He sat up and saw that he had several thorns embedded in his hosepipe (as Fred had once called it). Spots of blood were appearing. He began picking out each one gingerly, then rubbed the red marks with spittle on a finger tip. They formed a pattern. It was like a crown of thorns: a symbol of the Christian life, reminding him that this world was a testing ground, where we face cosmic challenges, which we must overcome for His sake.

He saw over the lip of the sheugh that Mary was laughing at his tumble. He frowned and kept his back to her as he tenderly extracted the little tusk-shaped, green hooks. Was this a punishment – or at least a warning – telling him that the stirrings he was beginning to experience more frequently now were wicked, profane? He must not yield to the temptation, in the dark of night, to tease himself, however exciting it felt! He must resist, deny, those base yearnings. He was slipping down the slippery slope to Hell, because he had discovered how to pull his stalk effectively - more like the way Sandy must've meant it was done, because it *worked*, it made him lose himself, it blew his socks off.

But he would have to try and will himself to not do it. It was evil! Self abuse, he'd heard someone say once, and now he knew what they meant! And hadn't he caused enough trouble? *And* suffered enough mental anguish, knowing, as he did, just what a disgusting thing he had done to – his *sister*, to poor wee Pamela. But, he sighed inwardly, there was no point in crying over spilt milk, no point in dwelling on the mistakes he'd made in the past. Life must go on.

When he had buttoned up, he moved along to a watering hole and squatted on his hunkers, to scoop up a drink of water.

"Don't drink out of the sheugh," Uncle Stan called over to him from the potato drills. "You can catch diseases from the rat's piss in the water."

He leaned forward pensively. "Why are you telling me this?"

"So's you don't do it and risk gettin' a disease," his uncle raised *his* voice in return.

For a short time his mind churned: he had had a mouthful – was he going to die? Who cares? Lethargically, he worked on. Later in the day, when they got to the end of the field, Uncle Stan set a potato on the summit of the pile on the cart and said, "The last yin."

"Are you gonna take this ground again next year?" Thomas asked.

"Are you lookin' to strike a deal?"

"No." He retreated, leaning against the cart and tumbling some spuds. Picking them up, he cushioned the impact of his brusqueness. "Sure, I know you'll be speakin' to Uncle Isaac about it. I was just ... askin'."

Laughing, Stan told him, "Oh, you be the businessman, son. Let that other oul' fella take a back seat. But look, I haven't thought about takin' this place from yous next year. With Mary's James goin' away, I'll have to see what way I'm fixed. Mibbe I'll git Hugh outta school. There's no point in him wastin' time sat in thonder when he could be out here, doin' somethin' useful. But no mind, we've plenty of time to surt it out, eh?"

"Have we time for tea?" Mary implored. "Let's head for home. I've got a wean wants seen to."

"We'd better mosey back to Islandreagh, though," he said. "The cows are waiting."

"Yeah," Fred added, "No rest for the wicked."

Does he mean me? Thomas was shaking inside as he got onto the tractor, but tried not to let his inner fragmentation show.

"Wasn't God a bastard!"

"Eh!" Fred looked round, taken aback by Thomas's outburst. "Look at what he did to Job."

"Thomas ...!" Fred was lost for words.

"God and the Devil, Good and Evil," he muttered obsessively. Things were piling up on top of him, things seemed to be out of his control. Nothing made sense anymore. "Black and White, there's a distinction, each has separate definition, but I don't see it at all. No! No! It's all black, black, black! It's all black!"

What the dickens was he on about? Sure, it was dark outside, but that was no call for this ranting. He was getting to be as bad as his mother. Isaac was coming, swaggering up the byre like the hero in a Wild West movie, so Fred ignored Thomas's dislocated rhetoric. The job in hand had long been deferred. They had kept the brown horny cow tied in the byre after the evening milking because she had been vicious last season - had dunted one of the other cows in the guts, so that it had had a dead calf and Isaac was determined there would be no more of that.

Fred put his arm around her neck, standing at one side of her head. Leaning over the byre stall wall, balancing on an oil drum, Isaac held her head tipped over by holding the horn down and ear forward. Thomas squeezed along the other side of the cow and began working on the first horn with a tenon saw. The cow strained her head and wheezed but her attempts to move were controlled by the two men. His arm pistoned with acquired dexterity. As the saw passed the halfway stage, blood began to seep from the incision. The heavy aroma of the blood was intoxicating. The saw sprinkled red drizzle along Thomas's arm and rolled up shirt sleeve. When the last of the horn gave way with a jolt, a bulb of plasma bulged at the wound like a mud spring beginning to bubble.

"I dunno why you prefer th' wee saw, I'd use the wire saw. Get a move on, bae. An' cut th' other yin nearer th' heed," Uncle Isaac instructed. "If a job's worth doin' at all, it's worth doin' well."

Thomas and Fred swapped sides. The horny cow shook her sore head from side to side, thumping the remaining horn on the top of the stall, near Fred's face. She bumped her tender spot, roared and bucked in the byre stall.

"Quit it! Quit it!" Isaac bellowed louder than the cow could manage.

They forced her to be still. Fred clamped his fingernails into her nostrils to hold her nose and yanked her head around severely. She breathed rapidly, shivering like a scared child. As she moved, tissue tore. Her dripping snotter was stained crimson. Isaac twisted her tail, then seized her horn and ear.

Thomas sawed as quickly as possible, wanting to get the operation over for both their sakes. The horn cracked and hung loose by the shell. He had nicked an artery, so a jet of warm, sticky blood spurted from the fleshy centre of the bared root. Trying to catch the hinged horn, he got squirted by the intermittently pumping jet. Isaac got hold of it and broke off the horn. He held the cow still as Thomas and Fred sidled out of the stall. When he let the cow go, this time she did not riot, but stood huffing and snorting. The stream of blood gradually lost power and splattered less and less over the stall wall. When the wound had congealed and the cow had recovered her composure, the chain was unhooked and Fred walked the grateful beast out to the Far Orchard, where the herd was picking at the grass.

"She'll find it funny for a while," grinned Fred.

"Like getting a tooth pulled," Uncle Isaac agreed.

"Life's like that, sometimes, eh?" Fred observed. "You get tied up, your tail twisted, terrible things done to you, and you think Destiny's got it in for you. But, really, when you look at it from the perspective of the Big Picture, it was all for the best, regardless of your personal feelin's."

"Mibbe," agreed Isaac. "After all, this is supposed t' be the best of all possible worlds."

"She's not a horny cow, now." Thomas's statement was made in an angry, hollow tone, as if the mind that constructed the comment was somehow absent and had set the words adrift in an endless ocean of sensation.

"He who has a why to live can bear with any how," was Fred's advice.

"He who has a saw can break the horn off any cow!" was Isaac's contribution to the erudition. "Come on away in fer yer supper, you two, an' let's quit this philosophisin' an' these poetry recitals. And your mother's got a surprise for afters for *you* th' night, Thomas." A corner of his mouth curled.

After tea, Thomas found out what the surprise was. Pat pat pat pat pat pat pa-at – pat pat pat pat pat pat pa-at.

"Why don't we get a horse churn like Kaye's horse thresher?"

His mother's attention was diverted from the board, where she was shaping butter. She looked up, watched her son plunging the handle into the wee wooden, barrel-shaped churn. "We don't make enough for that."

He continued the rhythm of plunge and *pull* up, plunge and *pull* up, plunge and *pull* up, plunge ... His arms were beginning to twinge, his shoulder blades were aching, there was a niggling tightness down a hamstring. The milk was hardly thickening at all. He looked across from his mother's work corner at the two men. His uncle had his hands crossed before him as he lay in his armchair, blinking occasionally. Fred had his head in a book.

"Is that Nietzsche?" Thomas disturbed him.

"It's your *Robber's Roost*," Fred grinned, exposing the spine.

"D' ye like the Zane Grey then?"

"It's a bit ... melodramatic."

"I'm fed up," Thomas sighed, after a while.

"Don't you give up." Uncle Isaac pointed a finger. "You would get lynched in the Army fer sayin' the like-a that."

"But the butter won't come."

His uncle frowned, surprised and angered by the audacity of him speaking back, but did not respond.

"It must be cursed by the Little People," said his mother.

"The wee skit ..." he almost used bad language.

His mother's eyes bulged. Uncle Isaac's head turned and even Fred's head turned. But he did not pay attention to their moral outrage. Instead, his mind was engrossed in his own endeavours. He set about the churning with a revised sense of application. He needed to use the Will to Power; he had to free himself of his human weakness and frailty. Yes, yes! His muscles began to surge with strength. He *had* the ability to defeat the Little People's ungodly spells and make the butter come. Come! Come! *Come!* It would come. God willing.

The spur was not the Hallowe'en Party, though he was looking forward to a night out. He laboured quite cheerfully, full of energy. His heart was light. He petted the cows and swept out the byre with excessive vigour. He had the lend of Terence's bicycle. But he also had a particular determination: he was going to visit Pamela and he was going to sort it out, once and for all, this time.

He had this nagging worry, maybe it would be born with two heads or something. And anyway, why couldn't they, if not marry, at least live together? If, as he had been led to believe, his mother and Uncle were living in incestuous sin together, why shouldn't he and Pamela do the same? Maybe it was the Gray Destiny, maybe it was in his nature to be like this. Could God have willed it so? Or was he an unwitting disciple of the Devil? All he knew was, this passion for Pamela that was burning in him was stronger than he was.

The evening meal, the wash in the parlour, the careful shaving, the hurried dressing, all seemed to take so long. He was wasting time here, he hurried out, to get motoring. The wartime restrictions meant that the front bike lamp was blinkered. He peered into the black night, swishing along the damp road hastily, with complete disregard for safety.

It was Doomsday: time to face the music. She had sounded a bit unsure before, so he thought he was in with a chance. But what if she turned round and *categorically* refused him? No, she wouldn't – she would see sense, especially when she knew how much he truly loved her. He wouldn't take 'no' for an answer this time.

He sped past the two churches: his own Dunadry Presbyterian, at the bridge and then, beyond the Clady Works, he passed their wee public elementary school and Muckamore Presbyterian church. He took it easy as he approached old Johnnie Fisher, who was sitting on his three-wheeler bike, with the wee cart behind it, parked at Agnes Hughes'. Johnnie was leaning over the garden wall, yarning. Agnes was throwing some meal to her chickens.

The chat between the housewife and the traveller gradually became audible the nearer Thomas got.

"Imagine, a nice fella like him, doing a thing like that. It's a disgrace, an outrage, if the stories I heard can be believed. Do you think he done it?"

"No smoke without fire. Like father like son. And like mother like daughter!" Johnnie turned his head as Thomas reached them. "'Lo, Thomas."

"'Lo. 'Lo. Kin y' lemme have half a dozen eggs, Mrs Hughes? Our hins are layin' poorly this weather."

Thomas pursed his lips; his throat was dry. And so they were *too* laying poorly, so he wasn't guilty of lying. What he was more perturbed about was this pair's talk he had just overheard. Despite his fears, Mrs Hughes didn't ask any awkward questions or confront him with any horrid, home truths. Johnnie remained suspiciously silent.

Thomas paid Agnes, thanked her and hurriedly moved off. He felt a searing heat at the back of his head as he rode away, not daring to look round; his ears were burning with their derision and scorn. Was it really him they were gossiping about? People must really despise him, to do it so brazenly, when he was so near at hand. Did they hate him terribly?

He pedalled on. He slowed as he began to go uphill, his legs feeling the change in rotation as he reached the crest. Soon, he was passing Ben's goat-house and was trundling down Summerhill Lane.

The dark bulk of the tenement building loomed before him. The riverside was strangely quiet at night – it possessed an eerie, ringing discordance during the silent hours, when the beetling mill was at rest. The blackout meant that there wasn't a chink of light glinting, for all of the block's numerous eyelids were tightly closed.

He rested the bicycle against the railing at the end of the gantry, which sloped up as a walkway to the upper level of homes. This was Alpha and Omega, the beginning and the end; the end of his loneliness and insularity, the beginning of an everlasting romance.

His precise footsteps echoed as he approached her door. It seemed the whole structure was shaking at the command of his resolute heels. At the door the noises of the inhabitants filtered through to his ears. His knocks seemed to be as loud as the hammerings of a hundred smiths, loud enough to wake the dead. There was a shadow at the two, thin, frosted panes of glass in the door. He sucked in a deep breath as the door slowly swung open.

"Oh, it's yourself. Are y' wantin' the wemen fer some work? Houl' on. Marbeth!"

"No. No, can I speak to Pamela? Houl' on, here. Here's somethin' fer yous."

Ben took the brown paper bag, peered inside and his face brightened a little. He muttered his thanks for the eggs and went off to get her. Thomas waited for quite some time, aware of the youngsters' squabbling inside and the others' lowered voices.

"Thomas Gray's here. He wants to see Pamela. He brought you a bag-a eggs."

"Wasn't that good of them?"

"What's he want to see *her* for?" he asked in an unkind tone.

Setting down the turnip she was hollowing out for wee Richard, Marbeth said, "Come with me, Ben." She tugged his arm and led him into the bedroom, where their eldest was ironing. "Aye, let's sort this out. He kin stand out there all night, as far as I'm concerned!" her husband snarled.

The children were shut out, while the grown-ups conferred, in voices as quiet as they could hush in the circumstances.

"What is it?" Pamela asked, seeing her father's face so hard. She was clearly much heavier now and even small movements, like her lumbering retreat from the ironing board as she sagged down on the bed, were exaggerated.

"Thomas Gray's here. What's he doin' here, to see a girl in your condition? So it was *him*?"

"No! I toul' Mummy who it was." She avoided her father's gaze.

"Leave the wee girl be."

"I want to know what that lad's here for."

"We're just friends."

"I dunno how you kin be friends wi' one of them Grays," snapped Ben. "Are you *sure* it wasn't him? I don't trust them 'uns, after the Hell they put your mammy through."

"How many times do I have to tell you, Ben, that was all a mix up. Why do you have t' bear a grudge? It was only Jean Gray's fool notions that made her do what she did. That's long dead an' buried in the past. Isaac's always had a job for Pamela an' me, hasn't he? Haven't they made up for it long ago."

"I niver heard of an apology from *her*, fer thinkin' you'd stoop so low as to try t' wheedle your way int' their money – silly oul' bitch!"

"Ben! Mind your language, in front of the girl."

"*Well*, an' so she is."

"It was a mistake Jean made, that's all. Let her stew in her own juice."

"Aye, she kin do that easy enough, fer she's an' oul' hypocrite t' boot! Sure, didn't she go an' get herself up the spout? At least you an' me had the daecency t' marry. She niver did! What surt of a man was it *she* dallied with, eh? One-a them oul' tinkers that's always hangin' about their place, wasn't it, eh? Some dirty oul' flea-bitten tramp, was that all the man she could attract? I'm not surprised! The sight of that God-awful, ugly oul' ... would put any *real* man aff."

"Keep your voice down, Ben, the children ... And don't be so unkind. She was brave an canny lookin' when she was younger. She's aged, that's all. Anyway, he's waiting, Pamela, to speak to you. Are you gonna speak to him?"

"Why *won't* she marry the other lad? It's not right! Who the Hell is he, anyway? Why won't yous damn wimin tell me any-damn-thin'? Tell me who he is, I'll make him marry you."

"He can't. Sure," Pamela attempted to state her case, "they've got no money, *he's* got nothin'!" Pamela began to cry, had to wipe away her tears with the back of her hand.

"Money's not an issue in a case like this."

"It doesn't matter, really, anyway. I don't want him. I don't! He's a beast! Sure, won't I be alright without any man at all?" she pleaded with her mother. "Nobody's goin' to want me now." Pamela struggled to her feet. She said to her mother, "I'd better go and speak to Thomas."

"Tell him to clear off t' blazes, if it's not his!"

"Ben," his wife remonstrated again, "have a heart."

He saw Pamela appear at the end of the hall. She went towards him slowly.

"Hello. Come in out of the cold."

He whispered, "Can I speak to you out here a minute?"

She did as he asked. As she raised her arms to slip on the coat, he could see her stomach sticking out. It revolted and frightened him, but he had no time to think about that, just now. She went out onto the gantry with him, pulling the door so that it clicked behind her, and they wandered away from the building, to the river's edge.

"Your eyes are red, have you bin cryin'? I heard somebody arguin'. Are they givin' you a hard time?"

"No, not at all. Daddy's just in one of his moods."

"Are yous havin' a party th' night?"

"The youngsters are fer lightin' a fire thonder, as usual," she nodded across the dark waste ground to the black mound. Our weans are goin' wild. As usual!"

"I'm off t' the Holestone. To James Mateer's. He has a perty every year. His farm marches a bit of ground we have up there. And he's right and great with Uncle Stan."

They stood side by side on the grass bank, which was already crisp with frost.

"I'm afraid there's talk about already," he said, recalling the bit of conversation he had overheard between Agnes and Johnnie.

She nodded disconsolately. "Aye. The scandal was bound to break sooner or later. I'm just glad you are here to give me moral support. There's not many men are as kind, are *gentle*men, like you. You understand. Is there something troubling *you*, Thomas? You seem all in a fluster about something."

He bowed his head, unable to catch her eyes. "It's this thing ... about me uncle and your mother ... an' all that."

"Don't you pay any heed to that story," she told him. He might be a friend, but there was no way he was going to call *her* mummy a gold-digger. She said defensively, "My mummy never did anythin' wrong!"

Not realising that the rumours she was referring to were different to the story he had picked up from Dickie, Thomas was elated and stunned by this miraculous information, which to him meant that she wasn't his sister after all. She *could* be his, after all! There was a God in Heaven!

"So," he cautiously asked, "we're still friends, aren't we? I'll come an' see you again, more often ...?" He moved to try and take hold of her.

"No, Thomas, my folks wouldn't be keen on the idea."

"What does it matter what they think?" he raged. "You should do what your heart tells you."

"That's been my problem," she taunted herself.

She thought about his offer of friendship. Perhaps she was being too hard on him. He couldn't help it if he was told the Gray's side of things. And it was nice of him to stick by her like this. Even Emily was less pally now. But no, it would be unfair of her to seek comfort in him. Folk would talk, it would be unfair on him.

"I appreciate your concern, Thomas. Honestly. I do like you, but ... It just wouldn't be fair."

He realised what she meant: it was unfair of him to force himself upon her, because he was unworthy of any nice girl: because *he* was

... like Sandy had said ... And if Sandy knew, the whole country must know. Being kissing cousins was one thing, but now that the enormity of her situation had emerged, he couldn't expect her to go so far as to tie herself down to a ...

"Aye," he said glumly, "I understand. *I'm* no good ... because of the *kind* of bastard I am."

"Don't put yourself down, Thomas."

"Pamela?" It was her father calling. "C'min outta th' coul', afore y' catch yer death."

"I better go in. I... I'm sorry if I've upset you ..."

He could tell by her tone that she was being genuine.

"I'll see y' about?" he asked earnestly. "Alright?"

He got on the bicycle and rode off. On the way to Holestone he felt like he'd been reborn and crucified all at the same time. He *had* been saved from a terrible fate. And even if he *was* a bastard he didn't care, except that it was putting Pamela off him. Her words cut into him like a knife: *it wouldn't be fair.*

This was like the trial of Job. But, he told himself, he should be thankful for the small mercy that at least she wasn't his sister after all. It didn't matter a hoot what his uncle had done, now that he was sure that he hadn't done the thing that Thomas felt was the most hurtful thing of all: be responsible for an unbridgeable abyss between Pamela and himself. Why had life this habit of building you up, only to slap you back down again, just when you thought you had found your El Dorado? If things were suddenly going right, for a change, why were they going wrong?

Nonetheless, he was relieved, more free of care and worry than he had been for ages, so the party seemed like a Heavenly experience in contrast to the long, darkening days he had just endured. Here, he was amongst friends. He knew what pleasure was again, after so long in his living Hell.

John Ussher was there with his girlfriend. When the lads were alone together, when Joan went off for a chat with Mary, Thomas told him what he had heard about Sandy's father dying and also the talk about Mr Thompson's antics as a Lothario, to which John listened with alert ears and eyes.

"I niver knew you were such a scandal-monger, Thomas."

"Ssh. Don't call me that. It's only chat."

John winked wryly. "I know you're a reliable source, Thomas."

He reciprocated with the news that James, in England for his RAF training, had sent a couple of letters recently. He had one on him and was passing it around for kith and kin to read, so let Thomas see it.

Dear Mother, Father, John, and all,

The basic training is fun, doing physical fitness training and drill and learning about military life. Some of these townees are unfit, but I find it easy and the assault courses are fun.

I am amongst a group of English, Scottish and Welsh lads, with only one other from home. Hopefully, my knowledge of tractors will stand me in good stead when we start the mechanics course soon. I am looking forward to tinkering with the aeroplanes. It is such an honour and a privilege to be here, doing my bit for King and Country.

I hope both of you and Elizabeth and John and all the family are in the best of form. Please pass on my regards to everybody I know. I won't detain you, as I know how busy you must be.

Your son,
for God and Ulster,
James

Mary had brought the new baby, to show him off.

"Do you want to see Daniel before we go home to bed-y-byes, Uncle Thomas?" she simpered.

Thomas obliged by tickling the baby's chin. Daniel gurgled, amused.

Mary chuckled the child, telling him a rhyme:

"Dan, Dan, the funny wee man,
Washed himself in th' fryin' pan,
Combed his hair with a donkey's tail
And scratched his belly with his big toe nail!"

Thomas recited for the baby the only rhyme he could remember (apart from his Uncle's Rabbie Burns):

"Matthew, Mark, Luke, John,

> Houl' the horse as I get on;
> Couldn't stand,
> Fell in th' fire an' burnt me hand."

John Ussher followed it up with his version:

> "Matthew, Mark, Luke, John,
> Hold the horse while I get on;
> Couldn't sit,
> Fell in the fire an' burnt me ..."

"Hip!" Mary tried to finish it for him.

"That doesn't rhyme," Thomas complained.

"It'll do rightly," she assured him.

The lads helped the men carry the big pieces of furniture out into the yard. When the room was cleared, he nabbed a chair in the corner and sat by Hugh Begley, watching the married couples and the courting couples and the pairs of spinsters and the wee children dancing to James Mateer's furious fiddle and the band's attempted backing harmony.

"They're ducking for apples out the back. Y' comin', Thomas?" Hugh Begley asked.

"Aye. I'm not in the mood for *The Gay Gordons* th' night."

They went in search of the other youngsters who were playing party games. They went across the field to the bonfire, which was over by the rocky place. It was impressive as its orange tongues licked the velvet sky, up on the stony outcrop. They could see no one about, so clambered up onto the large, natural platform. The heat of the crackling fire billowed towards them with the rises of the breeze.

"Deserted," whispered Hugh.

"It's like the burning bush," Thomas smiled, enjoying the warmth of the fiery hedge cuttings.

> Ardens sed virens
> *(burning but alive)*

"Like me, inside, burnin', consumed with a passion that's unquenchable, but still hanging on, still survivin'!"

"What are you bletherin' about? Where are they all? Maybe the evil spirits have got them," he said in a menacing tone.

"What d' ya mean, Hugh?"

"Don't you know about the pagan ceremonies the Druids had up here, at the Holestone?"

"Oh aye, is this more of this nonsense you were on about in the Isle of Man?"

"It's not nonsense, Thomas, it's true! And, don't forget, it's Hallowe'en th' night. The witches an' ghouls an' all will be out in force. Come on, there's nothing to be a-feared of." He climbed up onto the summit of the rocky mound. "Look, this is the Holestone itself. The whole district got its name from this stone."

"I've only ever seen it from the road."

"They used to summons the Little People, here. Touch it, feel the power! *It's tingling!* They say there's a special way of rubbing it, that makes the Little People an' all that mob appear. Maybe the Druids'll be out th' night, to cast their spells and worship the Devil and maybe even have," he intoned suggestively, "*a blood sacrifice!*"

"Don't be silly," Thomas said, hesitantly.

"Go on, then, scared-y-guts. Prove you're not afraid to touch the magic Holestone an' risk summonsing up the spooks."

Thomas tentatively touched the small, rough pillar. His fingertips rubbed the hole that was pierced through the standing stone, near its top. The gyrating flames of the bonfire behind him cast their half-light in such a way that the stone appeared to be pulsating. Could he feel a tingling? Not really, not just yet, but he turned to say to Hugh how majestic and unusual it looked -

"Waahhaahwaaahaawaahaaaahaawahaahaaahaawaahaaaahawaaha!"

"Aaaggghhh!" Thomas screamed. "Jesus, Mary and Joseph!" he touched his chest and fell to his knees with the shock.

The screaming gang of youngsters crowded round him, beating him on the back playfully. They held out in front of them their evil-faced, candle-lit turnip lanterns and waved them about, as if ritually wafting incense. As their wailing died, he laughed with relief, infected by their laughter.

"Got ya!" Hugh yelled above the shouting of the others.

"Some pals yous lot are!" he complained. His amusement was short-lived, had turned to suspicion - what was their motive for picking on *him*?

"What's the big idea, anyway, Hugh? Tryin' t' frighten th' life outta me!"

"They got me, so I had to get *some*body!" Hugh laughed. "You!"

You have not chosen Me, It is I who have Chosen you.

CHAPTER ELEVEN

A Good Heart

They were messing about, squealing and chucking straw at each other like toddlers. Mr Kaye heard the ructions and came in and told them off.

Rain was splattering in the yard outside. It was one of those beautiful dark days that feels wonderful because the falling raindrops look so impressive, because nature seems to be in complete command of all of creation, all seems wild and free, without Mankind being able to interfere. Their break was over, however, and the older people were returning from the Kayes' house.

They took their places again in the barn. Jean went up the ladder, to stand above her son's head. Maisie remained in the loft, with Terence. Isaac and Fred and the other men were below, to pass the corn sheaves, which were to be threshed. Thomas passed the loaded pitchforks hand over hand to his mother on the ladder, who raised them up to the small ones, in a regular rhythm. This was like a production line, like the conveyor belt manufacturing at the Ford factory in America that Fred had told them about. Thomas knew what he meant about it being bad for morale: it was no crack at all, this monotony.

Jean's feet bounced on the rung as she worked. She was wearing a grey skirt. A layer of petticoat was exposed as she stretched. It was like the lace lining that hung behind the curtains in Mrs Kaye's parlour. As her arms went up, the skirt went up, and he could see her sagging stockings – just a brief glimpse, before his eyes shot down to pick up the next pitchfork. Her ankle boot slipped, so that the arch caught the rung and her toes dipped down. Consequently, he could see the plain top of the stockings, the harsh stays, the stark flesh.

It was a game: spot the white. He began to count his conquests. It was like scaling a previously unclimbed mountain. He was tantalised by the unsatisfying glimpses of the summit.

It was the lunchbreak and the boys were chasing the girls in the playground. The leers and sniggers as he grabbed the fabric; the girl's annoyance as his fingers shook the pleats in the breeze, the way a housewife shakes out her washed sheets. Wee 'Carrothead' Sandy running after fat Emily. And then he spied *her* over in the garden, behind the toilets. So he snook over and cocked his head; he had her cornered by the hedge.

"Are you going to look up my skirt?"

Pamela stood impassively as his hand felt the rough underside of her grey school skirt, slid right up the slender little leg, beyond the catch of her knees. Bending over, he saw the top of her thighs, bridged by white bloomers – the sense of *awe* – his lingering gaze, as she stood there with that sweet, innocent expression in her eyes ...

And years after, when they were teenagers, during the Youth Club at the church hall, when they would all sneak up the ladder, into the loft that was used as a storeroom. It was the gang's den. They were the big yins then, the ones who mucked about – some tried smoking – and talked about fancying each other. That evening, they were all up there and there were too many of them missing from the hall so Mr Archer caught them on and chased them all out. Except that Pamela and Thomas were hid at the back, behind a big stack of chairs, so they were shut in, in the dark, now that he had turned off the hurricane lamp. And Pamela was scared of the dark, so held on to him until they heard someone going through the corridor below, going out to the bogs, and banged on the wee door till they unbolted it.

But while they were in there, alone together, when she was close to him, when her legs were rubbing up against his and he was too scared to move, because it was hard and he didn't want her to know – her legs then; that was the greatest feeling in the world, that smoothness, the warmth of those slender, shapely legs. When she chanced to lean over in the dark and her puddin', that soft place of hers, squashed against his thigh ... with her tender hands on his chest, his arm around her shoulders, to comfort her, his hand pressing against her arm ... that was the nearest he'd believed he'd ever get to Heaven. He sighed mutely as he relived his experience in that loft; that warm, dark womb of discovery, where he had once found the warmth of human flesh.

But that had been Pamela; whereas he knew this was wrong. Get these thoughts out of your head! He scratched his crown. And this was his *mother*, this was *evil*. Like Jesus said: if you commit adultery in your heart, it's as much a sin as committing the act itself. This was an assault on someone else's woman, his father's – whoever he was.

Eddie had been here this time last year, when they were threshing. It was nigh on five months already, since he ... An eternity. It was at the threshing last year, when the pair of them were in the loft – because Maisie and Terence were at school – that Eddie had told Thomas about the Family of Love.

He said some Blackmouth at his school had read about it. The Family of Love were a special sort of Calvinists in the dark days of history who believed in Communes. They said all sins are forgivable; if you're Elect your sin is forgiven – zap! If you're not Elect, you'll burn in Hell, whether you do good works or not. Which was half-right? Thomas wondered. But anyway, this lot indulged in carnal pleasures. He could see Eddie's smiling red face now, saying it must be a great way to live, he'd like to join.

Communal living, just like Comrade McCann's sort. Thomas had made the mistake of telling James Ussher about it! He was righteously indignant and pointed out that that kind of dirty behaviour should not be countenanced because it was an affront to Christian morality. Who was right? Could we really get away with ... well, if not murder, adultery? Fornication? If there was supposed to be forgiveness, why was God a wrathful God? Why did He want us to suffer? Why make *Jesus* suffer?

But there were no loving families any more. That must be the message, the moral to the tale; they disappeared because they were wrong, were heretics. They must be in Hell now; burning, screaming in eternal damnation, doomed by their carnality. That was the message: one kiss and you'll spend an eternity in torment!

"Thomas! Thomas!"

Who was that? Just a spooky voice? He looked down, looked up. No one was trying to attract his attention. He must've been mistaken. It was no one; it was nothing. It must've just been the wind swirling at the barn door.

It was Communion. That winter gloominess that darkens rooms and lets the shadows inhabit corners and crevices was visiting Dunadry Presbyterian, despite the electric. Dark skies outside had cast the countryside in dullness and wetness. They were finishing singing a psalm – the *Auld A-Hunderd*.

"All people that on earth do dwell,
Sing to the Lord with cheerful voice;
Him serve with mirth, his praise forth tell,
Come ye before him and rejoice.

Know that the Lord is God indeed;
Without our aid he did us make;
We are his flock, he doth us feed,
And for his sheep he doth us take."

The Reverend Dr Marsh was conducting the service in his usual sonorous tone. "Life is a quest for Truth.

Jesus is the Way
the Truth
and the Life."

Thomas pinched his earlobe nervously as the time approached. He glanced around the congregation. They were all in their dark suits, or their best dresses and hats, sitting solemnly, listening respectfully. Respectably.

He couldn't not do it now, they might all think it odd. It was such a big step, to do this. Was he ready? Did he love Jesus? He looked up at the window: the world beyond the arched frame of diamond-shaped panes was grey, was cold, was hostile. His mind repeated the Communion Table script:

'THIS DO IN REMEMBRANCE OF ME.'

His mother was shuffling her feet. He was tucked in between her and the wall. Condensation was running down the plaster, almost soiling his jacket shoulder.

He was too tightly packed in today for there to be any chance of escape. It was either do it or make a *really* big scene. He spotted Sandy. He'd done it and he was a only a couple of years older that Thomas. All the men treated him like an equal, now. He helped to take the Youth Club. If he sinned, it was only by accident. Why couldn't Thomas bring himself up to Sandy's level?

A voice at the back of the church was saying to someone, "What's Thomas Gray doing here? Sure, he ran away last time! He shouldn't be here at all. He's not a *real* Christian. He's a heathen. He's an imposter; he's not one of the Brethren."

Thomas cried out in his brain: I'm not a Heathen! I am a Christian! I mean, I want to be! Don't walk on by, be Good Samaritans. His tear ducts were bulging, were raw and pained.

He could smell that particular odour now, that distinctive Pamela Hart scent.

"Don't think of her," his mother's voice said in his head.

His eyes darted sideways. She was licking her lips, pretending to be listening to Dr Marsh. So, it was true, she could hear what he was thinking; and talk to him, as well. And them at the back of the church, whoever they were, they could, too? So, he knew the secret now, eh? Did this mean he was one of them?

Of course, his mother was quite right: he had made an eejit of himself, running after *her*, offering to marry her. And it wasn't even his baby. He should give his love to the only One who truly cares about any of us. To love a woman before God is spiritual adultery!

Give me the Grace to live as You ordain, he prayed. Let me be a good person, a good farmer, a good servant of Thine. You died for me. You are my Saviour. I will love You. Here is my heart, Jesus, I give it to You. Come to me, as I give myself to You. Amen.

The Elders were on their feet, passing the silverware, passing out the Eucharist bread and non-alcoholic wine. A juddering sensation seized him – from the pit of his stomach to his chest and down his left arm. He closed his eyes, leaned back, clamped his jaw. He felt himself drift upwards. He no longer felt he was in his body, but had become dislodged and had escaped out through the top of his head. He was looking down at his body, slumped in the pew, and upon his mother and Uncle and all the people he knew. He spied a white speck near the false fruit on his mother's hat and some of his uncle's poetry book came to mind:

>Ha! Where ye gaun, ye crowlin ferlie?
>Your impudence protects you sairly;
>I canna say but ye strut rarely
>   Owre gauze and lace,
>Tho' faith! I fear ye dine but sparely
>   On sic a place.

> O wad some Power the giftie gie us
> To see oursels as ithers see us!
> It wad frae monie a blunder free us,
>   An' foolish notion:
> What airs in dress an' gait wad lea'e us,
>   An' ev'n devotion!

He was hovering somewhere between their heads and the gallery. He swam forward, to fly, level with Dr Marsh's eyes. He waved an invisible hand. Yoohoo! Dr Marsh! I'm here, right in front of you. I'm up at your level, in the air. I'm a spirit, I'm a spirit – and I feel free! He descended and reentered his body.

Opening his eyes, he said to himself, this is *living*!

The silver plate was at their pew. He picked up a piece of bread and put it on his tongue. He felt it begin to dissolve. It tasted fatty, like bacon rind. The salty tang of bacon and a subtler feel replaced the initial sogginess; it was like the way a big bit of skin tastes when you bite it off from the side of your fingernail. It was a miracle: bread had become flesh. The goblet was cold against his lips. The wine was thick. It lodged in the back of his throat, so that he had to gulp down the congealed lump. It was warm. The taste of it remained on his pallet, the same way your mouth feels sticky after you've sucked a bleeding scab.

He'd swallowed Jesus! He had eaten the Body of Christ. It was spiritual cannibalism. But, to get the Spirit in you, you had to have the Body. He forced saliva into his mouth and cleaned his teeth by running his tongue around them. He had got a good heart now; he'd been saved by the blood of the lamb.

"... be with you all, this day and for evermore. Amen."

The service finished blissfully. The ritual over, chatter erupted and shoes clopped on the floor. He'd done it this time! He was born again of the Spirit!

He smiled at all the friendly faces as he was leaving and everyone was nice to him.

"My last milking!" Fred said, warming his hands at the big cast-iron potato boiler.

"When are you off?"

"I'm getting a lift down this evening."

Thomas was rushing about with hay. He stopped to talk. "I hear they tried to kill yer man Hitler. A near miss."

"I have my doubts about that man, now. I read recently that the Government's found out his lot have been unnecessarily cruel, put lots of folk in prison camps, tortured them for no good reason, and all. A British Fascist is different from a German Nazi. They're all repressed perverts, I reckon. Sadists. Old Freud knew a thing or two. What does it matter he was a Jew? He certainly wasn't biased, since there weren't any Nazis then. Yes," he poked out his backside close to the boiler, "I think we're on the right side in this one."

"You've changed your tune."

"There's no shame in seeing the light. To err is human ..."

"You don't know what you believe."

"'Can one live believing in nothing? Yes.' I don't believe in anything, for sure. Yet I can carry on, get by alright, without a God or something to believe in. If there is no God, then those who believe in God live believing in nothing. Or is that philosophical bull?"

"Paul once toul' me it's Catholic doctrine that ninety percent of people don't go to Heaven. Is that true?"

"I can't follow this talk about life after death," Fred replied. "How can a body that's rotted away to dust rise up again after centuries? There's nothing left! It's beyond me."

"It's ahead of you."

"I'm not scared of death. Everybody dies. *C'est la vie.*"

The wind was picking up, buffeting, as Fred hauled his kitbag over his shoulder and carried it to the car.

"I'd better be going. Mr McGuigan and I have a long drive ahead of us to Banbridge."

Thomas gave him a salute. Jean waved and shrieked above the wet wind from the half-door. Uncle Isaac shook his hand, wished him luck and went in, saying he was punctured. So Thomas swept out the byre alone, as the bad weather blew.

The byre door burst open. A shower sprinkled in. And out of the dark flurry came a draped figure. The lamp flames flickered violently. The man in the wide-brimmed hat closed the door behind him, without turning. Shaking his dripping body, he took off the hat and beat it against his thigh.

"Aren't you dead?"

"Do I luk like I'm dead?" he was amused. "I just came t' see how yous are getting on. Are you well?"

"Fine. Are you coming in to th' house?"

"Mmnn," he hesitated. "I'd like to, but I can't stop here long th' night. I've a wake to go to. Not me own," he smiled. "Time and tide wait for no man. I'm staying at a place near Ballymena until the new year."

"But aren't you ill?"

"It was nuthin'. So, what's new about Islandreagh?"

Thomas felt an urge to tell him about Pamela, but resisted. "Are you not married yit?"

How did he know to ask that question? Could he hear inside his head, like they could?

"What about thont wee girl from the Rabbit Hutches?"

"I couldn't be involved with her. I'm not ... that wouldn't do. I'm not in love with anyone. And no one's in love with me."

"You're wise to be choosy. When it comes to that surt-a thing, it's best t' be canny. They're only trouble, wemen. An' if iver, *when*-iver, I should say, you do go an' get mixed up with wan seriously – do it right."

"D' you think there's a right one waitin' fer me? Fer every man, I mean? Is there a Divine Plan – Order in the universe?"

Paul chortled. "I doubt if a buddy's love life is planned by inybody, let alone himself! And as fer a Design of the Universe, I think everything's very arbitrary, contingent, y'know, in its details. And even if it wasn't, I doubt if an individual's love life wud figure much in the calculations! It's up to us t' make the best we can of things. Don't fret about romance, Thomas. Don't be ... impatient. Are you still readin' Marx?"

"Well, I've still that buk you gave me, but I haven't had much time t' read over it much. I'm afraid I'm not a very faithful disciple, am I?"

"Few are, son. Not even Lenin. Certainly not Stalin. Forcing people to be Communists, instead of persuading them," he scoffed, "which is the best way. Democracy is more important that any ideology. Civil liberty, the freedom of the individual to make up his own mind. Or not, as the case may be. True liberty is freedom from evil. You believe what *you* feel's right and to Hell with everybody else. But I can't stand here gabbin' all night. I'm expected elsewhere."

As he opened the door again, Thomas asked, "Will you be back?"

"I'll come again," he assured him. As he climbed onto a big black bicycle that had been propped against the byre wall, he said, "Give my regards to Jean, for me, and your Uncle, and say I'm sorry I couldn't stop."

When he went into the house, Thomas did not dare mention it, in case it had not been real. Later on, in bed, he lay awake, wondering if it had been a dream. Before long, his fingers wandered down towards his privates again, to ease that nipping at the edge of his bag. His mind was soon engrossed in the tug-of-war between ignoring the quickening of his desire and the voice of morality that was telling him to resist it and not yield to temptation this time. As his thoughts slowly churned, he heard voices outside; the passers-by on the road were boisterous and they were laughing. He strained to hear what they were saying:

"... he's an eejit, but, isn't he?"
"... The bae that lives in thar?"
Laughter.
"... running after her ..."
"... eejit of himself!"

They laughed even louder.

What if his mother and uncle could hear this? What if they were awake? This ridicule! It was scandalous! And it hurt; the cutting words, the mockery, the cruelty.

Wet with sweat, Thomas opened his eyes. He leapt from bed and hurried through the parlour and across the kitchen. *Had* they heard anything? He listened at his uncle's door: not a sound. He tiptoed past the dresser and bent his ear to his mother's keyhole: a faint snoring. He hurried back to his own bedroom. They were both asleep. At least his shame hadn't affected them. Tiredness overwhelmed him now that his mind was at peace. Tension and fear were shed from his system as he slipped out of consciousness.

The witch was dead. Mrs Kaye had stopped in one morning to say hello and had found the old biddy stiff. The cold snap had got her. Ninety-seven, Mr Kaye said. He had organised the funeral, since she had no relatives round about. He said she had arranged with him in advance – several years in advance – to make sure the funeral was paid for and went smoothly.

An old woman was here, claiming to be a niece from Derry. She had a look at the shrivelled little corpse, as it lay in the pine coffin in the back room. Then, Uncle Isaac screwed down the lid. Mr Kaye, Uncle Isaac, Gerald and Thomas took hold of the coffin and moved it towards the door. But it was slightly too big to get through. So they tipped it at an angle. Still no good. And the clergyman, the niece and a few locals were waiting in the front room. They set it up on end, but it was too long to walk through the tiny doorway, so they put it down again. They looked at the window: no chance, far too pokey.

Uncle Isaac unscrewed the lid. It was passed out to the kitchen. The waxy, white-clad corpse was removed and laid on the bed. They turned the coffin on its side and got it through the door that way. Gerald and Thomas were instructed to carry the cold, stiff body to the next room. Mr Kaye suggested that they take the whole lot outside, rather than risk a repeat performance at the front door. The distressed looking niece was ushered out into the rain by the clergyman. At last the coffin was in Hennessey's horsedrawn hearse and the body was in the coffin and the lid was firmly screwed down on the coffin. Thomas endured the dreadful, wet afternoon with a shrivelled expression, which was only disturbed by the exacerbation of the nipping cold and pouring rain.

When they got home, Uncle Isaac told his sister the sad tale of Mrs Higgins's final humiliation. Thomas tittered manically throughout the telling; he rolled from side to side in his chair, unable to control his hysterical laughter. He retold the coffin scene with relish. His mother's glum face did not brighten when Thomas jocularly made the observation that you can't keep a good woman down.

"You mind what you're sayin', Thomas," his uncle warned. "Don't be speakin' ill of the dead."

"Aye," his mother agreed, "Or you might get your come-uppance."

"You're just grumpy because you're feelin' ill. It was that milk you drank upset your guts. I toul' you it was sour, not buttermilk at all." He suddenly flared into a temper. "Why can't yous ever listen to what I tell yous!"

His uncle and mother were startled, so didn't answer his bluster. He soon fell under the spell of a deep-rooted moroseness. Thomas was just depressed by having to touch that cold corpse, Jean told her brother, behind his back; his uncle was not convinced. But there was no time for Thomas to mope around at home: he had to set off for the York Road mill at Muckamore, to fetch a load of cinders, which uncle Isaac wanted to spread on the wee field, the one that had been an orchard, to give it a boost.

Ashes to ashes, dust to dust.

He steered the horse and cart round in front of the factory. He didn't mind a bit of drizzle. He had on his cap and the hessian bag he had over his knees would keep his legs dry. The bit of dampness in the air would keep the load of cinders from blowing about.

He muttered to himself about his mother: "I toul' her not to take it, it was adulterated. But, oh no, she knows best. You could smell it was off. 'Waste not want not!' Huh! Sure, the milk was clearly bad. Tryin' to poison herself, if you ask me."

He hopped off the cart when he arrived and went into the huge, high building. He was looking around for the foreman, making his way between the two great furnaces, when a familiar voice greeted him.

"Thomas! What are you doin' here?"

Pamela! Here she was. Was this his chance?

"I came to see about cinders. And to see my Cinder-ella."

She ignored his remark. He noticed that she was very big now and wearing a loose dress that hung out at the front. They stood in silence for a while.

Pamela thought of something to say. "I got a job in the office here, y'know. The work was gettin' too heavy for me at Clady, and anyway Mr Logue was givin' me a hard time. Daddy knows Walter Syms, that's how I got in here. Well, I'd better get back to work. Don't want to get into trouble, when I've only just started working here."

"Yes, I wouldn't like to get you into trouble. But can't you spare me a wee minute? I'd like to talk t' you." He had made up his mind to get it off his chest.

She looked him full in the face. "I don't think so. We're very busy today."

He reached forward, just as he had once before, but this time he was too quick for her to avoid him and he kissed her forcefully on the lips. They were in the dark abyss between the two roaring furnaces, out of sight of anyone, so she would not be compromised or embarrassed. And his hunch was vindicated, he thought, for she did not struggle. He felt a hand on his arm, and another gently touched his neck: she was responding – she was kissing him, too. He felt his lips against her moist mouth, sensed the motion as they absorbed each other's passion. This was a kiss, this *was* a kiss! This was love, oh this was loving.

"Thomas! What's got into you!" When they drew apart, her eyes were wide with amazement at what he had done.

He had to do it now, because it was driving him crazy.

"Change your mind!" he pleaded.

"Eh?"

"I can't change the way I was born. Can't you overlook my ... pedigree? Please, Pamela, think about it again."

"What are you on about, Thomas?"

Oh, she wanted him to spell it out again, to do it nicely, do it right.

"I love y' so much, Pamela. I do so want to marry you! Don't turn me down again."

"Again? You mean ... that time at the river, you were asking did I' want to marry *you*? I thought you meant, did I want to marry ... well, just in general, really. And I wasn't really sure. But now ... You mean to say, you really want to marry me?" She was stunned.

"Aye! And sure, when I asked thon night, at your house..."

"Oh, I thought you were only being friendly ... Well! I ..." her head bobbed, "... I don't think you should do this. But if you really want to ..."

He reached for her, hugged her, they kissed again. And it was long, long ... It was the tenderest, most perfect kiss in creation. So this was it, he had made it, he had found Paradise, Heaven, true love! He couldn't believe it, here he was, in the darkness of sensation, aware only of this kiss, aware only that he was joined – body, spirit and soul – to the most beautiful, wonderful, caring girl in the world. And he loved her and she loved him, and nothing else mattered!

They paused for breath and, as they were embracing, she asked, "And you really don't mind about ... my condition?"

"Well," he stuttered, blushing bashfully, "Sure, wasn't it as much my fault as it was yours?"

"Oh don't be silly, how could it be? You know you're not the father ..." she blurted out.

Stony silence. His grip loosened.

"Thomas? You *don't* know ... that ...?"

"How can I not be?"

"How *can* you be?" she asked dismissively. "You, of all people, ought to know about these things. You *must* know you're not the da. Sure, we didn't do anything that could even make you a candidate, did we?"

He shook his head half-heartedly, bewildered. "We might've ..."

"Thomas!" she lectured him as a mother does a child, "You know we didn't. But I thought that it didn't worry you that it's somebody else's? I thought you wanted me, despite that? You do, don't you? You still want me, don't you?" she pleaded. "I thought I could get by on my own, without a man. And I can't really have *him*; and I *wouldn't want* him as a husband, anyway. But I was kidding myself, to think I would be better off on me own. I do like you Thomas, you're the best friend I've got. We could make it work, we could be happy together. You do still want me, don't you? Is it still on?"

Thomas's face was wrung with distress and incomprehension. In his state of shock he demanded, "Whose *is* it, then?"

"I can't tell you that. For both your sakes."

"You want me to marry you, when you're someone else's woman? For God's sake don't tease me!" he bellowed.

And he hurried away from the furnaces.

The days were short. The end of the year was coming rushing. The purple mound of Lylehill sat level with the bank of clouds, yet the sun was brightening the wet land. There was a rainbow arched across the horizon. The cold air brushed back his hair as he bounced on the Ferguson to Umgall. He hadn't seen the house yet, but was told it was a palace now.

John had the calves penned already. "Hello. It's good of you to come an' gie us a hand."

"No bother at all. Sure yous are good to us. An' you reared those pigs for James, I hope he gave them till ye fer a reasonable sum?"

Thomas assured him, "He was very reasonable. Took a big luck penny aff, seein' as I'd all the bother wi' them. I should get a good turn at them. I'm gonna shift them up to the wee field that was the orchard sometime, now we've got it surted out. So, anyway, what's on the agenda th' day?"

"We're fer dressin' these boys. They're gettin' too big for their boots."

As John assembled his equipment near the crush, the sight of the sharp, slender knife caused Thomas's attention to prick up. The calves were going to be cut because if they weren't they'd become bulls, his consciousness reminded him.

They went down the yard and along the Ussher's back loanen, past the boggy field, towards the field of calves. Thomas paused at the gate of a field in which there was a flock of sheep. The ram was tupping a ewe.

As he watched, Thomas asked John, "You still goin' steady wi' that girlfrien' of yours?"

"Aye." John's eyes flitted from Thomas's face, along the trajectory of his gaze to the sheep and back again.

"D'you do *that* to her?"

"Thomas! You horny oul' ...! Well, surt-a ... We've not quite gone *all* th' way. Joan's a *nice* girl ... I didn't like t' chance me arm. I know *you* probably think I'm a bit of a wimp ..."

Thomas turned to stare earnestly at him as he asked, "So, don't you think it might give her a baby?"

"Well, aye," John humoured him. "Surely, if a buddy wasn't careful, it wud, alright. Right enough, a lot-a baes get caught out that way."

"An' a lot-a wimin get *caught* that way?"

"Aye." John eyed him suspiciously again.

"As I thought," Thomas murmured, staring across the field at the ram. "Sex is *real*."

"Wha'?"

"Nuffin'!"

As they rounded up the calves and walked them along the lane to the yard, Thomas recalled his fall into the thorns at Begleys' and realised that he might've damaged himself badly, he might've been dressed himself, by accident! But, he still didn't understand, who was the father of the child? Who was the *beast* that had done this wicked thing to his wee Pamela?

As they were closing the calves in the pen another caller arrived in the yard. It was Sammy Fee, the postman. He gave them his usual grave nod.

"Mon, let's go an' get Da," said John. "He's the expert at this job. He reckons when he's a bit older and not fit t' hump bales an' all he'll be a brain surgeon."

They went into the rebuilt house. Thomas cast a cold eye over the big new range and the modernisations and the new furniture and the lino on the kitchen floor, but he had little time to look around him, for Auntie Josie was in tears. Uncle George was sitting on the arm of the chair, with his arm around her. John did not speak, he merely drew the page from her hands in a slow, fearful manner.

He read it and, going to kiss his mother, held it out to Thomas. James was finished training and had gone to a frontline posting already? Or, he had ignored their advice and gone into the air? Or, worse, he had failed the induction process? Thomas read furtively: the Commanding Officer sent his sympathy – James had had an accident while training. He was working in a hangar, filling a tyre with an airline and there was too much pressure, the tyre had exploded. He had been killed 'outright' – was there any other way to be killed? Thomas wondered.

"I can't believe it." He was dumbstruck.

The immortal James Ussher, God's Ulsterman, dead? Never! What did it mean, that decent people like Willie Burns and Eddie Kaye and old Mrs Higgins and now James should die? What was the sense in being alive at all, if you only ended up dead? And James never even got off the ground. And Eddie never even got into the proper race. And Willie had nothing, just his oul' pushbike and his job at the Works. And Mrs Higgins had only an unknown niece to mourn her. And it all seemed so futile, so silly, that the they should go through the pains and worries of all their days, never to achieve anything much. *Was* life arbitrary, like Paul said?

He closed his eyes, but he saw James's face. Haunting him. And James was perfect, while he was a lowdown sinner. James had been so righteous, while he was a wretch. Why take James, Lord? Why do the good die young? Was it that this is Hell, this Life we're living, this inescapable round of toil and tears? The cows to milk and milk and milk and the desire that wells up inside but which you can't release, because you can't live like the way they do in the movies, where men are men and women lovers ... And all because of some unknown, dirty ... *beast*! He felt like he was falling, falling through the darkness, and he had nothing, no one, to cling to, and it was a nightmare – it was Hell.

He drove home in a state. The throttle was pulled back and he was racing along the roads, through the dark evening, ducking as each ghost swooped over the hedge at him and flew by his head.

He was thinking that if he took Pamela, if she would have him, it would mean her being unfaithful to the father. So what, if he loved her and she wanted him? And he couldn't help it if his parentage was the way it was. And sure, she didn't seem to mind. So where was the harm in it, just because other people said so? He loved her! He couldn't help it, he knew it was one of the most evil things in the world to do, but he loved her! She was *his*; she's committed adultery with *that beast*, not with him. And as for Margaret, that wasn't adultery because that was before he had kissed Pamela. And anyway, he still loved Pamela, even then. But was there even such a thing as love? Maybe people were all just animals, using each other!

The tarry fumes from the exhaust pipe that rose up from the bonnet in front of him made him choke. His eyes were smarting, so he drew out a rag to wipe them.

He swerved, seeing the bicycle just in time. The front wheel went in the ditch at the side of the country road. He was thrown clear as the tractor rocked.

"Y' alright?"

It was Albert Andrews, in his police uniform. Stunned, Thomas moved away from the hedge, where he had landed safely. The tractor had stalled. They inspected it. It was undamaged.

"What d'ya think you're playin' at?" the policeman began to scold him.

"James Ussher's dead. James Ussher's dead!"

Albert looked around, puzzled. "Where is he?"

Shrugging his shoulders, Thomas guessed, "Heaven."

"Was there someone with you on the tractor?" he asked angrily.

"No."

"Then what are you on about, son?"

"My cousin, James, he's died. He was in an accident. In England."

"England? Look you, less of your nonsense. Throwing me a red herring. You could-a killed us both, driving like that. Do you wanna be up playing a harp alongside ... whoever it is?"

"James Ussher. *You* know him."

"No I don't. And I don't care who it is. I'll be watching you, you mark my words."

"You're heartless!"

"Aye, that's right! And don't you forget it!"

When he got home, the dinner was over. His mother got his from the hob for him. He sat down at the table, only poking at his potatoes with his fork.

"What's the matter, son, not good enough for you?" she said, peering up from her sock darning.

"You don't care, do you?"

He lifted the iron from the table, where it was on its stand cooling, and launched it violently. It passed his Uncle and crashed through the wee pane in the jamb wall window.

His angry language had startled mother, uncle and dog. All three jumped with the crash. Help began barking. Thomas was shouting incoherently. His uncle was cursing, threatening to knock sense into him. Jean cried for them to stop it.

"You don't give a damn, do you?" Thomas accused his uncle.

There was suddenly peace. "About what?" they asked.

In tears, he sighed with exasperation. "That he's dead!"

"Who?" his mother asked. "Who's dead?"

He snapped, "I told you! James. James Ussher."

"Dead? James? Since when?"

"I told you," he asserted impatiently.

"No you didn't, son." Uncle Isaac was calm now.

"He got blown up."

His mother sucked in a sharp breath. "War is terrible."

"Not on active service. In the hangar. He was filling a tyre; it exploded. The letter arrived at Usshers' when I was there and we never even got the calves dressed. Spent all our time tryin' t' calm down Auntie Josie. Even Uncle George ended up cryin'."

"You never told us that," said Uncle Isaac.

"I did, I did, I did. At Usshers."

"But I wasn't at Usshers. I was *here*."

"I know! But weren't you tuned in?"

CHAPTER TWELVE

The Fall

There was a crisis. Isaac was adamant.

"Look at the way he flared up and threw the iron at me."

"He was just upset that James died."

"He didn't fly off the handle when Eddie died."

"He was very great wi' James."

"But Jean, the strange things he's been saying. And the way he's been creeping about. He's demented or paranoid or somethin' odd."

"Don't worry about him, Isaac. It's just the age of him. Young 'uns act up."

"I'm a-feared he's maybe goin' the way Tom went."

She held his arm, pleadingly. "Don't talk sich nonsense."

He got up and went to his room, but left the door ajar. Thomas came padding out to the kitchen in his bare feet. He went to the jug on the table and took a swig of milk.

"What are you doin' out of bed at this late hour, son?"

"It's so hot. The fires of Hell are consuming me."

He sat down and lifted his Zane Grey book and began reading. His mother left her darning and, making sure he wasn't watching her, slipped over to her brother's room.

"Did you hear that!" she whispered.

"He doesn't look very happy, does he? What do you suppose could be the matter?"

What did he say that for? Whispering about him in the corner, as if he couldn't hear them. God would punish them for that. In His own good time. Revenge is sweet.

Vengeance is Mine, saith the Lord.

They were against him! It wasn't the Devil trying to burn him in his bed, it was them! He put down the book and went out to the trough. He was filling a bucket when his uncle came to see what he was doing out there in his nightshirt and bare feet on such a frosty December night.

"What's the water for, son?"

"I'm gonna keep it by my bed, in case yous try to light a fire under me while I'm asleep and burn me at the stake."

They were at it again. They had Dr Moore in there and were conspiring to do away with him, sell him for experiments. He listened at the parlour door.

"No, no, I won't have it," someone was saying.

At last, someone was on his side! It must be the Holy Ghost: He'd stick up for Thomas, even if they would sell him into white slavery.

Pamela was waddling down the Rathmore Road, enjoying the bright sunshine, despite the December nip that was in the afternoon air. She was amusing herself with a rousing rendition of *Delaney's Donkey*, which she had learnt from listening to a 78 on Mrs Wilson's pride and joy, her only luxury in life, as she put it, her gramophone. Her merry singing became laboured, however, as pangs began to annoy her insides. She was frightened! These pains were *inside*: was it coming already? She stopped and the uneasiness seemed to stop. So she walked on. But another series of faint twinges began. It was while she was standing under a high hedge at the roadside wondering what she should do that Dickie Blenkinsop came cycling down the road.

Stooping by her, he greeted her cheerily. "I'm just on me way home for Christmas. We've finished our trainin' and I start at the wee polis station in Pettigo on the twenty-seventh. I got off at Templepatrick an' rode up round by me granny's at Loughanmore. It's great to be home again, fer a while!"

"I've just been up to my granny's, too."

"Isn't it incredible that we should meet like this? And it's such a lovely day. A real Christmassy feel. Life seems like one great big adventure for me at th' minute, wi' all the trainin' and this ... *freedom*, to cycle round after bein' cooped up in th' trainin' barracks fer ages."

"Aye, well it certainly has smartened you up a bit, anyway," she said, admiring his sharply pressed suit. He was lifting the pedal with his toecap, to head off again, when she held up her hand. "Don' go!" Pamela said through her teeth as a spasm shook her.

"What's the matter?"

"I feel bad, inside."

"Oh no! Not now! I'm supposed t' be off duty, y'know, Pamela. Come on," he dismounted and laid the bike in the verge. "We'd better get you sittin' down. It's too coul' an' wet out here. Can you walk a wee bit?" He let her hold onto him.

"I think so."

"We'll go in here," he said, leading her along and into Gray's yard. Seeing Thomas, he called, "Gie us a hand."

Thomas helped her inside and Pamela flopped into Uncle Isaac's armchair. He got her some tea from the ever-warm pot. "Will I get th' dacteur?" Dickie suggested.

"I feel okay when I sit down. The pain's gone."

"Are you sure? I don't know much about wimin's things," Dickie was exasperated.

"You shouldn't be out in your condition, you should be at home with your feet up."

"Oh, Mummy told me not to knock about as much," she confessed, "but I was bored in the house all day with nothin' t' do."

"You've stapped workin'?" Thomas asked.

"Aye." She winced again.

"What we need's a woman. Where's your ma?" Dickie asked Thomas.

"Down at the shap. She'll mibbe be stoppin' wi' Agnes Hughes an' all. She might be ages."

"Aw, well, maybe it's as well. I'm sure she wouldn't like to see you here, eh, Pamela? After all the dust she raised about your mother and father ..."

"That was a load of baloney!" Pamela snapped.

"Right enough, I know there's more than the one version to that tale." Realising his gaff, he said, "I'll go an' get th' dacteur. I've me bike, I won't be two shakes." Dickie made his way to the door. "You're a farmer, you know what to do if things turn out that way before I get back wi' th' dacteur."

"I know about cows an' sheep, but nuffin' about wemen!" Thomas protested. But he was away already.

"Don' look so worried, Thomas," Pamela smiled. "I'll be fine. Pregnant women get sore all th' time."

He knelt beside the chair and held her arm, which was resting on the arm of the chair. "But some women have problems! I don't want you to ... I'm worried for you."

She raised her hand and touched his crown, stroking his hair.

"I'll be grand. I feel more settled inside already."

"What's Dickie on about? I thought you said ... that *that* wasn't true?"

"He's got the wrong end of the stick, that's all."

Satisfied with her explanation, Thomas forced his feelings out.

"I'm sorry I was so ... nasty before. It was such a shock to think it's somebody else's baby." He lowered his voice. "But I do ... I don't mind, really. I do want you! Will you have me, after all?"

"That's nice of you, Thomas, but it's too late now. Besides, I couldn't let you do that. It would be just like him to think to himself you were doing it for *his* sake," she said angrily.

"I wouldn't be doing it for him, but for us. Who *is* this mystery man, anyway?"

"No, I can't say. It's best you don't know."

Dickie reappeared, so Thomas got up swiftly. Panting after his sprint on the bicycle, Dickie told them the doctor wasn't in. Pamela said not to fuss, she felt much better. She would go home. Dickie thought that it would be best if she got a lift down the road.

"You can't put Pamela on th' back of your bike," Thomas argued, "She wudn't balance praperly."

"Not on me bike," Dickie explained, "I'll go over an' see if Kayes kin take her down in their lorry."

"Oh, don't go to so much trouble." Pamela's plea went unheeded.

"Wouldn't the tractor do?"

"Where'd she sit?"

"I'll hook up the kyart."

"Far too bouncy! That surt-a contraption's enough t' give a nun kittens, let alone bring on someone in Pamela's condition."

"Don't fuss over me ..." she spoke up again.

"Aye, we'd better do that, then." Thomas conceded to Dickie's plan.

"I'll gwan over," said Dickie, leaving again. "Th' oul' polis initiative strikes again!" he said as he stood with his finger on the latch, tapping his temple with his free hand.

Thomas stared down at Pamela.

"And how's your invalid keeping? The wee dog?"

"Oh, Hop-Along Help! She's limpin' about like a good 'un. Can only run on three legs, has t' houl' th' ither wan up, but she gets by. I'll bring her in."

He went out to the yard and called. When the dog did not appear, Pamela saw him wandering round the back. He headed towards the fields, whistling. Then the latch clicked again and in walked Jean.

"What are you doin' here?" she asked, seeing Pamela alone in the kitchen, supping tea, in her brother's armchair.

"Hello, Miss Gray. I tuk not well, comin' down the road. Dickie Blenkinsop's away t' get Kaye's larry, t' get me a lift home."

"And where's Isaac?"

"Dunno. Thomas was here. He's just away out t' ... do something or other."

Satisfied, Jean carried her shopping bags over and lifted them up onto the folded down table. "And how's your mother keepin'?"

"Great, thanks. Daddy's well, too."

"Aw, well, as long as you have th' health, that's th' main thing, as they say."

"Mmm. I got a bit of jip walkin', just there now. Thomas has bin ever so kind, helpin' me out."

Turning from hanging her coat and scarf on the coat peg at the door, Jean squeezed her oval face and shot out, in a fearful tone, her disapproval.

"Are y' still at it? Still tryin' t' wriggle your way int' our pockets? Just like your parents before y'. Folk round here think I'm a daft oul' bird as has no sense an' didn't even know what was goin' on when I got tuk fer a ride, mesel'. An' that's as maybe, mibbe I was innocent of men's wicked wiles. But I sure as Hell wasn't fool enough not t' see how your da was eggin' your ma on t' marry our Isaac, rather than face the music himsel'!

"I've got you schemin' Harts worked out! Don't you come roun' here, thinkin' you kin fool my boy int' marryin' you when you're carryin' thon other scut's chile. Aye, by th' luk on your face, you didn't think folk knew about yous! But we're not so slow around here, us oul' wemen. We know what goes on round th' back-a th' goat-house, girlie! No wonder my Thomas is all in a quandry, not knowin' what t' think with you canoodlin' with him one minute an' some other scut th' nixt."

"I haven't been leadin' Thomas on, at all! I've been tryin' t' put him off! I know it wouldn't be fair," she said, struggling to her feet, "of me t' do that to him. We're friends, that's all. Why can't you oul' busybodies understand, I don't want to play by your *rules*, I don't want to live by your ... code. I want to live life my *own* way ..."

"Ack! An' make th' rules up as you go along?" Jean scoffed from where she was standing, at the end of the jamb wall. "It's a pity y' didn't move th' goalposts when thon other wee fella was kickin' his ball in your direction. You scored a bit of an own goal there, didn't you, my girl?"

Pamela sucked in sharply. "You can talk!"

"Your situation an' mine are *completely* different."

"Really?"

The lorry could be heard arriving outside and Dickie's feet running on the concrete ended their war of words. Pamela thanked Jean pleasantly in front of Dickie, as he helped her across the yard. He heaved her up the step into the cab, then got in himself, telling Pamela his bike was in the back. And so they drove off.

Shortly, Thomas went back inside, dragging Help on a length of rope.

"Don't bring that mucky thing in here," his mother ordered. "Where's yer Uncle Isaac?"

"Over at Duggan's, seein' if Patsy'll come over soon t' stick th' Christmas pig." He released the dog, which scampered off, tongue hanging out happily again, heading in the direction of the interesting-smelling hedgerows. "Where's Pamela?" He was worried: maybe she had got worse and was in the bedroom, being attended by the doctor?

"Kaye's man's been in the lorry an' tuk her hame. *And* th' wee lad Blenkinsop. And whatever other waifs an' strays y' brought in durin' the few minutes me back was turned."

"Is she going to be alright?"

"She's fine, physically."

"Didn't she leave a message?"

"What surt-a message?"

That she *would* accept his offer of marriage. That she *did* really love him.

"Anythin'?"

"No. She was just talkin' *brazenly* about how she was glad she's goin' t' be an unmarried mither. Honestly, some folk need their heads examined! What sort of girl in her right mind wud say a thing like that? It's a disgrace, isn't it?" Jean shook her head, as she unpacked her shopping bag.

His mood having suddenly become downcast, Thomas replied, "Aye. She seems t' be a right nice wee girl, but it just goes to show you how appearances can be deceiving."

Look at it: it's utter rubbish! He held the Father before him, his lip curling with disgust. He stabbed it in the face and midriff. He was going to feed the pigs in the orchard, so took it out with him and hid it in the bucket of gruel. When he was tipping the feed into their troughs, he quickly took out the stained carving and threw it inside one of the pighuts.

He stood for a moment, looking down sadly at his destroyed dreams, as the pigs snuffled greedily at the meal. *Was* he doing the right thing, in giving up? Maybe, if he kept at it, he would turn out to be the great artist after all. Maybe a review by that renowned art critic, Maisie Kaye, in a few years time, would pluck him from the obscurity of deepest, darkest rural Ulster and set him up on a plinth alongside the great Parisian sculptors; and his long ignored carvings of the Trinity would be displayed in the Louvre, hailed as world masterpieces, and he would be rich, famous, his company sought after by the crowned heads of Europe as he dined with them in places like the Palace of Versailles as Guest of Honour. But in his heart of hearts he knew he had failed.

He sighed, feeling completely drained of energy, and said to the pigs, which were more interested in rubbing their dirty, wet snouts through the dusty feed that in his artistry, "There, chew on that! It's no use to me. And *I'm* no use!"

When you give up your dream you die.

Patsy Duggan came to stick the pig. This year's Christmas bacon was a hefty Large White. Patsy was sharpening his knife. Thomas sighed deeply.

"What's the matter wi' you?"

"He's niver even pulled a hin's neck," teased Uncle Isaac.

"It's not the killin'," he said fiercely. "Just, it's so sad," he intoned.

"Don't be so saft. Here," Patsy offered Thomas the knife, "you kin do it."

"I've me own," he said, extracting his Bowie knife from his jacket pocket.

Patsy roped the pig and held it down. Thomas put a knee on its shoulder. He drew the silver blade around the squealing brute's neck, cutting deeply into the tough, bristly skin. The blood flooded out of the two purple-red lips of the incision. They collected most of the blood in a rusty tin bath, leaving the stuck pig hanging by its hind legs from the low beam in the byre.

When it came time to shave the porker, Thomas watched the expert. Its open eyes seemed to hate him. Its jaw was hanging open, showing the rows of sharp teeth. Thomas was sent to tip the bath of blood on the midden as Patsy began to scrape the body of the pig with a razor.

Alone in the byre, Isaac confided in his neighbour. "The lad's not well, Patsy."

" Aye, he sounds a bit ... disturbed."

Isaac tapped his crown. As the razor rasped, he said, "I dunno what t' do. Th' dacteur called in t' see Jean about her wimin's things, an' I toul' him. She didn't want me to. She thinks he's just under the weather. Right enough, it's not all the time, only a wee bit now and again, so's you'd hardly notice it. And if he says somethin' stupid to y' an' you ask him about it later, he says he doesn't know what *you're* talkin' about! But I'm worried it might be like what happened to Tam. Right enough, Thomas has been grand recently. But, like I say, on and off, he talks nonsense. The dacteur, he said if it wasn't too bad it might go away, but he'd be best to be seen." His voice shook. "They can't take him away. Our Tom ran about fer ages, sometimes he was alright, sometimes he had a turn ... But he always was a bit of a header. This is different. The lad was fine till recently. What kin we do?"

"Don't you worry none, me an' Mairaid'll be prayin' for yous."

"Oh, God," Isaac covered his eyes with his hand, "we sent the dacteur away and wouldn't let them take our boy. But if this gets much worse ... I just can't cope with it. This, on top of all me other worries. Jist whin I thought we were over the worse of it. Gettin' settled again after Jean's turns, the money side-a things pickin' up, not t' mention our past woes. Mind you, we brung them on oursel's."

"Nonsense, Isaac. You've done nothin' any worse than the rest of us."

"Ah, but I handled it all wrong. Like that thing wi' Marbeth. I was only visitin' her oul' mother afore she died. But, of course, Jeannie had t' think the worst – of her ain brother! Nobody thought anythin' *but* that the chile was Ben Hart's till Jean wint round sayin' the rumours about Marbeth an' me was all lies. An', of course, those rumours didn't exist till she did that! Sure, our ain mither and oul' Mrs Manson were great frien's, you'd-a thought Jean wud-a understood. An' wasn't it the cherry on the cake that the nixt thing you know, Jeannie was carryin' on wi' that rogue of a labourer, the first year he come here."

"I remember her singin' his praises!"

"Callin' *me* the blake sheep of the family! I toul' her he was no good. I tried t' prevent it. Luk at her, even now she still fawns over him ivery time he comes here t' see the boy, even though she's seen through him long since."

"Well," Patsy remarked, "I don't think much of his politics nur his heathenism, but he's a likeable enough buddy."

"Then, she said she wouldn't marry because he was ..."

"One of our surt, rather than yer ain?"

"Aye. But sure, that was only t' cover th' fact that he couldn't be bothered settlin' down."

"Well, I dunno about that. Lots-a folk are touchy about them things. And wimmin are touchier than men, in general, when it comes to religion." Patsy said, as the razor rasped on the pig's flesh.

"Aye, well, mibbe it was a bit of both; a bit-a reluctance on both sides."

"Does the lad know about his Da?"

"Oh, aye. We didn't say anythin', of course, but he's cottoned on by now, alright. He gave me a mouthful about it one night, when we were doin' th' milkin'. No, it's not that that's raggin' 'im."

"I hear thont wee girl of Hart's is expectin' this child that oul' Alex Thompson's lad is supposed to be responsible fer. Wasn't Thomas sweet on her? Mibbe that's what's rilin' him?"

Isaac pondered this for a moment. "He was only pally, the way youngsters knock about together. An' that was ages ago, anyway. Since she's been gestatin' he's really only seen her whin she's been here workin' wi' her ma. No, that sounds a bit too far-fetched. There must be more to it than that. I gist can't get iny sense outta him."

As he stood on the firm manure, spilling the sickly smelling contents of the tub over the back of the dunghill, Thomas noticed swarms of insects coming up out of his footprints and crawling over his boots and running up his leather leggings towards his body. He tried to swat the creepy-crawlies.

Then he saw that where there was a scab on his hand a fat, yellow maggot was trying to wriggle to the surface: he could see it through the flesh. Dropping the bath, he hammered his hand on the midden wall. Parasites!

"Yeeheeeheeheeaaaah!"

"What's the panic?"

"What's all this screamin' in aid of?"

Billy and Hugh were at the front of the dunghill.

"I hurt me han'," he stuttered. Then he shouted at them, "You're the Devil's advocates!"

"Naw, we're not quite that bad, though we are from the Government. We came about the scrap iron. Fer the war effort, like. We meant t' call by ages ago, but didn't get round this area till now. Got inny?"

"That oul' bathtub'll do, if it's no use t' yous," the other man suggested.

"This is the murder weapon," Thomas told them. "But you can have it if you want."

"Is your name John Christie, or summat?"

"I stuck a pig."

"Oh! Good for you," Billy humoured him.

"We didn't see your da about, is he at the market?" Hugh chatted as they threw the bits of scrap onto the back of the truck.

"Your uncle, he means," Billy corrected Hugh again.

Ignoring their jibes, Thomas said angrily, "He's talking to the Taig pig."

"Oh. That's a bad move," Hugh laughed. "Sir James wudn't like that, eh?"

"Sir James was shot down by Nietzsche."

They gave each other quizzical looks. When they had finished they thanked Thomas and he began walking back to the byre. But he overheard the criticisms they made as they were climbing back into the cab.

"A sheaf short of a thatch, that one."

"Bad blood! Bad breedin', must be!"

The laughter was unbearable. It wouldn't stop. Thomas clamped his hands over his ears, trying to block it out, but it laughed and laughed and laughed. He knew it probably wasn't real because it wasn't always there and, anyway, it was only recently he had noticed all this buzzing in his brain. It shouldn't be there, but he couldn't shake it out, he couldn't get it to stop. It kept on ringing in his skull, persecuting his mind, ridiculing him.

Christmas Day was special, for it was Thomas's birthday. It also had a relaxed feeling, that *Sunday* feeling. They got the cows milked at an unhurried pace, then settled to a big Ulster fry for breakfast. Thomas was in good form. It was a dry day, so he loaded the plough onto the cart and drove Mrs Simpson through Kaye's yard to the Meadows down the back lane.

He passed Terence on the loanen. "Merry Christmas!"

"And you. Say, why aren't you ploughing with the tractor? Is it busted?"

"Oh no. It's workin' well. But it wouldn't be right to use it."

"Why not?"

"Because it's an unnatural thing and today is a Holy Day."

The bare trees were still. The hedges were not rustling. No creatures were abroad to disturb Nature's tranquillity. He lifted off the plough and harnessed Mrs Simpson. The walk over the soil was made easy by the dryness of the loam. The sun was not visible, but a pleasant warmth penetrated his jacket, as if blessing him for the good work he was doing.

At mid-morning, his uncle appeared at the gate. He had two shotguns with him. They left the mare with her bag of oats and went hunting rabbits.

In the field by the stream they came across the first rabbit holes. They parted, taking a parallel route on either side of a grassy ridge. Thomas heard a report. He hurried up the slope. His uncle was aiming at a fleeing rabbit. He shot. It tumbled over. A group of rabbits scattered. One ran along the foot of the ridge. Seeing his uncle reloading, Thomas snipped off the safety catch and aimed at the fast moving target. He followed it with the barrel.

Isaac turned and looked up as the barrel swung at him. One eye shut, along the sight Thomas saw his uncle's pasty face: the hollow eyes beneath the cocked cap, ruddy nose and cheeks, stubbly chin. It was a look of amazement, stunned disregard, of resignation, that filled his view. His trigger finger wavered.

He lowered the barrel. He stared at his uncle. Isaac stared back. The old man swung quickly, raised his shotgun to his shoulder and with a swoop blasted the hopping rabbit. It flipped head over heels in the air and fell into a clump of bloodied weeds.

Isaac gathered up the rabbits and stuffed them in his bag.

"That'll do," he said.

Thomas unloaded. He walked to the lane with his uncle, then gave him the gun. The annual ritual was over. His uncle ambled up the lane. The branches that formed an arch above his head began to drip, as a light shower passed by.

He was a target, Thomas thought, as he continued ploughing. There seemed a spectacular elegance, a thrill, in the notion that he had the power over a life, over a death. A single twitch of the finger could change the course of history. Fight it, Thomas, fight it! He shouldn't think such things. This was an evil thought in his head. Kill the thought! Kill the thought! The thought was a demon and it would devour him! He mustn't think it, because even thinking it was a sin.

And one sin leads to another.

But he couldn't commit a sin, because he was Jesus reborn. Had he ever even blasphemed? Of course not: he was incapable of sin, for how could he take his own name in vain? His lips may have spoken harshly, but his heart remained pure. He was innocent.

As he ploughed, he projected a reel of film in the cinema of his mind: Billy the Kid climbed over the gate and pranced forward, fingers twitching near his holster, as he menaced towards Wyatt Earp. It was high noon, he realised, looking up at the sun. The gunslingers, in their ten-gallon hats, leather leggin's and spurred boots, gradually approached each other. The silver star badge on Earp's chest twinkled. Their mouths were pursed in mean determination.

"You're gonna get it," Billy the Kid was snarling.

The faceless sheriff's hand was twitching, poised by his holster. In unison, they drew. Blam! Blam! The sheriff fell.

Laughing to himself, he left Mrs Simpson again, snuffling in her nosebag, to go for his Christmas lunch. Thomas, why play these silly games? he asked himself. He couldn't help it! He told himself to block it out!

But his excitement was so great, he soon forgot about his daydreaming. He ran all the way up the lane, not even looking at the dark, closed-up, cottage, through Kaye's yard and along the road to the Orchards. He slowed to walking pace at the last turn of the road, to catch his breath.

His mother had the brown boxes all piled up on the jamb bench when he got to the house. He grinned broadly. He forced a parcel into his uncle's lap, as the elderly man sat by the fire, idly playing cat's cradle with a piece of string. Isaac freed his fingers and opened the paper bag. A new shirt.

"G'wan, y' big wean," Isaac urged, "get stuck int' your own."

The paper flew wildly. Thomas got three presents: an orange, a razor and a set of underwear. His mother handed another, saying it was his birthday present. It was a new Zane Grey novel!

He began to be bothered by the quadratic, and kept counting in his head, one, two, three, four, in sets of four. Then, if he strayed by one beyond the set, he had to not only start a new set, but his increasingly schizoid mind became obsessed with repeating the sequence until it was squared off:

$$\begin{array}{cccc} 1\ 2 & 1\ 2 & 1\ 2 & 1\ 2 \\ 3\ 4 & 3\ 4 & 3\ 4 & 3\ 4 \\ \\ 1\ 2 & 1\ 2 & 1\ 2 & 1\ 2 \\ 3\ 4 & 3\ 4 & 3\ 4 & 3\ 4 \\ \\ 1\ 2 & 1\ 2 & 1\ 2 & 1\ 2 \\ 3\ 4 & 3\ 4 & 3\ 4 & 3\ 4 \\ \\ 1\ 2 & 1\ 2 & 1\ 2 & 1\ 2 \\ 3\ 4 & 3\ 4 & 3\ 4 & 3\ 4 \end{array}$$

> One for sorrow,
> two for joy,
> three for a girl,
> and four for a boy.

"Well?" Jean was waiting for the answer to her question.

Thomas shook himself out of the trance. Don't lose the sequence, it's bad luck! he heard himself tell himself. But his brain was working on a reply.

"Sorry?"

"Do you want some mint sauce or not?"

"Yes, please."

He could hardly walk! Going back to the ploughing, his belly was filled out by the rich dinner. The walk behind the plough would do him good, get this grub digested.

There were no seagulls today. It was the cawing of black crows that competed with Mrs Simpson's jangling harness, as the scavengers followed Thomas as he followed the plough that followed the horse. A shrill, dastardly calling. Calling shame, shame, *shame* as they swooped behind him to pick for worms. The sun soon got low, so the ploughing had to be left for another day.

Pausing to survey the cloudy sky, Thomas cried to the breeze:

"Alright! it's over! I'm no artist. I can't even carve a block for the fire. And she ... *she's* never going to be mine, she's untouchable. That's the way it is. My dream is dead!"

When you give up your dream you die.

The sky was darkening again, and not just due to the nightfall, for more clouds were already racing to Islandreagh, to shed God's tears.

That evening the family went to the Begleys' Christmas Party at Holestone. It was a dark, moonless night, wet and cold, as they drove to their friends' house in the trap.

The Begleys Christmased in style: they had a brightly festooned tree in the parlour, even carol singing round the piano. Aunt Sarah provided sandwiches galore and punch and ginger wine and cake and even chocolate.

Thomas was nervous talking to John Ussher. He hadn't seen him since the funeral. Was he still touchy about James's death?

"How's things at Umgall?"

"Home's alright. Personally, not good. I split up with Joan."
"Oh."
"Thomas, come on out a walk."

Thomas followed him to the Begleys' stable. An outside light cast a yellow gleam across the yard. The gelding ignored them, turning its noble head away to reenter its slumber. John lit a cigarette and leaned against the wall. Thomas refused when the packet was offered. They listened to the softly falling rain. After a few puffs, John cleared his chest.

"She was two-timing me."
"That sounds great!"
"Well, it's not! It's enough to crack a buddy up."
"I know what you mean. I've had a few worries on me mind recently. But I'm over that, now. There's always somebody worse off than yourself."
"You're right there. Ach well, these things happen. People aren't perfect. Our family's the gauge of that."
"How do you mean?"
"We're both men of the world, Tommy, eh? You, me an' Trigger here know Uncle Tom Gray was a bit of a charmer, eh?"

Thomas nodded, waiting to catch John's drift.

"And, well, don't take offence, but there's your own case. Like, Auntie Jean was loved an' left, in a manner of speakin'."
"Now ..."
"I'm sorry to call a spade a spade, Thomas, but sure, I'm in a similar boat. Wasn't my ma expecting me when she got married?"
"Was she? Auntie Josie? *Really*?"
"I thought you'd-a guessed that one long ago."
"Never thought about it."
"Right enough, it's no big deal. So anyway, you see how it's not necessary to get het up about such things. Love 'em and leave 'em, like everybody else does. Oh, that bitch Joan! She strung me along good and proper!" He fumed for a while. "You and me, partner, we should be canny, like Uncle Isaac."
"Yes!" Thomas laughed. "Uncle Isaac, the confirmed bachelor. No women nagging him, telling him when to wipe his boots! Well, apart from me ma."
"Aye," John stubbed out his cigarette. "Love 'em and leave 'em, like Uncle Isaac.

Troubled by this insinuation, Thomas hesitantly asked, "Are you saying what I'm thinking?"

"Thomas! You little devil with your innocent smile! You don't fool me. Pamela Hart's the only one I know about, for sure. But then, everybody knows about that."

"My uncle ...?" He gestured in the air, twisting a hand at the wrist. "No way, not Pamela! He *couldn't* have!"

John grinned, drawing on his cigarette. "It's all over the country, I tell you. I reckon he's had a whole string of 'em. The oul' billy goat! A regular ram. Give 'em one and get out of it. Leave the woman holding the baby."

"John, Pamela's is his ...?"

"Sure, Pamela's is his! I thought you of all people would know all about it. It's all over the country. Joan used to hang about with Pamela Hart. I got to know her pretty well, meself. She never let on. Mind you, it's not a thing you discuss, is it, not wi' wemen? Polite conversation only, an' all that. Sure, isn't it often the case with things like that, you're the last to know about them. Like the way James knew about me long before I did. But then, he had an enquiring mind. To an extent. Pity he didn't enquire into tyre pressures. But ... Silly bugger!"

"But Pamela's supposed to be ..." his daughter. How could she also be carryin' his ... child? Thomas's mind raced. No, he couldn't do that!

But John had marched off across the yard back to the warmth of the party. However, the legacy of his gossip was a seed in Thomas's mind that was quickly germinating. A string of half-remembered gossip and innuendo haunted his consciousness:

More than one version to that story.
Loved and left, like Auntie Joan – in a manner of speaking.
Love 'em and leave 'em like Uncle Isaac.
Inbred bastard.
Whatever else your uncle might've done.
Who's the father? – Can't tell you – for both your sakes.
Marry me – wouldn't let him think it was for his sake.
He said he'd like to give her a kid.
Pamela's's his ...

Maybe the *worst* was true: maybe Pamela was his daughter *and* his lover and Thomas *was* his inbred bastard, to boot. Had she refused to marry him, to even tell him who the father was, because it *was* Uncle Isaac, and would shock him? John knew about it; and Dickie had even spoken in front of her about the other. Had she lied about not being Uncle Isaac's daughter? Of course, if that was the case, he couldn't marry her, pretend to be a father for his *own* da's child! In which case, it would turn out that the baby's grandfather was its father! No wonder she didn't want to get involved with the Grays anymore. What a mess it all seemed! Maybe he was the lowest of the low: the Gray to end all Grays.

But Thomas couldn't believe his Pamela would have been so evil as to do such profane things as – Thomas pictured her naked, on a four-poster bed, with *him* crawling up behind with an evil leer on his face ... Thomas blotted that out as hard as he was able.

It was all so mixed up in his mind. Thomas didn't know what to believe anymore. Just forget about it all, he told himself. What's done's done and it was none of your doing, whatever way it is. Let sleeping dogs lie. But as he was bolting the stable door behind him, he recalled something else that Pamela had said:

It wasn't something I could've prevented.

New Year's Eve: it was the Sabbath Day. There had been a fall of snow during the night, so the countryside was galvanised by a thin whiteness. Following the morning's chores, Thomas was in his room, reading his Holy Bible. He was reading the story in Genesis about Rachel's baby, Ben-omi: the son of my sorrow. Last week, Jesus was born – wasn't He the son of Man's sorrow?

He heard a knock at the door. Mrs Crowe had come early, to walk down with them. Thomas went through to the kitchen. He saw that she had with her a bunch of flowers.

"Well, Jean. How are you?"

"Fine, fine. We're all grand. Isaac's just away down to put the boiler on," she said, pouring her a cup of tea. "Thomas is in his ... Here he is."

"Good morning, Mrs Crowe."

"Good morning, Thomas."

Mrs Crowe began discussing the war news with his mother. Soon, she mentioned, "Did you hear about the wee girl Hart?"

Jean said, "Yes." She sighed. "The same old story ..."

"And on Christmas morning, too."
So soon? Thomas sat up straight.
"Oh, I didn't realise you meant ..." Jean began.
"Was it a boy or a girl?" Thomas asked.
"Don't you know?" Mrs Crowe looked at mother and son in turn. Their vacant stares prompted her story telling. "She had a miscarriage. On Christmas Day of all days. She was terribly ill, apparently. Critical, last I heard."

"Dead?" The breath upon which his gasp escaped carried him across the room and through the shaking front door.

"Thomas!" His mother called as he tore out of the house. "She's not dead yit, that I know of ... Did he hear me?"

Jean collided with Mrs Crowe in the jamb passage. "He's ... I expect he's goin' to give his uncle a hand."

"You said he wasn't quite himself this past wee while ..." Mrs Crowe probed sympathetically as they returned to their chairs and cups of tea.

"He's been fine this past week or so. A bit quiet, but on top form." Jean said as she sat down again. Her legs shuffled nervously on the cold floor. "Maybe it's time we were going, too, if you've to do the flower arrangement."

Mrs Crowe set down her tea cup and agreed, "Yes, it takes ages to do it right."

He ran, ran, ran without hearing or seeing or feeling or knowing. All he perceived was the blur of bare hedges, white with snow, and the black of the road where the wheel tracks were. The lumpy, icy road led along the familiar route, between the fields he had known all his days, to the dark grey stonework of the railway bridge. He reached into his jacket pockets and brought out his Bible and hymn book.

The station master's wife, at the door of their house beside the bridge, looked on in amazement, for as the books fell behind him to left and right, he cried,

"I am Chosen, the One!"

He ran along the side of the church, leaving flurried footprints in the crunching snow. He found the door at the side of the church open. There was no one in the boiler room, but the equipment was alive. He staggered on into the church building, going down the corridor, past the ladder to the loft and past the Minister's study. There were no Sunday School or Bible Classes this week, since it was still the festive season. The church complex was cold and lonely. From somewhere a deep voice was singing:

> "Abide with me: fast falls the eventide;
> The darkness deepens; Lord, with me abide:
> When other helpers fail, and comforts flee,
> Help of the helpless, O abide with me.
>
> Swift to its close ebbs out life's little day,
> Earth's joys grow dim, its glories pass away;
> Change and decay in all around I see:
> O Thou who changest not, abide with me."

Jean and Mrs Crowe were just reaching the end of the Rathmore Road when they met Paul McCann, coming along with his bag, heading for the Orchards. They stopped and talked. When he asked how Thomas was keeping, there was an awkward response.

"He wasn't himself for a while."

"He seemed to be actin' a bit funny this mornin'," Mrs Crowe enlarged on Jean's information. "P'raps he's gone to ... Summerhill, or somewhere like that?" she suggested.

"No, he wouldn't go there. D' you think, Paul, would you come down with us to the church an' see if he's there? I'm right an' worried about him. Maybe it would be best for someone to take him home, right away, if he's not in great form."

"Aye, surely, I've no objections. Sure, it's a grand, bright mornin' for a walk."

> "I fear no foe, with Thee at hand to bless;
> Ills have no weight and tears no bitterness:
> Where is death's sting? Where, grave, thy victory?
> I triumph still if Thou abide with me."

The door through to the front of the church was ajar. Thomas shouldered the door wide and, bursting in, saw a shape in front of him. The big, suited man turned slowly.

"I was just fer surtin' out the choir's stuff, you kin gie me a hand. Are the wemen here t' do the fleurs?"

Ignoring his uncle's questions, Thomas calmly took hold of the ornate Communion Chair and pulled it out from under the table and away back with him.

"Where are y' goin' wi' that, Thomas?"

"I'm goin' nowhere wi' it. But you're goin' back t' Hell wi' it, where y' belong!"

He spiralled round, raising up the heavy piece of furniture as his body turned. The edge of the seat struck his uncle on the head, throwing him sprawling over the table. Letting the chair swing on, he let go and it tumbled over by the font.

He leaned over the supine body. A trickle from the contusion on the head was beginning to drip onto the floor.

"I know you!
I know what you've done!
You're our father!
You're our brute!
You're a beast!
You're an oul' billy goat!"

As he extracted his Bowie knife from his inside pocket he said venomously to the unconscious Isaac, "Well, now I'm going to sort out the goat from the sheep."

He slit the buttons off the overcoat, ripped apart the pullover and tore open the shirt. He shredded the white vest until his uncle's chest was exposed. The point of the mirroring blade impressed on the flaky, pale flesh. His head felt numb; he hadn't self-control.

He sniggered, "This do in Remembrance of Me!"

Thomas closed his eyes as he hesitated. He saw himself pushing the blade down on the tight skin, just as he had done with the boar. He ignored the grunt of pain that Isaac seemed to breathe. Blood emerged. He dug deeper, slicing into the body as his imagined sacrifice struggled to regain consciousness.

"You raped her!" he heard his mind accusing. "And now you've killed her! Fether-a yer ain grandchild? Leave the wee girl t' suffer, wud ya? Y' dirty bastard!"

The layers of tissue parted. The space between the ribs welled with a mixture of fluids. He scooped aside some sticky plasma and saw the prize. He clawed into the cavity; his fingers poked greedily beneath the raw, pulsing lump and extracted the pulpy organ with conviction. He held it out under his palm, so that the tubes that stretched from beneath his little finger into the hole were taut. Then he sliced through each artery with a vicious tug.

Dropping the Bowie knife, he carried the slimy piece of flesh to the head of the table. The mouth was open, hanging like a stuck pig's jaw. There was no wheezing now, no breath at all. As if witnessing his own actions from another perspective, Thomas was aware of his face's purple-hot flush, the assertiveness of his grip as he clamped his free hand around the wax-pale cheeks and clean chin of his victim.

Thomas heard himself in his mad rage, bellow, "Here's your flesh and blood! I know you! I know!" And he saw himself stuff the weeping heart between the two rows of yellowing teeth ...

Thomas's eyes shot open. He raised the knife and held it limply in front of him as he screamed, screamed at the top of his voice, not even hearing the shrill cry that surfaced from his troubled spirit: "Give me *strength*!"

> "Hold Thou Thy Cross before my closing eyes,
> Shine through the gloom, and point me to the skies;
> Heaven's morning breaks and earth's vain shadows flee;
> In life in death, O Lord—"

The shouting caused the singing to cease. There was someone coming from the vestry. Thomas turned and was confronted by the Reverend Dr Marsh. The clergyman stopped in his tracks as he noticed the evil-looking weapon in Thomas's hand and the body on the Table, with the rash-like, red mark spreading over the temple, the bare graze spotted with blood. Thomas turned and, with eyes rounded and frantic, yelled wildly at the Minister:

"I am the Christ!"

"Come again?"

Thomas darted at the Reverend Dr Marsh, wielding the knife. In his furious temper he howled like a banshee, not at the clergyman this time but, seemingly, at the electric light above:

> "He careth for me? Balderdash!
> This is the heart of a heartless world!
> One sin leads to another!"

Thomas's blotched face turned to survey the vastness of the church, unusually quiet and empty because of the empty pews. He gazed at the scene of his shame, the body strewn over the table. His face revolved upwards once more, as if beseeching the beams. In complete and sudden contrast to his previous, brutal tone, he wailed melancholically:

"Father, why ... have I forsaken ..."

"You're not yourself!" the clergyman said furiously.

Dr Marsh moved towards him, reaching out to grab his shoulders. As he did so, the boy swung the knife up and round backhandedly. As the knife slashed across the Minister's eyes Dr Marsh hit out, instinctively, to defend himself. His fist struck his assailant on the nose. As the Minister staggered backwards and toppled onto his knees, covering his bleeding eyes with his hands, Thomas was punched off the step at the front of the church. As he fell down backwards, his head struck a pew.

When Mrs Crowe, Jean and McCann arrived, they found this disturbing scene. The widow woman knelt with the sprawling, howling, blinded Dr Marsh and comforted him. Paul strode forward to the Table and tapped Isaac's face.

"Out cold," he said, closing the shirt and jacket over the chest without more than an absent-minded glance.

When Jean saw the horror of the whole event – her son lying in the aisle, her brother's strange posture and his skull obviously injured, the Minister's face streaming with blood – she hardly knew where to turn. Mrs Crowe was already quietening the Minister, comforting him as she wiped the streaks of blood that were beginning to coagulate down his cheeks.

"He was blaming his uncle for something," the Minister stuttered to Mrs Crowe. "Didn't want to intrude – tried to pretend I couldn't hear it – but then his screaming shot the fear of God through me. The lad's barmy. He was saying such wild things ... I don't understand ..."

"Thomas is just a bit muddled at present," Mrs Crowe assured him. "He's obviously been imagining a load of baloney about an innocent man."

Jean told the Minister, "Some heartless folk round here have spread cruel lies about our family an' I thought, I prayed, Thomas wouldn't get his mind polluted wi' their ... false witness. But they've obviously been torturing him wi' their scandalous nonsense. No wonder he's been nearly twisted round the bend! But we didn't think he'd turn violent ..." Jean murmured. She was fighting back tears. "I didn't know he'd ... do the like-a this, attack one of his ain ..."

"Don't blame yourself," Paul said. He was straightening up the body on the Communion Table so that the head was supported. "Isaac's breathing fine, but he's got a nasty bump. I reckon his skull might be fractured. I'll go fetch the doctor."

"Wait," advised Mrs Crowe, "the first of the congregation will be arriving soon. Geoff Archer's usually here brave an' sharp – and somebody on a bike'll be quicker than you on foot."

Jean dropped her handbag as she hurried past the Communion Table. She floated down onto her knees in the aisle, to cradle her son. Having not moved the peaceful Isaac any more than a bare minimum, Paul went to them. As he kneeled down beside her, his eyes met Jean's. Both were sensing the sting of grief. He looked at the lad in her arms, was aware of the scent of the blood that was already beginning to mat in Thomas's fine, brown hair, and watched as her hands stroked the white face.

Blackness. Floating. Numbness. And, somewhere, the diminishing whispering of voices:

"What did you go and do this for, son? He never did anything to hurt you! All he ever did was try to do right by you. This wasn't necessary, there was no call for it at all! And anyway, it's not important where you came from, or what people think, or even how you end up. All that matters is that you're here and you're loved."

"Sometimes, you get the wrong end of the stick, eh? But you shouldn't let doubts and fears take over. Sometimes, things can be either black or white and, sometimes, things can be shades of grey. Didn't you know which was which? Above all else, you shouldn't take such things so much to heart!"

Then, the crowd came and, when they saw what had been done, they were amazed.